NICO

SARAH CASTILLE

D0191912

St. Martin's Paperbacks

This is a work of fiction. All of the characters, organizations, and events portrayed in this novel are either products of the author's imagination or are used fictitiously.

NICO

Copyright © 2016 by Sarah Castille.
Excerpt from *Luca* © 2017 by Sarah Castille.

For information address St. Martin's Press, 175 Fifth Avenue, New York, NY 10010.

ISBN: 978-1-250-10403-8

Printed in the United States of America

Our books may be purchased in bulk for promotional, educational, or business use. Please contact your local bookseller or the Macmillan Corporate and Premium Sales Department at 1-800-221-7945, ext. 5442, or by e-mail at MacmillanSpecialMarkets@macmillan.com.

St. Martin's Paperbacks edition / December 2016

St. Martin's Paperbacks are published by St. Martin's Press, 175 Fifth Avenue, New York, NY 10010.

10 9 8 7 6 5 4 3

To Mum and Dad, for sharing their love of all things Mafia.

ACKNOWLEDGMENTS

Thanks to my editor, Monique Patterson, and the very patient Alexandra Sehulster, as well as the St. Martin's team for polishing this book until it shone.

Thanks to my agent, Laura Bradford, my talented assistant, Danielle, and my bestest beta-reader Casey.

And thank you to the guy outside Il Terrazzo Ristorante, who took off his jacket and unbuttoned his shirt giving me an inadvertent peek at his wicked tattoo. You made me want a sexy Mafioso of my very own.

ONE

Act normal.

Mia raced through the Casino Italia, around brides-to-be, newlyweds, old men with bulging wallets, and young women in short skirts. She ran past slot machines, craps tables, and one of the highest stakes poker rooms in downtown Las Vegas. She pushed through the hordes of men crowded into the party pit to watch a sexy blackjack dealer dancing around a pole. And still she couldn't find the exit.

Which was fine if you were operating a casino and you wanted to keep your customers trapped in a never-ending party.

Not so fine if you'd just hacked their security system and stabbed a guard on the way out.

Not fine at all.

She paused by a Big Six wheel to catch her breath. A blond woman in a pink tutu ranted at a casino worker because the waitress hadn't returned with her drink. Mia wanted to tell her to take her chips to any other table. The house advantage at the Big Six was the highest of all the games in the casino. But she'd already caused enough problems today. It was supposed to be a simple penetration job—get into the control room, insert the USB, and go back to the office to hack the system—not an opportunity to avenge all women for every slimy sexist bastard who pinched a woman's ass.

And no, Mia didn't "deserve it" because she was dressed in a tiny black skirt, fishnet stockings, and a corset so tight her breasts threatened to explode over the top. She was just doing her job—although her real job just happened to be hacking into the casino's computer system and not serving drinks to the guys in the control room.

In a perfect world, she would have laughed off the pinch, walked out of the casino, and typed up a report for the owner who had hired her to test the security of his new casino. Unfortunately, very little about Mia's world was perfect, and it all suddenly came to a head when the guard in the control room decided to express his gratitude the sexist way.

So now he had a cute little tear in his security pants, courtesy of the knife she always carried in a sheath strapped to her thigh. Self-defense was a necessity for a girl growing up in a Mafia family, and habit had drawn the blade before her brain could pull the brakes. Big deal. It would give him character, a few stories to share over beer with the guys after work. Who knew he'd be so pissed? Or that a man his size could run so fast?

"Gotcha." A clammy hand clamped down on Mia's shoulder, yanking her back so hard she stumbled in the three-inch heels she wasn't accustomed to wearing. Her hand shot down to her thigh, but the guard was ready for her this time. He grabbed her wrist and twisted her arm up behind her back. "I'm taking you to see the boss. He's got zero tolerance for thieves.

"I wasn't stealing."

"You were doing something that wasn't right." With his free hand, he flicked on his radio and loudly announced that he had caught the "perp."

People turned their heads and stared. Mia's cheeks heated and she focused on the shiny, tiled floor, the looping, nondescript music, and the flashing lights of the slot machines. So much for not attracting attention. She'd never get another cyber-security contract if anyone heard she'd been caught in her own penetration test. The success of her business as a hacker and security consultant depended on keeping a low profile, and being frog-marched by a security guard through a high-end casino in somewhat provocative attire was as high-profile as low-profile could get.

Her captor walked her past two security guards, and through a set of sliding glass doors, into Casino Italia's high-stakes gaming salon. Men in tuxedos sipped on snifters of bourbon beneath crystal chandeliers, and women in evening dresses lounged on rich, red-leather furniture, or punched buttons on the five-hundred-dollar-minimum slot machines. Mia wished she had that kind of money to throw away, but she'd traded her Mafia princess life for the poverty of independence and the chance to carve her own little niche in the world, however small.

They stopped in front of a stained-glass door guarded by two massive bouncers in sleek, black suits. After a few quiet words were exchanged, one of the bouncers opened the door and gestured them into the ultra-exclusive private gaming suite. Exquisitely decorated in rich purple, gold, and chocolate, the design was contemporary in a classic way, with expensive lamps, walls of books with neutral-hued spines, dark wood furniture, and velvet sofas. The sounds of the casino melted away as the door closed behind them.

"Over there." He directed her past the unoccupied

roulette and blackjack tables to a large poker table where
five men in dark suits contemplated their cards. With a
rough jerk, he pulled her to a stop behind a man with
thick, dark hair, and broad shoulders, tapering to the narrow waist of his impeccably tailored suit.

He moved Mia slightly to the left and she caught a
flash of a gold Vacheron Constantin watch, the perfectly
turned cuff of a shirt, the sparkle of a diamond cufflink,
and just a few inches of thick, tanned forearm that made
her heart skip a beat.

Still holding Mia's arm behind her back, the guard
cleared his throat. "I caught this woman in the control
room, Mr. T. She was trying to stick something in the
main computer."

With the slightest lift of his finger, Mr. T silenced the
guard and Mia's heart kicked up a notch. She had grown
up around powerful men, but that simple gesture carried
with it an utter certainty that he would be obeyed.

The guard mumbled an apology and pulled Mia back
a step. "He doesn't like to be disturbed at the tables."

Mia checked out the man's cards over his shoulder and
quickly calculated the odds. If she'd been the one sitting
at the table with a stack of chips worth two hundred thousand dollars and a twenty thousand dollar bet on the
table, she would have folded, cashed out and run. Much
like she wanted to do now.

Mr. T threw down three cards, and Mia bit back a
gasp. He might look conservative in his impeccably tailored suit, but he was gambler. Not many people would
take that kind of risk, especially with so many players at
the table.

He turned at the sound, and her breath caught. God,
was he gorgeous. Movie-star handsome, he was sleek and
rugged at the same time. His ice blue eyes were a startling
contrast to the dark hair that curled at his temples and the

brows that furrowed at her distraction. Power, fierce and unyielding, radiated from him—and not because of his obvious wealth. It was something she sensed beneath the civilized veneer—something dark and dangerous, wild and ruthless; something that stole her breath, and left only a need so strong she couldn't move.

His lazy gaze slid over her face, to her throat, her breasts barely contained beneath the corset, her waist, her hips and down her legs to her heels. He didn't make any effort to hide his slow perusal of her body, of looking where he wanted with brazen unapologetic intent. Rather than finding it offensive, she found his scrutiny curiously electrifying, her body turning warm and liquid as she sank into the feeling of being caressed by his gaze.

"Enough." She was in this mess because she couldn't stand being objectified. So why was she putting up with it now?

Her words trailed off when his gaze sharpened on her. *Christ.* What the hell had she just walked into?

"Leave her with me, Louis."

He turned back to the table, considered his cards. He had a deep, movie-narrator voice, the kind that instantly pulled you into another world—a world of infinite possibilities, a world where devastatingly handsome casino owners let cyber-security specialists go.

Louis immediately released her and backed away with a mumbled, "Yes, sir."

Mia figured he must have worked here for some time to obey so quickly, or did everyone respond to Mr. T's commanding presence with instant submission?

Curious, she asked. "How do you know I won't run away?"

Mr. T looked back over his shoulder, and his lips curved. "I won't let you."

I won't let you. Something niggled at the back of her

mind. She'd heard those words before, spoken with the same intonation, the same hint of an accent. And his face . . . so familiar. As she struggled to place him, he lifted his drink, sipped the rich, amber liquid slowly, his corded throat tightening as he swallowed. Mia's pulse quickened, her mind filling with thoughts of what he could do to her with that beautiful mouth, how he would taste if she licked the Adam's apple at the base of his throat.

He lowered the glass and licked his lips, a predator ready to pounce. "Come." He rested his hand on the leather bumper and she joined him at the table, standing beside his chair.

"Bet." He flashed his cards so she could see he'd pulled two aces and a ten from the risky draw, giving him a full house.

Taking a chance that she'd been right in her assessment of him, she leaned over and pushed all his chips forward. Her breast brushed against his shoulder, and his body tensed, but it was nothing compared to the current of electricity that surged through her veins at the small touch.

"Two hundred thousand," the dealer announced.

Mia almost wept. Two hundred thousand dollars could get her a new apartment that didn't have a giant fungus growing on the ceiling from the leaky pipes upstairs that the slum landlord refused to fix. Two hundred thousand dollars could take her and her little sister, Kat, away from Vegas and set them up with a new, anonymous life where they weren't constantly being watched by their Mafia crime family. Two hundred thousand dollars could buy her a bigger office and pay for additional employees who could take on the growing amount of work her cyber-security company was generating. Two hundred thousand dollars would set her free.

"She's a gambler," he murmured when the man beside him called the bet.

"Maybe, I'm just lucky."

"Lucky people don't get caught trying to hack into my computer system." In one swift movement he stood, yanked the man seated beside him off his chair and smashed his face into the table. "Thieves don't belong in my casino." Blood splattered over the green felt and the man staggered back, holding his broken nose. It had taken only seconds. Silence filled the room. Adrenaline surged through Mia's body, freezing her in place as her mind tried to reconcile such brutal violence in such a sophisticated, elegant place. She had been right that Mr. T's civilized exterior did not reflect the inner man. He was the most dangerous of predators. Beautiful on the outside. Deadly within.

Mr. T hadn't even broken a sweat, but Mia could see the veins in his neck pulsing, his anger kept tightly in check. "Gentlemen." He gave the briefest of nods to the men at the table. "My casino manager, Vito, will be with you shortly to address the inconvenience." He turned to Mia, his narrowed, cool gaze holding her in place. "Come."

His voice didn't broach any argument, nor did the firm hand he placed on her lower back, or the slight pressure he exerted to direct her where he wanted her to go. He was even taller than she had thought, well over six feet, broad and muscular. She inhaled sharply at his touch, breathed in the fresh, spicy scent of his cologne. Given the violence he had just unleashed in the private salon, she had expected something wild and musky, reflecting the primitive, feral side of his nature.

"Where are we going?"

"My office."

She hesitated; looked back at the man on the plush carpet, his white shirt covered in blood. "Alone?"

"Yes, *bella*. Alone."

She was liquid sex.

Dark hair. Dark eyes. Curves all over the place. Creamy skin. Breasts almost bursting out of her corset. That little skirt barely covering her ass. Those high cheekbones and rosy cheeks. Those fucking long legs in those fucking stockings, the heels . . .

Nico hadn't paid much attention to the uniform his casino manager had picked for the waitresses, but on her it was so fucking sexy his dick got hard the moment she walked into the salon.

Usually he didn't get involved with the casino cheats, thieves, or the scammers who thought they could evade the hundreds of cameras and top-of-the-line security system he had installed when he renovated the old Lucky Duck casino on Freemont Street, but then soldiers from rival crime families were usually not stupid enough to walk into his casino much less try to cheat at a high-stakes table where Nico was seated, and sexy women didn't try to hack into his computer system.

He wanted to know everything about her. What she was doing in the casino control room? Why she didn't she flinch when he lost his temper at the poker table? And why she was so goddam familiar?

Nico steeled himself to do what had to be done as he walked the beautiful woman through his casino, a cacophony of alluring stimulation—bells ringing, siren-like lights flashing, slot wheels whirring, digital sounds beeping, the occasional simulated sound of change clanging—all meant to captivate and enthrall, giving the impression that everyone was a winner.

Although Casino Italia wasn't on the Strip, it had the same upscale décor to attract the high rollers who wanted a downtown experience without giving up the luxuries they would get at the high-end hotels. Everything was slick, burnished, and gleaming, from the red walls that were meant to evoke a safe, comfortable feeling, to the patterned carpets designed to mesmerize, welcome, and please the eye, and from the low mellow lighting to the soft, easing soundtracks to help gamblers get into a trance to encourage them to spend money. Nico had never run a casino before buying the Lucky Duck, and the psychology behind the redesign had intrigued him.

The woman didn't speak as he guided her through the maze of slot machines, poker and blackjack tables, past the crowds, around the craps tables and the roulette wheels. He slid his key card into a wood-paneled elevator and moments later they were on the tenth floor.

Nico ushered the woman into his office. Cold, austere, functional, and decorated in the casino colors of red, black, and gray, it had a small meeting table and chairs on one side, and a steel bookcase on the other. A place to do business, nothing more.

After closing the door behind her, he settled in the leather chair behind his chrome-and-glass desk.

"Sit." He gestured to the chair in front of her.

"I prefer to stand."

Nico expressed his displeasure with a scowl. As the Toscani family's highest-ranking *capo*—captain with a powerful and extensive crew working beneath him—he was unused to be being disobeyed. He answered only to the Toscani family administration: the boss, underboss, and *consigliere*, and even then he did only enough to maintain the illusion he was towing the party line. His uncle, Santo, now Don Toscani, had become boss after Nico's father's death. By rights, Nico, as the first son of the first son, was heir to head the family, but when he had come of age and made his claim, Santo had refused to step down.

"Sit," he said curtly. "Or I'll make you sit."

"By breaking my nose?"

He fought back a bark of amusement. She was all sass, despite her predicament, and when she didn't move, he was forced to drink in the full beauty of her lush body all over again. She was no ordinary thief if she knew how to find to the control room, what to do when she got there, and how to keep the interest of a man who would ordinarily just have handed her over to the police.

Legitimate businesses like Casino Italia had to be handled in a legitimate way, unlike the businesses in Nico's underground portfolio that spanned everything from loansharking to real-estate fraud, and from counterfeiting to tax evasion. He greased palms and oiled the wheels of business in Las Vegas and across California to Los Angeles. There was nowhere his influence couldn't reach— even in the territories carved out by the two rival Mafia families who were vying with the Toscanis for control of the city.

"Your nose is too lovely to break." He had to stop looking at her. He was engaged to marry a young Sicilian woman in the next few weeks—an agreement made between her father and Nico's father when Nico was six years old to cement a formidable alliance. He had never met Rosa Scozzari, but she was from a *Cosa Nostra* family many generations back. The alliance would legitimize Nico's status as heir to head the family, and give him the power to overthrow his uncle despite the fact that Nico was a bastard—the son of his father's mistress. A beautiful Italian woman was as much a symbol of status as a large house and a fancy car. Rosa would bear his sons, run his house, and organize social events. Sex and emotional attachment he would get from the mistresses every boss was expected to take as a further show of power.

"Is that meant to be a compliment?" She arched a perfect eyebrow and dropped one hand to the sweet swell of her hip. Bold and beautiful. *Cristo*. This woman was made to test a man's restraint to the limit.

"Do you want compliments?" He was more than willing to give them, starting with her magnificent breasts, her long, toned legs, the waist neatly cinched in the tight corset, and the short skirt that barely covered her ass. He made a mental note to give Vito a raise.

"I want to give you this, and get out of here." She pulled a letter from the bra cups of her corset and offered it to him and he strangled back a groan. His cock, already semi-erect from verbally sparring with the beautiful little minx, became fully hard as he imagined his mouth going where that letter had been.

"What is it?"

"A letter from my company confirming my identity and explaining what I'm doing here." She placed it on the desk in front of him when he made no move to take it.

Curiosity got the better of him, and he skimmed the short paragraphs. Mia Cordano, owner of HGH Enterprises Inc., had come to Casino Italia at the request of his casino manager, Vito Bottaro, for a pre-arranged security test. Vito's signature was scrawled at the bottom of the letter, but it was the woman's name that kept his attention.

Mia Cordano.

Nico spun his silver pen around his thumb as he studied her fidgeting in front of his desk, seeing her dark beauty in another light. An enemy light. "Cordano." The word was bitter on his tongue. For ten years his family had been involved in a *faida*—blood feud—with the Cordanos that had started the night Don Cordano killed

Nico's father in cold blood along with a young Toscani associate he had accused of defiling his daughter.

"Yes." She tilted her head to the side and her brow creased. "Do we know each other? You look familiar."

"Who's your father?" he asked, ignoring her question.

Her frown deepened. "Battista Cordano."

Don Cordano's daughter. The woman who had started a war. He remembered her now, although without the name he would never have recognized her ten years later and all grown up. She had been there the night his father had been murdered.

Memories gripped him, and he crushed the paper in his hand.

He had been so proud the night his father asked him to join him in a sit-down at Luigi's Restaurant with Don Cordano, the boss of one of the three leading crime families in Las Vegas. Don Cordano wanted permission to whack Danny Mantelli, an associate in the crew of one of his father's capos. Made men could only be whacked with the permission of a boss, and Danny had secretly been dating Don Cordano's teenage daughter—something strictly forbidden in the Mafia world. The women of made men—daughters, mistresses, and wives—were considered untouchable. Women were property and often the objects of passion. More than anything, passion could destroy the careful balance that existed between the Mafia families. As it had done that very night.

"You were at Luigi's." Bile rose in his throat, and for a moment he couldn't speak. Nothing in his life, not even the death of his mother when he was eight years old, had prepared him for the moment his beloved Papà had been murdered, his blood spilling through Nico's fingers as he desperately tried to save him. He had declared the *faida* that night. A man of honor could do no less, and a son had to avenge his father.

Her face paled as recognition dawned. "You're the boy who held me. Nico Toscani."

He spun the pen faster as he remembered holding Mia in his arms, trying to protect her from her father's anger. Don Cordano had been enraged that Mia dared interrupt the sit-down to beg for Danny's life, and he struck her so hard she fell to the ground

Raised in single parent households—first by his mother and then, for a short time, by his nonna after his mother died—Nico had a tremendous respect for women, and the brutality of Don Cordano's attack on young Mia had shocked and appalled him. Without thinking, he had stepped in to defend her. She wrapped her arms around him, held on tight. And in that one moment, in the midst of the horror, eighteen-year-old Nico came alive. He felt a sense of purpose and worth that he'd never felt as a bastard son—he was a protector and this sixteen-year-old Mafia princess who felt so right in his arms, was his to protect. When her father turned his gun on Danny, Nico covered her ears and pressed her face to his chest to spare her the horror of witnessing her boyfriend's death. And then she'd been ripped away and life as he knew it had ended with the crack of a gun.

He had no desire to rehash that night, or to hear what she had to say, whether it was regrets or apologies, thanks or accusations. He had lost not only his father, but also the fleeting glimpse of a life that could have been more than just following in his father's footsteps—a life with purpose and fulfillment. A life with love.

Mia was a brutal reminder of the emptiness he'd felt since that night, the black hole that had opened in his chest and couldn't be filled no matter how many women he took to his bed or how much success he achieved. He lived now solely to avenge his father and take his place as boss of the family.

Dropping the pen, he tossed the crumpled letter on his desk and vented his frustration. "*Cristo santo!* I told Vito to hire the best cyber-security firm in the city and he hired you?"

Mia folded her arms across her chest. "What do you mean by that?"

Nico made a dismissive gesture with his hand, trying not to focus on any one part of her beautiful body. "First of all, you're a Cordano. Second, you're a woman."

She gave an indignant sniff. "So what? Women can be hackers. A woman wrote the first ever C Sharp virus. Women speak at DefCon, one of the world's most prestigious gatherings of hackers. If you're not familiar with us, it's because most female hackers are interested in technology for what it does and not so we can break it or watch people suffer. We're not interested in cyber-vandalism. There's nothing clever about dismantling a system, and everything good about helping companies secure themselves against cyber attacks, which is what Vito hired me to do."

"Hacking is for men. This stuff . . ." He waved vaguely at her outfit. "Security work is for men. It's a dangerous business. It involves skill, deception, focus, and intelligence."

Her eyes blazed, and she crossed the floor to lean over his desk. "Intelligence? I was at the top of my class at UCLA. If you had even bothered to read the resume I sent your casino manager, you would have seen I've had contracts from multi-national corporations, state and local governments. I was even invited to submit a tender to the FBI. I got those contracts myself. I run a very successful business with the help of two on-site employees and a floating team of five online hackers."

She paused for breath, and Nico tried to tear his gaze

away from her magnificent breasts now only inches away from his face, but she wouldn't let him.

"This . . ." She cupped her breasts over the corset and gave them a shake, sending all Nico's blood down to his groin. "Ridiculous outfit is me doing my job and the only reason I was caught was because your security guard has the same antiquated, sexist, misogynistic attitude as you and decided to pinch my ass. I jabbed my knife into his thigh to defend myself as any woman being sexually harassed is entitled to do."

For the first time in his twenty-eight years, Nico had nothing to say. Captivated, entranced, and fiercely aroused by the infuriated, beautiful woman leaning over his desk, her face dark with indignant fury, he almost forgot she was the enemy—the daughter of the man he hated most in the world.

"If I hadn't been distracted," she continued, straightening up to Nico's abject disappointment, "I would have been in and out of your control room and hacking into your system as we speak."

"Exactly." Unable to contain the fierce arousal coursing through his veins, Nico pushed back his chair, and rounded his desk forcing her to take a few steps back. He perched on the edge of the desk in front of her, arms folded, legs spread wide, back in control of the room, of himself. "You were distracted. A man wouldn't have been distracted."

Her lips pressed tight together, she brazenly stepped between his parted legs. Electricity crackled between them, caused the air in the room to swelter. Unused to being challenged in any way, and never by a woman, Nico couldn't decide if she was coming on to him or about to rip out his throat.

She gave him a smile that was at once sultry and sweet.

"So you're saying"—she dropped her hand until it dangled just below his crotch—"that if I were to grab you right now, you wouldn't get distracted?"

Adrenaline pulsed through his body in response to her challenge, and he fought the urge to slide back on his desk. Not because she scared him—he was confident he could knock her hand away before she got close—but because he was so fucking turned on, he didn't know what would happen if she touched him.

Goddam fucking delicious.

He curled his hand around her neck, beneath the silken waterfall of her hair, and pulled her close, so close he could feel her breath on his cheek. "Do it," he demanded.

She met his challenging gaze, and he could almost taste her need, as thick and fierce as his own. Finally, her hand fell to the side and she wrenched out of his grasp. "You'd like that, wouldn't you? Well, you're not worth it."

Dio mio. If he didn't get rid of her, he'd have her over his desk in a heartbeat, stockings and panties torn away, skirt flipped up to bare that beautiful ass, hair wrapped around his hand, her back arched, and his name a scream of pleasure on her lips. "Goodbye, Ms. Cordano."

He expected apologies, embarrassment, some sign that acknowledged he had won that confrontation. Instead, he got a sniff.

"I'll send you my bill."

She turned and walked out of the room, back straight, head high, beautiful ass swaying gently as she walked.

He couldn't tear his gaze away.

Magnificent.

Irritating and utterly disrespectful.

Totally off-limits.

The enemy.

TWO

Unlike most Vegas locals, Mia loved the city at the tail end of winter. From the light dusting of snow that covered the hills in the Red Rock Canyon National Conservation Area, to the rain that turned the Interstate 15 into an angry mess, and from the gray skies that put everyone in a bad mood to the shortened days, it was a Vegas that most tourists didn't know existed, and with everyone huddling in doors in weather that the rest of the country embraced in spring, it gave the city an intimate feel.

It also meant she could indulge her passion for streetpunk clothing without worrying that she would melt the minute she stepped outside her grungy apartment. Today she wore a pair of worn, skin-tight black jeans, a graphic rocker shirt, and her favorite green cargo jacket. She'd paired it with her favorite Doc Martens lace-up boots embroidered with red flowers, and a cozy, oversized black wool hat that flopped from side to side as she walked.

By the time she reached the coffee shop two blocks away from her apartment in the John S. Park neighborhood of downtown, she was chilled to the bone and grateful for the fingerless gloves she wore on her hands. She picked up her usual double-shot Monday morning latte from the small, free-trade coffee shop on the corner and made her way to the pool hall where she rented office space in the upstairs suite.

"What happened on Friday?" Mia's bestie and second in command, Jules Rafferty, spun around in her chair when Mia walked through the door and into the open plan space.

A perpetually cheery, blue-eyed blonde with hot-pink streaks in her hair, a filthy mouth, and a sarcastic sense of humor, Jules had been an online hacker friend until Mia decided to take her business legit and set up a physical office.

Hired as a both an office manager and a hacker, Jules had found the newly renovated business suite above the pool hall. Decorated with exposed brick walls, timber beams and rustic accents, it was as "heritage" as Vegas could get, although the location left a little to be desired. Clients had to walk through the pool hall to get to the stairway leading upstairs, but Jules had convinced her it just added to their unconventional charm.

"How do you know something happened?" Mia unlocked her office door and Jules followed her inside.

"I just received a termination of contract notice by email from Casino Italia, so I figured the penetration test didn't go well."

Mia dumped her bag on the credenza, the only piece of furniture in the room not covered in computer equipment. She had four monitors set up in a U-shape around her desk, along with two hard drives and miscellaneous other equipment that would have made even the most hardcore IT guys drool. "Didn't go well is an understatement." She sighed and pulled a candy bar from her bag for a quick breakfast fix. Caffeine and chocolate were her morning mainstays, and even Jules' constant nagging couldn't get her to change.

"I had to dress in the skimpiest costume I've ever seen in a casino to get into the back room. Apparently that was an invitation for the guard to pinch my ass when we were alone, so I nicked him in the leg with my knife. He took me to see the boss . . ." She hesitated, choosing her words carefully. After running away from an abusive stepfather at the age of thirteen, Jules had been struggling to turn her life around when Mia met her online. She knew all about the underbelly of Vegas, from the pimps to the street gangs. Mia had told her about her Mafia family, but was careful never to tell her anything that would put her in danger.

"I knew him," Mia continued. "He's from a rival Mafia family. He didn't know his casino manager had hired us, and I didn't know he owned the casino. Needless to stay, things didn't go well between us."

Jules twisted her lips to the side. "That's gonna be bad for business."

Very bad for business. Mia had made her start when one of her father's capos asked her test the security of one of his legitimate businesses. After she pointed out the numerous flaws in his system and how easy it was to hack, he'd recommended her to another wiseguy. Mia quickly realized she had a vast pool of untapped clients who had been reluctant to hire civilian hackers to test the security of their businesses. Over the years, organized crime had embraced the digital age in every way from laundering money, to Internet scams, and who needed security more than the mob?

Mia kept her Mafia work above board, only taking contracts for legitimate businesses. As her reputation grew, she got calls from big corporates who did business with the mob bosses. When the work became too much to handle on her own, she contacted some of her online hacker friends and hired Jules and single mom Christine to help with on-site work. They now had a steady flow of quality work but because they worked contract to contract, the loss of the Casino Italia job would hit them hard this month.

"I guess I'd better return the outfit." She tossed the bag containing the go-go dancer outfit she'd appropriated from the casino change room on the table. "I don't want to be accused of stealing it even though the contract allows for the use of company equipment and attire."

Jules pulled the outfit out of the bag and laughed. "I wish I'd been there. I've never seen you in anything like this."

"And you never will." Mia didn't dress to show off her body. Growing up in a Mafia household, she'd quickly realized that women had little respect. When nothing she did could get her the attention she so desperately craved from her father, she'd expressed her displeasure by making a mockery of the pink, frilly, feminine clothes he expected women to wear by giving them her own punk-rock style, and forging a path in an online community almost totally dominated by men.

"Your dad would love it."

Mia took the dress and put it back in the bag. "Maybe I should wear it for the family dinner on Wednesday night. Then I won't have to spend my time justifying my life choices. Every time I wear my punk clothes home, Papa becomes apoplectic with rage and refuses to speak to me." She loathed going home for the family dinners with her abusive, domineering father, and her cool, detached mother who accepted her place as subservient to her husband and said nothing about the numerous mistresses he kept. Mia could have forgiven her that—after all she'd been raised in a very traditional Mafia family. But she couldn't forgive her mother for not defending Mia from her father's abuse.

"So what was the big boss like?" Jules leaned forward in her chair, her colorfully painted nails a startling contrast to the strategically torn tights she wore beneath a short black skirt. "When I think of casino owners, I imagine slick, slimy, and sleazy. In that order."

"He was . . ." Mia sucked her in lips, trying to encapsulate everything that was Nico Toscani in a few words. "Gorgeous. Young. Hot. Confident. Charming—"

"Whoa. Stop right there." A smile spread across Jules's face. "You like him."

"He's an angry client, a Mafia capo, and a family enemy," Mia countered. "He's also a sexist, arrogant, overbearing ass and in typical Mafia fashion believes women are useless and belong in the kitchen. He couldn't believe his casino manager hired a woman. He seemed to be more annoyed about that than the fact I'm a Cordano."

"I'm sure you set him straight," Jules said dryly.

Mia's lips quivered at the corners. "I threatened to squeeze his balls."

"Jesus." Jules burst out laughing. "I almost feel sorry for the guy. He pressed all your buttons at once, and you're not a forgiving type. What did he do?"

Her cheeks heated and she typed in the first of the five passwords she used to secure her system, remembering how her body tingled when she'd stepped between his legs, the electricity that crackled between them, the way his gaze had dropped to her lips and how she'd imagined what it would be like to kiss him. "He threw me out."

"So, when are you seeing him again?"

"I'm not." Mia looked up when she heard the front

door open. "He just fired us. And I told you, he's a family enemy and everything I hate in a man."

"Am I missing a meeting?" Chris joined them in Mia's office. She had been a struggling single mom working at the local library when they met, but her interest in computer hacking had led her to enroll her young daughter in Mia's coding class at the local community center. Mia and seen Chris's spark of interest, and helped her develop an online presence in the hacker world, eventually asking her to join her team when her business expanded. Toned and tan, and always dressed in sports clothes, she kept her hair in a short, dark bob so it didn't interfere with her obsessive fitness activities and would never be caught dead drinking coffee or eating chocolate at any time of day. She was the antithesis of every hacker Mia knew, which made her particularly effective for the kind of penetration test Mia had botched on Friday.

She filled in the details while Chris sipped her fluorescent-green protein shake.

"Maybe I should call the telecom company that called last week. They wanted us to hack into their rival's network to see what they were up to. I explained to them that we're good guys—white-hat hackers—and that we only hack to help businesses tighten their security. I said if they wanted to get involved in corporate espionage they needed to find themselves some black-hat hackers, or if they thought their rival was up to no good, a gray-hat hacking group would do. They weren't very happy. I'll bet if you gave them a call, we could land that contract."

"We're not that desperate," Mia said. "Once we cross that line, there's no going back." Chris didn't know that some of their contracts were for Mafia-run businesses, albeit they were legitimate, but she understood Mia wasn't interested in taking on any black-hat work. "Plus, we still haven't heard about that proposal we sent in to the FBI.

The RFP they sent out had a one-year time frame for them to consider the offers and that time is almost up. Fingers crossed they choose us."

"So what are we going to do about Casino Italia?" Jules asked. "That's a week of work lost."

Mia tucked the outfit away in her bag. "I went through all their systems, and checked their security. The only thing that wasn't completed was the final penetration test. I'll write a report and send the bill." Her lips quivered when she remembered Nico's shocked look when she stormed out of his office. She would give anything to be there when that cocky bastard opened the bill.

After all, it was what she had promised she would do. And in their world, honor was everything.

"Don Toscani."

Bile rose in Nico's throat as he bent to kiss his uncle's pinkie ring, the symbol of his power as boss of the Toscani crime family. He pressed his lips to the cold cluster of diamonds, and shuddered back the urge to rip the band off Santo's finger. That ring was Nico's ring—his father's legacy, handed down from oldest son to oldest son for generations. Every time he touched it, he felt the knife of his uncle's betrayal stab deeper in his heart.

Santo was three hundred pounds of ruthless, greedy bastard. He slicked his salt and pepper hair back with fistfuls of gel and only wore tracksuits over wife beater vests, with a heavy gold cross on a chain around his thick neck.

"Frankie." Santo spared a nod for Nico's closest friend and the top-ranking member of his crew. Although officially a Toscani family enforcer, who answered to Santo, Frankie De Lucchi had taken on the role of Nico's bodyguard when Nico became a *capo*—captain. Santo called on Frankie occasionally to deal with difficult situations, but usually his son, Tony, handled the jobs no one else wanted to do.

Frankie joined Luca, another friend and Nico's right hand man, at the back of the room near the door.

Usually Nico's most trusted associate, Big Joe, would stand guard in the outer hallway during Nico's weekly meeting with the don, but Nico had given him a pass today to deal with a work emergency. Big Joe was a good earner and had a legitimate business that he ran on the side.

"How is the casino business these days?" Santo gestured for Nico to sit beside his *consigliere*—trusted family advisor, Charles "Charlie Nails" Russo, on the other side of his huge, intricately carved wooden desk. Santo's office was designed to impress, with bookshelves filled with books he had never read, and statues and paintings chosen for cost rather than aesthetics. The room smelled heavily of cigar smoke from the Cubans he smoked on a regular basis. Nico's throat burned with each inhale, but he had long ago learned never to show any weakness, especially in front of the man who would take any opportunity to show Nico was not fit to lead.

"It's earning." That's all Santo cared about. That was all anyone in the mob cared about. A good earner was worth his weight in gold, and the hefty kickbacks Nico paid to Santo kept his uncle from sending out his enforcers to whack Nico in his sleep.

Nico's father had been all about respect, honor, and ensuring the continuation of the institution, the survival of the family. He had protected the people in his territory even as he squeezed them for cash. Santo didn't give a damn about anyone except himself and his son, Tony, now his underboss and seated to Nico's left.

"Good." Santo reached for a cigar, expertly flicking his

wrist to show off his gold Rolex. Santo was all about appearances. His mansion, in a guard-gated luxury Summerlin community, with spectacular views of the Strip was surrounded by a ten-foot-high electric fence. He had bought it from a movie star shortly after his self-appointment as boss of the Las Vegas faction of the New York Toscani family had been made official. He never resisted an opportunity to tell his guests about the famous people who had graced its marble halls, partied in the three swimming pools or played tennis on the regulation court nestled in the trees at the far end of his two acres of property.

Someone knocked on the study door, and Santo motioned for a pause in the conversation. A woman entered, carrying a tray of espresso and biscotti.

"Your espresso, Mr. Toscani." She placed the tray on a side table and served Santo, Charlie Nails, and Tony. "Anything for you, sir? She turned to Nico just as Tony rose from his seat.

"*Stupido cagna!* The espresso is cold. I warned you about that already." Tony backhanded the woman so hard she stumbled, and Nico caught her as she fell.

She gave him a grateful smile beneath her tears, and Nico helped her to her feet and put the tray in her hands.

"Go."

Nico was appalled, but not surprised by Tony's behavior. He had earned the nickname "Tony Crackers," not for a love of snacks, but because everyone thought he was crazy. Nico had known him since they were children, and even then it was clear something was wrong with his cousin. Tony had been caught torturing animals at a young age, graduating from insects to rodents and then to the family pets. Clever enough to hide his psychopathic tendencies from teachers and social workers, he'd made it through school and then dropped out to join the family business where he enforced his will with violence instead of words. He was known to be unstable, flying into rages for the smallest of reasons, and his crew was one of the bloodiest in the city.

Although tempted, Nico kept his views about Tony's abusive behavior to himself. This was not his house. The woman was not his servant. He could not disrespect his cousin and uncle by interfering in their private affairs. And no doubt, she would already be walking out the door as dozens had before.

"Where's the money?" Tony, his father's look-alike in clothes and demeanor, but one hundred pounds lighter and without the gray hair, held out his hand. Nico passed over an envelope stuffed with money—a percentage of the money his associates and soldiers kicked up to him from the loan sharking, gambling, protection and other rackets they ran under the protection of the family name. Anyone who failed to pay up, or was discovered running an undisclosed business, would find himself in a car going for a ride to the ocean, wearing a pair of cement shoes.

Charlie Nails frowned at Tony's lack of tact, but Tony had made it clear when he was appointed as underboss that he didn't give a damn what the old man thought of him. Charlie Nails had held the role of *consigliere* for Nico's father, and then for Santo after him. The *consigliere* was a supposed to be a close, trusted friend and confidant, an elder statesman of the family, but his support of Santo made him a traitor in Nico's eyes.

"Is this everything?" Tony thumbed through the envelope. "This is half of what you brought us last month." He shared a glance with Charlie Nails and smirked. "I thought you fancied yourself an old-style mobster. In the old days, the casinos were a license to print money. This is hardly enough to pay our staff."

Nico steeled himself to show an outer calm as he raged

inside. "That's just the casino money." He reached into the pocket of his double-breasted suit jacket, and pulled out a second envelope. "This is from the other businesses and the pay up from my crew."

Santo's eyes narrowed when Nico tossed the second envelope on the table. Although not a clever man, like Nico's father had been, Santo had a sixth sense for when he was being ripped off. "Is that everything?"

No, of course it wasn't everything. Despite the risk, Nico had several businesses on the side, including a nice little condo racket in which the main condo developers in the city exclusively hired interior designers controlled by Nico's associates, giving Nico a share of every condo development. His connection with the steelworkers' union had also given him a line into the rapidly developing construction of new casinos from a wave of foreign billionaires looking for a place to park their money.

Unlike his uncle, who had taken the family into the drug trade against *Cosa Nostra* rules, Nico was all about real estate. The online scams and Internet fraud that many of his associates claimed were the new wave of business were of no interest to him, nor were any rackets where he had to enforce his will through violence. Although he would mete out punishment if it was due, attracting the attention of the police and FBI was not the way he wanted to do business. Nico liked to talk to the people he did business with, he liked to make connections, and his casino was the perfect place to wine and dine potential partners before comping them a few evenings in the high-stakes room, and taking even more of their money.

"That's it." Nico moved to leave and Santo held up a hand.

"Since you're here and you are family, I want you to be the first to know. Tony's getting married."

Tony Crackers married? What kind of woman would agree to marry a man with a reputation for brutal violence?

"Congratulations, *cugino*." He shook his Tony's hand. "Who's the lucky woman?"

"Mia Cordano." Tony gave him a sly smile. "I heard you were with her the other night. I didn't know you were so close to the Toscanis."

Nico understood the implied threat, but he didn't address it because he was still trying to process the information. Political marriages were very common in the upper level of the Mafia, but usually the women involved in the arranged marriages were of a type—docile, submissive, fully indoctrinated in the *Cosa Nostra* culture, and willing to help the family through an alliance that would benefit both sides. He couldn't see an assertive, intelligent, sophisticated businesswoman like Mia Cordano marrying a violent, uneducated criminal like Tony Crackers unless she was forced to do it—and although some women were pressured by the families into marriages, how did one force a woman who so expertly wielded a knife?

"Vito hired her to do cyber-security work for the casino."

Santo sucked on his cigar, blew a ring of smoke. "You should keep better track of what your employees are doing, especially when we are involved in a *faida* with her family of your making."

"You don't support the *faida*?" Nico scowled. "What man of honor would not want to avenge his brother after he was shot in the back by a coward who didn't even have permission from the New York bosses for the hit?"

"Don't disrespect your uncle," Charlie Nails warned. "He has his reasons for doing what he does and they are not your concern."

Nico shot him a scathing look. Aside from some minor gambling and loan sharking, Charlie Nails, a lawyer, ran a legitimate law firm and helped the family out with legal issues as well as liaising with important "bought" figures such as politicians or judges. He had been a trusted and close friend of Nico's father, but Nico had no tolerance for a man who would sell his loyalty to the highest bidder.

Santo raised a hand to silence Charlie Nails. "He should know that his actions have led to this marriage. Don Cordano has eyes on his daughter. When he found out she had been seen with you, Nico, he called me with concerns about her safety. He accused us of disregarding the rules regarding the sanctity of women and children in the *faida*."

"That's bullshit and you know it. She was there for business. Her safety was never in question."

Santo waved a dismissive hand. "Both sides have lost many soldiers in this senseless war. Don Cordano fears for the life of his son, Dante, as I fear for the life of my Tony. We shared our concerns and discussed a truce. As a show of good faith, he offered one of his daughters in marriage to the Toscani family. It was not an opportunity I was prepared to pass up. The Cordanos have a solid foothold in the drug trade. Marriage will bring us together. Don Cordano thinks to gain strength through the union, but Dante is weak, not worthy to lead. Once Dante and the don are out of the way, Tony will have a claim to lead by marriage and he will take over as boss. Together, he and I will push aside the other *Cosa Nostra* families and take control of the city."

Nico pulled his pen from his pocket and spun it around his thumb as he struggled to hide his anger. His father had intended to pass the pen down to Nico when he became a made man, just as his father had done for him.

But he hadn't lived to see the day. Nico had only started carrying the pen after he was made, and he intended to pass it on to his son.

"My father has not yet been avenged," he spat out. "And what of all the soldiers and capos who will lose their lives? You dragged this family into the drug trade against *Cosa Nostra* rules. Everything my father tried to do for the family, you have undone. But this . . . betrayal of the other *Cosa Nostra* families, a full-out war for control of the city . . . How many will be left standing at the end?"

Charlie Nails, quiet until that moment, ran a hand through his silvery hair. "I have to agree, Santo. Not just because of Nico's father, Maximo, but because our involvement with the drug trade has already brought us to the attention of the FBI. When Maximo was boss, we were able to fly under the radar. If we expand our drug operation, and the bodies start to pile up, they are going to come down hard on us. Even if our men don't get whacked in the civil war you propose, they'll wind up in jail."

"Cazzo!" Even more volatile than usual, Tony reached for the weapon holstered at his side, and Santo held up a hand.

"Stand down. Charlie Nails is old and slow, and Nico is maybe upset that you have stolen his woman. But he understands that this is a sacrifice that must be made for *la famiglia*."

Nico's stomach tightened at the thought of his crazy cousin married to Mia, the girl he'd once held, trembling in his arms, who had become a beautiful woman who stirred a longing in him he had long thought dead. Did her father, Don Cordano, understand the risk? The danger she was in? "Did she agree to this?"

Santo laughed. "Don Cordano assures me she will do

her duty to her family. That's all we care about. Just as Tony will do his duty to ours to ensure the Toscanis are never without a boss of the pure Toscani bloodline. We are meeting them at Vincenzo's Trattoria on Thursday night to finalize everything, and they will be wed as soon as we can get it arranged."

"She's a fucking hot piece of tail." Tony made a lewd pumping gesture with his fist. "Not gonna be hard to knock her up and keep the Toscani line going."

The implication was clear. Santo was never going to step down. He had just declared Tony his successor to head the family, and if Tony had a son, Nico would lose control of the family forever. Not only that, once Santo allied with the Cordanos, he would no longer need the kickbacks from Nico's vast commercial operations. He would no longer need Nico—the illegitimate son of the man killed by the very family he now sought as any ally.

Which meant in the next few days, Don Toscani's associates would be taking Nico for a ride from which he would never come back, and Mia would be left to the mercy of a cruel, vicious man and a family who saw her as nothing but a means to an end. He wouldn't wish that fate on any woman, but especially not the woman he had connected with so long ago—a woman who made him feel felt worthy in the way a bastard son had never hoped to be.

"The pure Toscani line." Tony repeated his father's cruel words, as if reading Nico's thoughts.

"If we're done here . . ." Nico didn't wait for a response. He stood, and gave the barest nod of respect to Charlie Nails and his uncle. He had learned as a child not to rise to Tony's bait, but he could not tolerate any disrespect of his dead mother. A quick exit was the only alternative to a fight that would likely end with one of them dead. His mother had been the love of his father's life, but they had never been able to marry. To honor his family, Nico's father had gone through with a political marriage, just as Nico would do in the coming months. Nico could only hope his new wife would bear him sons so that no son of his *goomah*—mistress—would bear the stigma he did.

"We'll announce the wedding after church at Nonna Maria's house this Sunday," Santo called after him. "You can be the best man."

THREE

Benito "Benny" Romano parked his white Chrysler 300 outside a small run-down bungalow at the edge of Sunrise, a small community on the outskirts of Las Vegas. Across the street, a drug deal was going down between two boys, no more than fourteen, and a dealer who was only a year or two older. A mangy dog lay on the grass in front of the house, and a beaten-up pick-up truck was parked in the driveway.

Fuck. Gabe was here. He was never here on Tuesdays. Had he lost another fucking job?

He closed and locked the door and made his way through the overgrown weeds and up the sidewalk, stopping to move Daisy's broken tricycle and pick up Mr. Tickles who had been abandoned in the dirt. Christ. He gave Ginger enough money every month to afford a decent place for her and their daughter, Daisy, in a nice area of town. But, of course, with Gabe around, she'd have other plans for that money.

"Daddy!" The screen door banged open, and Daisy flew into his arms, her long blond hair a tangled mess, and her six-year-old hands sticky with sweets.

"Hey, baby. What are you doing up so late?" He scooped her up and gave her a hug, careful not to bruise her. She was too thin, but it seemed no matter how much money he gave Ginger, Daisy never filled out.

"Are you finished catching bad guys today? Did you bring something to eat?" She wrapped her skinny arms around his neck and bounced against him. "There was only beans in the cupboard for dinner today and I had them three times already this week for dinner."

"Ginger." He shouted her name, both out of anger and because he knew she'd be in the bedroom with Gabe and he didn't want that train wreck of a relationship in his face. "I got a sandwich in my bag. Daddy'll feed you good."

He only ever regretted his career choices when it came to Daisy. He'd been undercover with the mob four years when he met Ginger in a bar and took her home for the night. The nature of his undercover police work meant he couldn't have a normal relationship so he lived for his one-night stands. He hadn't expected that one night to lead to a lifelong commitment in the form of a little girl.

"Yeah." Ginger stepped out onto the porch, and crossed her arms beneath her generous breasts, almost busting out of her hot pink tank top. Those breasts were how he'd wound up in her bed in the first place. Daisy was how he wound up in her life.

"What the fuck did you do with the money I gave you last week? Daisy says you're only feeding her beans."

Ginger didn't even have the good grace to look guilty. Instead, she just shrugged. "Things are expensive. I gotta pay rent, utilities, car payments, the dog had to go to the vet . . ."

"You took the dog to the vet instead of feeding our child?"

"I knew she'd live. Scamper wouldn't." She gave him the look—that fucking look that drove him out of his mind, the look of a scheming woman who told a man she was on the pill when she wasn't because he was the first decent man to cross her path and she wanted to keep him. "You got no right to come in here and criticize how I raise Daisy. You chose your work over raising your kid. The criminals of Vegas get to spend more time with you than her."

He hugged Daisy to his chest. "I told you a hundred times, Ginger. It's not the hours. It's the danger. I'm doing stuff that could come back on you and Daisy, and I don't want either of you to get hurt."

She snorted a laugh. "What? You're afraid someone's gonna beat down our door 'cause you handed out a parking ticket? You just like to big yourself up when we both know you're a nobody. A beat cop who's never gotten off the street."

One day he'd tell her the truth. He'd tell her how he'd moved up quickly through the ranks of the Las Vegas police to become a detective, and how even that wasn't enough to feed his need for adrenaline. He'd tell her how he'd been offered an undercover job, and after it was done, he was hooked because the rush he got when he was shoulder to shoulder with the criminals, walking their walk and talking their talk, was like nothing he'd experienced before.

And he was good—damn good—able to fit into almost any social group, mimic their speech and body language, wear their clothes and drive their cars. No one had ever made him for cop, and no one ever would. He'd been undercover in the mob for ten years now, answering to another name, living another man's life. Although he wasn't a made man, he was a trusted associate. If they found out who he really was, they'd kill him where he stood. And then they'd go after his family—but only if there was a family to find.

Which was why he'd given up custody of Daisy to Ginger. Now all he had were visitation rights—every Tuesday evening, and weekends, if he was free.

The door banged and Gabe appeared in the doorway wearing only a ratty pair of sweatpants, a gold chain, and a ball cap. Ben had never seen him with his shirt on, and he felt surprisingly jealous of Gabe's rippling muscles, giant revolver chest tat, and washboard abs. Sure, Ben kept himself in shape. Although he was undercover, old habits died hard and he'd never missed a workout when he was a uniformed cop. He still worked out every morning, and ran five times a week. But Ben wasn't twenty-two any more. Nor did he take steroids that could be the only reason Gabe looked swollen like a circus balloon.

Gabe threw an arm over Ginger's shoulders and Ben caught the shadow of a tattoo on his arm. If he ever became a made man, he'd get a tattoo to mark the occasion, maybe a daisy for his daughter. Or not. As far as Ben knew, only one undercover cop had ever been made, and Ben was damn sure he would never be number two because his assignment was finally supposed to be coming to a close.

"Ben."

"Gabe."

"Kinda late to be showing up to take our little princess out on the town. A person might think you don't give two fucks about your kid." Gabe lifted his chin toward Daisy, and Ben's skin prickled. He'd had a bad feeling about Gabe the first time they met, and the feeling got worse every time Gabe looked Daisy's way.

"She's *my* fucking princess, and I got no say when I gotta do overtime."

"Don't swear in front of the kid." Ginger lit a cigarette and leaned against Gabe.

"I'm Daddy's fucking princess," Daisy said, delighted, knowing Ben wouldn't correct her. She was smart for a six-year-old. She already knew how to work Ben's guilt.

"And pretty like her mama." Gabe groped one of Ginger's breasts, and she laughed.

"We just went at it for two hours straight, and you're wantin' more?"

Bile rose in Ben's throat. He didn't want Gabe thinking Daisy was pretty, or calling her anything other than her name. Hell, he didn't want him anywhere near his little girl, but what the fuck could he do? He thought he was doing the right thing, giving up custody to keep her safe. Now he was beginning to think he had failed her.

Gabe grinned. "Maybe Ben will take her out for a midnight ride and I can fuck you on that pretty princess bed he bought for her birthday."

Ben didn't know if Gabe was a sick bastard or just messing with him, but unless he had probable cause he couldn't touch the fucker, nor could he call his handler, Jack Freemont, and ask him to send someone to arrest Gabe for being a dick.

Fuck. He needed to get out. Once the damn job was over, he would challenge the custody order. He'd go back to detective work. Regular hours. Steady income. Nice house in a nice neighborhood with good people around. No judge was going to deny him custody, especially after he explained how Daisy's home life had gone downhill since Gabe came on the scene with a full-on swagger and a car full of blow.

He checked his watch and shifted Daisy to his back so he could piggyback her to his car. He had a blue Volvo and a work truck he drove when he was in his Mafia skin, but when he drove out to the sticks to see Daisy, he used the Chrysler 300 the police had bought for him as a bribe the day he met Gabe and threatened to take Daisy and walk off the job.

Although he loved the thrill of undercover work, Ben was tired. It was becoming harder and harder to file reports about the activities of guys he'd come to like and respect—guys who considered him a friend. Yeah, they did bad shit, but most of it was done to other bad guys, and you had to be in the life to really understand. If criminals were whacking criminals and civilians weren't getting hurt, what was the benefit in locking half of them up? There would be an imbalance on the street, and that's when civilians would be at risk. And wasn't that supposed to be his job? Protecting civilians?

"C'mon, baby." He carried Daisy to his car. "We got about an hour before I have to go back to work. I'll take you for a quick bite to eat and then I'll bring you home and put you to bed."

"Don't hurry back 'cause her bed will be occupied for a bit," Gabe shouted after them.

"I don't like Gabe," Daisy whispered as he helped her into the car.

"I don't like him either." Ben didn't believe in hiding things from kids. He figured they were pretty smart these days, smart enough to know if an adult was lying to them.

"Can I come and live with you?"

He put her down beside his vehicle and crouched down on the sidewalk beside her. "I promise you, princess. As soon as my job is done, I'll find a way to get you outta here. We'll leave the city and go someplace where it's green all year 'round and there's trees and lakes and you'll never eat another can of beans again."

"As soon as all the bad guys are in jail?"

Ben opened his mouth to say yes, but nothing came out. He'd collected enough evidence in his first few years undercover to convict the top Vegas mafia bosses of multiple crimes. But the top brass in the police department had done fuck all with it. Whether it was greed or politics, Ben didn't know, but they refused to act. He'd had a hard time dealing with all the excuses and noise, the requests for evidence that wouldn't end, so he'd just put his head down and resigned himself to keep working until they got whatever it was they were looking for.

But things had changed for him when he was taken into a new crew with a new capo that he couldn't help but like and admire. His capo didn't allow gratuitous violence. He wasn't into prostitution or drugs. Although he loved the Mafia life, he craved respectability, and Ben understood that. As an unwanted foster kid, he had craved respectability too. Over the next few years, he earned the trust and respect of his new capo. His work on the crew was valued, appreciated, and rewarded. They were like the family the foster kid in him had always wanted, the friends he'd never made in the police department because he'd grown up wary of getting too close because he always knew he'd be moving on. It had been easy to agree to stay undercover year after year. But it became harder and harder to live with the fact he was betraying his capo's trust.

After ten years of guilt and deception, and constantly looking over his shoulder, thinking any minute he would be whacked, he wanted what everyone else had. A life. A family. Time to spend with his kid before she was all grown up. Friends he didn't have to betray.

"When I'm free, sweetheart, first thing I'm gonna do is come for you. I'll get that custody order changed and you can be my girl all the time."

Daisy rested her small hand on her cheek. "I'll hold that promise in my heart for when times are bad."

He didn't know how much worse things could be for her with her Mom a druggie and deadbeat Gabe in the house, but it was all he could give her for now.

FOUR

"Darling. It's been so long." Gina Cordano, Mia's mom, and the perfect mob wife, kissed Mia's cheeks and ushered her into the cool marble foyer of their Italian Renaissance home in the exclusive Henderson luxury community.

From the outside, the house looked like many of the other luxury homes in the gated area, all with awe-inspiring views and access to the canyon style golf-holes of the Rio Secco Championship Golf Course. However, security at the Cordano residence included wire fencing, CCTV cameras, and twenty-four hour guards as well as ten-foot high bushes for privacy.

Alfio, her father's top enforcer, closed the massive cathedral door behind her and punched in the security code. Before she understood what her father did for a living, Mia had always been amazed at her friends' families who did not lock themselves into their homes at all hours of the day. They routinely left doors and windows open, and wandered outside in their yards without the benefit of bodyguards or cameras. They had a freedom she desperately wanted and knew she would never have.

Mia wrinkled her nose at the overpowering scent of her mother's perfume and gave her a dutiful hug, trying her best not to crease her mother's linen dress. Not that it would matter. Her mother had a vast wardrobe and changed five or six times a day in her role as a symbol of her husband's power.

"You look nice, Mama. Is that Prada?"

"New season." Her mother smiled her perfect smile in her perfectly made-up face with her perfect haircut into a perfectly chiseled asymmetrical bob. Although Mia shared her mother's thick, dark straight hair, she had gone for a blunt cut as soon as her hair reached her shoulders, a look she knew her mother despised.

Her mother's gaze drifted down over Mia's black street-punk dress, the fake corset laced down the side, crinoline underlay and shoulder straps with silver buckles. Mia had paired it with lace stockings and her favorite thick-soled boots, calf-high with red roses embroidered on the sides.

"Your father will be disappointed to see you dressed like a punk-rock star. I have some last season Chanel upstairs in the spare room. Why don't you run up and find something to wear. He's not in a good mood tonight."

"Not in a good mood" was family code to mean he'd already taken out some of his frustrations on Mama, which was probably why her foundation was so thick and her arms were covered with a sweater. Mia's mother knew all the tricks for hiding bruises. It was part of being a good wife. Although her marriage had not been arranged, Mia's mother quickly found out she had been taken in by suavity and charm. Her husband had married her solely for her looks and connections, and the love he professed to have died on the day she said "I do."

Still, she had done her duty like the good Mafia princess she had been raised to be. She had given her husband the required son—and two unnecessary daughters—found and decorated a house to befit his status as a mob boss, raised their three children, and ensured she was always well groomed and impeccably dressed—the perfect accessory for her husband's arm at Mafia functions. She dutifully kept her mouth shut when he spent time with his mistresses, and in return enjoyed the benefits of his status as a Mafia don. It was a cold, empty existence and one Mia wanted no part of.

"I'm wearing a dress so he doesn't beat me," Mia said bluntly. "Unless he decides he now wants me in pink or Chanel when I come to visit, that's as far as I'll go. I wouldn't even come home if it wasn't for you and Kat." Or the fact her father would send his soldiers to hunt her down simply because he wouldn't tolerate disobedience in any form.

Her mother's lips tightened. "You need to accept who you are and the responsibilities that come with being a woman in a Mafia family. We have our place, and your life will be much easier if you just accept it and—"

"Don't." Mia cut her off. She had never been able to understand how her mother could want the life she led for her daughters. How could she not want them to be free to make their own choices?

"I just don't want to see you get hurt, darling."

"Then you should have stopped him every time he hit me, or when he broke my arm and beat me so badly I had to spend five days in the hospital pretending I'd been mugged." Her voice rose in pitch with the distress she always felt when she thought about that night. "You should have been there the night he killed Danny and left this mark on my throat." She touched the scar on her neck. "But you weren't. And the only reason he didn't kill me that night is because Nico Toscani saved me and lost his father as result."

She drew in a shuddering breath and brushed past her mother to head up the grand staircase as the memories flooded back.

Papà had been so angry when she burst into Luigi's restaurant that night, desperate to save Danny even though she knew there was no chance. And yet the blows he had dealt her when she pleaded for Danny's life in front of Don Toscani and his son were nothing compared to what he did to her to ensure her silence after Danny died—a silence to shield Dante from the deed he was commanded to do. Nico hadn't been able to save her as her father marked her with his blade. He had been on his knees, cradling the body of his dying father who had tried to save Nico from her father's wrath.

"Your father wants to see you when Dante arrives," her mother called up. "There's been a change of plans for dinner. Tell Kat it will just be her and I tonight. You and Dante are going out with your father."

Mia hesitated, tempted to ask why her father would want to waste an evening having dinner with her and Dante. He had never spent time with her without the rest of the family present except when he was beating on her for some perceived breach of the rules. But did she really want to know? Nothing to do with her father was good, so why ruin these few precious moments she got to spend with her sister worrying about something that she'd find out about soon enough.

"Kat?" She walked down the wide, carpeted hallway and pushed open Kat's bedroom door, only to be enveloped in a sea of pink. Kat was everything a Mafia daughter was expected to be, and, as a result, she had escaped their father's abuse growing up. But even if Kat hadn't embraced her girliness with the same passion with which Mia despised it, not even their father would have hurt her. Slim and fragile, with dark hair and wide, hazel eyes, Kat had a kind nature, a soft voice and a sweet, gentle disposition. She was the peacemaker in the family, empathetic to the point she would curl up and cry whenever Mia suffered her father's anger. Mia never understood why he directed all his abuse at her, but she willingly endured his punishments if it meant Kat would be spared.

"Mia." Kat jumped off the bed and threw her arms around her big sister. With Mia working in the city, and Kat busy with school and activities out in the suburbs, they communicated mostly online, but whenever they did meet, Mia realized just how much she missed her little sister, and how guilty she felt leaving her in the house alone. Dante had moved out long ago, and as Papà 's underboss, he helped manage the Toscani family capos as well as run his own crew.

"You cut your hair." Mia ran her fingers through Kat's thick, straight hair, now hanging just below her shoulders. "I like it."

"I did it for my eighteenth birthday, but Papà hated it." Kat sighed. "He said men like women with long hair, not women who dress and act like boys. I had to promise not to cut it again."

Mia's hand froze in place. "He didn't—"

"No." Kat let her go. "He doesn't hurt me like he does you."

Mia let out the breath she hadn't realized she was holding and sat on Kat's fluffy pink duvet. She had protected Kat when she lived at home, taking the blame when Kat did something wrong, intervening when she thought their father might lose his temper. When she'd finally had enough and walked out the door, she begged Kat to come with her, but Kat assured her Papa wouldn't touch her, even with Mia gone, and she'd been right.

Kat sat down beside her and leaned against Mia's

shoulder, threading their fingers together. Mia squeezed Kat's hand. It had taken her a long time to get used to Kat's physically affectionate nature. Their mother rarely hugged them, and the only touches she'd had from her father involved pain.

"Tell me all about school."

Kat filled her in on her classes, her friends, and her after-school activities. She showed Mia some of the paintings she'd done in art class and Mia flipped through Kat's portfolio, amazed at her sister's talent.

"These are good, Kat. Really good. Have you thought about going to art school?"

"I can't afford it on my own, and I'm afraid to ask," she said quietly. "After what you went through . . ."

Mia pressed her lips tight together. She'd applied for the computer-science program at UCLA without discussing it with her parents. When she received the acceptance form, she announced she was leaving home and suffered the worst beating she'd had since the night in the restaurant. But even bruises and a broken arm hadn't deterred her. As soon as she was able to stand, she'd packed her bag and walked out the door. She'd paid her way with scholarships, loans and by working two jobs while going to school. For the first few months, she lived in dreaded anticipation of seeing the family enforcers come to drag her home. But her father left her alone except to demand her presence once a month for a family dinner. They never spoke about it, and only Kat showed up at her graduation.

"He won't do that to you," Mia said. "You're special, Kat. He doesn't hate you like he hates me. And if you do want to move out and go to school, you can always stay with me."

"I couldn't leave Mama alone with him. He's nicer to her when I'm around, and I think she'd get very lonely."

Mia felt a twinge of guilt that she'd never had the kind of relationship with her mother that Kat did. Although her mother had always been there for her in every way but defending her against the constant abuse, they had never been close. Mia had just chalked it up to the fact they had very different personalities. Mia had never enjoyed shopping or getting her hair or nails done. She didn't care about entertaining, fashion shows, what movie stars were doing, or what celebrities were wearing. And her mother had no interest in computers, the Internet, gender politics, or feminist punk rock.

They talked until Mia's mother came to tell her Dante had arrived and she was needed in her father's study. Mia gave Kat a kiss on the cheek and went down the ostentatious stairway and along the marble hallway decorated with gilt-edged tables, replica Grecian statues and huge vases of flowers, to the back of the house. Alfio fell into step beside her, his footsteps surprisingly quiet for a man so large. He had been her father's top enforcer for as long as she could remember and never once had she seen him smile.

Mia knocked on the door to her father's study. After a few brief moments, her father called for her to enter. Taking a deep breath, Mia walked into the room that had seen the worse of her punishments and borne the brunt of her fears. Dark and gloomy, paneled in rich, dark wood and hung with thick green curtains, her father's study reminded her of something out of the Victorian era. He sat behind a massive desk in a throne like chair, that he'd had shipped over from his grandfather's house in Italy, along with most of the office furnishings. His *consigliere*, known as the Wolf for his peculiarly angled face, long nose, lean body and thick mop of gray hair, stood by his side along with Dante's massive muscle-head of a bodyguard, Rev, who had been with the family almost ten years.

"Papà." Mia bent her head in respect, not wanting to start out the meeting with a punch or a slap that would mean she would be more focused on the pain than on the real reason she had been summoned to the house. She spotted Dante standing by the window, and greeted him with a smile. "Hi Dante."

Tall and slim, with a long, thin face and chiseled cheekbones, Dante carried the heavy burden of being heir to the family. Although he had not inherited their father's vicious temper, or his ruthless streak, Dante never hesitated to do their father's bidding, and never challenged him, even when Mia was forced to bear the brunt of their father's rage. As a child, he had been a fun, teasing big brother, but he had changed when their father forced him into the life at the age of nine, sending him on errands for him and his men. After that, he had become detached and distant, and she still missed the Dante she used to know.

Dante gave her a curt nod, and Mia's smile faded. "What's wrong?"

"*Madre di Cristo!*" Her father snarled before Dante could answer. "You look like you're dressed up for Halloween." He took a deep breath and bellowed. "Gina! Get in here!"

Mia's mother, who no doubt had been waiting by the door in case she was summoned, rushed inside, her face pale and drawn. "Is something wrong?"

"I told you to make sure she was properly dressed. Look at her. She's an embarrassment to the family. How the fuck am I supposed to take her out looking like that?"

"*Mi dispiace,*" Mama stammered. "I thought you meant you wanted her in a dress, and she's wearing one. I did offer to give her some of last season's Chanel—"

"Shut the fuck up." He rose from the chair, pushed up his sleeves. Mia's skin prickled in warning, and her mother let out the softest whimper. After years of abuse, they all knew the signs, and they knew better than to run because running always made it worse.

Mia shot a look at Dante, noted the lack of tension in his shoulders, the disinterest in his face. He was taller than their father, younger, stronger, the first-born and only son. If she were Dante, she would protect her mother, protect them all. She would beat her father down and tell him never to touch her mother again.

Unbidden, an image of Nico came to mind, his broad, powerful shoulders and muscular arms, the way he had led her through the casino the other night, with his hand on her lower back, half guiding, half protecting her—the way he had protected her all those years ago. Nico would be able to put her father in his place with one well-placed blow. Not only that, he was a powerful Mafia capo; a formidable and ruthless man who took what he wanted, regardless of the consequences.

A man she did not fear, because she had seen the heart of him.

Mia had felt bold, reckless, and even brave when she threatened Nico in his office. Why couldn't she feel like that with her father? Why couldn't she be bold now?

"Don't touch her." Mia stepped back, placing herself between her father and mother.

Shock and disbelief clouded her father's face, and then a fury like she'd never seen before twisted his expression. "Stupid girl. Get the fuck out of the way. Your mother knew exactly what I wanted. She chose to defy me. She will be punished so she learns not to do it again."

"It was my choice to dress like this." She stepped back, pushing her mother behind her. "If anyone should be punished it should be me."

"*Dio mio*, I'll be glad to get rid of you." He closed the distance between them in two quick strides, and struck

Mia's face so hard, her head snapped to the side. Still reeling from the blow, she couldn't stop him from striking her mother and then kicking her when she fell to the floor.

"Dante. Get my jacket and pick up your sister. We don't have time to get her new clothes." He stepped over Mia's mother, and looked back over his shoulder. "Gina, the next time I use the words 'properly dressed' I want her dressed like you."

"Of course, Battista." Mama wiped the blood from the corner of her lip and pushed herself to sit, her legs folded under her on the plush, red carpet. "*Mi dispiace*. It won't happen again."

"Not for this one, it won't." He shot Mia a look of disgust as Dante steadied her with a firm hand on her elbow. After a few parting words to the Wolf, he stalked down the hallway, cutting a dark shadow through the light in his custom-made Italian suit.

"Where are we going?" Cheek throbbing, Mia followed her father down the hallway with Dante, Rev, and Alfio taking up the rear.

"Vincenzo's Trattoria."

Surprised that he would respond, Mia kept quiet as they exited the house. Rev climbed into the driver's seat of the family limo, and Alfio settled in the passenger seat beside him. Mia's father sat in the rear with Mia and Dante facing him.

"I want you to keep your mouth shut when we get there," Mia's father said as Rev pulled away from the curb. "I don't want to hear any attitude. You disrespect me or embarrass our family in front of our guests; you'll be one sorry girl when we get home. The clothes are bad enough."

Mia's skin prickled, and she looked over at Dante, but

he stared out the window in stony silence. "Who are we meeting?"

"Don Toscani and his son." Papà scrubbed his hand over his face. "It's time."

"Time for what?"

His face tightened. "Time to make yourself fucking useful to the family. You were seen the other night in a casino with Nico Toscani, dressed as a whore. You dishonored the family. You disrespected me—"

"I was working." She dared to interrupt him. "I was doing a penetration test—"

"Shut the fuck up," he barked. "You got yourself involved with the fucking Toscanis, now you're gonna be involved with them for life. You gave me an opportunity to contact Don Toscani and negotiate a truce to end the war between our families. I offered a marriage to seal the deal. We'll combine our drug-trade operations to push out the cartels and the street gangs for once and for all, not just here in the city but across the state to L.A. Not only that, we'll finally be able to get into the gaming industry through his nephew's casino. It's the perfect place to launder our money."

Shock stole her breath away. "You're asking me to marry Nico Toscani?"

"I'm not asking. I'm telling." He slicked down his hair. "And it's not that bastard son who put a price on my fucking head that you're going to marry. It's Tony. A son by marriage. He wants to have a look at you tonight. You aren't ugly. You've made yourself a marketable commodity. You'd better hope he can see past the ridiculous clothes."

"You think I worked hard in school and built a business so I could be a marketable commodity?" Her voice rose in pitch even though she knew it would rile him.

"Why the fuck else would you do it?" He leaned back in his seat, his silk shirt straining against his barrel chest, huge stomach hanging over his belt. "You're a woman. Your only value to me is political. We need this alliance to end the *faida* and increase the power of *la famiglia*. Once you marry Tony, his bastard of a cousin won't be a threat—he's not gonna be able to whack family and he won't have the power to challenge Santo anymore. I'd be surprised if he's still alive when you get back from your honeymoon."

All those years of trying to prove herself, to gain her father's approval, to show him she was good as a son, had been for nothing. He had never seen her as anything more than a piece of property to be maintained and traded away. In her heart she had always known it, but to hear the words from his lips made her feel sick inside. She wanted done of this, of him, of their sick, twisted, broken family, of *Cosa Nostra* rules and codes and culture. She had fought hard for her little piece of independence, and she wouldn't survive if he took it away.

"I am not marrying Tony Crackers." She looked over at Dante for help, but he continued to stare out the window. Her bad. Dante had never stood up to their father. Clearly, he wasn't about to start now. "I have no interest in getting married, and certainly not to a psychopath. The newspapers are now calling him the Butcher. Every time he has a dispute with someone, they wind up not just dead but massacred."

Her father waved a dismissive hand. "You'll marry who I tell you to marry, and you'll do what I tell you to do. We all have to make sacrifices. This is yours. We'll sit down, have a nice dinner, make the plans . . . I have invited Don Falzone, don of the Vegas faction of the New York Falzones to be there as a witness to the end of the *faida* and the marriage promise. The Falzones are the only other family strong enough to challenge us for control of the city, but once he realizes the might of our alliance, he will think twice before trying to push his way into our territory."

Did his greed have no end? She could read between the lines. Once he took out Don Toscani and Tony, the Falzone family would be next. Well, she refused to be a pawn in his game. "I have a business to run and a life to live away from *la famiglia*. I'm not getting involved."

His dark eyes grew cold and hard. "Forget about your little hobby. You'll be looking after your husband, having his kids, decorating your house, fixing that mop of hair . . . Doing all the shit the women do to make the men look good. If your business is making money, then Dante will take over."

Disbelief became anger in a heartbeat. "That's *my* business. I set it up. I paid for everything. I made the contacts. I brought in the contracts. No way am I handing it over to Dante. He doesn't know a damn thing about hacking or security. He can't even turn on his own damn computer."

She should have known what was coming, braced herself for the impact, but anger overrode instinct, so when he struck, there was nothing to protect her from his fist.

"Cristo." He smashed his fist into the side of her head. "How many fucking times do I have to beat you tonight? After all these fucking years, you still don't know your place. When you started doing work for friends of mine, that business became a Mafia business. Women don't do Mafia business. Women stay home, shut the fuck up, spread their legs, and do what they're told."

Stunned, Mia breathed through the pain, waited until she could see clearly again, until her ears weren't ringing and her head was no longer fuzzy. "You can't make me," she said. "The word 'yes' will never leave my lips.

Beat me all you want. I'll never marry into the mob."
She looked over at her brother. "How you could let this
happen, Dante?" she demanded. "Why didn't you do
something?"

"I did." Dante turned slowly to face her. "It was supposed to be Kat."

"*Dio mio.*" Her heart sank into her stomach. Sweet,
innocent, sunny Kat. "He'd destroy her."

"But not you." Guilt flickered across Dante's face
so fast, she wondered if she had seen it. "You're strong.
Smart. A survivor. If anyone could get through this, it's
you."

He was right. Kat wouldn't survive a week with Tony
Crackers. She was trusting, generous, innocent—an ar-
tistic soul who wouldn't survive the rigors of mob life.

Rev pulled up in front of Vincenzo's, a well-known
Italian restaurant and Mafia hangout at the edge of town
and bordering on an industrial estate. The location gave
it an air of privacy and kept the tourists away, but the food
kept those in the know coming back for more.

Mia's father turned to look at her, his face dark with
warning. "You gonna get out of the limo and meet Toscani's boy or do I send Rev and Alfio back for Kat?"

"Don't you dare touch her," Mia spat out as she opened
the door. There had to be a way out, and she would find
it, but in the meantime she would keep Kat as far away
from this mess as possible. "I hate you."

Papà snorted a laugh and joined her on the pavement.
Alfio joined them and put a hand on her shoulder, a
not-so-subtle warning not to run.

"After tonight that's not gonna be my fucking problem." Papà grabbed the neck of her dress and tore it, baring her throat and chest down to the crescents of her
breasts. "That should help the situation. Tony'll want to
know there's a woman underneath all those ridiculous

clothes. You try to hide it, but we all know it's there. You got tits, girl. Whether you want 'em or not."

She waited on the pavement for Dante to emerge, but when he reached for the door, Papà shook his head. "You've done what I asked you to do. I don't need you tonight. Rev will take you home. Wait for me."

Hand shaking, Mia tugged the edges of her dress together and followed her father into the restaurant. No matter what happened, she couldn't go through with the wedding. A Mafia marriage was for life. It didn't matter if there was cheating or beating, or if civilian law granted a divorce. *Cosa Nostra* would ensure that the two parties stayed together using whatever means necessary to get that message home.

And there was no way she could become a Toscani for the rest of her life.

FIVE

"Hey, sweetie. Wanna spend some time?"

"*Testa di cazzo.*" Nico slapped Luca's hand off his shoulder, steering his SUV with one hand. "You've been fucking too many hookers. You sound just like them."

Luca, a well-respected Toscani soldier with his own crew of associates, laughed. "That's 'cause you won't share what you've got going on in that casino. Young, drunk, available women in Vegas for the weekend all ready to party. How many do you invite up to your penthouse suite every night?"

"I'd tell you, but you can't count that high." Despite his tension about the operation they planned to carry out as soon as Vincenzo gave them the sign that everyone was in the restaurant, he was glad of Luca's joking mood. Luca had withdrawn after the tragic death of his newly-wed wife, losing himself in his work to the exclusion of everyone including his young son, Matteo.

Luca ran his hand through his thick blond hair, cut to stand up straight on top. With his hazel eyes, and rugged features, he looked more Nordic than Italian. "Anytime you feel like hosting another party, just let me know. I've decided to stick with casual hook-ups and one-night stands. No pain. No heartache. I won't fucking care if they get whacked, and I don't have to deal with little Matteo getting attached." He tapped Frankie on the shoulder. "Whaddya say, Frankie? You in?"

"Nah." Frankie shook his head, lost in thought. "I'll keep watch."

A prominent New York Mafia family had taken Frankie in when he was nine years old after his mother and father were killed in a revenge attack by the Russian mafia. Trained as an enforcer, he had been sent to Las Vegas by the New York boss to help the Toscanis in their bid to take control of the city, but he had quickly become attached to Nico's crew. He was more like a biker than a wiseguy, with his long dark hair, biker boots, and Harley belt, and he had the biker swagger to match, but he was fiercely loyal, and there was nobody Nico would rather have at his back.

Nico had never seen Frankie with a woman. No hookers. No girlfriends. No one-night stands. If not for the fact that Frankie had once confided in him after they'd had one too many drinks, that there was a woman he wanted but couldn't have, Nico would have pressured him more often to join their parties.

"You're missing out," Luca said. "Last time we had six girls up there skinny dipping in Nico's patio pool."

Nico pulled up in front of Il Tavolino, an old Vegas Italian restaurant that looked like it had seen better days. He pushed his weapon out of sight under his suit jacket. "So this is the thing I told you about." A *thing* was mob speak for an illegal act that was better left unsaid. "A friend of mine, Lennie, owns this joint. He says he has a problem." *A friend of mine* told Luca and Frankie that Lennie was a civilian as opposed to a *friend of ours*, a made guy in the mob. Usually, Nico's "friends" came to him when they had a problem, instead of Nico traveling to see them, but Lennie reputedly served the best cannoli in the city, and Nico was a sucker for sweets.

Gianni "Big Joe" De Cicco was waiting for them at the front entrance. Heavily muscled, a few inches shorter than Nico and bald as a stone, Big Joe had gotten his nickname due to his resemblance to a mob-friendly cop who'd been named "Little Joe." He was a mob associate who had been with the Toscani family for ten years— three of those with Nico's crew—and had proved himself loyal, honest, and trustworthy. Nico planned to open his books when things settled down so Big Joe could become a made man.

"Right on time," Nico said. "I'm gonna start thinking you're a cop the way you're never late. Luca's always dragging his feet and Frankie sometimes just doesn't show. Maybe you should share your secret."

"Don't want to let you down, Mr. Toscani." Big Joe gave a little shrug as if he were embarrassed by the attention. "I know what it's like to be counting on a guy and have him not show up. My plumbing business has a high turnover 'cause I don't put up with that shit. And if I won't put up with it from my guys, I wouldn't expect you to put up with it from me."

A retired jewel thief from Miami, Big Joe had moved to California to escape the heat of an FBI crackdown. He retrained as a plumber, started a business, and did some work for a few wiseguys on Nico's crew. Once it became known he did a good job at a low price, he became a hot commodity. Everyone needed plumbing work, and he quickly became the go-to guy for the mob. Eventually, Nico had taken notice, and now he worked exclusively for Nico and his crew, transporting stolen goods in his plumbing trucks between jobs fixing leaky faucets.

Lennie Minudo, the restaurant owner, was waiting for

them outside. Far from an innocent civilian, Lennie ran illegal craps games from his back room, and a small-time loan sharking business for the guys who lost big at his tables. He was dirty money, and Nico had no problem taking it off his hands.

As they walked into the restaurant, Nico felt like he'd re-entered the city's Golden Age—from the tuxedoed waiters and captains doing tableside presentations, to the magnificent plush banquets and the huge raised stage where a Frank Sinatra impersonator was singing "My Way." Vegas memorabilia and photos lined every square inch of the walls. Framed pictures of old movies stars sat alongside the Mafia greats—Bogart beside Bugsy Siegel, and Frank Sinatra beside Anthony Spilotro. Glass cases containing old 45s and sparkly shoes, an old-fashioned revolver, and a top hat and cane gave the restaurant an elegant feel. Nico had always enjoyed Vegas' old-school restaurants, but Il Tavolino was in an entirely different league.

"How long have you been here?" He pulled Lennie to the side as Frankie and Luca ordered their drinks.

"About two years now," he said. "This used to be the Golden Nugget back in the day. I bought it ten years ago and it took a long time to fix it up and decorate just right. Members of the Rat Pack used to come to the Golden Nugget and I got to keep all the pictures on the wall. Elvis Presley ate here, Joe DiMaggio, Tony Spilotro, and more."

"And the memorabilia?"

Lennie shrugged. "What can I say? I'm a collector, Mr. Toscani. It took me so long to fix this place up because I'd see something I'd just have to have and those things don't come cheap."

"Incredible." Nico took a walk around, soaking in the Old Vegas-meets-Old Hollywood decor. If he ever had something that was just his, bought with clean money, decorated to his taste, and solely for his pleasure, it would be this.

He felt a curious longing as he joined Frankie, Big Joe, and Luca in the booth. It was the same feeling he'd had when Mia had been in his office. Something so unexpected and foreign he had dismissed it right away.

"You guys want something to eat? Drink?" Lennie offered them a menu. "Everything is on the house."

"I'll tell you what we're gonna have," Nico said, waving away the menu. "Make us a little of this and a little of that, maybe some antipasti, some mussels with gorgonzola, a little strozzapreti with wild boar sauce and rigatoni with spicy sausage and peppers, and maybe some tiger prawns with a little cream and basil, and then we'll have cannoli. Lots of cannoli. How does that sound?"

"Very good, Mr. Toscani."

He enjoyed his meal, smiled as Luca and Frankie ribbed Big Joe about his punctuality, but his mind was on the saucy little temptress he'd caught in his casino. He'd directed Vito to send a notice terminating the contract, but when he received a bill with the words "As promised" scrawled across the top, he couldn't help but laugh. No one else would have dared send him a bill after what had happened at the casino. That she had, made him want her even more. He had met few women in his life who would stand up to him, fewer still who would defy him. And none he wanted to see again.

After the dishes were cleared, he waved Lennie over and thanked him for the meal. Business was never conducted until after the food was done, and that was Lennie's sign to explain his problem.

"I got thieves on my staff, taking from the cash register, hauling away food and booze," Lennie said, wringing his hands. "And I got problems with drug dealers loading my customers up with coke. The dealers are attracting some rough characters. They cause fights in the bar, and I can't call the police because if they find out about the dealers then I'll lose my liquor license and my craps tables. My friend down the street, he says he pays you every week and you help him out with security issues. I was just wondering if I could get in on that, too."

Nico bit back a laugh. When he'd cleaned up Lennie's friend's restaurant, he'd sent the thieves and druggies down here with the sole purpose of getting Lennie to call and ask for the same protection the Toscanis offered his friend. The ultimate goal was to bust them out, a classic scam in which the mob offered to clean the place up for a fixed weekly fee, and then over time offered to drop the fee for a piece of the action. As the mob worked its way into the business, they would section off tables for their permanent use, order excess supplies on credit to sell on the black market, and launder money through creative bookkeeping. When the owner's credit and reputation were shot, the building would be burned down for the insurance money.

Nico didn't bust out innocent civilians, and now that he was here, he didn't want to bust Lennie out either. Burning down the restaurant would be a fucking tragedy. The memorabilia Lennie had collected was irreplaceable.

"I'll tell you what I'm gonna do." Nico outlined a plan in which Big Joe would come by every day for a week or two to weed out the crooks and clean the place up. Nico would ensure Lennie was never bothered again, and in return Lennie would give him twenty percent of the business and the best table in the house whenever Nico stopped by for a meal.

Frankie, Luca, and Big Joe stared at him like he'd grown another head. This discussion usually happened months after the first visit when the owner was dependent on the mob for protection and had no way out. But Nico didn't intend to play the game to the inevitable conclusion. He wanted a piece of the Il Tavolino, but he wanted Lennie to run it.

"Mr. Toscani. Please." Lennie held out his hands. "Twenty percent is too high. I'm up to my ears in debt. How about I pay you something every week and you come by whenever you want for a meal on the house?"

With a sigh, Nico stood. "You come to me for help. But when I offer my protection, you negotiate?" Nico held up a box of matches he'd swiped on the way in. "Does that sound respectful to you? I come out of my way to see you, and you insult me? Is that how you treat a business partner? Your customers? I don't think this business is worth saving. How about I burn the fucking place down right now?" He lit a match and threw it on the white cotton tablecloth. Big Joe, Luca, and Frankie jumped up as the tablecloth burst into flames.

"No. No. Please don't burn it down." Lennie begged, dropping to his knees as a waiter rushed over with a fire extinguisher. "I'm sorry, Mr. Toscani. Please. It was a very generous offer. I wasn't thinking."

Nico held up a hand, warning the waiter back. It would be a shame to let the restaurant and all the precious memorabilia burn, but sacrifices had to be made to ensure no one ever challenged his authority. Nico told people how it was. There was no negotiation. "You're right. It was generous. Too generous." Nico watched the flames climb down the tablecloth and lick the red velvet banquette while sweat beaded on Lennie's brow. "I'll take thirty percent of the business, and Luca here is gonna be the manager. You'll be his assistant and you can teach him all he needs to know about your business."

Nico didn't look at Luca, knowing his friend wouldn't be happy with the plan. Luca already had a restaurant to run, as well as his other businesses. But he had turned that small place around and made it into one of the best Italian eateries in the city. Nico had no doubt he could make a success of Il Tavolino, too.

"Yes, of course. Thank you Mr. Toscani." Lennie glanced nervously at the flames. One more second and the banquette would catch fire, the sprinklers would turn on, the memorabilia would be destroyed, the fire department would show up and the entire evening would turn out to be a waste of time. Nico motioned to the waiter and the fire was quickly doused while Lennie wilted on the floor with a mumbled thanks.

Luca tapped Nico on the shoulder and spoke quietly in his ear. "I got a call from one the associates we sent to watch Vincenzo's Trattoria. Don Toscani and Tony are there along with Don Cordano and his daughter, as well as a bunch of bodyguards. But get this. Don Falzone is there, too. Might be something else is going on—something bigger than just a wedding. You want to go check it out? It's only a couple blocks away."

Nico had been trying all day to think of a way to stop the wedding. The marriage would put a huge obstacle in his quest to avenge his father. And the thought of his sexy temptress with Tony made him want to punch something. Maybe if hadn't met her before, seen that the fire courage she showed in his office were the truth of her essence, he might not have given their union a second thought. After all, his marriage to Rosa Scozzari would give him the power to overthrow both his uncle and Tony, even with the Cordano alliance. But something about Mia intrigued him—something much deeper than her beauty—and he was determined to find out what it was before Tony or some other wiseguy bastard stole her away.

"We'll take a walk." Nico brushed past a shell-shocked Lennie and headed for the door.

"I got no problem popping that fucker Tony, if you want," Frankie said, coming up behind him. Frankie had more kills under his belt than any other Toscani enforcer, and no compunction about pulling the trigger. And yet he was the most loyal and trustworthy man Nico knew. There was no one he would rather have at his back.

"We're not murderers," Nico snapped. Santo and Tony had taken the family down a path that would make his father turn in his grave. When Nico's father had been boss, civilians were considered untouchable, drugs, human trafficking, and prostitution beneath them, and the only people who got whacked were people like them.

Luca's phone buzzed again, and his eyes widened as he checked the message. "We'd better hurry. There's been gunfire. Multiple shots. Something big is going down."

Run. Run. Run.

Mia heard the words as if they were far away. She tried to move but her feet were planted firmly on the floor. Frozen in shock and fear, she tried to make sense of the stillness around her when only moments ago the restaurant had echoed with gunfire—of the darkness, when there had been light.

"Papà?" Her father had been sitting at the table facing her, his eyes cold and hard as he assured Tony Crackers that underneath the punk clothes she had the same tits and pussy as any woman, and she'd been trained to obey. Alfio, who had been escorting her back from the restroom, had grabbed her chin and twisted her head so Tony could see the bruise on her cheek.

Where was Alfio? He'd released her when the lights went out. She'd heard gunfire, a grunt, and a thud. Many thuds. And then the noise stopped, and Alfio's clammy grasp slipped away.

Carefully, she edged her foot to the side where he'd been standing and made contact with something soft. She didn't like Alfio. He'd always been cruel when carrying out her father's orders—holding her too tight, shoving her too hard, his hands surreptitiously touching her when her father wasn't looking. But she knew him—had known him since she was six years old—and in the darkness, better the devil you know than the one you don't.

"Alfio?"

Still nothing. She didn't know how long she'd been standing there when she heard a sound. The creak of a door. Footsteps. She drew in a shuddering breath and willed herself to move. Where was the sense of self-preservation that had built up the walls to shield her heart after Danny died? That had allowed her to endure the horror of being dragged back into the Mafia world she had tried so hard to escape?

Shaking, she bent down, felt around Alfio's body for his gun. Bile rose in her throat as she touched his warm skin, followed his arm to his hand and then, finally, to the cold, hard steel of the weapon lying beside him. She wrapped her fingers around the handle and stood, turning to the door just as the lights came on.

She blinked as her eyes adjusted to the light, tried to make out the blurry figure in front of her. Tall, broad shouldered, dark hair, well-cut suit. Her vision cleared and dark eyes met hers. Familiar. Her tension eased until he raised his gun. Mia slid her finger through her trigger. Her father may have despised her for being born a girl, but at least he'd taught her how to shoot.

"Holy fuck," a man's voice said from behind her. "Holy fuck, Nico. They're all dead: Don Toscani, Don Falzone, his underboss, coupla dudes who musta been bodyguards. Did she kill them all?"

Seemingly unconcerned by the gun Mia had pointed at his chest, Nico lifted a querying eyebrow.

"No." Mia shook her head. "It wasn't me. The lights went out. There were shots. And then . . ." She couldn't bring herself to turn around and see all the dead bodies so she gestured vaguely behind her with her left hand. "This."

"Drop your gun." Nico's voice, low and deep, rumbled through her.

"Drop *your* gun." She didn't know where she'd found the courage to defy him, but the minute she lowered her weapon, she would be vulnerable, and she'd had enough of being vulnerable tonight.

"Have a care, " he warned. "Frankie is behind you and he won't hesitate to add to the death toll tonight."

She didn't know who Frankie was, but if he worked for Nico, there was no way he would put Nico's life at risk by shooting her while she held a gun.

"So shoot me." Her instincts were screaming at her to get the hell out, but she forced herself to stay in place. As long as her weapon was pointed at Nico's chest, she was in a position of power, and she wasn't prepared to give it up.

"Tony is alive," the voice said behind her. "So is Don Cordano. They aren't moving, but they're still breathing."

Nico's gaze flicked over Mia's shoulder, and his jaw tightened almost imperceptibly as a chill settled in the air. "Are you sure Don Cordano is still alive, Frankie?"

"He doesn't have to be."

Mia felt something cold and hard press against the back of her head, and she tightened her grip on her weapon.

"We're the only ones here." Frankie lowered his voice. "We could make it look like everyone in the restaurant was killed in the shoot-out. You could have your revenge, your ring, maybe some Toscani pussy, too."

"I'll shoot you if you touch him." She stared at Nico, holding the gun steady. Although she bitterly hated her father, had imagined him dead hundreds of times in hundreds of different, painful ways, she couldn't allow Nico to shoot him when he was down, especially when he wasn't guilty of the crime. He was still her father. Family. And blood ties ran deep. So deep that he'd taken the blame for Nico's father's death all these years to protect Dante—a secret their family had vowed to carry to the grave.

"He owes me a life," Nico said, his eyes blazing.

"He's no threat to you right now."

Nico's face twisted with hate. "My father wasn't a threat. He had his back turned. He didn't have his gun out. He was trying to save me."

"I know," she said softly. "I was there. I feel your pain. I lost my Danny, too, and every day I have to look at his killer and every day I wish him dead. But not like this." Nico might be dressed as a mobster, but that night at Luigi's she had seen something else—the essence of the man. He was kind and compassionate. Protective. Caring. He didn't know her, but he had tried to spare her the sight of Danny dying. And when her father tried to beat her, he had protected her at the cost of his father's life.

"He should know he is paying for his crimes," she said. "He should suffer as he made us suffer. He's my father and I despise him, but I can't let you take the life of an unconscious man. It's morally wrong."

"Don't listen to her. You've been waiting ten years. This is your chance. Do it," Frankie urged Nico. "Do it before anyone else comes. If you're worried about her, I'll take care of the problem."

Sweat beaded on Mia's brow. *Taking care of the*

problem meant Frankie was prepared to ensure she didn't walk out of the restaurant alive.

Nico lowered his gun and walked toward Mia, his expression vacant, seemingly unconcerned by the gun in her hand. Frankie gripped her shoulder, forcing her to turn with him as he pressed his weapon to her head. Mia gasped when she saw the carnage behind her—the restaurant red with blood, glass shattered, tables torn apart, the walls riddled with bullet holes, bodies on the floor, her father slumped over the table, covered in blood.

Madonna. Flashbacks of the night at Luigi's restaurant assailed her.

Danny lying dead on the floor. Nico holding his dying father. The sickening sharp scent of blood mixed with what had once been the comforting scent of tomato sauce. Dante with the gun in his hand, horror on his face. And her father laughing—laughing because Dante, who had never wanted to be part of the family business, and couldn't even kill a spider, was finally a made man.

Nico leaned across the table and put two fingers on her father's neck, feeling for a pulse. Disgust curled his lip, and he aimed his gun at her father's back.

"Please," she begged, the word dropping from her lips before she could catch it. "He's unarmed, defenseless, and it looks like he might die from his injuries anyway. Do you really want his death on your conscience?"

"I gotta lot of deaths on my conscience," he said without looking up. "None of them keep me up at night."

"But this will." She gritted her teeth, hardly believing she was trying to save the life of the man who had meant to force her into a marriage she didn't want. "I know what kind of man you are. I saw *you* that night at Luigi's. You showed me your humanity, your compassion. If you won't do this for him, do it for me. Please don't make me watch him die."

"You don't know fuck all about me." Nico's eyes darkened almost to black, and in that moment she believed him. She'd changed the night Danny died. Maybe he had, too.

Frankie yanked on her hair, pulled her head back. "You are one crazy fucked-up bitch. You want him to spare a life after you just killed all these men. You should be happy he's finishing the job."

"I didn't do it. I told you that. Look at the walls, the tables, the . . ." Her voice broke. "Bodies. My father. That wasn't done with this handgun I'm holding. It was an assault rifle. I heard it."

"So how is it everyone got hit, your father is still alive, and you didn't get a scratch on you?"

She wondered that herself, but she had no answer. "I don't know."

Frankie released her hair, and pressed his gun to her head again. "Last time. Drop the weapon. I have no hesitation pulling the trigger."

"I won't drop it until Nico gives his word he won't kill my father."

Nico studied her, his face an expressionless mask. "Do you have no sense of self-preservation?"

"Do you have no sense of honor?" she shot back.

"Nico. C'mon man." Frankie's voice rose almost to a whine. "I hear sirens. Shoot the bastard and let's get outta here. We can take the bitch. Hold her for ransom. If she did just whack two bosses and try for another, everyone will want a piece of her."

"Fuuuuuck." Nico screamed and fired six bullets into the table in front of her father. He yanked on his tie, loosening it from his neck. "Take her. We'll find out what really happened here."

"I gave you my story," she protested.

Nico closed the distance between them, pressing his

chest against the barrel of her gun until the pressure of his advance forced her to drop her arm or risk shooting him.

He stared at her, his fathomless eyes sending a chill down her spine. There was no trace of the man she'd met in the casino the other night or even the boy who'd held her the night Danny died; he was every inch the dangerous mobster he was reputed to be—cold, vicious, ruthless, and, depending on the rules of Toscani succession, now the boss, the new Don Toscani.

"You gave us a story." His words were ice. "As soon as we get out of here, you'll give us the truth." He gripped her chin so hard her eyes watered.

"You can't take me." She grabbed his wrist, tried to pull his hand away. "I'm a . . ." She trailed off, unable to bring herself to claim the protection afforded to women in the Mafia. She'd spent her whole life fighting against the archaic Mafia rules that deemed women worthless, useless, property to be traded away. She had pushed back every time her father tried to force her into the Mafia princess mold, struggled to win his approval for her skill and intelligence and not for the fact that she had breasts and a womb. How ironic that now, in a matter of life or death, the only thing that could save her was the one thing she had always resisted.

"Woman." He finished the sentence for her. "I am very aware you are a woman, or you'd be dead already. It's the reason I let you go in the casino. However, *Cosa Nostra* rules don't protect women who involve themselves in Mafia business, and this . . ." He gestured vaguely around the restaurant. "Counts as being involved."

"I didn't . . ."

"I hope not." He trailed his finger down her throat to the crescents of her breasts bared by her torn dress. "You're too pretty to kill."

SIX

What a fucking mistake.

Nico scrubbed a hand over his face. His soldiers had reported that the bosses and bodyguards from the restaurant massacre were confirmed dead on arrival at the hospital, and Tony Crackers and Don Cordano were in surgery and expected to live. He should have killed them when he had the chance. No doubt in a few short days Tony would challenge Nico to succeed Santo as head of the family, and he would have to go after Don Cordano all over again.

He picked up his pool cue and glanced across the Toscani clubhouse where his most trusted soldiers and associates sat around the card table playing poker. Big Joe and former boxer, Mikey Muscles, had racked up most of the chips, but there was none of the usual banter. The world as they knew it had been shaken to its foundations. Never in the history of the U.S.-based *Cosa Nostra* had an attempt been made to kill three bosses—Don Cordano, Don Falzone and Don Toscani—in one night, and the repercussions of tonight's massacre would be felt in New York and as far away as Sicily. With Santo dead,

Nico and Tony would be locked in a battle to control the family, taking time and resources away from his quest to avenge his father by killing the man who murdered him.

What had come over him in the restaurant? He glanced at the woman tied to a chair on the other side of the room and immediately wished he hadn't. He'd rushed into the restaurant expecting to find an army. Instead he found her. All lush curves, and long silky hair, full pouting lips and dark eyes the color of the warm, rich chocolate his nonna used for dipping her *biscotti*. She was so unlike the young girl he'd held in his arms the night his father died. And yet she had the same courage and determination, the same sense of justice and inner strength. But now they were coupled with a whole lot of sexy and a generous helping of sass.

He chuckled, remembering the venom that had spilled from her pretty lips as they dragged her to the vehicle. She was one hell of a fighter. Frankie had been forced to tie her hands with a curtain tie to save them both from serious injury.

But what to do with her? She wasn't a docile, pampered Mafia princess, groomed to do her father's bidding. Hell, he wouldn't be surprised if she had pulled the trigger to get out of the marriage, in which case, he had a right to vengeance on behalf of the Toscani family, as did the new boss of the Falzone crime family. Did he offer her to the highest bidder? If she was innocent, he had to let her go. Mafia rules prohibited involving women in Mafia business. He couldn't even hold her hostage, or trade her for the man he should have killed tonight.

She was definitely woman. His gaze raked over her body, lingering on her chest where her torn dress only barely concealed the swell of her breasts, before dropping down to her black leather shit-kicking boots with flowers embroidered on them. *Christ*. Those damn boots called to him, spoke to the wild side that he had inherited from his mother and repressed in a bid to become everything his father hoped he would be.

He tore his gaze away and looked at her face, marking the wide bruise across her cheek, her black eye, the blood splattered on her hair and skin. He felt a flicker of anger that someone had hurt her. Ironic, really since he might have to kill her.

Nico maintained his position as the most powerful capo in the family with direct acts of violence or with violence carried out on his behalf. Reputation was everything. The minute he showed mercy or tried to be a peace broker, his younger and more vicious soldiers would seize the reins of power from him. He had made an uncharacteristic tactical error tonight when he walked away from Don Cordano, and the repercussions could be severe. He couldn't make the same mistake again.

"What's the news?" Frankie and Luca joined him at the pool table as he took his shot. Nico thought best when his hands were busy, and pool was his favorite game.

"Tony's alive." He watched the four ball drop into the corner pocket. "He's in the hospital under guard. Vincenzo's is crawling with cops. Our man in the police department is giving me regular updates. The police have been all over the restaurant parking lot and they are combing the area. They haven't found the murder weapon yet. They think it was one shooter and he managed to get pretty close before he opened fire."

"Or she," Luca said.

Nico's gaze flicked to Mia. He couldn't believe she had killed all those men in cold blood. When he'd turned on the lights, her face had registered only terror and shock, not guilt, satisfaction, or the fear of being caught. And if she had been responsible, the police would have found the gun. There hadn't been enough time for her to run and hide it. And it wouldn't make sense. Why go back?

Frankie gave an irritated grunt. "You gonna question her?"

"Yeah, I'm gonna question her. I didn't bring her here to sit and look pretty."

Luca grabbed a stick from the rack on the wall. "Cut Nico some slack. We don't all want to walk on the dark side like you."

Nico felt a tightening in his gut. He was losing Frankie. Ever since Santo and Tony had dragged their crews into the drug trade, Frankie spent more and more time alone, taking on jobs for Santo that no other soldier would touch. Every time he returned, he seemed less of the Frankie who had first come to Vegas, and more a dark version of himself.

"Forget about it." Frankie made a rude gesture and walked over to the makeshift bar in the corner.

"He needs a woman." Luca chalked his cue. "Someone who really gets him. Maybe you should ask if that girl who's coming from Sicily has a sister."

Nico doubted his prospective bride would "get" him either. No one really understood his wild side except his mother. As a teenager, he'd learned how to hide the wildness beneath a veneer of civility, how to leash the beast and walk among men. He had been on his way to becoming a man worthy of walking in his father's shoes when fucking Battista Cordano put a bullet through his father's heart.

And now he had his enemy's daughter tied to a chair in the middle of his fucking clubhouse. So what the fuck was he doing over here?

"Keep everyone busy," he said to Luca, making a quick

decision. "I'm going to talk to our little assassin and decide if this is the night she finds herself dead."

Mia twisted her wrists trying to loosen the ropes that secured her hands to the back of the chair. If she could just get free before Nico closed the distance between them, she could try to fight him off, or even make a run for it, although she had no idea where she was or how to get out.

When Frankie had slowed the vehicle in front of the rundown auto body shop, after a circuitous drive around the city, she thought she might be able to escape and find help. But she was quickly disabused of that notion when he parked around the back and led her into a deceptively large workshop that had nothing to do with auto-body repairs and everything to do with a secret meeting place for the Toscani mob. With a wet bar in one corner, a pool table in the other, a couple of card tables and worn out couches, and a nauseating odor of beer and cigarettes, it was everything she imagined a typical Mafia clubhouse would be.

Off course, she'd have to get past Nico's soldier, Luca, who had joined them as they left Vincenzo's, and now hovered near the door. Luca was tall, although not as tall as Nico, his shoulders broad, hair blond and spiked up on his head. He seemed more laid back than the dark, glowering Frankie who had pressed Nico to let him interrogate Mia as soon as they walked through the clubhouse door.

Her wrists scraped against the rope, and she grimaced. Something cracked on her cheek, and a brown flake dropped to her lap. Blood. So much blood. She had a vague memory of it spattering on her during the massacre, had seen it on her hand when Nico turned on the lights.

Nico's gaze stayed steady on her as he crossed the

floor. He'd removed his tie and suit jacket as soon as they entered the clubhouse, and unbuttoned his collar just enough for her to see the hint of tattoo on his broad chest. Unlike her father, who wore a suit even when he sat down to dinner, Nico seemed uncomfortable in the traditional mob attire. She imagined him in worn jeans and a T-shirt, maybe a leather jacket and a pair of boots. He had the swagger to carry it off, the presence to wear anything and command a room, and a hint of dangerous wild that his suit could contain.

God, what was she doing? He was the enemy. A kidnapper. A fierce, ruthless mobster who, no doubt, was considering whether it would benefit him most to kill her, hurt her, or ransom her to the highest bidder. And what was she? A victim. At the mercy of men. The story of her fucking life.

His brow creased in a frown as she studied his handsome face. Was it the chiseled jaw, the chiseled cheekbones, or the hair that was slicked back like he fancied himself James Dean that drew her? Or was it the power rippling beneath the surface? Why couldn't he have been a civilian? Maybe a lawyer or an accountant or the CEO of a software company? Looks like his were wasted on the mob.

Mia trembled when he stopped in front of her, then caught herself, stilled her body. For all that she hated her mob family, and despised her father, she was Battista Cordano's daughter, Mafia royalty, and she knew better than to show her fear.

"So, this is the real you." Nico gestured vaguely to Mia's clothing. "Not what I expected."

Indignation gave her the courage to overcome her fear. "Apologies if I don't fit the stereotype of a typical Mafia princess."

Something cold and dangerous moved in his dark eyes.

"I got that when I walked into Vincenzo's and saw you standing in the middle of a massacre with a gun." Nico's gaze raked over her body, openly lingering on her chest where the torn dress barely concealed her breasts. "You seem to attract trouble wherever you go."

"It's this life. No matter how hard I try to run from it, it always seems to find me."

All business, he grabbed a chair from a nearby table, straddled it in front of her, and rested his arms on the back. Her gaze drifted to his powerful forearms, the soft hair, strong wrists, and Toscani tattoo. Sexy. She'd never thought a man's arms could be arousing, but she couldn't tear her gaze away.

"What were you doing there? Tell me." His voice was pure steel, sharp and biting.

A shiver of excitement ran down her spine. She wanted to obey and resist, both at the same time, but a life of secrecy in the mob overrode her desire. "I can't tell you."

"I don't want to hurt you, *bella*." He reached out and touched her cheek.

Unable to read his intentions, Mia shuddered.

"Shhh." He rubbed his thumb gently over her skin and held it up for her to see. "Blood."

Papà's blood. A wave of emotion threatened to breach her walls at his hushed voice and gentle touch after all the horrendous events of the evening. She dipped her head so he didn't see her falter. "I wasn't there by consent. Well, not real consent. So now you know the truth. You can let me go."

"No."

"Could you at least pretend to think about it?" She tipped her head to the side, looked up at him through her lashes, hating herself as she did. But this was a matter of life or death, and she couldn't let pride take away her only advantage.

His eyes sparked, amused. "If you killed those men, you will die either by my hand or another. If you didn't, then you are safer here with me until the shooter is found."

"So you kidnapped me and tied me up to protect me?" She almost laughed at the irony. Only in death could she finally be equal to a man in the Mafia world.

"Some might say I'm protecting myself." He reached out and tucked a wayward strand of hair behind her ear, his touch so gentle, it was almost a caress.

Uncontrollable desire pooled in her stomach. Anticipation and fear warred inside her as his touch lingered. "Are you afraid I'll grab a gun and try to shoot my way out of a room full of wiseguys?"

His fingers trailed down her neck, rested in the hollow at the base of her throat. She felt the throb of her exposed pulse, as heat swept through her body.

"I'm not afraid of girls with guns, *bella*. They either don't know how to shoot or they don't have what it takes to pull the trigger."

"Then you've never met a woman like me." Her hoarse, throaty voice betrayed her desire.

He leaned forward, whispered in her ear, his voice dangerously seductive. "No, but I'm looking forward to our acquaintance."

Her body turned to liquid heat, but before she could retort, he pushed himself up and rounded her chair.

She felt his hands on her wrists, and the ropes gave way. He massaged her forearms, gently running his thumbs over her tender skin. His touch sent an electric spark through her, wicked and hot. How would it feel to have those hands on her most intimate parts, his powerful body covering her own?

"Are you letting me go?"

"I'm letting you clean up." He led her to a small hallway along the side of the clubhouse and gestured to a filthy, decrepit washroom, all rusted pipes and peeling wallpaper. "You can wash in here."

Thrown off by Nico's sudden change in demeanor, Mia turned to close the door only to find him in the doorway.

"Can I have some privacy?"

"No." He leaned against the doorjamb, folded his arms, his muscles straining beneath his fine cotton shirt. Her nipples tightened at his hot, unwavering stare.

With a sigh, she turned to the sink her gaze sweeping over the grungy bathroom for anything she could use as a weapon or a means of escape. She spotted a window over the toilet, and a thrill of excitement shot through her. Although too small for a man, she was pretty sure she could squeeze through. If she had oriented herself correctly, it opened into the alley they had driven down as they came around the garage. Forcing herself to look away, she washed her face, cringing when the water in the sink turned pink.

She felt Nico's hands on her shoulders, turning her to face him. He dabbed at her cheeks with paper towel, wiping away the blood and water. Something flickered and flamed inside her, desire pushing fear away.

"Who did this?" he demanded, his fingers brushing over her sore, swollen cheek.

Mia opened her mouth to answer and closed it again. Family business was never discussed outside the family, and she would be a fool to forget who he was. A predator. And a dangerous one at that.

"It must have been the same person who did this." His finger traced along the tear in her dress to the crescent of her breast, his touch feather light on her skin. Unnerved by the arousing effect he had on her body, Mia slapped his hand away.

His expression hardened, any hint of softness gone. "A little respect, *bella*."

"Respect goes both ways."

A cool stare. "So it does."

Her gaze moved over his face, searching for the man behind the mask. Instead she found something raw and primal—lust, barely contained, as fierce as her own.

Electricity crackled in the air between them. He cupped her jaw with his hand, his eyes narrowing on her mouth. She saw the pulse throb in his neck. He wanted her. And in that moment, she wanted him like she'd never wanted a man before.

Their staring contest was interrupted by a broad-shouldered, stocky man, bald, but with a thick, brown beard. "Sorry to interrupt, Mr. Toscani, but Mikey Muscles just got a call from a friend of ours. He's got that . . . uh . . . information you asked for."

Just like that the connection between them broke. Nico's hand dropped, leaving her bereft, and she released the breath she hadn't realized she was holding.

"Look after her, Big Joe." Nico waved dismissively in Mia's direction. "Don't leave her alone."

"Sure thing, Mr. Toscani." Big Joe looked over at Mia, and for a second she saw concern flicker across his face. "You got . . . um . . . a civilian woman in there? Is she your . . . ?"

"My prisoner." Nico turned away without another look in Mia's direction. "Make sure you tie her up when you take her back to her chair. She might look harmless, but the minute you become distracted she'll take a knife to your balls."

Mia wished she had her knife now as he stalked away as if nothing had happened between them. But maybe she'd imagined it. After all, what could happen between two family rivals, one of whom was a dangerous misogynistic Mafia bastard, and the other a punk rock hacker who couldn't tell her Gucci from her Gaultier?

"So what did you do to get yourself kidnapped by the mob?" Big Joe took Nico's place in the doorway, his face creased with consternation. "We've never had a woman prisoner before."

"He thinks I killed six men with a machine gun."

"Jesus Christ." Big Joe blew out a long breath. "Did you do it?"

"Of course not. Do I look like a murderer?"

Big Joe shrugged. "All sorts of people kill for all sorts of reasons. There's not really a look to them. Maybe it was crime of passion, or sometimes people who've been abused just snap."

"The only person I passionately want to kill right now is Nico." She turned back to the sink to wash her arms and neck, taking her time as she formulated a plan. Maybe Nico was right that she would be a target outside, but better a moving target than a sitting duck.

"You know Mr. Toscani?"

"I thought I did. Now, I'm not so sure." She tipped her head to the side, tried to force a blush. "Could you give me a minute to . . . ah . . . use the restroom?"

Big Joe shook his head and kicked at the stone holding the battered door open. "Sorry, love. Not going to happen. Mr. Toscani said not to leave you alone."

Damn it. She needed that door closed. She scrambled to find some way of convincing him to leave her alone and came up with the one thing she would never in a million years have imagined she would say, a betrayal of everything she had fought against when she realized her father despised her for being a girl. She hadn't been able to make herself play the woman card in Vincenzo's, but since it was clear Nico wasn't going to let her go, she had no choice.

"It's . . . um . . . that time of the month." Mia glanced around and lowered her voice, feeling no small bit of remorse for falling back on the stereotypical alpha male fear of all things period. "It's kinda messy to watch. And really, there's nowhere I can go in here. Look at this ass. There's no way I can't fit out that tiny window, and if I don't deal with it now, it's just gonna leak all over the place, drip on the floor—"

"Whoa." Big Joe held up his hands palms forward, and took a step back as if she might infect him. "Okay. Woman things. Not a big fan. You can close the door to do . . . what you gotta do. I'll be right outside. But don't take long."

"Thanks." Mia dragged the stone inside and closed and locked the door. She'd never had to escape from anywhere before, but she'd seen it in movies. Taps were good. They made noise, and in this rusted out, leaky bathroom, a lot of noise. Too bad they had her damn purse. She could have just called for help.

Heart pounding, she climbed on the toilet and peered through the glass. No bars. No lock. But then who would be stupid enough to break into a Mafia clubhouse? Maybe the same type of stupid person who would try to break out. She slid her hand around the window frame and cursed under her breath. It was sealed shut. She would have to break the glass, and even with the tap running it would draw attention. Well, she'd already dipped a toe in the water, might as well go for a swim. Mia turned off the tap and shouted through the door. "Do you have any tampons?"

"Fuck." Big Joe muttered. "This is why we shouldn't take women prisoners." And then loud enough for her to hear, he yelled. "I'll get Cherry. You stay put or I'm not gonna care that you're a girl, and I'll treat you the same as I would any dude who tried to escape."

"It's not like there's anywhere I can go, especially not

in my condition," she retorted as she quickly hefted the rock. When she heard his footsteps fade away, she turned on both taps and flushed the toilet for maximum noise, then threw the rock through the window. The glass cracked and splintered, shards clattering over the toilet tank and onto the floor. Mia froze, certain that someone might have heard, but when the footsteps didn't return, she untied her boot and put her hand inside, using it to clear the small shards of glass from around the window frame. Slipping it back on, she climbed on the tank and pushed herself through the window.

"Cherry's coming." Big Joe knocked on the door. "She's got your . . . girl stuff."

"Great! Boy do I need it." Mia yelled over her shoulder, realizing as she hung half in and half out of the window, that the forward approach wasn't the best idea. But now she was stuck, and her ass clearly was bigger than she'd thought because no matter how much she wiggled, she couldn't get through. She scrambled, kicking the wall and the toilet tank as she tried to shake herself free. Her undone boot came loose and tumbled to the floor. No time to retrieve it. With one last shove she pushed herself through and tumbled headlong into the garbage bags piled below.

"Open up, honey." A female voice called out. "I got what you need right here."

Mia pushed herself up and limped for the road, her booted foot thudding on the sidewalk. She heard a shout, the splinter of wood, and the slam of a door. She sprinted away from the garage, her heart pounding so hard she thought she might break a rib.

Run. Run. Run.

She turned the corner and raced down the empty street, the thrill of escape tempered by the loss of her boot and the reality of being on the run from three crime families who all thought she was responsible for the massacre. If she didn't make it home . . .

No. Defeat wasn't an option. Tonight, she wasn't a victim. She was free.

And she intended to stay that way.

SEVEN

"Are you sure you need me there?" Mia folded her arms and leaned against the wall in the bedroom of her brother's lavish penthouse, all cool marble and floor-to-ceiling windows with incredible east to west views of Las Vegas. Three days after her dramatic escape from the Toscani mob, life was back to the crazy kind of normal that was Mafia life.

"It's a matter of respect." Dante adjusted his tie, his gaze on Mia in the mirror. They shared the same dark eyes and olive skin, but his hair was fair where hers was dark, and his face was sharp and angular where hers was smooth. "With Papà in the hospital, I'm the acting boss, and I want the whole family to be at Don Falzone's funeral to show our support. We aren't enemies with the Falzones like we are with the Toscanis," he continued. "And in this time of upheaval we need to keep our allies close."

Mia rarely participated in mob-related events, and then only under duress. In her mind, the day she walked out of the family home was the day she was done with the mob, and with their father now in the hospital, there was no one to force her to go.

"It's not safe," she protested. "The Toscanis will be there." And in particular, the dangerously handsome, Nico Toscani, who made her feel the kinds of things she shouldn't feel for a family enemy who had kidnapped her and tied her up, albeit for a very short time. "What if they told everyone I was responsible for the massacre?"

"No one would dare pull a trigger on holy ground. And the police found the murder weapon over a mile away. I've made sure all the families know you weren't responsible. They wouldn't have believed it anyway. You're a woman. And it's been three days since it happened—long enough for the message to be passed along." His voice rose to a pleading tone. "Please, Mia. I need you. It shows my strength to have the entire family with me. I'm asking, but you know Papà would make you come."

She couldn't refuse her brother. Although he'd never been there for her in the way she'd always thought a big brother should be, he was still family and he had saved Kat from Tony. "I'll come for you, not for him. You know how I feel about Papà."

Dante's lips tightened. "He may be hard on us, but he cares about the family."

"Hard on us?" She stared at him aghast. "He beats me. He killed Danny right in front of me. He tricked you into shooting Don Toscani by telling you the don had pulled a gun. And he got away with the lie."

"He saved me," Dante snapped. "He let everyone think he pulled the trigger. I wasn't a made guy. It was an automatic death sentence for killing a boss without approval from New York, no matter what the circumstances were."

Mia put her hands to her hips. They'd had this argument again and again over the years, but no matter what she said, Dante refused to accept the truth. "He had to save you because he's the one who told you to do it. If he hadn't taken the blame, he would have had no son and heir. I don't understand how you can excuse what he did, how you can think he cares about anyone except himself."

"Why are we going over this again?" he snarled. "It's been ten years. What does it matter?"

"Obviously it matters to the Toscanis or they wouldn't have started a war." And, no doubt, it mattered to Nico or he wouldn't have kidnapped her the other night.

Her cheeks heated, and she looked away. Although it didn't make sense, she hadn't told anyone about the kidnapping. Why incite more violence? For some reason, she hadn't felt threatened by Nico. Why wash the blood off her face if he intended to harm her? Despite his cool composure, she'd sensed passion within him, and a hint of the compassion she'd seen the night Danny died.

"Maybe this can be a chance to mend fences." She walked over to the huge, floor-to-ceiling window, stared out over the city spread out below. "Since Papà is in the hospital and Don Toscani is dead, you could ask for a meeting with Nico as the new Don Toscani, offer reparations—"

"The Wolf says Nico won't be the new boss. Tony will be the successor."

Mia turned and caught a flicker of guilt cross Dante's face, but it disappeared so quickly, she wondered if she'd seen it all. "Tony Crackers? Nico is the first son of the first son."

"He's also a bastard." Venom laced Dante's tone, and Mia frowned at his sudden change in demeanor. "His mother was his father's mistress. There were only daughters from his father's legitimate marriage. The Wolf says that gives Tony a stronger claim."

Mia felt a growing sense of unease. She'd heard that Tony survived the shooting, but with his father, the former Don Toscani, now dead, he wouldn't be forced to go through with the marriage their fathers had arranged. Or would he want to? "Dante . . . ?"

"How do I look?"

Mia pushed her misgivings aside and forced a smile. "You look like a boss."

"Acting boss until Papà is out of the hospital. And you can be my secret underboss. I've got the password to his computer and all the accounts." His face reddened ever so slightly and he looked away. "I need your help to find a way to free up some cash without Papà knowing."

"Oh God, Dante. You aren't gambling again, are you? After Papà bailed you out last time, I thought you were going to get some help." Dante had had a gambling problem for as long as she could remember, sometimes running up debts so high her father had to send out his enforcers to deal with the bookies who tried to collect. No matter how much Papà threatened, Dante couldn't stop, maybe because he knew Papà couldn't disown his only son.

"I was on a roll at the craps table at the Golden Dream, Mia. I've never had such a long run. You should have seen the crowd! The atmosphere was electric. And there was this beautiful blonde who would blow on the dice before every roll . . ."

"I'm not getting involved."

Dante knew better than anyone how much she loathed the family business, how determined she was to separate herself from her father's criminal enterprise. There was no way she was getting mixed up in her father's affairs, especially to feed Dante's gambling addiction.

"We can talk about it after the funeral." His voice had a pleading edge that made Mia cringe. Dante became a different person entirely when he was on a gambling high.

"We'll have to do it another time. I'm teaching a cod-

ing class for girls this afternoon at the community center.
I have to leave right after the service."

Dante's gaze flickered over her floral black lace dress,
with its black underlay, deep V-neck and lace sleeves. She'd
paired it with knee-high black socks, a pair of thick-soled
Doc Martens shoes, and beaded jewelry.

Mia tensed under his scrutiny. Her father never held
back on expressing his disdain for her sartorial choices.

"At least you wore black." Dante held out his hand and
Mia let out a quiet breath. He wasn't entirely his father's
son.

"I always wear black," she said. "It's the kind of world
we live in."

Mia hurried along the sidewalk away from the church.
She'd done her duty. Everyone had seen her, and Dante
was now busy shaking hands and playing politics on behalf of their father, while Kat and Mama smiled dutifully
beside him. Although she'd wanted to get him alone to
ask if he'd been serious about drawing her into the family
business, she wasn't prepared to spend any more time
with her family and she was running late for her Sunday
afternoon class.

Her tension eased when she turned the corner and
spotted her cherry red 1993 Mustang convertible parked
in the shadow of a tall, brick apartment building. Although it had been well-used when she bought it and
was now in even rougher shape, it was the first thing that
was truly hers, paid for with the money from her first security contract after she started her business.

She unlocked the door and slid into the seat, trying to
push away memories of the funeral, the shiver that had
slid down her spine when she looked out over the sea of
mob bosses, captains, soldiers, and associates from the

three Las Vegas crime families. They had come together ostensibly to mourn the death of one of their own, but in reality to see how the power vacuum would shake out. She had narrowly escaped being part of that. Married into the mob. Imprisoned for life.

Mia turned the key. The car turned over but wouldn't start. After several tries she slammed her fist on the dashboard, hoping the little jolt would shake it awake, but no such luck. Maybe it was a quick fix. She had twenty minutes to get it started before she'd have to call a cab. With an irritated groan, she grabbed her tools from the back and popped the hood.

Doing her best not to get grease on her dress, Mia leaned over the engine and proceeded to go through her usual four-step check.

"Need a hand?"

Startled, she drew back, dropping her wrench, only to freeze when Nico stepped out of the shadows. Damn. She hadn't seen him at the church service, but it made sense for him to be there. Every boss and capo would have attended Don Falzone's funeral out of respect.

"Ah. It's Mr. Mob Boss." Her stomach gave a nervous twist. "Are you planning to kidnap me again?"

A smile ghosted his lips. "Only if you've got an assault rifle tucked under your dress. And a little discretion, *bella*. You never know who is listening."

Mia's cheeks heated. Nico was right. The feds were everywhere, trying to bring down the Las Vegas families after decimating the mob in New York. It was why the top *Cosa Nostra* bosses had implemented the rule that no associate could be made unless he had put in ten years as a soldier, the theory being that no federal agent was going to give ten years of his life to go undercover and infiltrate the mob. Dante's bodyguard, Rev, had only just been made after a long ten-year wait.

"No assault rifle." She held up her empty hands.

"Then no." He handed her the small black handbag she had taken to Vincenzo's the night of the massacre. "I believe this is yours."

"Thank you." Their fingers touched when she took the bag and she felt the now familiar zing of electricity spark between them. She couldn't believe that he'd returned her bag. Not only that, he'd apparently sought her out to do so. It wasn't typical mobster behavior, but then Nico wasn't like any wiseguy she knew.

Nico's gaze flicked to her open hood. "It appears you need some help."

"I can fix my car myself." Part of her wanted to turn around and show him just how competent she was at fixing her engine, but the other part warned her not to turn her back. He was a made guy, a criminal, and a very dangerous person to be around. She had no doubt, if she had been responsible for the massacre, he would not have hesitated to kill her. And yet, she couldn't forget the night he'd shielded her from Danny's death, nor could she forget the touch of his hand on her cheek . . .

"You weren't afraid to accept my help at Luigi's," he murmured softly. It was a challenge that dared her to respond, but she didn't like being manipulated.

"I'm not afraid. I just don't need it."

His eyes gleamed as if she'd fallen into a trap. "Then you won't mind if I watch."

"Why?" Mia bristled. "Do you think women can't fix cars, just like you think they can't be hackers?"

He pressed his lips together and Mia almost laughed. So easy to read. Yes, that's exactly what he thought.

"Don't answer or share your misogynistic views with me, or I'll be tempted to pull out my knife and do some serious damage." Her hands found her hips, and she glared, although she felt more amused than angry when he lifted a warning eyebrow. Yeah, she dared to threaten him because for some crazy reason he didn't scare her. "I do, in fact, know how to fix cars because practically everything that can go wrong with a car has gone wrong with mine—the radiator burst, the voltage regulator busted, the carburetor spews gas, the ignition wire broke, and I've had more flat tires than I can count. I had to take an automotive-repair course just to keep up."

He laughed, the sound darkly sensual. "Of course you did. You've already proven yourself to be a very resourceful woman. But sometimes it doesn't hurt to accept help when it's offered."

"From the man who kidnapped me and tied me to a chair? No thanks. I think I'll pass." Even if he hadn't kidnapped her the other night, she wouldn't have accepted his help. She was used to going it alone. From enduring her father's beatings to surviving her dysfunctional family, and from working her way through university to setting up her own business, Mia had always been a one-woman show. Jules was the only person she had ever let close, and even she didn't know everything about Mia's past.

When Nico didn't move, she waved her hand in the direction of the road. "You can go."

He chuckled and bent to pick up the wrench. Every movement he made was smooth, calculated, tightly controlled. She had a sudden desire to shake that control, strip off the thin veneer of civility and see what lay beneath.

"What's so funny?"

"It's been a long time since anyone dared dismiss me quite that way." He held out the wrench and she took it from his hand, careful this time to avoid any contact.

"So you can accept help," he said, amused.

"I accepted a wrench."

"A poor-quality wrench. It only has twenty-four teeth

in the ratchet handle. You're going to have trouble if you try to fit it in any tight places. You'll have to move it fifteen degrees to reach its limit, but a handle with sixty teeth has to be moved only six degrees to turn a nut as far."

She blushed. With money tight, she'd bought the best socket set she could afford and resigned herself to put in the extra work over splashing out for higher-quality tools. "So you know your tools. Am I supposed to be impressed?"

This time he laughed out loud, his smile transforming his face.

"I can only hope. Nothing has worked so far. I also have some familiarity with fixing up old cars. Among other things." His finger skimmed over the hotness on her cheek, as if he didn't believe her embarrassment was real.

"Fixing to steal them? Like you stole me?"

"You wound me, *bella*." His face softened. "I give you my word I mean you no harm."

"The word of a mob boss," she said bitterly.

"My word as a man." He placed his hand over his heart, his fingers resting on his double-breasted suit jacket, a smile playing over his beautiful lips.

She looked at him, considering. He didn't appear threatening. There were a few other people on the street, so they weren't alone. It was daylight. He was somewhat amusing, pleasing to look at, and he appeared sincere. Also, she was desperate. Time was running out. She had never missed a class, and she didn't intend to miss this one. "If you don't mind getting your fancy suit messed up, Mr. Mob Boss, you could give me hand checking it out."

"Pleasure." He carefully removed his jacket and tie, folding them neatly on the seat of her car. Her mouth watered as he removed his cufflinks and rolled up his sleeves. He was sexy in a suit, but with his broad chest and powerful shoulders straining beneath his fine cotton shirt, sleeves rolled up to bare his corded and inked forearms, dark and dusted with hair, he was something else entirely—dark and primal, fiercely masculine, and oh, so tempting.

"*Bella*?" His soft voice pulled her out of a fantasy of those strong arms holding her down, pinning her to the bed, his powerful body hammering into her, deep voice rumbling with a growl.

She dipped her head; let her hair swing down to hide her face. "Sorry. I was . . . distracted."

"I know the feeling." His eyes darkened almost to black, and he joined her beside the car. "What have you tried so far?"

She liked that he didn't just push her aside and take over like most guys would, and that he accepted she knew what she was doing. So far, he was behaving like a gentleman, but he had a steep hill to climb to regain her trust after what he'd done on Thursday night. "I have a good spark, clean air filter, and solid compression."

"Fuel pump?" he offered.

"It's got a carburetor, so I figure that's the cause of the fuel-delivery problem. Maybe a sunken float, rust in the jets, or it might just be gummed up."

They worked together for a short time, sharing ideas. He hadn't lied about his knowledge about cars, but Mia knew all her Mustang's quirks and eccentricities. With his jacket and tie off, and his sleeves rolled up, away from the places where appearances mattered, he was different. His lethal edges were tempered with a slightly sardonic humor that matched her own. Although he was no less the dangerous, seductive, powerful mobster, he had a softer edge, and his comments and suggestions were considered, respectful of her experience. When she checked her watch and realized time had run out and she needed to call a cab, she was almost disappointed to leave.

"I'll have to come back," she said, finally. "I'm teaching a class at a local community center, and if I don't get a cab now, I'll be late."

Nico straightened. "I parked at the end of the block. I'll give you a ride."

"Are you kidding?" She snorted a laugh. "You and me in a car together? First of all, our families are enemies. Second, you are a known kidnapper. Third, I can't show up at the community center with a wiseguy."

He looked affronted. "How would they know?"

"How could you be anything other than a wiseguy?" She gestured vaguely, trying to encompass the entirety of his fine Italian wool suit with its mobster sheen. "You're kicking it old school in that suit. Modern mobsters dress down so they don't attract attention."

"I have no fear of attracting attention."

Mia smiled despite herself. "I'm just saying, you're not really a suit kinda guy. I'll bet when you're alone, you kick back in jeans, T-shirts, leather jackets, and boots."

His gaze dropped to her feet. "Boots like the one you left behind?"

"Actually, I'd like that boot back."

Nico's eyes flashed, and he licked his lips. "It's very valuable to me. A souvenir of the first person ever to escape from my clubhouse. It comes with a price." He closed the distance between them, and Mia's heart drummed in her chest. He was so close she could feel the heat of his body. There was nothing terrifying or lethal about him as his hand slid around her waist. He was all hard, hot, deliciously sexy man.

"What price?" she whispered, looking up at his lush, sensual mouth, his lips only inches away from hers. She imagined all the wicked things that mouth could do to her, and her blood ran hot through her veins

He stroked a thick finger along the line of her jaw, his eyes locked on hers, dark with passion, his lids heavy with desire.

"Tell me." She felt drawn to him, as if there was a magnetic current pulling them together. She moved closer. Their bodies touched, and she felt the unmistakable ridge of his erection press against her stomach. If he kissed her now, would she slap him or kiss him back? She really didn't know.

"I'll take you where you need to go." He stepped away, breaking the spell.

She released a ragged breath, her body pulsing with unfulfilled desire. "You want me to accept a ride to get my boot back? That's the price?"

"Yes."

Still, she hesitated. It was no small thing he offered. If they were seen together, the repercussions could be severe, not just for them but for their families, too. And yet, how much worse could it be? Their families had already been at war for ten years. And if she texted Jules the details of his car, texted again when they arrived . . .

"Do you know what you're asking? Even this"—she waved at her broken-down car—"was crazy. Us talking on the street is crazy."

"Some risks are worth taking." He leaned in, brushed his lips over her cheek, his breath warm against her ear. "Say yes," he whispered.

Mia had never been averse to risk. Every time she confronted or defied her father, she took a risk that she might not make it out of his office on her own two feet. She had taken a risk the day she tried to save Danny, when she sent her application form to UCLA, and again when she'd dared move away from home. She'd taken a risk to start her own business with only bank loans and savings from her internship as capital. She'd taken a risk when she'd accepted the help of a mobster.

Suddenly, she didn't care about the consequences. She didn't have to be a victim. She didn't have to run scared. She could choose this. Choose him. She could follow her gut instead of the rules, and her gut said go.

"Yes."

Nico pulled his Cadillac Escalade away from the curb. He was out of his fucking mind. He had come perilously close to kissing Mia on the street, and only his fierce self-control had enabled him to pull back before he threw them headlong into disaster. So what the hell was he doing now with Mia Cordano in his car?

Frankie clearly wondered that, too, from the way he had scowled when Nico told him he'd meet him at the Sunny Heights community center. Frankie's job was to protect Nico. He couldn't do his job when Nico wasn't with him. Nico understood that, but there was no way he wanted Frankie glowering in the back seat with Mia in the car. He wanted her all to himself.

"Black Escalade." Mia ran her hand over the dashboard. "Why am I not surprised?"

"Because you suffer under the illusion that all wise-guys are the same."

Her lips quivered in a smile. "How many guys in your crew drive either a Cadillac or a Chrysler 300C?"

Fuck. She was killing him. That sass. That smile. Her strength and determination. She wasn't intimidated by him. Showed no fear. He'd never met a woman quite like her. And the way she handled her tools, tested her engine. Sexy. As. Fuck. "We're talking about me."

"And your big ass, alpha Escalade," she teased. "Didn't your mother teach you not to show off?"

His hands tightened on the steering wheel. "My mother died in a car crash when I was seven." He regretted the words almost as soon as they left his lips, not just because he'd dampened the heat between them, but also because he rarely shared personal information, and especially about his mother.

"I'm so sorry," she said softly. He liked that about her, too, the sudden flashes of softness behind the tough exterior. Hell, there wasn't much about her he didn't like.

"It was a long time ago." True, but he still had vivid memories of his mother, her energy, her laughter, her singing, and the sadness in her eyes every Saturday morning when his father had to leave them to return to his regular life. They had one day a week with him. Never more.

"Our world really isn't that big, but I know nothing about you, except by reputation, and even then I didn't connect the you from Luigi's with the ruthless violent mob boss who rules the street of Vegas with an iron fist. I think it's because I tried to forget everything about that night. I didn't even know who you were. I barely even saw your face." She toyed with her purse. "If it's all true, the things they say about you, I should run screaming in the other direction."

"You don't strike me as the running type." He switched lanes, glancing in the rear-view mirror at Frankie following close behind them.

"I'm not."

She had more courage than many of the men on his crew, an inner strength that intrigued him. And yet she was sweetly feminine, challenging his primal nature to protect and possess.

"I'm surprised we never bumped into each other," she

continued. "Or maybe we did and I just didn't recognize you."

"I spent some time at Berkeley studying business." He swerved to avoid a pedestrian and Mia threw an arm over the center console for balance. Taking advantage of the opportunity, he threaded his fingers through hers and rested the pad of his thumb on her wrist so he could feel the throb of her pulse. He couldn't explain the connection he had with her, but every touch sent a jolt to his groin, unleashing a hunger he could barely contain.

"An educated wiseguy." Her hand relaxed beneath his. "You are different. I went to UCLA to study computer science. My father wasn't happy about it."

"I'm surprised he let you go." If he ever had a daughter, he'd never let her out of his sight. He knew exactly what men were like, and given the direction of his thoughts right now, if he found out his daughter was out with a boy, he'd be in his car with his weapon all ready to give someone a serious headache.

"He tried to stop me." Her hand curled beneath his palm, and her pulse kicked up a notch. "He broke my arm. This one." She lifted her left arm slightly and he tightened his grip, reluctant to let her go.

"He'll pay for all his crimes, including what he did to you." They were not idle words. Nico did not toss out threats the way many mobsters did, hoping to gain compliance through words alone. He followed up each threat as if it were a promise so that it might serve as a warning to all who might defy him.

A curious expression crossed her face, part longing and part guilt. "You mean that, don't you?"

"Yes."

Traffic slowed to a crawl as they hit the I-15. Mia glanced at the clock in the console, and Nico gave her hand a reassuring squeeze. "We'll make it on time. I know a short-cut."

"Does it involve some monster truck driving over the tops of all these vehicles? Because if so, I am fully on board."

He shot her a sideways glance. "You like monster trucks?"

She shrugged. "It's a guilty fascination thing. Who wouldn't want to get into their vehicle and smash all the obstacles out of the way, knowing there was very little risk of getting hurt? Unfortunately, I've never had the opportunity to give it a try. I smash virtual obstacles instead."

And no doubt she did it with the same focus and determination with which she approached every task. "Is that what you're teaching this afternoon?"

Her face brightened. "I run a weekly coding class for girls age nine to thirteen, and then one right after it for teenagers. I want to teach girls to become passionate builders—not just consumers—of technology. It's becoming a basic skill, but girls aren't getting involved. They need female role models, and unfortunately there aren't many around." She told him about the class as they inched along the fifteen. She was passionate about encouraging girls to get involved with computers and shifting the balance of a world that was dominated by men.

He was drawn to her energy, her enthusiasm, her passion for helping girls succeed, and her desire to change the world, one line of code at a time. Nico had never felt that kind of passion, except in his desire to avenge his father. He wouldn't trade the Mafia life for anything, but he was damn sure his eyes didn't light up when he talked about busting out Lennie Minudo so he could take over the Il Tavolino restaurant or greasing a few palms with the unions to ensure the companies he controlled won the bids for the construction of new casinos. He was the darkness to her light, dismantling the world, one racket at a time.

After dropping her off, he sat in his vehicle waiting for Frankie. How was she going to get home? Although there were a few families around the community center, it wasn't the kind of place a woman should be walking around alone. He'd already seen a few members of a small-time street gang, a drug dealer he had run out of his territory a few years back, and an assortment of underworld characters that would only stand out to someone who ran in the same circles. And what about her car? His lips tugged in a smile when he recalled her vintage Mustang. If he didn't have to make a show of status, he would be riding in a vintage vehicle, too. Not a Mustang, but something luxurious and comfortable with a dollop of exclusivity and style—maybe Dean Martin's Facel Vega HK500 with the V8 engine, or the Dual-Ghia that Dean Martin loved. Or, if he wanted something closer to home, Sinatra's T-Bird.

He made a quick call to a mechanic who owed him a favor. Told him he had two hours to pick up Mia's vehicle and get it fixed and over to the community center, making it clear failure wasn't an option. A few years ago, the guy had come to him asking for help because another garage had opened down the road and he'd lost all his business. Nico had sent a couple of wiseguys down to pay the new garage owner a visit, explained to him there wasn't room for another garage in the neighborhood. Maybe he'd like to relocate. The guy showed a bit of attitude, told Nico's boys to piss off. His garage burned down the next day. Electrical malfunction. The mechanic understood he'd sold his soul to the devil, and Nico had just called to collect.

He spotted Frankie walking up to the vehicle and lowered the window.

"With all due respect . . ."

"Don't." Nico held up his hand. "You're about to say something disrespectful, and right now I'm not in a mood to bounce you down the street. I am well aware of the risks."

He looked up; saw Mia through the window with a cluster of little girls around her. Every time she turned around, another one was clinging to her clothes. He wouldn't have pegged her as a nurturing type, but they obviously adored her. But then, what was not to like?

When Frankie made it clear he wasn't going to leave, Nico left his vehicle and they grabbed a couple of espressos from a small café around the corner. Just as he was about to call the mechanic and remind him about the meaning of keeping his word, he saw a flash of red and the familiar lines of Mia's car coming down the street. He and Frankie reached the curb just as the vehicle pulled up beside them.

"Car is a piece of shit." The mechanic handed Nico a set of keys. "I can't believe it's still working. I did my best with it, fixed the engine problem and tried to make it as safe as I could, but to be honest, it's not going to last."

Nico tucked the keys into his pocket. "*Grazie*."

"No problem." The mechanic hesitated, and Nico knew he wanted to ask if they were even. But when the mob did you the favor of putting a competitor out of business, the debt would never be repaid. "Guess I'd better go. One of my guys is coming to pick me up."

"Did someone spill the Holy Water on your fucking head in church?" Frankie shook his head as the mechanic walked away. "You a good Samaritan now? Nonna Maria's gonna have a heart attack."

"For a guy who doesn't talk much, you can't seem to shut the fuck up today." Nico left Frankie's side when he saw Mia emerge from the building. "Gimme a minute."

"What are you still doing here?" Mia's brow creased in a frown when he stopped in front of her.

Nico gestured to her car. "A friend owed me a favor. He fixed the engine. Tuned up a few other things."

He waited impatiently for her reaction, tried to discern what she was thinking from the puzzled expression on her face. Usually he didn't care what people thought about his actions, but he cared about this. For some reason he didn't understand, he wanted to please her.

"Why?"

"You needed your car," he said simply.

Far from reassuring her, his words seemed to cause her concern. "But you hardly know me, Nico." Her voice rose in pitch. "And I can't pay for it."

"It was a small thing, *bella*. A favor between friends." His heart thudded in the silence, a pounding only he could hear.

"Are we friends?" She tilted her head to the side, studied him.

"We aren't enemies."

She smiled, giving him a glimpse past the tough exterior to a gentle, sweet softness that made his chest ache with longing.

"*Graze tante.*" Her Italian was soft, smooth, and utterly sensual, conjuring up visions of hot sweaty, summer nights, naked bodies tangled in sheets, and erotic moans of pleasure.

"*Prego.*" Pride suffused his veins, followed by an almost primitive satisfaction that he had pleased her. And although she didn't know it, he had protected her. She would be safe now in her vintage vehicle. "How was the class?"

"Good." She held up a small disc that resembled a circuit board. "They made me a present."

Nico didn't know what the hell it was, but it made her happy so he smiled. "Very nice."

It was a banal conversation. Normal. And yet they were not normal people living in a normal world. Even as they talked, he was watching for danger—suspicious cars, men loitering on the street, undercover agents, snipers on the roof, wiseguys out for a stroll . . .

She tucked the present away in her purse, fidgeted with the zipper. "I guess I'd better get going. It's my day off and I have stuff to do."

He didn't want her to leave, but he couldn't think of a reason to ask her to stay, and he didn't want to endanger her any further.

She unlocked her car, hesitated. "How did you start it without a key?"

He put his hand in his pocket, fingered the spare key the mechanic had made for him. "I have a lot of friends. They have many skills and owe me many favors."

"I guess I owe you one now."

His blood heated, rushed to his groin, her soft, sensual tone as potent as if she had grasped his cock. When she closed the distance between them, it was all he could do to keep his hands by his sides. He hadn't arranged for her car to be fixed so she would owe him, but if she wanted to repay the debt, he wasn't going to complain.

"How's this?" She placed her hands on his chest, leaned up, and kissed his cheek.

His self-control shattered.

Her kiss was so utterly unexpected, so breathtakingly sweet; his body reacted before his mind could process the danger. In a moment of madness where he gave in to the wildness he kept so closely in check, he yanked her against him and crushed his mouth against hers in a kiss as fierce as the desire coursing through his veins.

"Oh God." She moaned, wrapped her arms around his neck.

Nico pressed her soft body against him and pushed his tongue between her lips, sweeping her mouth with ravenous intent as he drank of her sweetness like a man dying of thirst. He had never felt so alive. So utterly consumed by desire he would risk everything for a kiss.

Their tongues danced together; their hearts pounded in unison. He twisted his hand in her hair and trailed kisses down the graceful column of her neck. He was a physical man, experiencing life through his body more than his mind, and right now he was overwhelmed with the need to bite her, taste her, breathe in her scent, see and touch every inch of her beautiful body, mark her, and stake his claim.

"Boss."

Frankie's voice pulled him out of his lust-fueled haze, and he growled his displeasure, pulled Mia against him, driven by a primitive desire to protect the woman in his arms. *Mine*.

"You're exposed. We're in Cordano territory. You wanna take it inside?"

Mia shuddered in his arms. "I'd better go."

Before he could protest, she pulled away, leaving him standing on the sidewalk, so fucking hard he ached. She slid into her vehicle and closed the door. The roar of her engine shattered the silence on the street.

"Mia."

She lowered the window and blew him a kiss.

"Thanks for the ride."

EIGHT

"You gotta get me out, Jack."

Ben looked around the twenty-four-hour diner, but at 2 A.M. in a roadside diner outside Mesquite, an hour away from Las Vegas, they were very much alone. The waitress had just refilled their coffee cups and was now chatting with the cook by the kitchen door.

He'd been meeting with his handler at the same diner every Sunday night for the last three years, drinking the same coffee poured by the same waitress and leaving the same tip. But tonight was supposed to be different. Tonight was supposed to be his last night. He'd called Jack during the week to let him know he was done.

"We're begging you." Jack made a show of wringing his hands. Although he wore a ball cap to cover his bald head, and a leather jacket over a polo shirt, he looked like a cop. Ben didn't know if it was the thick neck, the big shoulders, or just the set of his jaw, but something about Jack screamed law enforcement, which was why they had to take their meetings out of town.

"Just a little longer. There's something in the works. Something big. So big the higher-ups won't even tell me anything except that if you leave now, all your work, undercover, will be for nothing."

"Fuck." Ben balled up the resignation letter he had printed off just before he left home. "Everything's gone to shit, Jack. Three bosses were hit in one night. It's a dangerous time. We've got capos and underbosses fighting to be boss. We've got soldiers wanting to be capos and associates wanting to be soldiers. The Falzone and Toscani families have destabilized and we're not just looking at civil wars within those families, but wars between the three top Vegas crime families as they grab for power. All our work collecting evidence on the top bosses and the guys who worked with them is useless now. We can't put dead men in jail."

Jack shrugged. "I don't see how that changes things for you. If you just keep your head down and continue to do what you do, you shouldn't be in any additional danger."

"Are you fucking kidding me?" Ben slammed his cup on the table, gritting his teeth against the urge to shout. "Every family is gonna open their books, Jack. They're gonna want to make up as many associates as they can to increase their numbers. I've been there ten years—three of those with Nico's crew. If they come to me and tell me it's time to get made, I can't refuse. No one refuses. They'll give me a contract to whack someone, and then what am I gonna do? It's been hard enough doing my job without breaking the law. No way am I going to execute someone, even if he is a bad guy. But if I don't go through with it, they'll kill me, and I got a little girl who needs her dad more than ever since Ginger's taken up with her new man, Gabe."

He had given ten years of his life to bringing down the mob. Ten years, three relationships, and the first six years of his daughter's life. And until the triple hit on the three bosses, it had been worth it. But now two of those bosses were dead, and most of the evidence about the murders, assaults, arson, extortion, kidnappings, and racketeering he'd collected over the years was worthless. Locking up the bosses would have made the Las Vegas *Cosa Nostra* crumble from within as everyone turned rat to flee the sinking ships. Nothing could decimate an organization faster than a loss of trust.

"The higher-ups need intel on the new administration that's gonna take over," Jack said. "They also want to know who had the balls to pull the trigger. So far we've got nothing. The murder weapon was found a couple blocks away. No prints. No registration number. Forensics got nothing in the alley where it was dumped. We've got no witnesses to the crime."

"You think they're gonna tell me? I'm not a made man." Ben sipped his now cold coffee, wincing at the bitter taste.

"We have faith in you, Ben. You've gone deeper than anyone in the department ever has." Jack hesitated, the coffee cup near his lips. "Maybe too deep."

"Fuck that."

"You got a written report for me?" Jack lifted an eyebrow, and Ben shrugged.

"No time." He'd given up filing reports a long time ago, unable to commit the betrayal of his crew to writing. Now he just gave Jack brief selective verbal updates that would satisfy his obligations but keep his capo and crew out of the line of fire.

Jack sucked in his lips and let out a long breath. "I'm getting pressure from above. They need to know what's going on."

"I'll get something to you next week." *Fuck*. He was so done with this. Living a lie, answering to a different name, struggling to stay on the straight and narrow when he'd spent ten years living in the gray.

"I'll make sure everyone understands you want out. And they're not asking for years, here. Just a couple of months, and then you'll be free."

Ben leaned back in his seat and sighed. Of course he wouldn't just walk away. He'd been a policeman since he turned eighteen, fulfilling a dream he'd had for as long as he could remember. His dad had been cop before he'd been killed in the line of duty—a single parent after Ben's mom died giving birth. With no relatives to look after him, Ben had wound up in foster care, but law enforcement had been his dream—a way of keeping the memory of his father alive. Sticking with the job was the right thing to do. The honorable thing. And if it meant he could also protect his boss, and his closest friends in his crew, well, that would be okay, too. "Okay. But if I hear anything about getting made, I'm walking away."

"Good man."

"I got a personal favor to ask, though." He wrapped his hands around the cup to warm them, although his coffee had long gone cold. "This is just between you and me. If it's not something you can do personally, then tell me, and I'll find another way."

Instantly serious, Jack nodded. "Anything. All these years you never asked for a favor and you got plenty owed to you."

"I told you before, Ginger's taken up with a new guy, Gabe. I got a bad feeling about this dude. Gut instinct has kept me alive all these years. Don't like how he treats Ginger. Don't like how he looks at my little girl. Can you check into him? See if he has any priors? Any connections? I've been a shit dad, but if he's a danger to my little girl, I want to get her out."

"Leave it with me," Jack said. "I'll see if we can send Social Services around."

"You guys need a refill?" The waitress stopped at their cracked Formica table, holding her coffee pot above the booth. Shy and pretty, with long blond hair she wore in a ponytail, and wide blue eyes, she rarely engaged them in conversation although she'd been serving them for years.

"That would be great, sweetheart. Thanks." Ben pushed his cup along the table, and she filled it up.

"Everything okay here?" Her cheeks flushed, and she looked away. Damn she was cute.

"We're good. Just need the bill." Ben gave her a smile. If things hadn't been so crazy, he would have chatted with her a little more, tried to find out how come a pretty girl like her was working the graveyard shift for three long years, but he didn't even have enough time for Daisy much less for pursuing a woman he couldn't have. And look how it turned out last time.

"One day, I'm gonna have a woman like her," Ben said after she left the bill on the table. "Pretty. Soft and sweet. I'll have a normal life, nice house. Daisy and a couple more kids."

Jack snorted a laugh. "You'd be bored. You're an adrenaline junkie, Ben. This job is your fix. There's only a certain kind of man who could do what you've done for ten years, and he's not the man with a sweet wife, a nine to five job, and a white picket fence."

"So what? I'm gonna be undercover for life?"

"I dunno." Jack threw a few dollars on the table to cover the bill. "Maybe you get out and you want back in. Or maybe you're already in so deep, you're already gone."

NINE

"So how was the funeral?" Jules looked over her shoulder when Mia walked into the office on Tuesday morning. Jules had taken Monday off to take a course at UCLA as she slowly worked toward getting her computer-science degree.

"Good."

"Good? As in it was a big party? People had a great time singing and dancing and boozing it up in church? Aunt May got it on with the priest? Little Johnny drank the Holy Water? Someone pissed on the altar? Or are you just not listening to me?"

Mia dragged her gaze to her irritated friend and laughed. Jules always poured the sarcasm on thick when she was annoyed. "I'm listening now."

"Funeral?" Jules lifted an eyebrow in censure.

"Same as all funerals." Mia sighed. "Depressing. Although, I was shocked to see mobsters from rival families in church and no bloodshed. I wasn't sure if the restraint was out of respect for the church, the family of the deceased, or because everything is so unsettled.

Although . . ." Her lips quivered with a smile, and Jules patted the chair beside her.

"Ah. Something interesting. Sit down and give me the goods, and while you're talking you can help me with this. I can't figure it out."

Mia pulled up a chair beside Jules and stared at the code on Jules' screen, trying to make sense of the only thing that usually made sense in her life.

"I'm guessing you're distracted for a reason other than that rush job you did over the weekend." Jules pulled up another screen to show Mia her various attempts to hack into the client's system. "My weekend was okay. I'd give it a C-plus rating." She tapped the keyboard and brought up another screen of code. "I went to a fancy country club with the cousin of a friend of mine. Met a British tennis pro. He invited me to his room for a drink. When we got there, he was painstakingly polite to the point I had to strip down and lay on the bed to get the message across."

"That's great." Distracted, Mia stared at the screen, wondering what she would have done if Nico had invited her out for a drink instead of kissing her on the street. Or had she kissed him? She'd definitely initiated that sordid little encounter. Or had he? After all, he was the one who decided to get her car fixed. But she'd accepted the ride . . .

"I think those cavemen were on to something with the whole grab-the-woman-you-want-and-drag-her-to-your-lair thing," Jules continued. "It loses something when you have to do all the work.

Nico was definitely the caveman type. He'd kissed her like he wanted to devour her. If Frankie hadn't interrupted them on the street, she didn't know what would have happened. Once she had a taste of the power and passion he kept so tightly leashed, she wanted more. He was utterly irresistible. Those dark, brooding good looks, his magnificent body, and when he spoke Italian in his deep, sensual voice . . . Her knees went weak just thinking about him. She'd taken a big risk kissing him on the cheek like that, but when he pulled her into his arms and sealed his mouth over hers, it felt so right.

She didn't know why she'd run away when he clearly wanted her to stay, only that she'd suddenly felt exposed, open in a way that she'd never been before. He'd breached her walls and she needed to shut them down.

Jules gave her a nudge. "See if I missed anything when I was writing those lines of code to turn our website into an international porn hub and telling the FBI to go fuck themselves."

Mia startled, and her cheeks heated. "I wasn't listening again. I'm sorry. I was so busy this weekend, and Sunday after the funeral, I bumped into Nico . . ." She trailed off, not wanting to say more. But it was already too late.

"Nico? The mob boss dude who caught you in the pen test?"

"Yeah." She tapped on the keyboard, corrected Jules' mistakes. "He helped me work on my car when it didn't start, gave me a ride to my coding class, and then got someone to fix my car while I was teaching and had it ready for me when I came out."

Silence.

"Jules?"

"Isn't that the same guy who kidnapped you and tied you up, and you had to escape out a bathroom window? The one you described as the most dangerous and powerful capo in the city and a mortal enemy of your family?"

Mia shrugged, suddenly regretting that she'd finally decided to share the story with Jules. "He was sorry."

"I'm sure he was," Jules muttered. "Sorry you got away."

"It wasn't like that."

"Did he say the words?" Jules lifted a quizzical eyebrow? "Did he get down on his knees and beg your forgiveness? Did he say, 'Mia, I am so terribly sorry I kidnapped you, threatened to kill you, tied you to a chair and forced you to escape out a window and flee for your life. It was horribly wrong of me. I will never do it again. Please, please forgive me'?"

"No. But he kissed me. Outside the community center. I've never been kissed that like that in my life. I didn't even know a kiss—"

"You kissed an enemy mob boss in the middle of the street?" Jules ran her fingers through the pink streak in her hair, her telltale sign of agitation.

"Technically, he's a captain, not the boss. I don't know who their boss is going to be. Probably his cousin, Tony, because he was the underboss and usually the underboss becomes boss. And we were on the sidewalk, not the middle of the street. His bodyguard was standing right there. And yes, he's a Toscani. It was a bit of a risk—"

"A bit of a risk?" Jules voice rose in pitch. "Not that I understand Mafia politics, but I've seen *West Side Story* and *Romeo and Juliet*. They don't end well. And the *Godfather* movies? Even worse. There are no happily ever afters. No running through a field of flowers or riding off into the sunset together. No saying 'I do' and nine months later out pops a baby mobster and all the Mafiosos drink champagne together and dance the Macarena at the christening. It's all bullets and cement shoes and fish in newspapers and horses' heads in the bed and people killing themselves because their true love is dead."

Laughing, Mia stabbed her fingers on the keys. "Maybe things will be different now with the new bosses in place."

"And maybe you'll get yourself dead, and I'll be so

damn angry because you know I can't make it without you." Her voice hitched, and Mia's heart squeezed in her chest. She'd helped Jules through a difficult situation shortly after they met online, and when Mia finally scraped together enough money to start up on her own, Jules was the first person she called.

"He's not like anyone I've ever met." Mia gave up even trying to make sense of the numbers on the screen. "He's strong, powerful, very confident, and very dominating. But he's got compassion. I saw it the first time I met him, and I saw it when we met again. And he's got a wild side—he's a bit of a risk taker. Very intense. He reacts quickly to things. I kissed him and suddenly I was in his arms, and he was kissing me like we were alone. Ravaging might be a better word."

"You're playing with fire," Jules said. "That's all I'm going to say. Not that you would listen to your best friend." She hesitated, tapped the keyboard. "Are you gonna see him again?"

"No. Are you kidding?" Mia shivered. "I only just escaped being married off to his cousin like a prize cow. I'm not interested in getting involved with anyone in the mob. Plus, I don't trust myself around him. I would probably rip off my panties and throw him on the nearest piece of furniture the minute he walked into the room."

"Sure." Jules didn't sound convinced. "Although, if I met a dude so hot he made me want to rip off my panties, I might not care if he was a mob boss or an enemy soldier. Maybe I should stop wearing my comfy cotton briefs in case I meet a man like that. Satin and lace are easy to shred, but I'd probably lose a leg if I tried to tear off my Fruit of the Looms in a frenzy of lust."

Mia laughed despite herself, and her tension eased. Her phone buzzed, and she checked the screen. Dante. Again. He was probably just stressed about his new role as acting boss. Dante didn't handle change well, and with their father still in the hospital after the shooting, he had a lot on his plate. Well, she didn't want to get involved. She tucked the phone away and left Jules to get to work.

Late-afternoon, Chris joined them after spending the day at a pen test out of town. "There's a guy in a suit downstairs in the pool hall looking for you," she said, dropping her report off in Mia's office. "I told him to come up, but he says he'll wait down there for you to finish. I'm not sure if he's a client. He was tall, dark, and handsome, but kind of intense, and he had some interesting friends with him—a biker dude, some muscle head in a Giants' cap, a hot hunk of blondness, and a couple of guys in black."

"Three guesses who that might be." Jules snorted a laugh from her desk outside Mia's office. "Someone liked the amuse-bouche so much, he's back for more. You want me to hold the fort while you go meet your man?"

"He's not my man," Mia called out. "We have a meeting in half an hour, and I have work to do. I'm not going to just drop everything and go running because he showed up." Did he really think it was that easy? One kiss and she was at his beck and call? What about the family feud, the kidnapping, or the fact he had issued a vendetta against her father that had restricted his movements for the last ten years? What if that's all Mia wanted? Just one kiss.

After the meeting, she sent Chris and Jules home, and called down to the bartender, a friend who was more than willing to do a little recon for her. Nico was still there, he said. Playing pool with his friends, having a few drinks, and chatting with the ladies.

Clearly, he was prepared to wait her out. Time to take control of the situation. She finished her work for the day and tidied up her office. Before locking up, she pulled out her pony tail holder, and made a quick check of her clothing—black tank top with semi-sheer lace panels on the front and back, black combat pants loosely wrapped in studded belts and chains, and lace-up black leather boots.

Badass. That should put him off if he was here for a repeat performance of what happened outside the community center. Wiseguys didn't go for punk hackers in thick-soled boots. They went for women who looked hot, dressed well, and could increase their power and status by making other mobsters jealous.

She made her way down the stairs and stopped in the doorway to the pool hall, looking through the crowd for Nico. She spotted him right away, sitting at a table in his fancy suit, fully engaged in a conversation on his phone, his hands waving in the air as if the person on the other end could see his agitation. Mia drank in every delicious inch of his powerful presence as she walked through the bar to meet the mobster who had come to call.

He sensed her before he saw her. The soft thud of her boots, whispers in the air, the intoxicating scent of her perfume. Not wanting to ruin the moment, he kept his eyes averted until he finished his call. When he finally looked up, he saw an angel, dressed as the devil, to tempt him beyond original sin.

"Hello, Mr. Mob Boss."

Hunger like he'd never known before took over him at the sound of her voice—husky and throaty in a way that made him think about pushing her to places where they would both lose their self-control.

She tapped her foot, and his gaze dropped to her boots. *Cristo*! She rocked her sexy punk clothes like no other woman he'd met, and more than anything he wanted to get under her skin. He wanted to know what made her tick, what music she listened to, what she liked to eat, and whether her apartment was as offbeat as her clothes. He wanted to know what it was about her that made a powerful Toscani capo with an empire to run want to spend the evening in a pool hall waiting for her to appear.

"Mia." Her name on his lips was a sensual treat. "You're lucky I'm a patient man."

She snorted a laugh. "You are not a patient man. A patient man would have waited to bump into me on the street or at a wedding or a funeral, of which I expect there will be many after people see you here with me. An impatient man lays siege until he gets what he wants."

"Do I get what I want?" He leaned forward and licked his lips, his entire being focused on her. An entire SWAT team could have run into the building throwing grenades and shooting machine guns, and he would have been totally unable to drag his gaze away.

"Depends what it is."

"How about you in my bed?" He wasn't usually so direct with the women he was trying to seduce, but playing it safe wasn't going to work with a strong woman like Mia. He had to prove himself worthy and he could only do that by taking risk. Although he tried to convince himself he had come to honor a debt, the reality was he couldn't stay away.

"You've wasted one of your three wishes. Try again."

Nico frowned. "I thought I was forgiven."

"Because I accepted a ride from you, and you fixed my car? Because I gave you a little thank-you kiss? Gratitude for a kind deed doesn't equal forgiveness. And forgiveness doesn't equal sex."

Sex.

His assessing gaze drifted down her body, taking in the quick flutter of the pulse in her neck, the slight flush on her cheeks, and the bead of her nipples pressed against her thin tank top. He felt the impact of her desire deep in his groin. *Fuck*. Thirty seconds with her and he was perilously close to losing his self-control. Again.

"Are you done checking me out, Mr. Mob Boss?"

Cristo. Every word from her mouth went straight to his cock. Women didn't talk to Nico with amused disdain. They didn't accept his gifts and walk away. They didn't make him wait three hours in a pool hall for the honor of their presence.

"You are a beautiful woman," he said honestly. "You deserve a man who knows how to please a woman in bed."

Her lips tipped at the corners, and she walked without hesitation between his parted legs sending all the wrong messages to the right part of his body. "And that would be you?"

"Yes."

Heat sizzled in the air between them, and she dropped her gaze but, not before he saw the truth in her eyes. Yes, she wanted him. But she was going to make him work damn hard for the privilege of finding out what she hid beneath those badass punk clothes.

Boldly, he smoothed his hand up her thigh to curve around her hip. Pulling her closer, he gestured her down, pressed his lips to her ear. "You are wet for me, *bella*. Hot. I hear your need in the quickness of your breath, see it the flush in your cheeks, your nipples tight and begging for my touch, and if I stroked you, gently rubbed my thumb over your clit, you would come for me, and you would scream my name."

Her breath hitched, ever so softly, and then she pulled away. "Save the sweet words for the women who are awed by your mobster charm."

"Play nice," he warned. "I brought you a present." Nico reached under his chair and pulled out her boot. "I always keep my word."

Mia's smile transformed her face from suspiciously annoyed to delighted, in a heartbeat. "A booty call," she murmured, reaching to take it. "How thoughtful."

"Ah. Ah." He held it out of reach. "Where's my something extra?" No good mobster repaid another without adding a little extra, a premium to compensate the other for the inconvenience of doing the favor in the first place. If Luca had no cash for lunch and Nico gave him seventeen dollars to cover his meal, he would pay back twenty. It was loansharking, but with class, and it was the way their world worked.

She reached for her purse, hesitated, her gaze falling on the pool table. "Care to make it interesting?"

Wrong words to say to a gambling man. Or maybe they were the right ones because his evening plans to pick up the weekly nut from Lennie for the security work they were doing suddenly became a low priority.

"Everything about you is interesting," he said. "What do you suggest?"

"A favor." She licked her lips, lifted a perfect eyebrow. "Or can your massive ego handle losing to a girl?"

"I won't lose." Nico almost felt bad about the bet. After his father's death, he had worked his way through his grief in the Vegas pool halls, playing until he was good enough to consider going pro. Not that he ever would ever leave the Mafia, however tempting a civilian career as a professional pool player might be.

She laughed, a low, sexy chuckle that he felt deep in his chest. "So arrogant."

"You love it," he teased. "You've never met a man like me, a man who can challenge and respect you, a man worthy of a woman like you."

"Isn't that the truth." Her smile faded, and she dipped her head and looked away.

Before Nico could question her further, she leaned over the table to rack the balls, giving him a perfect, beautiful view of her lush ass outlined in black sequined denim and wrapped in chains. Her top rode up, and he caught a glimpse of creamy skin and the sensual curve where waist met hip. Overwhelmed with the urge to touch her, he curved one hand over her hip, rubbed his thumb over the bare skin of her lower back.

She looked over her shoulder, gave him a sultry glance, and ever so slightly wiggled her ass, making the chains on her belt rattle. "Do you like it like this?"

Luca choked back a laugh, reminding Nico that they weren't alone. Heat flooded his veins, and he was instantly seized with images of Mia down on the table, naked in chains.

"I'll break," he said. As if she hadn't broken him already. After that look, he would follow her to the ends of the earth.

Turning, he took his shot, scattering the balls as he tried to collect his thoughts and focus on the game..

"You're solid." She patted his arm, and his muscles went rock hard beneath her touch.

With a quick grab, he closed his hand around her wrist, and pulled her forward. He pressed his lips to her ear, inhaled the soft fragrance of her perfume. "Are you trying to distract me because you're afraid you'll lose?"

"I'm practicing my sympathy pat for your bruised ego when I win." She pulled away, turned so her hip brushed against his shaft, hard beneath his jeans. It couldn't be anything but deliberate, and his body responded accordingly. *Fuck*. If he took off his jacket, the entire pool hall would know what he was thinking about the beautiful minx on the other side of the pool table. Maybe that was her plan.

In a rush to finish the game, he ran out all his balls without giving her a shot. On the second break, he had to bank in both the four and the five but missed a thin cut on the six down the rail when she bent over to tie the lace on her boot.

Mia arched an eyebrow. "You might have warned me before we started that this was going to be a hustle." She leaned over the table across from him, her tank top falling just enough to give him a perfect view of the crescents of her beautiful breasts and the enticing valley between them.

A hustle, indeed.

"I know what you're doing, *bella*," he called softly.

Mia took her shot, sank her stripe. "Playing pool?" she offered.

"Playing a game that you aren't going to win."

Frankie handed Nico a beer, and he took a grateful sip. But nothing could quench the fire raging inside him. Not just because he wanted her so much that he could barely breathe, but because it had been a long time since he'd played the game with an opponent who challenged him, and who was going to make him work for every minute he got to spend between her pretty thighs.

Mia sank three balls in a row, each shot more difficult than the next. She was a straight shooter, but not a pro, and she was giving him a run for his money, if not through skill, then by unintended seduction. Each time she bent over and wiggled her ass, Nico suffered an exquisite torture as his mind conjured up all sorts of images that involved Mia naked over the pool table with his hands on her hips and his cock deep inside her.

He also imagined beating the shit out of the guys drinking beer in the corner, who hadn't taken their eyes off her since she'd walked into the hall.

"Do you know them?" He gestured to the men who had drawn his attention.

Mia shot them a quick glance. "Yeah, they're here a lot. They've asked me to join them a couple of times, but I always turn them down. Something about them makes my skin crawl. But they don't seem to be able to take 'no' for an answer."

Nico didn't need to hear more than that.

"Frankie. Luca." He tipped his chin in the direction of the unwanted audience. Words weren't necessary. They would have his back and watch over Mia, too.

"*Scusa, bella.*" Pool cue in hand, he walked over to the two men, assessing their size and strength. The blond had an inch over him in height but little in the way of muscle, whereas the skinhead in his muscle shirt, his arms covered in tats, looked like he knew how to fight. "Gentlemen. You seem very interested in our game."

"It's a free country. We can watch anything we want." The blond sipped his beer while the skinhead smirked beside him.

"Watch something else."

The skinhead tipped his neck from side to side, a universal sign of challenge that the primal side of him could not ignore. "You gonna make us, suit boy? You afraid your hot friend's gonna leave you for a real man? I've had a taste of that pussy . . . "

Nico didn't hear the rest of his words. Overwhelmed by a possessiveness that was both savage and fierce, he slammed his pool cue over the skinhead's skull, breaking the stick in two.

"Holy fucking shit. You're gonna pay for that." Seemingly unaffected by the blow, the skinhead leaped from his chair so fast it toppled behind him.

Frankie came up beside Nico to deal with the blond

as Nico plowed his fist into the skinhead's smarmy face. *Fuck*. It felt good to unleash the beast. He countered an incoming jab with a left hook and traded punches until he saw an opening to sweep the skinhead's leg. Following him down to the ground, Nico let loose, oblivious to everything but the need to ensure the bastard never looked in Mia's direction again. By the time the skinhead was groaning on the floor, his face covered in blood, Luca had paid the bouncers to clear the crowd and look the other way, and Frankie had taken care of the blond friend.

"You don't look at my girl." Nico kicked the man on the ground, careful not to get blood on his Italian leather shoes. "She's not a fucking piece of meat. You don't come back to this pool hall. You don't come to this end of town. You do, and you're dead. Get the fuck out."

His heart thundered in his chest as he straightened his jacket and tie. "Follow them out," he said quietly to Luca. "Take their phones. If the cops show up, call Charlie Nails. He knows what to do."

Nico had a bead on the top brass in every police station in the city. He'd given the details of the corrupt cops on his payroll to Charlie Nails who could handle both the bribes and any legal problems that arose. Unless the feds were involved, no member of Nico's crew ever spent a night in jail.

He half expected Mia to be gone when he returned to the game, but she was still there, leaning against the table, casually sipping a drink, like she was just waiting for him to come back from the bar.

"I should be disgusted by that brutal display of violence, or at the very least, terrified." She bent over the table, took her shot, left him with a tough bank.

"Are you?" He didn't want to know, but he did.

"Make that last shot, and I'll tell you." She chalked her cue, one hand twisting back and forth over the polished knob while the other slid up and down the smooth, wooden stick almost as if she were pumping . . .

"Mia." He gave a soft growl of warning before easily making the bank. With adrenaline still pumping through his body, and the object of his desire close at hand, failure wasn't an option.

"What? Feeling distracted because you're in a sprint to the finish? Do you prefer it long and slow before you sink your balls? Or are you off your game because you just finished beating a guy to a pulp because he was checking out my ass?

"Jesus fucking Christ." He threw his stick on the table and yanked her against him, driven by a primal need to conquer and claim. The moment their bodies touched, lust, wild and raw tore through him, and his voice, when he uttered his demand, was thick with desire. "Tell me."

She licked her lips, slowly, sensuously, her tongue sweeping the lush pink bow until it glistened before she whispered in his ear. "I don't know if it's because it was you, or because you did it for me, but it was so fucking hot, all I want to do is get you alone, tear off your clothes and—"

And he couldn't wait. Not one more second. He had to have her.

Now.

TEN

She knew she was in trouble even before he grabbed her hand.

He'd been like a caged lion when he returned from the fight, only half-focused on the game, the other half on her. If he hadn't been so good at the game, she could have used his distraction to her advantage, but he wasn't just good, he was amazing. Professional level. Not a straight shooter like her.

Now she owed the mobster a favor, and as he tightened his arm around her waist, she was in no doubt what that favor would be.

"Anyone in your office?" His breath was hot against her neck, making her shiver despite the heat in the room. Her stomach knotted, her arousal soaring as his free hand glided over her curves. His fingers toyed with the hem of her shirt, bunching it up the back as he slid his hand beneath the cotton, exploring her bare skin with a whispered caress. Possessive. As if the rest of the evening was a forgone conclusion. Which, after he'd just beaten a man to protect her, it was.

"No." She wanted him, had wanted him since she

walked into the pool hall, and she wasn't afraid to let him know it. Usually she kept her hook-ups discrete and short-lived to protect her dates from her father. But this wasn't a man who needed protection. This was the man her father feared.

With a groan, he spun her around, dropped his hand to her waist and ground his hips into her ass, as the hot, sultry sound of Peder's "The Sour," played over the speakers. She was wet as much from the knowledge he wanted her, as from the way he handled her body, like he knew exactly what he was doing, like he was totally and utterly in control. And yet only a few minutes ago, he had been lost in a battle frenzy, a predator subduing his prey.

She tilted her head to the side and looked over her shoulder at him. His face was dark with desire, and she felt his low rumble of pleasure in every inch of her body. She wiggled against him and his free hand snaked under her shirt, moving upward with obvious intent. Mia slammed one arm over her breasts. Yes, she wanted him, but not with everyone watching.

"Don't deny me." His words held a dangerous, primal undertone, one that sent a thrill of fear through her body.

"I have no intention of denying you, or myself." But one of them needed to exercise some restraint, and it clearly wasn't going to be him.

He gave a grunt of satisfaction, and swept his fingers over her shoulder, pushing her shirt aside. His mouth was warm against her skin as he kissed her shoulder, licking and tasting her, teasing her neck with the scrape of his teeth. Her blood turned to molten lava and streamed through her veins.

"Not here, Nico. I know most of these people."

"Upstairs." He slipped to her side, one arm around her waist, paused to say a few words to Frankie. She grabbed her bag and her boot, and he guided her through the pool hall to the back stairway leading to her office.

It was dark, but she didn't turn on any lights, letting the faint glow from the pool hall, and the exit lights guide her up the stairs. When she reached the door to her office, she turned. "Should we tell—?"

His hands wrapped around her ribcage and he lifted her, shoving her back against the wall. Hot and hard, his body pressed against her, forcing her thighs apart to accommodate his hips. He was rough, demanding, and as wild as she had imagined he would be.

Before she could catch her breath, his hand fisted her hair, and his mouth was on hers, ravaging her with a kiss that turned her body liquid. Her bag and boot fell to the floor as his tongue plundered her mouth. Fierce and hard, he took everything she gave him, and demanded more.

"Bare yourself to me," he demanded against her mouth as he pushed up her shirt.

Mia unfastened her bra, freeing her breasts from their restraint. Nico gave a low feral growl and shoved a thick thigh between her legs, pushing her up so he could wrap his hot mouth around her nipple.

This was what she fantasized about at night, alone in her bed. A man who knew what he wanted. A man who could take control. A man who feared nothing and would never yield. A man who would never hurt her.

Need coiled deep in her lower belly as he sucked her nipple into his warm mouth. She squirmed against him, her pussy slick with want. But there was no escape. He had her pinned, his body hot and hard against her, his rock hard shaft branded into her hips.

"Don't move." He turned his attention to her other breast as his hands dropped to her ass, fingers digging into her flesh as he rocked her over his thigh, teasing her clit with small jolts of pleasure.

Through the partially open door in the hallway below, she could hear the murmur of voices, laughter, the clack of pool balls, and the faint strains of Hozier's "Take Me to Church," But in the dark, secluded stairwell she could only hear the rasp of their combined breaths as they moved against each other, and the thunder of her pulse in her ears.

"We should go inside," she whispered.

He lowered her to ground, but instead of releasing her, he tugged at the button on her jeans.

"Nico!"

His hand slid into her panties, over her soft curls, stroking through her labia, slick with her juices.

Mia moaned softly, and Nico captured her clit between two thick fingers, fuzzing her brain with need.

"They wanted you," he said roughly. "If you'd walked out of the pool hall alone, they would have followed."

She rubbed against him, her hips twisting and grinding for the climax he held just out of reach. "I can take care of myself."

"You don't have to take care of yourself when you're with me." He pushed his fingers inside her, curled them to rub against her sensitive inner tissue. His powerful body surrounded her, pinned her, his muscled chest blocking her view of everything but him.

Mia tried to fight the orgasm that was rising fast, unstoppable. But he was relentless, his fingers working her without mercy until her climax hit her in a rush of white-hot heat. She bit his shoulder to muffle her cries as her hips jerked against him, and an exquisite wave of pleasure crashed over her senses.

He continued to stroke her, drawing out her orgasm until she sagged against him, panting her breaths. "Well . . ." She rested her forehead against his shoulder. "I guess we don't need to go inside."

Nico tipped her chin up, and she saw the answer in the darkness of his eyes.

Her heart skipped an excited beat. "Maybe we do."

Hand shaking, she opened the lock, and willed herself to calm. That had been incredible, but unsettling just the same. Some primitive part of her liked the idea of being chased, caught and ravished by a man so dominating, so utterly in command of himself and the people around him, that he had only to lift a finger to have them do his bidding. And yet giving up her control went against everything she had fought for with her family—recognition of her worth, a status equal to her brother. Respect. An end to the violence that had overshadowed her life.

She needed to regain some control of the situation. Make sure she wasn't making the biggest mistake of her life by giving in to the chemistry that burned between them.

The lock opened with a click, and Mia walked inside and turned on all the lights. "How about I show you around?"

Nico let out one slow, ragged breath after another as Mia showed him around her office. Although he tried to pay attention, his mind wasn't on the exposed brick walls or the finished pine floors. He needed to pull it way back, calm the fuck down. Never had he been so aggressive in his pursuit of a woman. Never had he come so close to losing control. But hell, when she appeared in the pool hall, his plans to drop off her boot went out the window. She was the most sensually alluring woman he had ever met—beautiful, brave and strong—and he wanted her, wanted to touch her more than he needed to breathe.

What was it about her that turned him inside out? It

was more than her physical attributes that got to him. So much more. And that made her dangerous.

For reasons other than the obvious, he needed to stay away from her. It wasn't just because she was the daughter of his enemy or because she distracted him from his goal, but because she reminded him that he had a heart. After watching his father die in his arms, he'd locked that part of himself up tight. He'd lost both parents and he wasn't prepared to go through that kind of pain again.

"So this is where Jules and Chris, my two on-site staff, work," she said, unaware he was only half-listening. "I have six online hackers who help me as well from remote locations."

"Where do you work?"

"Over here." Mia walked into an office, hidden behind a sheet of frosted glass. Nico followed her and listened patiently as she described her set-up with four screens and three hard drives as well as the bits and pieces she had picked up over the years.

"So you can test my system from here?" Nico settled in Mia's chair, welcoming the moment of respite to gather his thoughts.

"Yes, but I would need that USB I brought to the casino put back into your hard drive to finish the test. Your security guard, Louis, took it from me."

"Nico pulled out his phone and typed a quick message to Louis a.k.a Mikey Muscles. "Five minutes. It will be done."

She gave him a puzzled frown. "You want me to test your system now?"

"I'm interested in what you do, *bella*. Not just what's underneath your clothes, although I still plan to take them off you before the night is done."

Laughing, Mia gestured Nico to her spare chair. "Then

you'll need to move your dominant alpha self over to the side. I need to sit front and center to run the tests."

With a grunt of disapproval, Nico shifted to the side and draped his arm over Mia's chair, trying to find a position that would not be too restricting for his painfully erect cock.

"I see you have to lay claim to the chair, even if you're not sitting in it." Amused, she settled beside him and picked up her ear buds.

"What are those for?"

"I need music when I work." She clicked an app on her screen. "It helps me focus. Do you want to listen?"

Curious, Nico took the offered ear bud and placed it in his ear.

"What do you listen to?" Mia asked, scrolling through her playlist. "You didn't have anything personal in your office so I couldn't figure you out when you dragged me there to give me a tongue lashing."

What would she say if he told her he loved the Rat Pack? The Old Vegas-meets-Hollywood style? He'd never shared his nostalgia for the old days with anyone; pushing aside anything that might distract him from his goals to be the man his father wanted him to be.

When he didn't answer, she tilted her head to the side and smiled. "Come on, Mr. Mob Boss. Just one song."

He loved her gentle teasing, her nickname for him, the way one side of her mouth quirked with a smile when she thought to cajole information from him when he would have told her almost anything she wanted to know. "Sinatra's 'Strangers in the Night.'"

A grin spread across Mia's face. "You old romantic mob boss, you. So, you like the oldies?"

"My mother collected old records. She used to play them for me." He cut himself off abruptly. This wasn't the time to get nostalgic for the days when he'd been a young boy who lived for his father's visits, and the nights he and his parents danced around the small apartment his father paid for to keep Nico and his mother close by. Those days were gone, buried the night his mother died when she tried to take him away from Vegas to start a new life—a life in which she could be someone's wife and not just a mistress. Love wasn't enough, she tried to explain only moments before they were hit by an oncoming car, and his world turned dark.

Mia reached over and squeezed his hand, a small gesture that conveyed both sympathy and understanding without demanding further explanation. He was grateful for her silence and for a few moments he just watched her scroll through her playlist.

Finally, she looked over and grinned. "I'm going to introduce you to something new." She clicked on the screen. "Welcome to the modern world of feminist punk rock."

Instantly, Nico's ear was assault by noise. "What the fuck?"

"Give it a minute," she said loudly. "It's 'Rebel Girl' by Bikini Kill. It's about female bonds."

Nico didn't know what a Mafia princess was doing listening to a song about female bonds, but he suspected she had never played it in her house when her father was within earshot. "It has a good beat," he said, for lack of anything better to say about the music that was as far from Sinatra as music could get.

Mia laughed as she typed on the screen. "You'll like the next one even better. It's 'Oh Bondage! Up Yours!' by X-Ray Spex, about people who think girls should be seen and not heard and what women think about that."

"Does all your music make a political statement?"

"I suppose it does," she said. "I usually only share it with my close friends and the girls in my coding classes."

He endured a few more punk anthems while Mia typed, and then he recognized a tune. "I know this one. That's Gwen Stefani. So they aren't all political."

Mia gave him a mischievous look. "That opening riff is nothing short of iconic. She's a punk queen. Her parodic takedown of misogynistic stereotypes is pure genius."

Nico tapped his thumb on the desk in time to the rhythm. He couldn't remember the last time he had just sat and listened to music. The family business had consumed every waking moment of his life. Although a lot of wiseguys chilled out in the club, or hit the strip joints or brothels looking for some female entertainment, Nico worked. His father had told him at an early age that nothing good in life came easy, that success came from dedication and focus, that a man could lead only by example, and that example had to be one of hard work and sacrifice. He was a practical man. A good boss. Nico wanted nothing more than to be like him.

Mia talked him through what she was doing, testing back doors in his system, trying to insert viruses, and break passwords. He enjoyed watching her work, the way she bit her lip when something wasn't going her way and her utter focus on the screen. The businessman in him could see the advantage of having someone with her skill in his crew. Although his main business was real estate, there was money to be had online. But women were not part of the mob. And a woman could never be made.

"Looks good," she said. "Secure against the usual kind of attacks. Maybe not against the FBI, especially if they hire someone like me. I actually submitted a proposal to work for them last year. They put out a tender for cybersecurity work, and I thought why not? I'm just as good as any of the hackers I know, if not better. But I never heard back so I guess they picked someone else."

He gave a bitter laugh. "You were going to work for the FBI?"

"Sure. Just because my family is in the crime business doesn't mean I have to be in it, too."

Nico leaned back in his chair and stretched out his arm, brushing his fingers over the smooth skin of her shoulder. "You can't get away from it. Once you know the lines can be crossed, you can't go back. It becomes part of your DNA."

She stared at him aghast. "You're saying because I grew up in a Mafia family, I'll wind up being a criminal, too?"

He couldn't understand her anger when he was stating a simple fact. "I'm saying you'll innately take risks normal people won't. You won't see the lines between lawful and unlawful as fixed and unbreakable. Instead, you'll see them as fluid and malleable." When her frown deepened, he gestured to the screen. "You stole a uniform, impersonated a waitress, and broke into my control room to do the penetration test."

Mia stiffened, shifted in her seat. "It was all aboveboard. Vito knew what I was doing."

"But it's not something anyone could do," he said, choosing his words carefully. "Just like hacking isn't something anyone can do. Regardless of why you do it, many would see it as wrong. And yes, you keep it all legal, but it's a very fine line."

With an irritated sniff, she turned away and stared at the screen. Amused that she was annoyed that he had pointed out what he thought of as an engaging quality, he wrapped an arm around her waist and tugged her up.

"Come here, *bella*. I wasn't criticizing. I like that you aren't afraid to take a risk. I like that you aren't straight, that you try to help people in an unconventional way. I like that you have one foot in my world and one in the other."

He pulled her into a straddle over his lap while the Queen of Soul poured liquid sex into his ear, drowning out the warning niggle at the back of his mind.

Mia raised an eyebrow in mock disapproval. "I just played you the top twenty feminist songs of all time, tried to introduce you to a new genre of music, and you decide you want a lap dance to Aretha Franklin's 'Respect'? I hope you appreciate the irony."

"I respect you. If you want me to stop, I will." He put his hands on her hips, rocked her gently against his aching cock, the ear bud wires dangling between them, connecting them. "But if you're offering . . ."

Her smile lit her face, warmed his heart. He had put that smile there, and there was nothing he wouldn't do to see it again.

"I don't give lap dances to suits." She reached for his tie and deftly undid the knot, pulling it off Nico's neck with a soft hiss. His fingers clenched tight on her hips, and all his blood rushed to his groin.

"Undress me, Mia," he demanded. "I want to fuck you into oblivion."

She pushed his jacket over his shoulders, and he released her long enough to let it drop to the seat behind him.

"Tell me what you like," she said softly.

"You."

"I like you, too," she murmured as she undid the buttons on his shirt one by one, her soft hands an exquisite torture on his skin.

"Tell me another song you like. Something modern." She tugged his shirt out of his pants, parted it, her hands smoothing over his chest. He unclasped his holster and placed his weapon on the desk before shrugging out of his shirt. Unlike many of the wiseguys on his crew, Nico worked out daily. Not just because he took pride in his appearance, but also because violence was part of the life and he needed to be in top physical condition to be able to enforce his will in a way that would garner respect.

"AC/DC's 'Thunderstruck.'" It was how he was feeling now with this beautiful, sexy woman on his lap, her hands warm against his chest, her hips grinding against him as she wiggled to the beat. A delicious agony.

"You like AC/DC?"

"I liked it so much, I once threw a brick through Luca's window so I could hear it better."

Mia sat up. "Did you just tell a joke, Mr. Mob Boss?"

"I don't joke, Mia. Ask him."

Her smile faded. "I don't think that's going to happen. You're forgetting who I am."

Nico's stomach tightened in a knot. He had not for one second forgotten who she was. But he didn't fucking care that she was the daughter of his enemy. He wanted her. End of story.

Mia pulled back, studied his bare chest. "You're inked," she said in delight. Her fingers traced the lines of the word inked beneath his pec. "*Trust.* Why did you choose that?"

"If we don't have trust in our world, we have nothing."

"And the dagger?" She tilted her head as she studied the handle of the dagger tattoo that reached from his belt to his sternum.

"A commitment to protect my family."

"And this?" Her throaty voice made it almost impossible to sit still, and he shifted in his chair when she pressed a kiss to the tribal design on his right side.

"Warrior's mark."

"God," she whispered. "I love your ink. I don't know any mobsters like you."

He fisted her hair, tugged her head to the side, deeply satisfied that his body pleased her. "There are no mobsters like me." He kissed his way down the column of her throat and nipped the sensitive skin where her neck joined her shoulder. Her thighs tightened around his hips, and she rocked against the broad thickness of his cock. Sharp waves of hunger pulsed through his veins. He could lose himself in this woman. They were connected in a way he didn't understand but he knew he couldn't live without.

Nico's phone buzzed on the desk. He wanted nothing more than to turn it off, but it was a ringtone that Luca and Frankie used to warn him if something was wrong. He reached for it, and the message he read killed his desire in an instant.

"Get dressed." He stood so abruptly, she only just caught herself before she fell.

"What's wrong?"

Nico reached for his gun. "We have company."

ELEVEN

"Who is it?"

Mia ran to the window and peered through the blinds, but she couldn't see much in the dimly lit parking lot save for the vehicles of the customers from the pool hall below.

"The Wolf." He spat out the name, and Mia's blood ran cold. Her father's *consigliere* was as cruel and brutal a man as her father, and he held as much power in the family as Dante. If Mia's father hadn't groomed Dante to take over from the day he was born, the Wolf would have assumed the role of acting boss while the don was in the hospital.

"The Wolf?" Her breath left her in a rush. "He never comes here. Are you sure?"

"My bodyguards know who he is." Nico grabbed his shirt, shook it out. "Is there a reason he might be looking for you?"

"I don't know. Dante left me a lot of messages that I haven't answered. I think he needs some help with the business, but it's not something I want to get involved in so I've been avoiding his calls. Maybe he sent the Wolf to track me down." She straightened her clothing. "You have to get out. If you go down the back stairs—"

"I'm not leaving." He checked the magazine in his gun, peered out the window.

"You can't shoot him, Nico. He's our *consigliere*."

His gazed turned feral. "Then you'd better hope he's unarmed and means you no harm."

Her heart kicked up a notch. The Wolf couldn't find Nico here. Their families were still at war, and she was alone with the enemy. Either the Wolf would think she was betraying her family or that Nico had forced her. Neither of which promised a happy ending.

"How about the window?" She yanked up the blinds. "You can get out here. There's a fire ladder—"

"I am not running, *bella*." He rocked his neck from side to side, each little crack ratcheting up her fear.

Desperate, she looked around the room. "How about the closet? You could hide there. Or in one of the empty offices—"

"I don't hide."

"Nico!" Her voice rose in pitch. "He can't find you here. You know that. You know what it means."

"If I wasn't prepared to deal with the consequences," he said evenly, "I would never have come."

Caught in a maelstrom of emotion, anger, fear, and frustration, she grabbed a pen off her desk and threw it at him. "But *I'm* not prepared. I didn't think it through. And now someone's going to get hurt."

His gaze pinned her, cold as ice. "You're afraid of him."

"I'm more afraid of losing my freedom and independence than I am of being hurt." She was also afraid to open herself up, show any weaknesses of vulnerabilities, including her interest in a man she shouldn't want. Her father would find a way to turn this fling with Nico against her. Whether through pain or humiliation, he would do her harm. And Nico . . . Her stomach knotted. She couldn't go through the Danny situation all over again. She couldn't watch another man she cared about die.

"So he has hurt you."

She shivered at his lethal tone. He was right, but she would never admit it. Several times, her father had sent the Wolf to punish Mia for her disobedience when he couldn't do it himself, and he had seemed to relish the task. The Wolf had no limits. There was no line he wouldn't cross. He had been born into the mob, served as *consigliere* for her grandfather at the end of his rein and for all the years her father had been in power. Although he was in his early sixties, he kept himself in shape and could beat a man unconscious without breaking a sweat.

"All the more reason for me to stay," he said into the silence. "I'm not afraid of any man. I'll protect you."

"Please," she whispered. "Please go."

"No." He leaned against the window, facing the door. "I'll wait here, and I make no promises if I hear anything that causes me concern."

Stubborn ass. Well, she would just have to keep the Wolf in the main part of the office and get him to leave before Nico lost his patience. He had impressive self-control, but she'd seen what lay beneath the surface. If he would beat a man half-unconscious for looking at her, she could well imagine what he might do if the Wolf touched her.

Someone pounded on the door. Taking a deep breath, she walked through the office and unlocked it. The Wolf pushed his way past her, stalking into her office with one of her father's enforcers behind him. Beyond the doorway, she saw Frankie and Big Joe coming quietly up the stairs.

"Can I help you?"

The Wolf scowled, his eyes darting around the office as if he'd expected to catch her doing something wrong. She shuddered, thinking just how much worse the situation could have been if Nico's bodyguards had not been outside to warn them.

"Dante has been trying to get in touch with you all day." His cold, black eyes hardened. "You show the *capo bastone* disrespect by not answering his calls."

Brave, knowing Nico was in the room behind her, Mia shrugged. "I was busy at work. He's never had an issue with that before. He knows I'll eventually call when I'm done."

The Wolf's eyes narrowed. "I see your attitude has not improved even after your father put you in your place the other night."

Mia bristled. Yes, he was *consigliere*, but she was still the daughter of the boss—Mafia royalty—and he owed her some respect. "My relationship with Dante is nothing like my relationship with my father. I'm surprised he would send you here. This isn't something Dante would do, and certainly he would never send a *consigliere* with a message that one of his soldiers could deliver."

The Wolf closed the distance between them, stopping only a foot away. The enforcer stood in the doorway, as if to remind her there was no escape. Mia trembled, braced herself against the desk behind her, but refused to back down.

"A soldier would be ineffective at dealing with your disobedience. Only Don Cordano and I seem to have the ability to keep you in line."

"I left years ago," she snapped. "No one keeps me in line."

The Wolf barked a laugh. "You don't seem to understand that things have changed. When Don Cordano heard about how you dishonored the family by whoring yourself out to a Toscani in a downtown casino, he realized he had been too lenient. The marriage to Tony might have fallen through, but Dante needs someone who understands financial and computer matters by his side. This . . ." He waved vaguely over her office. "Little hobby is done. What freedom the don allowed you is gone. You will return to the house and assist Dante until Don Cordano decides otherwise."

"And if I don't go?"

"Do you really want to test me?" He brushed a rough finger over the small scar on her cheek, a reminder of the night he'd hit her, and sliced her cheek with his ring.

"Fuck you." She slapped his hand away.

"Maybe next time." He reached for her arm, but before his fingers even closed on her skin, he was no longer in front of her. Instead, Nico had him up against the wall, one hand around his throat, the other on the trigger of a gun pointed at the enforcer in the doorway.

"Drop your weapon or I'll break his fucking neck."

The enforcer placed his weapon on the floor and Frankie came up behind him and yanked his hands behind his back. Big Joe leaned in to grab the weapon, his chest heaving as if he had just run a marathon.

"There's two more downstairs," Big Joe puffed. "Luca's dealing with them."

"You would dare touch the daughter of your don?" Nico pressed the barrel of his gun against the Wolf's throat.

"You would dare touch a Cordano woman, Toscani scum?" The Wolf wheezed out as Nico's hand tightened around his neck. "But then she's a whore and slut. Fitting for a Toscani bastard."

Nico moved in a blur. One moment the Wolf was up against the wall; the next he was bruised and bloody on the floor, his mouth a wreck of teeth.

"Big Joe. Get her out of here." Nico nodded in Mia's direction, his voice devoid of anything but cold, lethal fury as he drew his weapon from its holster.

"Come on, love. Let's go." Big Joe gestured to the door.

Mia shook her head. "I'm not going anywhere. This is my office. My fight."

"Take her." Nico's sharp command awakened fear in her heart. "Now."

"I won't be ordered around. Not by my father. Not by the Wolf. Not by anyone." She stiffened her spine. "I won't leave my office unsecured, especially if you plan to kill my family *consigliere* in cold blood."

"Your office will be safe." Still, he didn't look at her, but she didn't need to see his eyes to know death lay within them. "Trust me."

Trust. The word was etched into his skin. But trust didn't come easily in their world; it had to be earned, and she didn't trust him. Not yet.

"I'm sorry, Nico. I can't do that."

His anger was a knife blade that cut through her heart. Tension thickened the air between them, and a curious silence filled the room. Nobody said no to a mob boss, and especially not one who had earned his position of power through blood and pain. But Mia had grown up defying her father. No matter how many times he punished her, she never backed down. Every family dinner was a battleground. Every interaction a fight. She didn't know why she felt compelled to disobey him, only that she knew the day she gave in was the day she lost what little respect he had for her. Not once did he break her, and she sure as hell wasn't going to break tonight.

She shivered at Nico's glacial stare, realizing only as her blood chilled in warning that she'd made a serious tactical error. At home, with just her family within earshot, she could challenge or disrespect her father without causing him to lose face, but here, in front of both the Toscanis and the Cordanos, she had left Nico no way out.

"Hey, you got any employees who could come and help out?" Big Joe asked into the silence, his voice low, cajoling, as if he was trying to ease the tension. "Make sure our guys don't touch anything they aren't supposed to, maybe do a little cleaning, and lock up after we're gone?"

"Yes. My friend, Jules." Mia shot Big Joe a thankful look. Obviously, very politically aware, he had used very specific language to suggest a way out that would give Nico a way out without causing offence or disrespect.

"Whaddya think, Mr. Toscani?" He turned to Nico. "You're my boss, and if you say get her out of here, then I'll get her out. I'll toss her over my shoulder and carry her if I have to. But getting her friend in might be another possibility." His gaze flicked to the Wolf and back to Nico. "After you're done, of course."

Nico didn't respond, but she didn't expect him to. His will was absolute. As far as he was concerned, she was already gone and the reality was there was fuck all she could do about it. Still, Big Joe had given them a way out that would allow Mia to escape humiliation and ensure her office was secure, so she decided to play along.

"If you approve," she said to Nico, biting back her anger. "My friend Jules could come and keep an eye on things. Although I don't see why—"

She cut herself off when Nico's face turned stony. *Okay.* Time to shut up and take advantage of the extraordinary opportunity to make a graceful exit that involved walking and not being carried out like a sack of potatoes.

"I'll call her when I get outside." She grabbed her purse, and swept past Nico, standing over the Wolf's twitching body like a predator over a kill. Frankie moved to the side to allow her to pass, and she stepped over the enforcer and made her way down the stairs, Big Joe behind her. Once outside, she called Jules, tried to explain the situation without alarming her friend.

"All good?" Big Joe gestured to a blue Volvo. "I'll take you home and come back for your car. We got a coupla extra guys out here. Frankie doesn't like to take any chances with the boss."

Mia drew in a ragged breath. "Thanks for what you did back there."

"No problem. After ten years, I think I've got a handle on Mafia politics. You can't tell the boss right out he might have missed an option, but there's ways around it."

"I mean for showing me some respect," she said. "That's not something I see much. In my family, if your boss tells you to put the dog out, you put the dog out. You don't try to spare the dog's feelings."

"Well, ma'am." Big Joe scrubbed his hand over his face. "You're not a dog, and you said you didn't want to go."

Mia laughed bitterly. "It doesn't matter what I want. I'm a woman. In this world, I'm nothing. You should have picked that up when he said, 'Get her out of here' instead of 'Mia, I think we should take you someplace safe, what do you think?' Or 'Mia, I'm about to kill a man in cold blood in the middle of your office, and I don't want you to watch.'"

Big Joe's nose wrinkled ever so slightly like what she'd said was distasteful. "I've never seen Mr. Toscani treat any woman with disrespect. All the women he's been with—"

"I don't want to know." She felt a stab of jealousy at

the thought of Nico with other women. Had he seduced them the way he seduced her? "I thought Nico was different, but I was wrong."

She heard a loud crash and looked up just as the lights in her office flickered off. No doubt her office would be destroyed by morning. And Wolf . . . Her stomach clenched. She was so tired of picking up the pieces. Her life had been shattered the night Danny died, her illusions about what it meant to be part of a Mafia family destroyed in the time it took to pull the trigger. She'd thrown out everything soft and feminine she owned the next day, remade herself in kick-ass punk as a "fuck you" to her father and because the anger in the music soothed her soul. Only the ink she'd secretly gotten a few years later reminded her of her femininity, gave her strength for the punishments that would never end.

Big Joe's phone buzzed, and he pulled it out and checked the screen. Tucking it away, he opened the door to his vehicle. But as Mia moved to enter, he hesitated, as if he had something to say.

Mia frowned. "Is something wrong?"

"I don't want you thinking the wrong thing about Mr. Toscani," he said. "He's a good guy. The best. He treats everyone with respect. But sometimes in the heat of the moment—especially when a guy is trying to protect someone he cares about—he doesn't think straight. Maybe all he wants is for his woman to be safe, and he doesn't use the words he should."

Mia's heart warmed to Big Joe. If her father could inspire this kind of loyalty in his men, he wouldn't need to use his fists to keep them in line, and he wouldn't be constantly looking over his shoulder, worried that they would betray him. Instead, he could turn all that energy into the family business, and his power would be unrivaled.

"I'm not his woman."

"I don't mean any disrespect, ma'am," Big Joe said. "And I don't have a woman of my own, so I could be wrong. But since I'm supposed to sit outside your place all night to make sure you're safe under pain of death, I think you are."

TWELVE

Mia wound her way through the crowds on the Freemont Street Experience with Jules in tow. Like most locals, she usually avoided the five full blocks of pedestrian heaven featuring a huge arched canopy of computerized lights, a massive sound system, shows, live bands, a slot machine-inspired zip-line attraction and free-flowing booze. When she wanted to game or play pool, she headed to the smaller, local casinos or occasionally to the Strip.

She pulled Jules to a stop outside Casino Italia. It had all the glitz and glamour of its predecessor, but with a modern touch. A massive banner hung over the sleek chrome and glass facade, advertising the hotel's current show—a hip-hop rapper who was in high demand.

"He owns this?" Jules smoothed down her little black dress, a radical departure from her usual T-shirts and jeans. Mia didn't think she'd ever seen Jules dress up before, and certainly not in heels.

"I knew mobsters had money," Jules continued. "But this takes it to another level."

Mia didn't want to admit she'd also been shocked to discover Nico owned the casino. Over the last two years, she'd heard rumors about the renovation of the old Lucky Duck hotel, but she'd never considered it might be mob-financed and especially not by a capo as young as Nico. With the money now required to set up a casino in Nevada, most of the renovations and new developments were handled by large corporations or foreign investors, with the mob taking their cut through deals with regulators, unions, legislators, and developers.

"Come on. Don't stand outside gawking." Jules tugged on her arm. "It's Friday night. I want to party and meet your man, not necessarily in that order."

Mia bristled. "He's not my man."

"Then what are we doing here?"

"It's business." At least that was what she told herself when she convinced Jules to join her.

In the three days since Big Joe had escorted her home, she'd had second thoughts about billing Nico for a service that hadn't been completed, so she'd taken a second look at his system and flagged a few areas of concern. When neither he nor his casino manager returned her calls, she'd decided to pay him a visit.

After all, she'd been hired to do a job, and her professional reputation depended on doing it right. If that meant she had to see the misogynistic bastard again, well she did owe him a thank-you for dealing with the Wolf. Not that she needed him to come running to her aid, but it had been nice to know someone had her back. She was still waiting for the fallout from that disastrous visit. So far, the newspapers hadn't reported the discovery of a body, but she knew without a doubt her father would have something to say when he got out of hospital. Too bad she couldn't bring Nico along.

"I'm calling bullshit on that one," Jules said. "Look at you all dressed up in your short black dress, laced up the sides, with that naughty crinoline underlay, the bare shoulders, and your long sexy socks. Men go crazy for stuff like that. If it was business, you'd be wearing a suit. You like him."

"He's insufferably arrogant, condescending, controlling, bossy, violent, and dangerous," Mia shot back. "He does what he wants regardless of what people think or feel or what the consequences might be, and he's pretty much as off-limits as a man can get in my crazy, fucked-up Mafia world. He kidnapped me, hustled me at pool, and then it was all hands on deck to claim his prize. I mean, who does that? And after I let him into my office and . . ." Her voice hitched. "Showed him my stuff, does he ask what I think about leaving after he beats the crap out of the Wolf? No. He says, 'Get her out of here.'" She paused for breath, and Jules laughed.

"So that's a yes, you like him. Guess I'm here as your wing woman tonight."

"It's business," Mia insisted as they walked into the casino. "You're here as my associate."

"Well then I'm gonna get hammered, and I'll write off my drinks."

Mia opened her mouth to refute Jules again, but she had to accept that Jules was right. Despite all her protests, and all the reasons why it was wrong, she wanted to see Nico again. It just wasn't easy to let down her guard. The security test gave her an excuse to step out from behind the walls that had sheltered her for so long, to open herself up, to take the one risk she had always been afraid to take.

"Looks like we're gonna have to buy you a few drinks, too." Jules gave her arm a squeeze and they walked inside.

Casino Italia was a mix of old and new. Shades of gray and red dominated the upscale decor. Mia liked the unique mix of young/hip and retro Rat Pack Vegas vibes with live entertainment and vintage slots with levers; not so much the scantily clad dealers busting out of their skintight outfits as they leaned over the gaming tables.

In addition to sound effects and other noise—clapping, cheers, bells, sirens and whistles—the casino played a mix of soft, repetitive and easy listening music, as well upbeat and stimulating Top 40 hits, all psychologically designed to manipulate customers into dropping the maximum amount of cash.

Mia had to admit that the casino renovation was a smart move. The Downtown revival was picking up steam. Only a few blocks away, two of the city's oldest hotels were being redeveloped, and the Freemont Street Experience was beginning to draw the younger, wealthier crowd away from the ostentatious grandeur that was the Strip.

She led Jules past the massive central bar where bikini-clad bartenders gyrated to fast-tempo intrusive music, and over to the high-stakes room. Louis stood guard at the door in his blue security uniform, his head shaved since the last time she'd seen him.

"I'm from HGH Enterprises." Mia handed over her card, hoping Louis wouldn't recognize her now that she was dressed in normal clothes. "I'm looking for Nico Toscani. It's a business matter. Is he here tonight?"

Louis smirked. "You planning to break into the control room again? Or are you here to dance?"

"It was business," she snapped. "And we sorted it out. Is Nico in the high stakes room or not?"

"No, ma'am." He pulled out his pager. "I'll see if I can track him down."

One moment became five minutes, and with Jules chomping at the bit to explore, Mia had almost lost her patience by the time Louis pointed to a man pushing his way through the crowd, his coiffed silver hair a perfect match for his shiny silver suit. "That's the casino manager, Mr. Vito."

Although Mia had talked to Vito on the phone and communicated with him by email, she had never met Nico's casino manager in person, and she held out her hand to greet him.

"Ms. Cordano. A pleasure to meet you at last." Vito shook her hand. "Mr. Toscani is occupied tonight and asked me to extend his apologies." He handed Mia an envelope. "He asked me to give you these comps, and he hopes you enjoy your visit."

"Thank you." Mia's cheeks flamed although there was no reason why Vito would think her visit was anything other than business. Her hand tightened on the envelope as disappointment speared through her chest. She hadn't realized how much she was looking forward to seeing Nico. And Jules was right. It wasn't about the security system. It was about him, and the way she felt when she was with him—beautiful and brave, wanton and wanted, instead of bruised, broken, and alone.

"I guess I'll just email the cybersecurity report, and you can pass it on. Call me if you have any questions." She moved to return the envelope, but Jules snatched it from her hand.

"That's lovely. Please thank him for us."

"Why did you take it?" Mia followed Jules to the cashier. "He doesn't want to see me. I shouldn't have come here. Why don't we just go back to your place with a bottle of wine?"

"He does want to see you." Jules joined the line-up with the chip comp in her hand. "If he didn't, the guard would have just told you he wasn't around. But Vito-Magneto from the X-Men just came to see us instead. He gave us comps encouraging us to stay. Read the signs. He's here. He knows you're here. Give it some time.

Sometimes guys are more scared of their feelings than we are."

"He doesn't have feelings. He's a mobster."

"If you really believed that, you wouldn't be here." Jules handed the chip comp to the cashier. "You're always looking out for people. You pulled me off the streets. You gave Chris a chance to make a new life for herself and her daughter. You're giving back to the community by teaching coding to underprivileged girls. You look after your sister, and even your mom when your dad hurts her. Now I'm looking after you. I know it was hard for you to come here. But this is the first guy you've liked since I met you. The first guy you've actually put yourself out on the line for. Are you going to let him go so easy? He took a big risk to see you the other night. So why don't you take a risk, too? I mean, look where we are. If there's place to take a risk, it's in a casino. And given what he did to protect you, I think the odds of you winning are pretty good."

"Jules . . ."

Jules handed Mia a stack of chips. "It's Vegas, baby. Time to live a little."

"I'm very disappointed in you, Sammy." Nico drove his fist into the hustler's gut. "I thought we had an understanding. I did you a favor, and you were supposed to return that favor by keeping your business out of my territory."

"*Testa di cazzo.*" Frankie stepped to the side as Sammy fell.

Sammy's hand hit a discarded soda can, and it clattered down the alley toward Luca who was keeping watch with Mikey Muscles. No one ever came down the narrow alley at the back of Nico's casino, but with so many drunken tourists around, they couldn't be too careful.

"It was an honest mistake." Sammy wiped the blood off his mouth. "I thought I'd swapped out the ring by mistake, so I swapped it back."

Nico hit Sammy with a left hook, and Sammy's head snapped to the side. "Honest is not a word I'd use for a man who sold a $50,000 three-karat diamond ring almost two hundred times."

Sammy had a good thing going until Frankie caught him hustling on Toscani territory. He would hang around pawn shops and offer the ring to innocent civilians at a bargain-basement price. At his insistence, the sucker would take the ring to the pawnshop, or even a jeweler to have it appraised. Sammy would make a big show of being shocked by the appraisal, and would pretend to reconsider the price. During the negotiation, he would switch out the real ring for a fake, pocket the cash and disappear into the crowd. Unfortunately, he'd just made the mistake of selling the ring to one of Nico's casino dealers. And since everyone in the casino was under Nico's protection, Sammy had a price to pay.

Nico stepped aside as Frankie went through the hustler's pockets, removing his wallet and a bag of rings, including one in a red velvet pouch. Nico landed a few more punches, breaking Sammy's nose. Not that Sammy's looks would matter anymore. He had been warned before, and now he would become a lesson for all the other underground slime who thought they could operate in Nico's territory.

Sammy slumped to the ground and moaned. Nico jerked his head and the two associates keeping watch opposite Luca and Mikey Muscles picked him up by the shoulders and dragged him away. Usually Frankie dealt with scum like Sammy, but after receiving Vito's message that Mia was in the casino, Nico needed an outlet for his frustration, and Sammy had the misfortune of trying to pull a hustle at the wrong time.

For four days, Nico had tried to stay away from Mia. *Cosa Nostra* came before blood family, and blood family came before the man. With his succession hanging in the balance and an agreement with the Sicilian Scozzaris to be honored, Nico had no place chasing after a beautiful, sexy hacker in crazy boots and punk clothes with dubious taste in music, who made him so damn hard when she refused to do his bidding, he couldn't think straight.

"What are you gonna do with him?" Frankie handed Sammy's wallet to Luca and leaned against the wall. He lit a cigarette, and Nico's lip curled. He'd given up asking Frankie to quit. Steeped in violence and darkness, the Toscani family enforcer had few vices and little tolerance for suggestions about how to live the life the Toscanis had given him after his parents were killed in a savage attack by the Russian mafia. If he wanted to spend his days with a cigarette in one hand, and a bottle in the other, who was Nico to judge? They had all given their lives to the mob. They'd all suffered. And yet they would never leave. The mob was family. Until death did you part.

"Something public." He adjusted the knot on his tie, and smoothed down his jacket. He hated fighting in the damned suit, but presentation—*la bella figura*—was as important as action and without the veneer of civility, he would scare the civilians away.

Luca tucked the wallet into his pocket. "You want Frankie to do it? Or you want to open the books and give the contract to Big Joe?"

Big Joe had put in the ten years of service to the Toscani family necessary to become a made man, three of those with Nico's crew. The only thing standing between him and his button was a contract killing. It hadn't always been that way. In the old days, a good earner could make his bones solely by participating in an execution and not pulling the actual trigger. Big Joe was a solid earner. A good guy. Loyal. Trustworthy. Easy going. He didn't smoke, didn't do drugs, drank but never drove, argued but never lifted a hand to any member of the crew. He was the perfect mobster in a world of imperfect men.

"I'm not ready to open the books yet." Nico only accepted new made guys when he had the time and resources to support them. But now, with everything in crisis, he wasn't prepared to take on the additional responsibility of policing another soldier, no matter how good an earner he might be.

Frankie and Luca preceded Nico into the casino with Mikey Muscles taking up the rear.

"Is she still here?" he asked quietly, as they emerged onto the casino floor. Mikey Muscles had been tasked with liaising with Vito about the unexpected visitor.

"Yes, sir, Mr. Toscani. I got a live feed into the security cameras in case you wanted to check up on her." He handed Nico his phone.

Pausing in the doorway, Nico watched the short video clip of Mia on the screen. *Madonna.* Why the fuck did she have to dress like that? Every damn male in the bar was watching her dance in those lace-up boots, that tiny dress, and those sexy socks that just begged a man to follow them under her skirt just to see how far they would go.

He watched her dance on the stage beside the bar, her body undulating to the music. She was more titillating than the scantily clad go-go girls dancing up a storm on the counter beside her. Was it the corset part of her dress that pushed her breasts up obscenely high and emphasized the narrowness of her waist and the swell of her hips? Or was it those fucking socks that bared a flash of creamy thigh? Or was it the strength of character the out-fit conveyed—that she knew what she liked and gave fuck all what anyone thought.

She looked up, straight at the camera. Danced in a cir-cle giving him the full picture of what he was missing, flipped her frilly skirt just enough to show the curve of her cheek. She had to know he was watching. She had to know what would happen when she gave him a glimpse of something he shouldn't see.

Something he wanted.

Something he would have. Tonight.

"I like your socks."

Mia smiled at the pleasant-looking man in the polo shirt and chinos dancing in front of her. "Thank you."

"I like your skirt, too." He moved awkwardly to the music, like a dad who had forgotten his rhythm, although he didn't look older than twenty-five.

"Thank you."

"I'm Richard," he said stiffly. "Is it okay if I dance with you?" He did a zombie jerk of his arms, and Mia bit back a laugh.

"Yes."

After four rounds of vodka shooters, two games of craps, a Mai Tai, and some decidedly bad luck on the Big Six wheel, Mia was ready for some action. If it happened to come in a preppy package with a blue collared shirt sporting a little pony on the chest, then she'd take what she could get; she'd given up on Nico showing his face several hours ago.

"I like your boots, too. I don't meet a lot of girls who dress like you." He made a not-too-subtle adjustment of his chinos, and Mia looked the other way as the beat slowed. She wondered what he would think if she told him he was dancing with a mobster's daughter who spent her days hacking computers.

He moved closer and put his arms around her, still trying to find the beat. She leaned her cheek against his crisp, cotton shirt. He smelled cool and fresh, faintly of soap and aftershave. He was nice. A gentleman. He had tassels on his shoes, and his shirt was well ironed. This was the kind of man she should go out with if she didn't have to worry that he would get shot in the head by a father who only cared about her for her value as a prize cow. Not a dark, dangerously seductive mobster with a fierce scowl, who overwhelmed her so quickly she lost her inhibitions and let him finger fuck her until she climaxed in the hallway outside her office.

Her skin prickled with heat. Was Nico watching? Resisting the urge to look around, she leaned closer to Richard. If Nico couldn't be bothered to leave his office, then she'd give him something to watch. There was something between her and Nico, some kind of chemistry she didn't understand. Although she was scared to open herself up to such a dominant, powerful man, to show the vulnerability she had hidden for so long, she was determined to explore their curious connection. And if he didn't show, she was pretty sure tall, blond, and tasseled would be happy to take Nico's place in her bed tonight.

Richard's hand slid down to her ass, and her hopes shot up that this night might not end as badly as she thought it would.

"Is that okay?"

Mia was momentarily lost for words. She'd never been asked by a man if it was okay to squeeze her ass in public. But if that didn't draw Nico out, nothing would. "Squeeze away."

He laughed and held her tighter, rocking her from side to side until she thought she might get seasick. She looked for a stationary object to focus on to make the nausea go away and found a glowering mob boss instead.

Nico.

A giddy thrill swept over her. She hadn't felt anything like it since high school when the senior she'd been crushing on showed up at her soccer game just to watch her play

But, unlike the senior who had asked her out after the game, Nico wasn't smiling.

He took his time perusing her body, his scrutiny thorough and avid, his heated gaze lingering on the bare expanse of skin between the top of her socks and the bottom of her dress.

Damn. Nico was by far the most breathtaking man in the bar, the most beautiful man she had ever seen. He was impeccably dressed, as usual, in a perfectly fitted dark suit and blue silk tie, but his dark hair was slightly ruffled, just begging to be smoothed down. That tiny imperfection hinted at the wildness that rippled beneath the surface, the predator that watched her with hungry eyes.

His gaze dropped, sharpened on the hand on her ass.

Ah. A miscalculation. She didn't want the nice man to get blood on his shirt. "I'm really sorry." She gently disengaged Richard's hands from her ass. "My boyfriend is coming." She directed his attention to the bar. "My friend, Jules, is single, though, and looking to hook up with someone tonight. She's over by the bar—pink streak in her hair. And thanks for the dance."

Before he could respond, she pushed him gently in Jules's direction and turned just as the sea of dancers parted, waved aside by two burly bouncers who had appeared out of nowhere. Nico stepped into the space only just barely cleared by her new friend.

"*Che cazzo fai*—what the fuck are you doing?"

She lifted an eyebrow at the strong words. Did he even

realize he was speaking Italian or how sexy swear words could sound in the language of love? "Dancing."

"Not anymore." He wrapped an arm around her and pulled her close, claiming her with his body. His hips moved to the XAmbassadors's "Unsteady," so smooth they were one with the beat, and she felt the thrum of desire between her thighs.

"Maybe I wanted to finish my evening with Richard." She circled her arms around his neck. "He was very nice."

Nico snorted. "You'd eat him alive."

"You don't know anything about me," she said, indignant. Why couldn't she have a nice guy like Richard? They could see movies, go for walks in the park, build a house with a white picket fence, have babies . . .

Because she belonged to the Mafia, and they would never let her go.

"I know everything I need to know about you," he whispered in her ear, his lips brushing over her sensitive skin. "I know you're going to be wherever danger is at. I know you aren't afraid to take risks or you wouldn't be in my casino. I know a man like that would bore you to tears."

She shivered, drinking in his deep, rich voice. Her panties were wet with her desire, and she was damn sure Richard, with his zombie dancing and baggy chinos, hadn't turned on the tap. Not a drip.

Their gazes met, his eyes so dark they were almost black. Mia sucked in a deep breath, desperate for air. She didn't know if it was the alcohol in her blood, the heavy beat of the music, the darkness around them, or the fact it felt like they were alone despite the sea of people, but she felt awake when she was with Nico, alive in a way she hadn't been since Danny died. It was a heady, addicting feeling and the more she had, the more she wanted.

"I actually came about your security system."

"Bullshit." He thrust a thick thigh between her legs. "You came to see me."

"I can't access the system without you, so yes, I came to see you."

They were no longer dancing, but their bodies were still moving, grinding, his hand on her ass, his lips in her ear. "You want me. I can feel your wetness against my thigh, the heat of your body. I can smell your arousal, *bella*."

She did want him. And from the press of his erection against her hips, he wanted her, too. Why play games? She was bold in business, why couldn't she bold with her personal life, too? "What are you going to do about it?"

"*Dio mio*, you test a man to the limits." He fisted her hair, tugged her head back. "I'll tell you what I'm going to do. Tonight I'm going to fuck you like the bad girl you are. You're gonna learn who you belong to. Your voice is going to be hoarse from screaming your pleasure. And when we're done, you're gonna beg me for more."

Mia tried to rein in the runaway lust train that was on a crash course to tear off his clothes in the middle of the bar. Nico was different tonight. Wild. Raw. Uncontained.

"I wanted to tell you your password isn't secure." She drew in a ragged breath, struggling against her own desire. "It should really have a mix of upper and lower case letters, some symbols and numbers."

"Fuck the password." He nuzzled her hair, ran a possessive hand over the curve of her hip. "Someone breaks into my system, they steal from me. They steal from me, they die."

"So, I'll just reset it to Mr. Mob Boss, then, shall I?"

His hand slipped under her dress to run up the inside of her thigh. "You keep talking business, and I'll find something else for that smart mouth to do."

She moaned softly and his eyes blazed with sensual

heat. "That's right, *bella*. Tell me how bad you want me, and I'll give you what you need."

"You seem to get off bossing me around. I didn't appreciate what you did at my office."

"I kept you safe." Beneath the screen of her dress, his finger pushed the damp cotton of her panties aside while he kept his body close, shielding her from view. "I'll always keep you safe. And you're gonna hate how much you like it. Now, turn around or I'm gonna slide my finger in your hot, wet cunt and work you hard right here on the dance floor."

Since 'no' didn't seem to be an option, she turned as stared into the crowd seething in front of them. Nico yanked her against him, her back to his front, and his hands on her waist, spanning her stomach. He didn't miss a beat as he rocked them from side to side, rolling his hips against her with the kind of sinfully sexy moves she had only ever seen on the big screen.

"Good girl." He leaned down, feathered kisses along the sensitive curve of her neck. Mia lost herself in sensation—the pounding of the bass vibrating through her body, the sweet slide of alcohol through her veins, the energy of the crowd dancing to the party that was Vegas, and the heat that was Nico pressed up against her.

"I'm not a girl."

"No, you're not. You're all woman. My woman." He wrapped her hair around his hand and tugged her head to the side, baring her neck for the erotic nip of his teeth. A tremor ripped through her body. Fuck Papà. Fuck her family. No one could stop her from taking what she wanted, and she wanted this man. The enemy. Dark, dangerous and utterly delicious.

She turned in his arms, and her breasts pressed up against his chest, her nipples taut and throbbing. Nico grabbed her ass and pulled her against him. His scorching gaze slammed through her, melting her from the inside out. He licked his lips, leaned down until she could feel the heat of his breath on her lips, until he was so close she only had to reach up for a little taste.

"We're leaving," he murmured, pulling away seconds before their lips met.

"Good. Let's go." She nuzzled his neck, breathed in the fresh scent of his cologne. "I think you comped me a room. Let's use that."

"No." Gritting his teeth, he gently detached her hands from where they had sunk into his very tight ass. "I'm taking you out for dinner."

She gave him a puzzled frown. "I don't need to be wined and dined. I'm quite happy to go upstairs, tear off our clothes, and continue what we've started."

"You deserve more." He threaded his hand through hers and led her through the crowd. "But make no mistake, *bella*. I am going to pleasure the fuck out of you tonight."

THIRTEEN

"So nice to see you, Mr. Toscani. I've got the best table in the house ready for you and your guest." Lennie swept the door open and Mia preceded Nico into Il Tavolino.

Always on the alert, Nico checked out the other diners as Lennie led them to their table. Was that guy in the bowling shirt hiding a weapon under his table? Was that suit heading for the restroom going to pull a piece out from beneath his jacket? Were the two guys in track suits talking by the bar connected, or just stopping for a bite to eat after hitting the gym?

Lennie seated them in front of the stage, and Big Joe sat at a table a discrete distance away. He was Nico's second pair of eyes, and Nico trusted him to have arranged for guards to be at every entrance to the building.

"What are we gonna eat today, Lennie?" He waved the offered menu away.

Lennie made a few suggestions that Nico ignored.

"You know what? I'll tell you what we're gonna have. Make me some *prosciutt'*, a little *antipasti*, some *arancini,* a little *caponata*, polenta with gorgonzola, some chicken masala, then when we're done with that bring us a little red mullet in onion sauce. How's that?"

"Very good, sir."

Mia coughed discretely and he caught her frown. He'd ordered lots of food. Wasn't it enough?

Lennie's gaze flicked to Mia and back to Nico. He looked decidedly uncomfortable, like he'd been squeezed between a rock and a hard place. "Anything else, Mr. Toscani?"

What the fuck? "You unclear about something I said?"

Mia gave an irritated grunt, and curled her hand around her water glass, clutching it so hard her knuckles turned white. Something niggled at the back of Nico's mind, but before he could work it out, Lennie backed away with an obsequious bow.

"*Mi dispiace.* I'll get that order to your table right away."

"Never had a problem with Lennie before." He reached for Mia's hand, and she moved it away.

The niggle in his mind became a prickle of warning. *Fuck.* Of course. Not everyone liked mullet.

"You don't like the food? I'll tell Lennie to make something else."

"I like it," she said, her tone clipped. "But I would have preferred to have been asked."

Asked? He always ordered the food. He was the man. It was his job. And women ate what the men ate because men knew what was good. She needed to understand that when it came to matters of protection and providing, he was in charge.

"I'm the ma—"

She held up a hand, cutting him off. "Don't go there. Just. Don't."

He felt the slightest twinge of regret that he hadn't asked her opinion, especially since she'd been very careful not to disrespect him in front of Lennie. Given her views on empowering women, her restraint was a gift of immeasurable value.

"Next time, *bella*, you tell me what you like."

Would there be a next time? Did he want to get involved when he still had the Scozzari engagement hanging over his head? The only possible future they had was one in which Mia became his *goomah*—mistress.

Nico felt a curious tightening in his chest at the thought of putting Mia through what his mother had been through. Yes, there was love, but there was also a lot of jealousy, sadness, and pain. And what if they had a son? Would he really want a child to bear the stigma he had borne, growing up a bastard in a culture where marriage was a sacred bond? Nothing had come easy for Nico. He'd had to fight for what little respect he earned. And everything he achieved had come with a price.

"This place is amazing." Mia gestured to the photographs on the walls nearest them—classic prints of the heyday of Las Vegas, showgirls in the fifties, the Rat Pack in the sixties, Sinatra, Liberace, and the classic hotels—the Flamingo and the Riviera.

"Those were the days," Nico said, grateful for her attempt to smooth over what could have been an abrupt end to the evening. "Big names. Best acts. The hotels were all trying to outdo each other. Money flowed. The Mafia ran the show."

"You really do like the oldies. Is this restaurant yours?"

"I have a part-interest."

She laughed, the shadows fading from her face. "Soon to be a full interest, I expect. I know how those part-interests work. It would be a shame if it burned down."

"It won't. I protect everything that is mine." He cupped her jaw, brushed his thumb over the curve of her cheek. "Everything."

Mia studied him for a long moment, and then she tipped her head, rubbing her cheek against his palm.

Forgiven.

He felt something uncurl inside him, and liquid warmth flooded his body, spreading out to his fingers and toes.

"So you're a history buff?"

"Just Vegas." Nico reluctantly released her when a waiter came to refill their water glasses. "The idea of creating something out of nothing, this incredible city in the middle of the desert . . . I would have liked to be part of it." He hesitated, reluctant to share more, but no one had ever shown much interest in his secret passion. "My father would have hated all this. He was a very practical man. Very traditional. Very committed to the family and the business. He was very New York. Being sent here to set up the Las Vegas faction was a punishment to him. He said the only good thing that came out of it was that he met my mother."

"His *goomah*?"

"Yeah." He sipped the ice water, felt a cool rush through his veins. "It was hard on her. They loved each other, but there was never a chance he would marry her. Her family had nothing to offer. And, of course, *Cosa Nostra* marriages are forever, so there was no possibility of divorce once he married my stepmother." He downed the rest of the glass, trying to take the edge off the bitter memories with the icy burn. "I built the casino in my mother's memory. She was Vegas—a dancer in one of the shows; she loved to sing and dance, gamble and party. I run it clean. Respectable. For her. If I could do that for the family, I would."

"You want the family to be respectable?"

"What bastard wouldn't?"

"Nico . . ." She moved close to him, stroked her fingers through his hair in a soothing gesture that did much to ease a pain he had never realized he carried in his heart.

"Love isn't worth the pain," he said.

"Love created you." She pressed a kiss to his cheek, as she whispered in his ear. "A dangerously delicious, sexy, handsome mob boss."

If love felt anything like how he was feeling right now, he would be able to take on Tony and the family and the Falzones and even the fucking Sicilians with one hand tied behind his back. He would be able to fly to the fucking moon, dive to the bottom of the ocean, catch a star and bring it back to the earth. Would he feel this way for his Sicilian bride? He'd always been resigned to a loveless marriage, but then he'd never had a taste of what he might be missing.

A growl of pleasure rumbled in his chest. "That's Mr. Mob Boss, to you."

She gave him a seductive look through the curtain of her lashes. "I hear mob bosses like to seduce geeky hackers."

He slid his hand under the tablecloth to stroke the bare skin below her skirt. "I thought you were the one seducing me," he murmured. "Coming to my casino wearing those fucking hot socks, and this dress that just begs a man to take it off, dancing like you're fucking, letting another man touch you . . . You had to know I couldn't stay away."

"That makes two of us."

For a long moment he didn't move. If he'd had any doubts about her reason for showing up at the casino tonight, he had none now.

She reached over, loosened his tie. "Why the suit?"

"The suit goes with the business."

"Is that what this is?" She brazenly slipped the knot and undid the first button on his shirt. "Business?"

It should be about business. The business of revenge. The business of making his family strong again. But she was making it so damn hard, giving him those long, searching glances, breathing deep so he couldn't help but watch her breasts rise and strain against the tight bodice of her dress, licking her lips so he could watch the flick of her little pink tongue and imagine her lush mouth wrapped around his cock.

"There is nothing businesslike about what I want to do to you right now," he growled.

"So I'm at the mercy of a ruthless, horny mob boss?" She slid the tie off his neck and dropped it in her lap, an invitation he was unable to refuse. There was nothing he wouldn't do for her in that moment. He was totally and utterly at her mercy.

"Ruthless?" he asked, struggling for control, and no small bit amused.

Her cheeks flushed a delightful pink. "I know your reputation."

"In business or in bed?"

"I've seen what you do for business." She undid the next two buttons of his shirt, feathered her fingers over the throbbing pulse on his neck. "I'm waiting to see what you can do in bed."

Sexytimes countdown with a horny mafia boss:

Five minutes: Nico yanks Mia from the booth, heedless of the way her dress rides up as she slides across the soft, plush surface of her seat.

Four minutes thirty seconds: Nico shouts for Lennie and tells him he'll using Lennie's office. Orders Lennie to keep the food warm and the drinks cold. Snatches Lennie's key.

Three minutes thirty seconds: Big Joe frantically calls

the guards stationed around the restaurant, and tells them to secure the back hallway and office area.

Three minutes: Nico half drags, half carries Mia through the restaurant to the back hallway with Big Joe running behind them. People rush to get out of Nico's way. Mia murmurs apologies and mutters excuses—sick relative, death in the family, car accident, medical issue, urgent need to tear off clothes and have hot, wild sex. No. Wait. Scratch that.

Two minutes: Nico unlocks office door and yanks Mia inside. Brief pause to tell Big Joe to stand guard and not to disturb Nico unless someone dies, and even then, only if they are family.

One minute thirty seconds: Nico slams and locks door. Pushes Mia up against the wall. Plasters his body against hers and kisses her so hard she gasps for breath.

Thirty seconds: Nico reaches under Mia's dress and tears her panties away. Mia congratulates self on not wearing her comfy cotton briefs.

Twenty seconds: Nico yanks on laces holding bodice of her dress closed, slips shoulder straps over Mia's arms. Dress falls to filthy office floor. Nico growls with pleasure as he helps her step out of it.

Ten seconds: Bra whisked away. Nico tells Mia to leave her socks and boots on. Mia guesses it's not because he's worried about the floor that looks like it has never been washed.

Five seconds: Nico says, "Spread your legs for me, *bella.*"

Finally.

One second: Nico makes long leisurely perusal of Mia's naked body, making her overheat. Eyes go wide when he notices her ink.

Pause in sexy times countdown.

"*Madonna.*" Nico breathed the word, and sudden panic

coursed through Mia's body. She was ready now. She was wet now. She wanted him now.

"Fuck now. Look later." She reached for his belt.

"No." Nico clamped her wrist and drew her hand away. With his free hand, he traced the delicate lines of the tattoo on her side, following it down to the pink petals that covered her hip. "How far does it go?"

She half-turned to show him the delicate pattern of flowers that extended from her ribs, down her side and over her hip, the last few vines ending just beside her mound.

"Beautiful," he murmured.

"The flowers are tiger lilies." She blushed, slightly embarrassed by his intense scrutiny. "They are the only flower that will continue to grow in the vase after being cut. The meaning of tiger lilies I liked best was, 'I dare you to love me.'" She dipped her head, shrugged. "They kind of sum up all my emotional issues growing up in the kind of family I did. They give me hope."

Nico pressed a soft kiss to each flower, working his way down her hip. "If I had to pick a flower for you, this would be it. Bold and beautiful and wild."

Her arousal dropped to a slow, throbbing pulse and she turned again to show him the rest of her ink so he wouldn't get distracted again. Her fingers dangled over her right hip. "This is my favorite piece."

"*Molto bella.*" He studied the intricate tribal design that wound its way over the front of her hip, beneath where her panties should have been, and down her thigh, interweaving pink butterflies, roses and thorns with the words, "Love me as I am" inked along the top.

"You hide a lot beneath your clothes." He crouched down in front of her, traced along the wing of a butterfly with his warm, wet tongue, sending a delicious shiver down her spine.

"Well I can't have any ink where my father might see or he would kill me. This is all mine. Something he can never take away. All my secrets for you to see."

"You are a work of art. I could look at your beautiful body for hours." He pressed a kiss to her stomach, and she ran her fingers through his soft, thick hair.

"You could do other things to my body for hours, too." She lifted her eyebrow in hopeful suggestion, encouraged by the naked desire on his face. If he didn't give her what she needed soon, she'd have to take matters into her own hands.

He gave a dark laugh. "You have no idea."

In one fluid move, he stood and lifted her against him, one hand under her ass, the other behind her head, holding her still for a fierce, wicked kiss.

She gasped when his teeth nipped her lip. Instantly, the dingy, windowless office, and the scents of yeast and stale grease faded away beneath a deluge of need so extreme she shamelessly ground her hips against the firm ridge of his cock.

"If you keep working that pussy against me, I'll have no choice but to fuck you so hard everyone in the restaurant is gonna know what's going on." With two easy strides of his long legs, he carried her to the desk. One sweep of his strong arm, and he cleared it of pencils, pens, and papers. "You're going to be very acquainted with this desk because every time I sit in my office, I think about how fucking sexy you looked that night we caught you in the casino, how hard I was when I had you standing between my legs, how I wanted you naked in front of me, your pussy bare, begging me to make you come."

"I thought you'd be thinking about how I was ready to cut your balls with my knife."

He gave a snort of laughter as he lay her down on the

cold, hard surface, positioned her boots on the edge. "You wanted me. Just as I know you want me now. Spread those legs. Show me how wet you are for me. Show me where you want my cock."

So arrogant. A delicious thrill of defiance shot through her and she snapped her legs together, daring him to push, challenging him to show her just how far he would go, how dangerous he really was.

"Do you really want to play that game?" He leaned forward and kissed her, softly, deeply, giving her a taste of the power he kept so tightly leashed. "I'm a hard man, and I'm going to take you hard and I'm going to take you rough and I'm going to want things from you that might be difficult to give. But you are always safe with me. Do you understand that?"

Safe. She hadn't known that was what she needed to hear, but the words undid the knot in her chest. She'd never felt safe before. Not when she was forever at the mercy of her father.

"Yes." She cupped his face between his hands and returned his kiss as she spread her legs wide.

"Very nice, *bella*." He pulled the chair around and settled himself in front of her, wrenched her legs farther apart. "Are you as sweet down here as you up there?"

"What are you going to do?" Her voice came out breathy, soft with anticipation. Of course she knew what he was going to do, but she'd never been with a man who had given her that pleasure, had no idea about her role in the process or how it might feel.

"I'm going to taste your sweet pussy, and then I'm going to make you come so many times you're going to beg." He slicked a thick finger through her folds. "You're going to beg for my cock."

He was so dominant, so utterly confident in everything

he did. She licked her lips, threaded her hands through his soft hair, and hung on for the ride.

Nico gave a low growl of satisfaction as he feathered kisses over the soft curls covering her mound. She moaned, angled her hips up for more, but he moved down to her inner thighs, alternating butterfly kisses and little nips of his teeth over her skin until he reached the sensitive crease at the top of her thigh. She shuddered, her body taut with anticipation, but she wasn't prepared for the molten wave of heat that rushed through her body when he gave her slit a long, luscious lick.

"Oh God. Nico. Please." She pulled on his hair, tried to tug him where she wanted him to go, the only part of her that his tongue hadn't tasted.

"Mia." His voice was hard with warning and she released him, balled her hands into fists as she tried to think of anything but the ache between her legs.

He nudged her thighs open wider and ran the pads of his thumbs along her labia, spreading her wide.

A moan ripped from her throat. She had never realized how exquisitely sensitive that area could be, and her legs trembled violently with a fierce surge of need.

"Hands over your head. Grip the edge of the desk."

"I want to touch you," she protested.

"You want to be in control. Trust me, *bella*. Let go with me and I'll catch you when you fall."

Well, it wasn't like her hands would be tied, although the idea of being totally restrained sent a thrill of fear through her body. Mia raised her hands and curled them around the edge of the desk, her back arching off the wooden surface.

"Very nice." Gently at first, and then with more pressure, his hot, wet tongue traced the sensitive edges of her labia, circled her clit.

"Oh God." Mia angled up for more, and Nico placed one hand on her hips, pressing her down. "Lie still and take what I want to give you."

She struggled to stay still, as he pushed two fingers deep inside her, alternating gentle licks with firm thrusts, brutal sucks with light glides. She closed her eyes and focused on the soft brush of his hair against the sensitive skin of her inner thighs, the sharp edge of the desk beneath her fingers, the hard surface keeping her from sinking into oblivion.

"Don't stop," she groaned, writhing on the desk as she fought the firm press of his hand against her stomach. "Don't stop."

He made a growling noise deep in his throat, and then he sucked hard on her clit and pulsed his fingers upward.

A whirlwind of sensation caught her and threw her into her climax without warning. She bucked against him, threw one arm across her mouth to muffle her cries as pleasure crashed over her like a tidal wave, cresting again and again with every hard pull of his mouth. He added a third finger and pumped deep, drawing hard on her clit until she came again. And again. And when she dared ask for more, he made her come so hard she screamed.

"Nico!"

"Tell me what you need."

"I need you." She drew in a ragged breath. "I need you inside me."

He eased back, kissing her inner thighs as she lay trembling on the desk. How could she want to come again after she'd come more times this evening than she had in the last year? But she did. She wanted to feel him inside her. She wanted to feel his hard muscles above her, watch that magnificent body pounding into her as he took his pleasure. But more than that, she wanted to see him lose control. She wanted the beast as well as the man.

His hands travelled up her sides, tracing the vines and flowers. When he reached her breasts, he leaned over her body and licked and sucked her nipples until she felt her arousal climbing again.

"Now." She pushed herself up on her elbows, and he backed away. Fearing she might be denied, she gave him what she knew he wanted. "Please, Nico."

"I like to hear my strong, sexy hacker begging for my cock." He carefully removed his jacket and tie, hanging them on the chair as he stood. She bit her lip when he stripped off his shirt to reveal his toned, inked, muscular chest.

"One day, I want to lick all your tattoos," she murmured, her gaze dropping to his waist as he undid his belt.

"I don't think I'd last long enough for you to lick them all once you touched me with that little pink tongue. I'd have you on your knees so fast, showing me what else that mouth could do, you wouldn't have time to take a breath." He shoved down his fine wool trousers and the boxers beneath revealing his thick, heavy cock.

"Oh." She let out a breath of anticipation.

"*Cristo.* You test a man's willpower to the limit." Nico snagged a condom from his back pocket and tore it open. He fisted his cock, pumped the hard flesh until a bead of precum glistened at the top and rolled the condom over the slick head.

"Don't make me wait any longer."

Nico tipped her face up and crushed his lips to hers, his tongue diving deep into her mouth. "Lie back," he murmured against her lips. "I want to see you and those fucking sexy socks when I'm inside you." With a firm hand on her chest, he pushed her back. The scorching heat in his eyes as his gaze raked over her body both scared and aroused her. She had no doubt he would fuck her with the same ruthless intensity, the barely leashed power that had made him the most feared mobster in the city.

A shiver ran down her spine, and Nico leaned forward, brushed his lips along the taut line of her neck. "Shh."

"I want you so badly." She moaned softly. "I'm so wet. I've never wanted a man like this."

Hands around her ankles he spread her legs wide. "There are no men for you. Not in the past. Not now. Not in the future. There's only me, and I'm gonna fuck you so hard you never forget. You're gonna feel me for days, *bella*, inside and out."

"I like your dirty talking." She arched her back against the hard desk, tilted her hips, so desperate to feel him inside her she didn't care how he reacted to her challenge. "But you're talking too much."

As if he'd reached the end of his control, he yanked her against him to meet the powerful thrust of his hips, burying himself inside her, his body taut and straining.

Mia gasped as she tried to adjust to his thick, hard shaft, the exquisite fullness of being so completely filled, the connection she felt as he pushed deeper into her body.

"If I'd known how good you'd feel, how hot and wet and tight your cunt would be, how much of me you could take, I would never have let you walk out of my office at the casino." He braced himself on the desk and began to fuck her with hard, hammering strokes. His hips pistoned back and forth, his powerful muscles bunching every time he surged forward, his cock driving her closer and closer to the edge.

"Maybe I should have made good my threat that night." Her voice was hoarse, thick with desire.

"One touch and you would have been mine. You are mine, Mia. If I find you with another man, his screams will echo in the desert for years." He shuddered, as if he was fighting for control. With a guttural groan, he hooked her leg around his shoulder and drove deep.

"Let go for me." He slid his finger over her clit and her orgasm ripped through her body, a white-hot burst of pleasure that scorched her very soul. Nico hammered into her, drawing out her orgasm, until he stiffened and groaned, his cock pumping his release deep inside her.

He collapsed over her, taking his weight on his elbows. "You are so goddamn fucking sexy." He nuzzled her neck, nibbled Mia's ear. Still dazed from the roughest sex she had ever had, she stiffened, and he pulled away.

"Did I hurt you?"

"No." She ran her hand down his back, felt his powerful muscles ripple beneath her touch. It was hard to believe that she had just fucked a wiseguy after all her years of trying to distance herself from the mob. He was arrogant and controlling, ruthless and violent, and yet she'd glimpsed another side to him—the man behind the mobster, who was protective and caring and deeply passionate about the things that meant the most to him.

She felt no shame embracing her feminine side when she was with him, because he respected her and appreciated her strength. He made her want something she had never allowed herself to want before, to free the part of herself she had buried away when Danny died. She could see herself with him—a man who was not threatened by who she was or what she did. A man who could be in control but not control her. A man who could keep her safe. A man who had no fear of her family.

"If you'd told me the night I walked into your casino that we would end up here like this, I would have called you crazy."

"I couldn't decide what I wanted more that night," he said, brushing a kiss over her temple. "You naked and on my desk or tied up and used as bait for your father."

Guilt speared through her when he mentioned her father, bringing her to her senses. What would he do if she told him that Dante was the one who pulled the trigger? How could she continue this when she was keeping a secret from him that he would see as the ultimate betrayal?

Nico helped her up and turned to dispose of the condom. Mia scooted off the desk and pulled on her clothes. By the time she was done, Nico had dressed and was back to his impeccable self.

"What do we do now?" She stuffed her shredded panties into her purse, suddenly overcome with how reckless she had been. What would her father do if he knew she was consorting with the enemy? Or maybe he knew already.

"We do what all Italians do when there is a food waiting for them." Nico pulled open the door. "We eat."

FOURTEEN

Ben parked his vehicle and turned off the engine. His unscheduled meeting with Jack was four hours away. Jack had given no reason for the change in day, but Ben hoped it had something to do with the end of the assignment. In all his years undercover in the mob, he'd never seen craziness like what was going on right now. People were going to get hurt. Good people. People he cared about.

Until he'd joined the new crew, he would sit in his apartment with the TV blaring and a beer in his hand before his meetings with Jack. He would handwrite a report of all the criminal activity he'd witnessed in excruciating detail, listing names, locations, and descriptions—anything that might help the DA with the big case that never seemed to get off the ground. But tonight, he wasn't in the mood. He hadn't been in the mood for two fucking years.

He respected his boss. Admired him. He was loyal, honorable, and protective of his family, his crew and the people in his territory. But right now he was distracted. And that meant he wasn't listening for the rumbling of the storm. And there was a storm coming, no doubt about that. Ben had friends who passed him intel the Mafia could never get. Snippets of information from other undercover cops that told him something big was brewing. Good thing Ben had his boss's back. He just had to find a way to tell his boss he needed to get his head back in the game or he was going to lose more than his heart.

His own heart ached because tomorrow was supposed to be one of his days with Daisy. But when the boss called and told him he had guard duty in the morning, he couldn't say no. He'd had guard duty all day today, too. Now it was late—too late. But maybe he could stop by and say good night. Give her a hug. Maybe she'd even still be up. Ginger always partied on a Friday night.

Half an hour later, he pulled up outside Ginger's house. The lights were all on, and music was blaring through the windows. No chance of Daisy sleeping through that. He knocked, but when no one answered, he pushed open the door and stepped inside.

"What the fuck are you doing here?" Ginger looked up from the couch, slurring her words as Ben walked into the living room. Her shirt was pushed up around her neck baring her breasts and she had a blanket over her legs. Her hair was a crazy tangle around her head, and her eyes were dilated so wide they looked black. A needle lay on the carpet beside an empty beer can, and Ben fought back the urge to shout so he didn't disturb Daisy.

"Are you shooting up when our little girl is in the house? Christ, Ginger. Cover yourself. Look at you. What the fuck happened to that sweet girl I met in a bar seven years ago."

"Gabe rescued me from the drudgery of motherhood." Ginger pulled down her shirt, sucked on her cigarette. "You should take a hit sometime. He's got a line on some good quality stuff. Might help you pull the stick out of your fucking ass. And what the hell are you doing here anyway? What the fuck time is it?"

"I'm just here to say good night." Ben turned away, feeling sick. He had to get off this case for Daisy's sake. Ginger was a disaster waiting to happen. And Gabe . . .

"Ben." Gabe stepped into the hallway in front of Daisy's door. He was wearing nothing but a pair of track pants loose around his narrow hips, his junk clearly outlined by the thin material. He was all ink, toned pecs and smooth muscle, the kind of body every man dreamed about having if he had ten gallons of protein powder, a steady supply of steroids, and no job so he could spend twelve hours a day in the gym.

Ben frowned when Gabe didn't immediately get out of his way. "I'm here to see Daisy."

Gabe tipped his neck from side to side, making it crack. "She had a busy day. She's all worn out."

Every hair on the back of Ben's neck stood on end, every nerve ending flared in warning, every instinct that had kept him alive ten years in an organization that would kill him if they discovered he was a cop, screamed danger. "Get out of my way."

Gabe smirked, stepped to the side, forcing Ben to brush past him to open the door. "We were just having a bedtime story. It's our nightly ritual since her daddy's not about."

Ben's hand opened and closed, hovered near the gun holstered by his side. He imagined pulling it out and shoving the barrel into Gabe's throat, pushing him up against the wall the way his pals in his crew did with anyone who pissed them off. But Ben couldn't cross that line. Even thought he was undercover, he was still an officer of the law. He couldn't beat someone up because of a smirk.

"Stay the fuck away from Daisy."

"Kinda hard since we're living together. Me and Ginger and your pretty little girl."

Walk away. Walk away. Gabe was baiting him and he couldn't risk a fight. If Ginger called the police and he was arrested, he risked having his cover blown because Jack would have to come and identify him to have him released. Every Mafia family had cops on the payroll. Someone would tell his boss. He'd be taken for a ride, and he'd never come back. His boss had zero tolerance for thieves, traitors, and rats. He had a reputation for being merciless with those who displeased him, and protective of those under his care. If Ben asked his boss for a favor for Daisy, Gabe wouldn't live to see the sun rise again.

Ben walked into the dark room and closed the door behind him. He was a cop, and he had to follow the rules, and the rules didn't allow asking for favors from the mob.

"Daisy?"

Daisy shot out of the bed and threw herself into his arms with such force that Ben stumbled back against the door.

"Hey, sweetheart." He kissed her forehead. "I came to say good night."

She squeezed him tight, plastering her thin body against him, her fingers digging into his back.

That warning prickle came back, and he forced himself to take a breath. "You okay? Anything wrong?"

"I want to go out of here," she whispered.

"Okay." Ben stroked her head, trying not to let his anxiety show. When he'd come by during the week to visit, she hadn't been interested in doing the things they usually enjoyed doing together. She didn't want to play in the park, go for ice cream, or hang out at the mall going on rides and buying sparkly jewelry and clothes. Instead, she clung to him, holding his hand as they walked around, her body plastered against his side. Whenever he sat down, she curled up on his lap and pulled his arms around her. She didn't even want to talk, and his Daisy loved to talk. But she hadn't been as agitated as she was now.

"You get dressed, and we'll head out."

"Please, Daddy." Her body shook, and she shuddered in his arms. "Take me out of here now."

His throat tightened and he had to force out the words. "What's wrong? Did Gabe . . ." He couldn't say it, didn't want to hear his biggest nightmare had come true, because if it had, there was no law he wouldn't break to avenge his little girl.

She shook her head, and he released the breath he didn't even know he was holding.

"Please," she whispered.

"Sure. We just gotta put some clothes on you. We'll go for a ride somewhere." He detached her fingers and looked around the tiny room for some clothes.

"I don't want to go for a ride. I just want to sit with you." Tears trickled down her cheeks and Ben thought his fucking heart would break. He wanted to take her away from Vegas, but if he walked off the job, he would have to go into witness protection and that meant leaving Daisy behind unless he could sort out the custody issues before he left.

"Anything you want."

He found some clothes and got her dressed before he carried her out of the house. The next few hours went by in a blur. He picked up a prepaid phone, drove around until he found a safe, quiet spot to park overlooking the city, and settled Daisy on his lap. She listened to the radio with him until finally fell asleep. Ben gently placed her on the back seat and covered her with his jacket, before giving Jack a call on his secure line.

"I'm not going to make it tonight." Ben leaned against

the vehicle, looked out over the peaceful, residential neighborhood spread out below him.

"I haven't heard from you all week," Jack said. "You haven't filed those reports you promised me. What the hell is going on?"

"I'm real worried about my Daisy being in the house with Gabe."

Jack gave a sympathetic murmur. He had a wife and two girls, one of who was the same age as Daisy. "I did the basics on Gabe for you. No criminal record. Not even a parking ticket. He's got a valid driver's license. Pays his taxes. Last job was as a cement mixer for a construction company. No current employment. I hit a roadblock internally when I tried to dig deeper. Some kind of clearance issue. There's nothing else I can do."

"Fuck." Ben thudded his fist against the wall. "What about the social worker? Did she stop by the house?"

"Daisy is at the bottom of the list because there is no evidence of abuse—no reports from doctors, teachers, coaches, or neighbors. They are totally overworked, so she's got a low priority."

"Something's wrong with her, Jack." Ben scrubbed his hand over his face. "She wouldn't talk about it. And things with the crew are getting way the fuck out of control."

"I wouldn't know since you aren't filing any reports," Jack snapped. Ben braced himself, pretty damn sure he knew what was coming next.

"I've been cutting you some slack over the last year because I know it's a matter of life or death for you every day," Jack continued. "But the higher-ups started getting concerned when they heard about things going down involving your crew and we weren't hearing about it in your reports. We're worried about you, Ben. I'm worried."

"Forget about it." His hand closed in a fist. "I gave you

more than enough evidence to convict the top bosses and the department wouldn't act. If they hadn't dragged their feet for the last year, those bastards would be in jail, and the families would be on self-destruct. Now the bosses are dead and we're starting from square one. You think I have time to write reports? And because I don't, you question my loyalty? You tell me you can't help my kid even though the reason she's unprotected is because I've spent ten years of my life on this assignment? No fucking way."

"We're pulling you out," Jack said. "We think you're in too deep, and this stuff with Daisy is compromising your ability to do your job. Our recent conversations have had more to do with her than your work. You're putting yourself and the investigation at risk."

"This stuff with Daisy?" Ben fought back the urge to smash his phone on the nearest rock. "I think something's going on in that house. She's scared, Jack. That's not 'stuff.' That's a crime. This is what we're supposed to do. Protect civilians. Protect my daughter."

Jack sighed. "I know you don't want to hear this, but you might be overreacting. You're not thinking straight. It's been a tense situation, and we didn't really consider the ramifications of that massacre at Vincenzo's on you. Our psychologist thinks you just might be projecting your anxiety on Daisy. After all, Gabe's been around for a while, and you never had any concerns about Daisy until just after it happened."

"Holy. Fucking. Shit. I can't believe you just said that." Ben felt like the rug had been ripped from under his feet. Projecting? Not thinking straight? That didn't sound like Jack. He was a straight-up guy. Never went for that psychology shit. What the hell was going on?

"Listen, Ben." Jack's voice dropped to a low, cajoling tone. "You come to the diner right now and someone will come to get you. I've already finished all the paperwork for witness protection. You'll be sent away until the situation is all sorted out and they make all the arrests. I'm not sure how long that's gonna be, but you'll be safe until it happens."

If Jack had made the offer weeks ago, Ben would have jumped at the chance. He'd wanted this. Wanted out. But now that it was offered, he realized it wasn't what he wanted at all, and he couldn't believe he'd been begging Jack to make it happen.

"What about Daisy?"

"She can't go with you because of the custody order. Only way would be if you took Ginger, too, but I'm guessing that's not going to happen."

"No fucking way." He couldn't stand being around Ginger for ten minutes, much less forever.

"So Daisy will stay in her current situation—"

"No." He barely managed to keep his voice low so as not to wake his sleeping daughter in the car. "Absolutely not."

He could hear Jack's sigh of exasperation. "Well, what then? You won't come. Daisy can't go with you because it be would be considered child abduction. What do you suggest?"

"I'll get a fucking court order." He stared out over the city he'd come to after he left foster care, his stupid teenage head full of dreams of taking down the mob. "I'll keep my head down and do my job. I'll call you ten fucking times a week if you want. I'll file the fucking reports. Meantime, you're going to push harder to get Social Services out to see Daisy. When Daisy is mine again, that's when you'll pull me out. In the meantime, I'll deal with Gabe."

"You'll deal with Gabe?" Jack's voice rose in pitch. "What the hell does that mean?"

"It means that I'm going to find out what's going on,

and if that fucker hurt my girl in any way, the streets are going to run red with his blood."

"Jesus Christ," Jack shouted. "We're cops, Ben. We don't do vigilante justice. I'll give you two weeks to sort yourself out, then custody order or not, you're done."

"Don't back me into a corner when my little girl is a risk," he warned. "If you're that worried about me, tell the fucking department to pull some strings with the judge."

"I'll pass on the message, but you're making the wrong decision," Jack said. "You're in way too deep, Ben. You're thinking like a wiseguy, talking like a wiseguy—hell, you're acting like a goddamned mobster."

Ben turned off his phone, and checked on Daisy, still asleep in the vehicle. Jack was wrong to overlook the benefits of Mafia-style vigilante justice. There was no administration or red tape to go through. No legal proceedings or victims' rights. There was the fucker who had scared his girl. And there was the bullet that would go through his head.

Would he go to jail if he pulled the trigger? Or would he become a made man?

FIFTEEN

"Your father wants to see you."

Mia looked up from her terminal in the community center computer lab. She had just logged in to for her Saturday morning coding class. Rev stood in the doorway, filling the space with his pumped-up bulk. Her pulse kicked up a notch. Usually her father summoned her over the phone. Rev was his top enforcer, entrusted with keeping Dante safe. That her father had pulled him off bodyguard duty to come and get her told her this was one meeting she did not want to attend.

"I'm teaching a class."

He walked toward her, idly kicking at the chairs as if they were pebbles. He wore a sweatshirt, sleeves torn away to showcase his massive biceps, and ripped down the chest to reveal his revolver tattoo.

"He wants to see you now."

Mia opened up the web browser, watching Rev out of the corner of her eye. She had come early to set up her class, and there weren't many people in the education wing of the community center on a Saturday morning.

"*Now* will have to be in two hours when I'm done."

When the web browser finally opened, she quickly logged in to her personal email, and then froze. What was she doing? Who was she planning to email? She'd been called to her father's office dozens of times and never once had she asked for help. She had weathered all sorts of storms alone, suffered many beatings, and always managed to make it out alive.

"Now means now."

But this was a different type of storm. First, Rev was here, and it was clear he wasn't going to take no for an answer. Second, she had still not been called to account for what happened with the Wolf. Third, she had been indiscreet last night going out in public with Nico. And fourth, well, if anyone had been watching when he dropped her off at home, there would be no doubt they were more than business acquaintances. At least he hadn't accepted her invitation to come inside..

"What if I refuse?" Who could she email anyway? Jules wouldn't be able to help her. What about Nico? She didn't have any way to contact him except through the casino, although she was pretty sure he would jump in his car and race to the community center if he thought she was in danger. Even the thought that there was someone who had her back made her feel stronger inside. But asking him for help would just escalate the war between the families. There had been enough bloodshed already.

"Then I'll get to put my hands all over that pretty curvy body when I carry you out." He moved toward her at a slow, steady pace, as if he had no fear that she might escape.

"That might attract some unwanted attention. Especially if I scream." She sent a quick email to Jules asking her to come down to the center ASAP to take over the class, and added a small note at the end about being dragged to her parents' house. As an afterthought, she added a scared emoji, and hit send just before Rev's meaty paw clamped down on her arm.

"You're not gonna do that 'cause I don't think you want Don Cordano to be any more pissed at you than he is now. He's got Kat and Dante in his office, and he's been raging at them for the last hour." He yanked her out of his seat. "He's using Kat as a substitute for you."

Mia stared at him aghast. "He hurt Kat?"

Rev's face turned hard. "Yeah. Wasn't nice to see. Or hear. But it wasn't my call."

"I'm coming." She grabbed her purse, but froze when she heard a knock at the door.

"Everything all right in here, ma'am?" Big Joe walked into the room.

Mia bit back a smile. Nico had meant what he said when he promised to keep her safe.

"Yes, thanks. I just . . . have to go home. There's a . . . family emergency."

Big Joe's gaze flicked to Rev. His eyes widened for the briefest of seconds, and then his face smoothed to an expressionless mask.

"So what's this?" Rev chuckled uneasily. "We got cops taking computer classes for little girls now?"

"Cops?" Mia looked from Big Joe to Rev and back to Big Joe. "He isn't a cop. He's . . ." She trailed off considering just how much worse the imminent beating would be if Rev told her father Nico had someone from his crew watching over her.

"A . . ." She frowned at Big Joe, willing him to fill in the blank.

"Dad looking to sign his girl up for the class," Big Joe said quickly.

Okay. She could work with that, although the tension in the room was so thick she could cut it with a knife.

Obviously they knew each other, but why did Rev think he was a cop?

"How old is your daughter?"

"Six." Big Joe's eyes didn't leave Rev as he spoke, and she couldn't decide if it was fear she saw in their blue depths or anger.

"This class is for girls nine to thirteen, but if you put your name down in reception, I'll ask them to give you a call if I get enough interest in teaching something for younger kids."

"Sure thing." Big Joe jerked his chin at Rev. "So you know this guy?"

"He works for my father. He's here to escort me home so I have to cancel today's class, otherwise I would have signed you up myself."

Big Joe frowned and she figured he was struggling to reconcile his instructions to keep her safe with the fact she'd pretty much told him she was being forced to leave.

"It's okay," she assured him, worried that Rev might start asking questions about their awkward conversation. "You can go . . . sign up your little girl."

"Our little girl." Rev smirked. "She's got two daddies now."

Mia could almost feel the waves of anger rolling off Big Joe. What the hell was going on? Rev clearly didn't know Big Joe was on Nico's crew because usually if two soldiers from feuding families bumped into each other, there would be some kind of fight. But they obviously had some kind of connection, and Rev's cop comment niggled at her brain. Was Nico in danger?

"She's got one daddy," Big Joe spat out. "And he's got a fucking bead on you."

Rev laughed, tipped his head from side to side and cracked his neck, a habit that was really starting to annoy

Mia. "You got nothing on me. And what the fuck would you do if you did? Write me a parking ticket?"

"Why do you think he's a cop?" Although Mia hated Rev, and had no desire to enter into any form of conversation with him, she had to ask the question. If Big Joe wasn't who Nico thought he was, or if he was some kind of undercover cop, she needed to know, not just for Nico's sake, but also for her own. Knowledge was power, and that kind of information could buy her some very important favors.

Rev shrugged. "Because he is."

Big Joe drew in a ragged breath and his eyes hardened, his entire body so tense Mia thought he might explode. She'd never seen this side of the usual affable and easy-going Big Joe. But then she was beginning to wonder if she knew him at all.

"Ma'am." Gritting his teeth, he turned and walked down the hall.

Mia glanced over at Rev, his eyes distant in contemplation. "I just need to tell him something about the course. I'll be right back." She pushed past him, but before she reached the door, he snatched her purse from her hand.

"A little insurance policy." He held the purse out of reach. "Not that I need it. I've got guys stationed at every exit. No way am I going back to Don Cordano empty-handed."

With a huff of annoyance, Mia ran down the hall after Big Joe.

"Wait." She caught up to him at the reception desk. "Why does he think you're cop?"

Big Joe turned, quickly blanking his face. "I didn't want my ex to know what I really did for a living." He shrugged. "She's not a discrete person, if you know what I mean. And I didn't want this life to touch my little girl.

So yeah, I made up a story about being a traffic cop. It was a good way to explain the odd hours and why I couldn't always be around. Then my ex took up with that loser, and I didn't see any point in changing the story. I figured, the less they knew about me, the better. Looks like that was a good choice 'cause I didn't know he was a made guy or part of your father's crew."

Mia's tension eased. "I was worried for a second there. I thought maybe you were an undercover cop and you were going to take Nico and his crew down."

"No, ma'am. Nico and the crew don't have anything to fear from me."

Maybe not. But she hadn't suffered through years of abuse without developing the ability to read the smallest nuances of expression as a matter of survival. Big Joe said all the right words, but the throb of the pulse in his neck, and the cold stare from a man she knew as a nice guy mobster told another story, one that she would unravel as soon as she got a chance.

"Nico, can you and your boys eat?" Nonna Maria greeted Nico, Luca, and Frankie at the door of her modest home. As always, her gray hair was tied back in a bun, and she wore her worn, red apron tightly wrapped around her doughy middle.

"Always. But I didn't ask to use your house for the meeting so you could feed us." Nico kissed his grandmother on both cheeks and followed her into the kitchen, every surface covered with pots, food, dishes, and utensils, the air thickly scented with tomato sauce and parmesan.

"It's just a little something." His nonna shook her head. "You're too thin. Look at your uncle Santo before he passed. He ate well."

Santo ate too well, and had to rely on Tony to handle

discipline and enforcement. By contrast, Nico stayed in shape and could hold his own in any fight. His father had taught him that a leader who could physically dominate was more effective than a leader who had to rely on others to enforce his will.

After the obligatory testing of the dishes his nonna had prepared, he headed into the oak-paneled dining room where the men of the family were waiting. Decorated with faded seventies wallpaper, and stuffed with ornate wooden furniture shipped from Italy by his now-deceased grandfather over fifty years ago, the dining room was the heart of his nonna's home and the place where all family business was conducted.

Nico had waited two weeks before requesting a meeting with Tony to discuss the family succession out of respect for Santo's death and Tony's injuries. His developing relationship with Mia was making him rethink his commitment to the Scozzari marriage, and he needed certainty in at least one area of his life.

Tony had not yet made a formal declaration of either support or challenge, and although Nico suspected Tony would not step down, he needed to hear it from his mouth so he could plan his political strategy going forward. If Tony decided to challenge him, Nico would need the Scozzari family support to push him aside. If he didn't, Nico would be in a position to avenge his father without needing the support of the New York bosses, although his developing relationship with Mia added an unforeseen complication he hadn't fully resolved.

After the usual five minutes of kisses and greetings, the men sat down to eat. Tony, Charlie Nails, and Paulie Onions, a powerful capo in what was once Santo's crew, sat on the left. Luca and Frankie sat on the right. As Nonna Maria's adopted son and head of her house, Nico sat at the head of the table, and enjoyed a small moment of pleasure when Tony scowled.

Nico worked his way through dish after dish including crostini, lasagna, stuffed peppers, veal piccata, risotto, and ricotta pie while Nonna Maria hovered over his shoulder telling him to take more. Talk was of neutral matters—politics, family, city infrastructure and stray bits of gossip—but tension was thick in the air. Business was never discussed until the food was eaten and with the amount of food on the table, the idle chatter lasted a long time.

"I'm glad to see you're recovering," Nico said to Tony as he finished his last bite of cannoli. Nico had a sweet tooth but only when it came to his nonna's desserts.

"A bullet in my shoulder and one near my heart and I'm still standing." Tony puffed out his chest. "That bastard is looking at a long, painful death when we catch him. Three bosses. Can you fucking imagine who would have the balls to do something like that?"

"The Albanians." Nico leaned back in his chair. "They're moving into our territory. I'm sending men out every day to deal with them, but as soon as we put out one fire, they've started another."

"My crew is having problems with them, too," Tony admitted. "But once we have the alliance with the Cordanos, we'll have the power to put them in their place."

Nico stilled. "What alliance?"

"I've been in talks with Don Cordano since he returned home from the hospital." Tony smirked. "We share a bond from our bullet wounds. He says his family will uphold the agreement made with my father to join the two families through marriage. I plan to marry Mia Cordano after an appropriate mourning period for my father." His dark eyes glittered in challenge. "I figure she must be wild in bed under those crazy clothes. But that will just make taming her more fun. She needs a firm hand, and I'm the one to give it to her."

Every muscle in Nico's body stiffened, and he fisted his hands so tight under the table his fingernails dug into his skin.

"Something wrong?" Tony leaned forward, toyed with the knife beside his plate. "Are you upset that you'll need a new cybersecurity consultant or that I'm taking your fuck toy away?" He jammed the knife into the table point first and it quivered upright. "Or maybe you're disappointed that I'll be the new Toscani family boss? You wouldn't dare challenge me when I have the Cordano family support."

Charlie Nails and Paulie laughed. Nico's heart thudded in his chest as a potent cocktail of possessive and protective anger surged through his veins. He wasn't surprised that Tony knew about him and Mia. Everyone in the Mafia spied on everyone else. But had Mia consented to this? Had she come looking for him in the casino on Friday night for a last fuck knowing that she was about to marry his cousin? Nico had no love for Tony, but he did believe in the sanctity of marriage—at least when it came to women. Although men were expected to have mistresses, women were required to be faithful to their husbands from the time of their engagement until death. Had she sought him out at the casino out of genuine interest, or was he supposed to be a last hurrah?

"What does Don Cordano get in return?" Nico struggled to keep his voice calm and even. "Is this all so he can sleep well at night?" The alliance would mean the end of Nico's vendetta against Don Cordano. He would be denied his revenge in the interests of peace between the families. Tony had to know that he was taking away the one thing Nico had lived for since his father died.

"That's between Don Cordano and me." Tony grinned. "But I will tell you it has enough value to him that he has agreed to put us in touch with his key drug suppliers. I've been trying to corner the market in heroin for the last few years, but Don Cordano has the missing piece—connections with the biggest Mexican cartel, and once I'm in good with them, we won't need the Cordanos anymore."

"You plan to take over the Cordano territory? You don't mean to end the war, do you?" Nico's stomach twisted in a knot. "You want more bloodshed. More lives lost. More wiseguys in jail. That's what will happen when you get involved with drugs. My father believed that. His father believed that. Look what happened in New York. Every family that got involved with drugs imploded. Drugs attract the feds. They attract the street gangs and cartels that don't live by a code of honor, and have no issue taking civilian lives. I have tried to bring respectability to the family. Your ambition will destroy it."

"My ambition will make this family great again." Tony pounded his fist on the table. "And the alliance with the Cordanos will ensure I have the power to make it happen."

Tony didn't know about the marriage Nico's father had arranged with the Scozzari family in Sicily. If Tony married Mia, Nico's Sicilian bride would be the only way he could save the family from certain destruction. With the Scozzari alliance, Nico would be able to avenge his father's death and the deaths of all Toscanis who had fallen to Cordano soldiers in the war.

Nico pulled his pen from his pocket and spun it over his thumb. He had to put personal feelings aside, just as his father had done. Although Papà loved Nico's mother, Papà loved his family more. He had married his wife for the powerful alliance that came with the union, and he wouldn't have risked the security of the family, even for the woman of his heart.

All his life, Nico had wanted to be like his father—a man of honor and respect, selfless and loyal, devoted to the family—a man whose blood had run through Nico's fingers when the damn Cordanos shot him through the back.

Duty or desire?

Ruin or revenge?

"Mia." Mama pulled open the door, dressed in mourning black out of respect for the fallen bosses. Many Mafia wives wore black all the time to honor the brothers, cousins, husbands, or fathers who had died in the endless wars for power. "So nice to see you again so soon."

"Seriously, Mama?" Mia pushed past her mother and into the hall as Rev headed down to her father's office. "Do you really think I'm here for a social visit? Rev was sent to drag me here against my will. He told me Papà hurt Kat. Where is she?"

"They're waiting for you in your father's office." Mia's mother swallowed hard and twisted her gold bracelet around her wrist. Mia remembered the night her father had given the bracelet to Mama, praising her as a good wife. Only later had she discovered that Mama had seen him with his mistress but had done her duty and kept her mouth shut.

Mia stared at the bracelet. "How bad is it?" Her mother never fidgeted or sweated or appeared anything less than fully interested in whatever a person had to say. She had perfected the look of a porcelain doll even though she was shattered inside.

"Your father is very stressed." Mama gave her a wan smile. "He's still recovering from his injuries, and poor

Dante mishandled something to do with the business—
you know he's not good with numbers—and we have lost
our *consigliere*."

"The Wolf is dead?"

"I'm afraid so. They found his body this morning."

Mia felt a chill through her veins. Had Nico really
killed him? She'd never seen him as angry as when the
Wolf threatened her, even the night he'd held his gun to
her father's head in the restaurant. But was she really surprised? Even she knew of Nico's brutal reputation in an
almost barbaric conflict. Her father had lived in fear of
Nico for years, never leaving the house without a slew of
bodyguards, and keeping the family locked behind a high
wire fence.

"And, of course, you were seen in public with Nico
Toscani, which is just one more thing to add to his stress."

Mia stared at her mother and looked down the hall.
Mama had just given her fair warning that the next half
hour was going to be bad. Very bad. Maybe worse than
anything she had experienced before. She had a sudden,
overwhelming urge to ask for help. But only person
who could help her was the last person who would walk
through that door.

Nico.

She had opened herself up to him, and he liked her for
who she was—with her dyed black hair and her ink, her
feminist anthems, her punk clothes, and the attitude that
brought out the worst of her father's anger. He was interested in her work, respected her business, and made her
feel both feminine and strong. She felt good when she was
with him. Like two halves made whole. Like the woman
she was meant to be. A woman powerful enough to take
on her father and win. Alone.

"Okay." She took a deep breath and walked down the
hall, with her mother following behind. "I can do this."

"Be strong, darling."

Mia looked back over her shoulder when she reached the door to her father's office. "I've always been strong, Mama. I just don't know if it will be enough."

A guard Mia didn't recognize let her into the office, and she staggered back from the blast of heat. Her father had closed the thick, velvet curtains, and lit a fire in the fireplace. Four guards stood at attention near the windows, and another two stood behind his chair. He wore his usual dark suit and blue tie, his broad, angry face was twisted in a scowl. There was nothing to suggest he'd suffered a life-threatening bullet wound just over two weeks ago, and she wondered just how badly Kat, seated in a chair in front of his desk, had been hurt.

"Papà. I'm glad to see you are home. Kat, are you—?"

"Don't lie to me, Mia." Her father cut her off with a bark of anger. "You've taken advantage of my absence to whore yourself out to the Toscanis yet again. And by the time I'm done with you, I'm certain you won't be glad of anything."

Well, at least he didn't drag things out. She stiffened her spine and met his glare with one of her own. "I'm doing work for his company."

"Enough." He thudded his fist on his desk. "The guard who went with the Wolf to your office after you refused Dante's requests for help told me what happened. Nico Toscani was with you. He attacked the Wolf, and now the Wolf is dead."

"It was work," she insisted.

God, oh god. Please don't let Nico have killed him.

"Is this what you call work?" Dante closed the distance between them, and held up his phone. She grimaced when she saw a picture of Nico and her kissing outside her apartment building in a way that could not even remotely be construed as businesslike.

"It started off as business," she said quietly.

Red-faced and shaking with rage, Dante rounded on her. "You betrayed the family with the enemy. He wants Papà dead."

"Technically, he wants you dead," she murmured, quietly enough that only he could hear, annoyed that Dante would dare to give her a lecture. Yes, she'd crossed the line, but it was her father's line, not his.

Dante lifted his hand as if to strike her, and anger flared through her. If he dared to touch her, she would unleash a hell like nothing he'd ever experienced before. She had suffered through years of abuse from her father; she was not going to accept it from him.

"No, Dante," Papà said. "She's too stupid to see that he's using her to get to me. Hitting her isn't going to teach her anything." He motioned to Rev and the guard nearest the window. "Put Kat over the table."

"What?" Mia made a move toward her sister, not realizing two guards had come up behind her. They grabbed her arms, holding her back.

"You are done with Nico Toscani," Papà growled. "You won't see him again. I promised the Toscanis a Cordano bride and I won't have the family honor smeared by going back on my word. You will marry Tony, as we agreed. And then Nico will pay for what he has done."

"I'm not marrying him."

Papà laughed. "Oh, I think you will. You're a strong girl, but you have a weak heart."

Mia watched in horror as Rev and the guard dragged Kat to the large meeting table at the side of her father's office. "Leave her alone."

"Dante." Papà's gaze didn't leave hers. "Remove your belt. Beat Kat until Mia changes her mind."

"No!" Mia struggled against the guards holding her, realizing too late why her father had so many in the room.

"She doesn't have anything to do with this. This is between you and me." She looked to her brother. "Don't do this, Dante. You can say no."

"No, I can't." With grim determination, he unbuckled his belt and tugged it off while the two guards pinned Kat face down on the table.

"Dante!" Kat's soft voice rose to sob. "Please. No."

"Hurt me." Mia thrashed in the guards' arms, kicked and twisted to get away. "Whatever you're planning. Do it to me. Hurt me." She struggled, tried to reach her knife, but the guards were too strong, their hold too firm.

"That's the problem." Papà leaned back in chair and sighed. "I can't hurt you. No one can hurt you. The more I beat you, the stronger you got. Even when I broke your fucking arm, you packed your bag with one hand and walked away. So I thought to be done with you. Leave you to the wolves. And what do you do? You bring dishonor to the family. You spread your legs for a man who issued a vendetta that has cost us many lives. A man who wants to kill your father. And when I tried to end the war, arranged a good marriage, you refused to obey. You refused to do your duty to your family. Until I threatened Kat. That's when I realized I was giving you the wrong kind of pain."

He nodded his head, and Dante whipped his belt across Kat's thighs, striking just below her floral cotton skirt; the crack of leather on flesh as sharp as the shot of a gun.

Kat's scream echoed through the room, speared through Mia's heart.

"No." She stared at Dante aghast. "Dante, don't do this."

Dante's face tightened, and he turned away, but not before she saw darkness in his eyes. If there had been any bit of goodness left in her brother, it was gone now, destroyed just as her father had destroyed so many.

Dante struck Kat again and again. Her screams filled the room, her calls for Mia, their mother, for mercy. Bile rose in Mia's throat, anger and frustration and hatred twisting her insides, but she couldn't say the words to bind her to Tony for life, because if Kat was now fair game, who would protect her if Mia was gone?

"Stop." Her father lifted a hand and Dante dropped his belt, chest heaving, a sheen of sweat over his brow. "I had hoped it wouldn't come to this but Mia obviously needs another form of persuasion. Rev, give Dante the poker from the fire."

"No." The word dropped from her lips in an agonized whisper and she watched in horror as Rev lifted the poker.

"You and Kat are nothing to me," her father said. "Nothing but property that I will use to gain an alliance that will increase the power and wealth of this family and end this ridiculous vendetta that has gone on too long. Once you are in Tony's hands, he will get rid of Nico for me, and you will not be distracted from your duties as his wife."

Horror turned to rage, and she bit one of the guards holding her. He released her with a yell, and she managed to use the distraction to twist away from the second guard. But he was fast. Before she could move toward Kat, he grabbed her hair. Heedless of the pain, Mia scratched and clawed and kicked in a bid to get free. Statues toppled. Vases shattered. If she needed to break her arm to save Kat she would. If she lost a handful of hair, so be it. And if they killed her, at least she wouldn't suffer the pain of watching Dante destroy the only good, beautiful thing left in their twisted, ugly family.

"*Basta!*" Her father yelled, spittle collecting at the corner of his mouth. "*Che cazzo fai*—what the fuck are you doing? Why won't you stop fighting me, and accept you will never win?"

"Because this will destroy Dante as much as it will destroy Kat and me." She felt another pair of arms around her, ropes twisting around her ankles and wrists. "I'm fighting to save us all."

Dante's lips twisted in a snarl. "You're too late to save me. I was destroyed the night I was made."

Rev blew on the poker and it glowed bright red.

"Mama!" Kat screamed, struggled on the desk. "Mia! Help!"

"Shut up, Kat. She won't come." Dante yanked up her pink T-shirt. "You should know that by now."

"I'll do it," Mia yelled. "Whatever you want. I'll become a Toscani. You'll have your fucking alliance. You have my word. Just let Kat go."

"Excellent." Her father motioned to Rev. "Give Dante the poker."

"What?" Mia sagged in the arms that held her. "No. I said I would do it."

"I want to make sure you honor your promise," her father said. "Because if you don't show up for the wedding, this will be the least of her suffering." He looked over at her brother. "Do it."

"What's happened to you, Dante?" Mia's voice was hoarse, thick with defeat as he raised the poker. "What have you become?"

"I'm the monster Papà always wanted me to be." He pressed the burning poker against Kat's lower back, and Mia sank to her knees, drowning in her sister's scream.

SIXTEEN

Mia smoothed down her bright pink Chanel dress as she walked up the stairs to the private dining room of Bella Via, a new ultra-modern Italian restaurant on West Flamingo Road. Her matching pink heels tapped softly on the hard wood. Her mother had given her the ridiculous outfit years ago when she still had hope Mia would accept her role as a Mafia princess, but Mia had never even taken it out of the dress bag until tonight. She wobbled slightly on the last stair and chipped one of her freshly painted nails as she grabbed for the railing.

Damn. She knew it wouldn't last. She was just not cut out for couture. Well, she'd better get used to it. If everything went according to plan, she would do what she had vowed never to do—marry into the mob. But she would do it on her own terms.

"Ms. Cordano." A waiter in a formal tux bowed when she crossed the landing. "Your party is waiting."

"*Grazie.*" Mia forced a smile, prayed it wouldn't crack the thick coating of foundation Jules had applied for her before she left her apartment. How did her mother wear this stuff every day? With the high-necked shirt, the fitted skirt and the tight jacket, she felt trapped. If any of her father's goons found her here, there would be no possible way she could run. She'd have to hang herself with the strand of fake pearls around her neck. She almost wanted to hang herself now. Although she was perfectly made up on the outside, inside she was screaming, desperate to be free.

"Okayokayokayokay." She took a breath, tried to calm her thudding heart. This wasn't such a big deal. People asked for help all the time. It didn't mean she was weak, just that she had finally come up against a problem that she couldn't solve on her own. And it wasn't like she was asking for help from a stranger. She knew Nico. Liked him. Sure, it was a little unconventional to ask someone to marry you after one date, but hadn't he said he liked that about her? And it wouldn't be forever. Just until Tony found someone else to marry and she found a way to keep Kat safe. They wouldn't even have to live together. They could get on with their separate lives and just make the occasional family appearance so their union looked legitimate. Although how Nico would stand in a room with her father and not want to pull the trigger, she didn't know.

"Are you okay, miss?" The waiter looked back over his shoulder, and Mia nodded.

"Yes, thank you. Lead the way."

She followed him down the hallway, paused as he opened the door. She had left a message for Nico through the casino the day after her father had so brutally branded Kat. When four days passed and she hadn't heard from him or seen Big Joe or any of his crew parked outside her office or apartment, she began to worry. Had she just been a conquest to him? Had he lost interest after he got what he wanted from her? By the time Vito called to let her know Nico would meet her on Friday, she had almost convinced herself her plan had no hope. But it didn't mean she wouldn't try.

Taking a deep breath, she walked into the private dining room. She had picked Bella Via for its mix of warm contemporary and cool minimalism. Industrial padded chairs surrounded long, rustic wooden tables. Stark white walls contrasted with a polished wooden floor, seamlessly blending traditional and modern. She hoped Nico got the message.

She drank him in as she entered the room. His suit tonight was midnight black, deep and lustrous, and his tie was a mix of burgundy and blue. He had cut his hair since she'd seen him last, and she missed the wayward strands that hinted at the wildness that he hid inside.

I'll always keep you safe.

God, she'd missed him. The urge to run into his arms and beg him to make the monsters go away was almost overwhelming.

He rose from the table to greet her, and she quickly crossed the room and held out her hand, hoping to set a businesslike tone for the meeting. "Thanks for coming. I was beginning to think you didn't want to see me again."

"Things have been busy." He stared at her outstretched hand and frowned. "What the fuck?"

What the fuck, indeed. Her father had promised the Toscanis a Cordano bride. And since Tony wasn't the only Toscani bachelor, she just had to make Nico an offer he couldn't refuse.

"It's nice to see you, too."

"This isn't you." He gestured to her clothes, and his nose wrinkled. "You don't dress like that." He gestured to the bun on the top of her head. "You don't wear your hair like that." He waved his hand as if in distress. "You don't look that. What the fuck is going on?" He seemed agitated tonight, angry, and not the Nico who had kissed her passionately in her doorway and whispered sweet things in her ear.

"I have a proposal for you." She took her seat, and dug her newly manicured nails into her palm. If this was going to work, she needed to maintain the facade of a cool, composed businesswoman who had come to discuss a merger and acquisition, and not let him see the shaken, desperate woman who had no other way to save her sister except by doing the one thing she had vowed never to do. "Please, Nico. Hear me out."

Saying his name seemed to break through his angry agitation, and he took his seat on the other side of the table. "What business proposal?"

Mia reached into her briefcase and pulled out a contract she had drawn up at her office earlier that morning. "A . . . merger. One that would serve both our interests, and that of our families as well." Hand shaking, she handed him the contract. Nico placed it on the table in front of him without even reading the first line.

"I don't like legalese. Talk me through it."

Her stomach clenched. It would have been so much easier to just sit and watch him read, but to explain it all to his face . . . See the rejection instead of hear it.

She folded her hands on the table. "I know you and your cousin have both declared as acting boss of the family. Obviously, there can't be two acting bosses. I'm offering you a way to come out on top. An alliance. A merger, of sorts."

"Did Don Cordano send you?"

She cringed inwardly at the sound of her father's name, the memory of Sunday night still fresh in her mind. "No. This is just between you and me."

"There is no you and me. I heard about you and Tony. Congratulations."

Ah. So that was why he hadn't returned her calls. Taking the plunge, she said, "I was hoping it could be you instead." Her cheeks heated under his scrutiny, and she had to force herself to meet his gaze.

He stared at her aghast. "You want to marry me?"

"It doesn't have to be forever," she blurted out. "Just until everything settles down. My father will be enraged, but once the deed is done, there's nothing he can do. We'll be married in the sight of God, and the New York bosses won't approve a hit on you because the alliance will end the war. Our marriage will also fulfill the agreement between the families—a Toscani marrying a Cordano. You will have the power to secure your position as boss of your family. After a year or so, when the alliance is running smoothly, we can get the marriage annulled and go our separate ways. I have no desire to trap you, Nico. I just . . ."

She couldn't bring herself to tell him about Saturday night. Lessons about keeping her mouth shut had been drilled into her head from her earliest years. Given Nico's protective nature, she had a feeling he wouldn't agree to an alliance with her father if he knew what he had done to Kat—or at all, if he still wanted to avenge his father. But more than that, she didn't want him to agree because he felt sorry for her—that would just lead to resentment later on. She wanted him to agree because of the benefit he would get—the best outcome in any business arrangement.

Silence.

"I can be everything you need a mob wife to be." She waved her hand over her sickly pink outfit, even as bile rose in her throat. "I learned from the best. I can dress the part, act the part, and be the part. I can be the perfect adornment, the perfect hostess, and the perfect wife. I can dye my hair back to its original color, put the punk stuff away." She gave a wan smile. "I can learn how to cook and keep the house tidy. I'll even listen to Sinatra . . ."

She trailed off when he didn't respond. "Nico?"

A desperate ache formed in Mia's chest as he stared at her, his face an expressionless mask. She'd considered all her options, and this was the best she could come up with. If he refused, she'd have to get Kat and go on the run. Although she was tech savvy, she knew there was nowhere to hide if the Mafia really wanted to find them. Kat was young. She didn't deserve a life of fear, a life where she was constantly looking over her shoulder.

"I'm sorry, *bella*," he said, finally. "But I have to decline."

"Why?" She didn't want to know, but she did.

"I'm engaged."

"Ah." Her breath left her in a rush. Of all the scenarios she had imagined, of all the responses she had prepared for, she hadn't even considered that he might be with someone else. But why wouldn't he be? He was rich, powerful, devastatingly handsome, charming, protective and utterly compelling. She had been a fling for him, but nothing more. Her world fell out from under her and for a moment she couldn't breathe.

"I'm sorry. I didn't even consider . . . I thought when you . . . when we . . . that was wrong of me." She pushed her chair away, and her napkin fell to the floor. "I feel so stupid. I mean, it's not like we were in love or anything, or I thought it would be real, but I was desperate . . . my sister . . . I needed help, and . . . of course, you can't—"

"Mia." A pained expression crossed his face, the first hint he felt anything for her at all.

"No. It's okay. You don't have to say anything else. I knew it was a bad idea anyway. I don't want to be married into the mob. My whole life has been about escaping my Mafia roots. I'm sure I would have made your life a living hell in the short time we were together, even if it wasn't real. I would actually be a terrible mob wife. I can't cook. I'm awkward in social situations. I always use the wrong fork at the table. I'm not easy to live with. I'm very messy, listen to loud music, dress weird, eat a lot of unhealthy food, and I never screw the top on the toothpaste. I'm glad you found someone who does want the life, though. I'm sure she's perfectly lovely." Her bag fell off the end of the chair as she slid off her seat. Hand shaking, she bent to pick it up and rose too quickly, snagging her stocking on the rough metal piping of the chair.

Her face flamed, and her pulse beat so hard all she could hear was the frantic pounding of her heart.

"Mia. Wait." Nico stood, his chair making a high-pitched shriek as it scraped over the floor.

Suddenly the enormity of the situation hit her in a rush, and she began to unravel. For five days she had focused on this meeting, hope giving her the courage to carry on. But now there was nothing to hold her up, no one to catch her as she fell. She stepped back to get away, stumbling on the uncomfortable, unfamiliar heels. She grabbed the chair for balance and tipped it backward to the floor.

No. She was not going to humiliate herself further by falling on her face. She steadied herself, took a deep breath and then turned and walked out the door as the run in her nylons zipped up the back of her thigh.

Nico opened the throttle on his Ducati Superbike and turned off the road toward the Valley of Fire State Park. The winding roads through colorful cliffs, and past Lake Mead, were the best part of the journey. Usually he rode to relax and take his mind off all the responsibilities of being a capo, the constant need to assert his power, the delicate balancing act between illegitimate and legitimate businesses, the risk of violence, and the even greater risk of being caught. But today, he saw nothing except the asphalt rushing up to greet him, felt nothing but the cold mountain air on his face, and heard nothing except the rev of his engine and the pounding of his pulse in his ears.

He wanted to get away, and yet the road would take him back. Back to the promise he whispered as his father died. Back to the legacy his father had left him and the responsibility of caring for a family that was now a mix of crime and blood.

From the Cadillac he drove, to the Vacheron Constantin watch he wore, and from his Brioni suits, to his Italian leather shoes, he was everything his father wanted him to be. And yet there were chinks in his armor. Small defiances that only his mother would understand: the ink on his body, the leather jackets, boots and jeans he preferred to wear, the bike he rode weekly into the desert in search of something he hadn't realized was missing until he held Mia in his arms.

He wanted her.

He wanted her with a ferocity that took his breath away.

He wanted her with every drop of his bastard blood.

He wanted her on his bike and in his bed. He wanted her by his side and beneath his body.

What would it be like to have a woman with her strength by his side? A woman who defied convention, forged her own path, and knew her own mind. A woman who at once challenged and infuriated him, seduced and resisted him. A woman who was prepared to sacrifice herself for her family, to give herself to him for the rest of her life.

And he'd said no.

Torn between doing his duty to his family and following his heart's desire, bastard in all ways, he'd said no.

Nothing in his life had cut him as bad as watching her

crumble. There was nothing in his life he regretted more than causing her pain.

What the fuck was he supposed to do?

He had rehashed the terrible meeting over and over in his mind, and every time bile rose in his throat, and guilt wracked his soul. He remembered everything in painfully excruciating detail—the way her hand shook when she gave him the contract, the chipped, painted nails, the mask that hid her beautiful skin, her clear discomfort in the hideous pink outfit, the bun that hid her glorious hair, the way she wobbled on her heels, the hope that had shattered in her face.

His heart ached at the thought of his brave, strong Mia; so desperate she would dress in the clothes she hated and offer herself willingly into a life she despised, so afraid she would ask for help.

No.

He had destroyed her with just one word. He had destroyed himself.

Nico leaned into the curves as the road wound back and forth through the park. Faster, faster, so fast adrenaline pumped through his body, a heady mixture of excitement and fear. One slip, and it would all be over. One slip, and he would die his father's son but not his own man.

He slowed the bike. Pulled up at a lookout. Stared over the mountain pass. Luca pulled up behind him, reminding him a boss was never truly alone.

"Everything okay, boss?" Luca dismounted, patrolled the gravel as if danger was afoot.

"Yeah. Just taking a minute. Then we'll head back to the city." Luca and Frankie were the only soldiers in his crew who knew how to ride, so they took turns on guard duty when Nico went out on his bike. Big Joe would be coming up behind them in his vehicle, just in case they had problems with their bikes.

"I always come up here when I have girl trouble," Luca said.

"I've never seen you with just one girl." Luca had become the manwhore of the club after his wife died, going through women so fast, Nico couldn't keep track.

"That's why I come here. Every time I start thinking about getting serious with some chick, I come here and remind myself why I'm not doing it all again. If what we had was love, it isn't worth the fucking pain."

Nico dismounted his bike and stared out over the valley. He had learned that lesson when he watched his mother cry every Saturday after his father went back to his wife. And he'd learned it again when she'd decided to run away with Nico in search of love, and died in the attempt. As always, his father had it right. A political marriage would keep his heart safe and his mind focused on what he needed to do to ensure the success and survival of the family.

If Mia married Tony, she would become part of the family. Nico would see her every Sunday at Nonna Maria's family gatherings. He would see her as he saw her today, everything that he loved about her hidden away beneath the veneer of a respectable mob wife, everything he wanted, crushed beneath the weight of tradition, her wings clipped when she had only just gotten free. How could he bear to see her fire gone? What would he do if he saw even the hint of a bruise on her beautiful face?

Tony wouldn't have exclusive rights to "crazy" after that.

"You didn't love Gina?" Luca had married Gina in a shotgun wedding after getting her pregnant. He'd never expressed any discontent about the situation, and they'd seemed happy together, especially after Matteo was born, but she was not the kind of woman he would have ever picked for Luca. Too brash. Too loud. Too shallow.

Too needy. Luca had taken to carrying two phones, one just to field her constant calls, and the other for business.

"Who the fuck knows?" Luca fiddled with the zipper on his jacket, and Nico realized they'd never talked about Gina's death before. He had never witnessed the utter destruction of a man, until he went with Luca to identify her body. He'd assumed love had crushed Luca's soul, but now he wondered if something was going on.

Nico's hands tightened around the railing. His entire life had been about the family—duty, honor, and revenge—and the best thing for the family was to stand aside while Tony married Mia. The marriage would provide a short-term benefit in the form of a truce between the families, and a long-term benefit in the form of increased family security and power after he married the girl from Sicily, and dealt with Don Cordano and Tony in a permanent way. It made perfect business sense. It was what his father would have done. But it didn't align with the yearning in his heart.

"I don't want to speak bad about her," Luca said into the silence. "I cared about her enough to marry her when I could have just walked away. And she gave me Matteo. When he was born, I thought there might actually be a heaven and maybe I did something right in my sorry life because God sent me an angel of my very own."

"Yeah, I know that feeling." Big Joe joined them at the railing. "First time I realized I had a heart was when I held my kid in my arms. One day maybe I'll find a woman who makes me feel like that, and my fucking heart will start beating again."

Nico's heart had started beating the moment he laid eyes on Mia, and it had stopped when he gave her up to Tony.

"Your talents are wasted in the mob." Nico mounted

his bike. "You two should be writing fucking greeting cards."

Nico wanted vengeance, but he wanted Mia more. Vengeance had left him empty inside, blind to what was going on around him, deaf to the rumblings on the street as Tony secretly gathered more and more power in anticipation of the day Santo was whacked. If he had been on the ball, he wouldn't be on his back foot in the fight for control of the family. If he had thought and planned ahead, he would have been able to secure his power the day Santo died. Mia offered him more than just an opportunity to save his family. He could save her. He could save himself. He could make his heart beat again, and he could give it away.

"Where are we going next, boss?" Luca mounted his bike.

"Back to the city. I'm getting married tonight."

SEVENTEEN

Bang. Bang. Bang.

"Mia! It's Nico. Open the door."

Bang. Bang. Bang. He thudded again on the motel room door. Big Joe had confirmed Mia was inside with her sister. They had no time to waste.

He heard the bolt slide and chains rattle. The door opened and he pushed his way through with Luca and Frankie behind him. "Let's go. If I could find you, your father won't be far behind." He spun around, startled when he saw her gun. If he'd expected a broken, tearful, terrified woman, he was sorely mistaken. He had come to rescue a kitten and found a tiger instead.

"Put that away." He waved a dismissive hand. "We have to leave right now."

"Jules called and told me you were coming. Get out." She backed up, pushing a girl behind her. Taller than Mia, and slim, she shared Mia's long dark hair and dark eyes, but her face was more oval than heart-shaped, and she wore light, floaty clothes covered in flowers, a decided contrast to Mia's black outfit—all leather, chains, and laces.

"We don't have time for this," he said impatiently. "I'm here to help." Nico scraped a hand through his hair. It had taken all day to track them down using his network of contacts and calling in favors.

"Come." He gestured again to the door, and Mia shook her head.

"Thanks for the effort, but I'm not going with you. I'm done with the mob. This is a family matter, and I'll deal with it my own way."

Damn stubborn woman. "You asked for my help," he gritted out. "I'm giving it to you."

"I asked, and you refused. I realize now I didn't need your help. We'll be fine on our own. I hacked my father's phone. I'll be able to track them and keep us safe."

Cristo mio. "I came to marry you, Mia. You can't get safer than that." Once he had the marriage certificate, he would use the threat of the alliance to oust Tony. He would take over as boss of the family, get close to Don Cordano and whack the fucking bastard. He figured Mia would no longer have any objections. Although, he didn't know what Don Cordano had done to her sister, it was bad enough that she had thought to offer herself up to him as a mob wife to save her, and when he refused, to take her sister and go on the run.

After Don Cordano was out of the way, Nico would make Dante the notional head of the Cordano side of the family, cement the alliance, and Mia and her sister would be protected. Everyone would live happily ever after. Aside from the Scozzari family agreement, which he had yet to address, and the small matter of a few grumblings from New York, it was the perfect plan.

"Married?" Her beautiful face twisted in a scowl. "I'm running away because I don't want to be married to the mob. Maybe you didn't pick that up when you mentioned you were engaged."

Nico frowned. Obviously the engagement was no longer an issue since he was here offering to marry her. He was a good-looking man. Fit. Wealthy. Powerful. Very skilled in bed. He hadn't expected her to find the idea quite so distasteful, especially since she had come up with it in the first place. "It's the only way. We're not strangers, *bella*. You're not an unattractive woman so it's no hardship for me. And we get on fine."

"I'm not unattractive? We get on fine?" She threw the words back at him, her voice rising in pitch. Sensing a heaping dose of disrespect coming his way, Nico ushered everyone out of the room with instructions to take Kat to his Escalade and guard her until he and Mia were ready to go.

"Those aren't reasons to get married," Mia snapped, after the door closed. "And what about the part where you told me you were engaged? All this time you've been lying to me, leading me on."

Dammit. How could he get through to her? "Your alternative is getting married to a man who means to break you, who will take everything you own, and destroy everything you are, a man who plans to start a war with all the families in the city. Dozens of lives will be lost."

"Or I could run away with Kat." She put her hands on her hips, clearly not appreciating the gravity of the situation. "And then I can hack into all his accounts, and destroy him financially. He'll be too busy worrying about his money to come after us."

Nico closed the distance between them. "*Mi bella*," he said softly. "We still deal in cash for that very reason. Your father is desperate for an alliance, and you and your sister are his best way of securing one. He will not let you go easily. You will always be looking over your shoulder. But I can keep you safe." He reached for her, and Mia slapped his hand away.

"I don't trust you anymore, Nico. I'd rather take my chances on the run than forever with you."

"If a divorce is what you want, and the time is right, I will be willing to break with tradition and petition the New York bosses to let you go." It was an easy promise to make because he knew they would never say yes, but he could see in her eyes that it was a deal breaker, and if he'd learned anything in this life, it was how to close a deal.

"*Let* me go?" Her eyes flashed, and despite her bitterness, it just made him want her even more.

"It is the man's prerogative."

She bristled at his words. "And that right there is the problem."

"Would it help if I told you I have never met or spoken to the woman I am engaged to? That my father arranged the marriage when I was six years old? I have been in touch with the family only sporadically over the years. But she means nothing to me save for an alliance that I would need only if you marry Tony."

"You want to use me," she said bitterly.

"No, *bella*. Marriage is not something I have seen bring any joy to people, and it is not something I ever wanted. Even the old-school political marriages never sat well with me. I regret that my reaction to your proposal caused you pain." He reached for her, stroked her cheek. This time he wasn't denied, and she shuddered beneath his touch.

"I felt humiliated."

"*Mia, tesoro . . . non era mia intenzione ferirti*—I never wanted to hurt you."

"You grovel well in Italian," she said, her voice softening. "It seems it's not just the language of love."

Taking a chance, Nico drew closer, brushed a kiss over

her forehead. "If I have to marry, I want a willing partner. I can protect you with this marriage. I can protect your sister. I can end a war. We may not have love between us, but we have respect and a commitment beyond ourselves."

Nico felt a curious stab in his chest. He cared for Mia. So much that the thought of losing her had almost been unbearable. But he didn't want to call it love. He'd lived through the devastation of his mother's tears, and watched men crumble. Love was not an experience he wished to have.

"If we do this," she bit out, "and I'm not saying yes, you won't be telling me what to do. I'll continue working, and you won't interfere with my business."

"Of course, you may continue to work." He smiled, tasting success.

"What would you expect of me?"

His lips quivered at the corners. "What you offered. You would have to play the role of a proper Mafia wife. You would need to dress and act the part in public."

Mia snorted. "Submissive."

"Supportive," he countered, stroking her cheek. "But when we are alone together, I want this." His finger skimmed the crescents of her breasts, just visible about the V of her T-shirt. "I want you the way you are, with your kick-ass boots, your torn stockings, leather and lace, and these outfits that drive me fucking crazy with the need to tear them off you. I want your angry feminist punk music, and your silver chains, and the ink that tells me you are not a conventional woman." His hands found her hips, and he drew her toward him. "I want your strength, your sweetness, and all your sass."

She twisted her lips to the side, considering. "I'm not wearing a wedding dress."

"If we want everyone to believe it is real, it needs to look real. We can rent something just for the ceremony. Ten minutes at most. I have an associate who runs a store on the Strip. Anything else?" He cupped her face in his hands, stroking his thumbs over her soft cheeks.

"No more sex. It will complicate things."

That was unexpected. And totally unacceptable. "I can't agree to that," he said firmly. "If we get married, even if it isn't real, I want everything." He smoothed one hand over her curves. Even the simple negotiation with her was making him hard; there was no way he could share a bed and keep his hands off a woman who aroused him the minute she walked into a room. "I want a marriage in every sense of the word. You will live with me, sleep in my bed, and give yourself to me. You will be mine. Completely. In every sense of the word."

"Until it ends," she added. "Because when the war is over and you're the boss, and we've found a way to keep Kat safe, we won't need each other anymore. And you did say you would agree to a divorce."

"Until it ends." He agreed with great reluctance, not just because part of him didn't want it to end, but also because he knew it wouldn't end. She didn't seem to understand that, in a way, this was a sacrifice for him, too. He had never wanted a marriage, and the one he had envisioned was one where his heart would never be at risk.

Mia fiddled with the zipper on his leather jacket. He had forgone his suit and vehicle for the speed and freedom of his bike in his pursuit. "The sex part is going to make it harder when it's over. Especially if I have to see you dressed like this."

"Are you afraid you might fall for me?" He leaned in and nuzzled her neck, breathing in the light, floral scent of her perfume. His Mia was a study in contrasts. With a soft moan, she tilted her head to the side, giving him better access, and he feathered kisses down her neck.

"I'm afraid you won't let me go," she whispered.

She was right to be afraid. Nico had never considered marrying any woman other than Rosa Scozzari, but if had to pick a woman it would be Mia. She intrigued and challenged him, enticed and excited him. She was brave, intelligent, and confident; the most sensual woman he had ever met.

He pulled her into his arms, his hand coursing over her body, in and out of her delectable curves. "You are a hard woman to resist. You are courageous, selfless, beautiful, and bold. I want to own every inch of you. I want my hands in your hair, my lips on your breasts, and my cock buried inside you. I want to take you in every way a woman can be taken. I want you to come with my name on your lips." He slid one hand under her T-shirt, cupped and squeezed her breast.

"Well, that's better than 'We get on fine.' "

He turned his attention to her other breast, rubbing his thumb over her nipple until it peaked beneath her bra. *Christ.* He ached for her. If not for the fact her father was on the hunt, and his men were waiting outside with Kat, he would take her right now.

Her nails dug into his scalp, and the pleasure pain almost sent him over the edge. "Okay. Sex can be part of the deal. It helps that I find you somewhat attractive."

"Somewhat?" He gently bit her nipple, and she gasped.

"Your ego is already so big I have to step around it. I'm not about to feed it anymore."

"There is no bigger ego boost than having a beautiful woman agree to a fake marriage proposal so she doesn't have to marry a psychopath," he said, amused. "Are we done with the conditions?" He eased his thigh between her parted legs. He wanted her so badly he could barely breathe, his body thrumming with a need to claim her so everyone knew she was under his protection.

"Did you kill the Wolf?"

Whoa. He hadn't seen that one coming in from left field, and it served to take his arousal down a notch. "Business matters are not shared with wives," he chided gently. "You agreed to follow the rules."

"I'm not your wife yet."

"But you will be, and the rules now apply. Ask me any question, *bella*. Make any demand. But not that."

She gritted her teeth, pressed her lips together, and he almost regretted what they were about to do. Mia would have to struggle hard to fit into the mold of a Mafia wife, and he didn't want to see her wings clipped in any way.

"I'll need a bottle of vodka before the ceremony and one glass."

Nico kissed her softly; relieved she had backed down on her question about the Wolf. "Just what I always wanted. A drunk bride."

She laughed, the tension finally leaving her face. "When do you want to do it?"

"It's Vegas. The question isn't when can we get married, but how many Elvises do you want at your wedding?"

Only one Elvis attended the wedding.

One Elvis. Two witnesses (Kat and Big Joe). Two best men (Luca and Frankie). Three bodyguards, including Louis, who she now knew was a member of Frankie's crew and went by the nickname Mikey Muscles. And a bridesmaid who wouldn't stop talking.

"I still can't believe this." Jules shook her head as the officiant, an associate of the Toscani crime family, directed Nico where to stand in the tacky Vegas chapel. "One minute I'm chilling with some Netflix and boom, two hours later I'm standing in a chapel with Elvis and bunch of mobsters. Nico sure doesn't waste any time." She leaned over and whispered in Mia's ear. "You don't have to do this. I can get you out of town. I have friends who will take you in. You never wanted to marry into the mob. Don't get caught up in it now."

Fraught with nerves, Mia didn't even try to respond. Jules hadn't stopped talking since they arrived at the small wedding chapel that was owned by a "friend" of Nico's. It was everything she had never imagined her wedding would be. Giant vases filled with plastic plants, fake Grecian columns, an explosion of silk flowers and a raised, red sparkly stage. Pictures of Vegas adorned the cream-colored walls, along with tacky Vegas mementos and a portrait of Elvis in a cheap wooden frame. Behind the stage, a giant pink heart, trimmed with flashing red lights gave the room a perpetual strip-bar glow. With every breath, she inhaled the scents of incense, sweat, and cheap perfume. It was as fake as the marriage was going to be.

Mia smoothed down the hideous polyester dress trimmed in sequins and plastic beads, but there was little she could do to subdue the giant skirt, much less the padded shoulders and huge leg of mutton sleeves. Nico had suggested going for the most traditional dress so no one would have any doubts about the authenticity of the wedding. All fine and good for the man who got to wear a sleek, black tux. Not so good when his idea of traditional meant the victim of an 80s throwback meringue explosion. If Pussy Riot could see her now . . .

"Oh. My. God." Jules filled the awkward silence, when

the officiant indicated he was ready to begin. "I'm going to cry."

Kat dabbed her cheeks with a tissue, and Big Joe put a comforting hand on her shoulder. Nico had ordered Big Joe to take Kat to his apartment and guard her after the wedding, but Big Joe had gone one step further and taken Kat under his wing. He had looked after her while Mia and Nico got the marriage license and rental clothes, and posed for the pictures that Mia hoped would never see the light of day. Mia was confidant Kat would be safe with him. He had shown his protective side when he faced off with Rev at the community center, but the whole cop thing was still a worried niggle in her mind. Most mobsters lied to their families about what they did, but Big Joe was such a straight-up guy, so black and white, that it wasn't hard to imagine he really was a cop.

Still, an unfounded accusation could have serious repercussions. Maybe after the wedding was over and the dust had settled, she would take him aside and get some answers. She liked Big Joe, and if he was an undercover cop, that would give him enough of a warning to get out before she went to Nico with her suspicions. He knew, probably better than her, how Nico dealt with traitors, and if he chose to stay after that, there was nothing else Mia could do.

Even after a couple of shared shots of vodka with Jules, Mia's pulse pounded when the officiant, a justice of the peace dressed in an Elvis costume, complete with wig and a rhinestone guitar slung across his body, flashed a gold incisor and opened his book.

"Dearly beloved, we are gathered together here in the sight of God to join Nico Giuseppe Salvatore Toscani and Mia Alessandra Cordano in Holy Matrimony; which is an honorable estate, instituted by God, signifying unto us the union that is between—"

"*Cristo.*" Nico cursed under his breath.

"That's correct." Elvis raised a warning eyebrow, and continued. "Christ and His Church; and therefore not entered into unadvisedly, but reverently, discreetly, soberly and in the fear of God—"

"Is there a faster ceremony?" Nico said, abruptly. "Something where we can get married without the fear of God?"

A disgruntled Elvis cleared his throat. "We do have the ten minute quickie elopement ceremony with no religious references, although you did pay for the full religious version."

"Fast is good." He looked to Mia for confirmation, and she nodded. Since it wasn't meant to be forever, it was probably best not to have a religious ceremony. Nico might not fear God, but she'd been raised Catholic and she didn't want to take any chances.

Elvis flipped through his book and smoothed out a page. "Ladies and gentlemen, today we have gathered together to celebrate the marriage of Nico Toscani and Mia Cordano. Marriage is a sacred promise between two people who love, trust and honor each other, and who wish to spend the rest of their lives together. Two souls share—"

Nico coughed, cutting off the officiant's words. With a slight frown, the officiant put down his book, picked up his guitar and strummed through a few bars of "It's Now or Never." Nico gave a soft grunt of displeasure, and Mia's anxiety faded away beneath the amusement of watching Nico struggle with his self-control. If he couldn't even make it through a simple civil ceremony, how would he ever make it through a proper Catholic ceremony that included an hour-long mass? She felt a pang of sadness when she thought about the real marriage that lay in his future with the woman who would one day be his wife.

"Marriage is more than a contract," the officiant continued after putting down his guitar. "It is a commitment to take that joy deep, deeper than happiness, deep into the discovery of who you most truly are, deep into the essence of your being, deep into the soul—"

Another cough from Nico. "We get the deepness. Move on. This is supposed to be the shortened version."

With a raised, fake, bushy eyebrow of disapproval, the officiant read. "It is not to be entered into lightly, but thoughtfully, responsibly, and reverently. Marriage is forever. And it joins families as well as hearts."

Mia's stomach knotted at the serious words, reminding her that this marriage was a sham. It not meant to be forever, or even a joining of hearts. Nico had made that perfectly clear back in the hotel.

"Do you have the ring?"

Nico pulled a small red velvet bag from his pocket and took out an enormous diamond ring.

Elvis whistled low, losing the thin veneer of civility to show his Mafia roots. "Now that's some rock. You sure you want the shortened version? For an extra five hundred, I can give you a private show of the King's best works." He picked up his guitar again and strummed "Wear My Ring Around Your Neck."

Mia stared at the gaudy stone set up high on a thin gold band. "It's . . . sparkly. And huge. Very huge. Are you sure no one is going to chop off my arm to get it? I mean . . . it's not an ordinary diamond."

Guilt flickered across Nico's face. "No, it isn't. And if anyone tries to touch you, his life won't be worth living."

"No threats during the ceremony, please." Elvis segued into "Big Boss Man," as if he issued that kind of warning every day. But then he was a mob associate, so maybe he did.

Nico scowled. "Get on with it."

"The marriage ring seals the vows of marriage and represents a promise for eternal and everlasting love." He handed Nico a card. "Read this and put the ring on her finger."

Nico glanced at the card and then met Mia's gaze. "I will love, comfort, honor and protect you; forsaking all others to be faithful to you until death do us part."

Emotion welled up in Mia's throat as he pushed the massive ring on her finger. Although she had never given much thought to marriage, hearing the beautiful words, knowing they weren't real, made her ache inside with longing.

Elvis sang a few bars of "Are You Lonesome Tonight," and Mia choked back a sob.

"You okay?" he asked, pausing mid bar.

"Yep. Fine. That was just so beautiful." She stiffened her spine, reminded herself of why she was doing this and how much better it was that she was marrying Nico and not crazy Tony Crackers.

After Mia repeated the pledge, and they exchanged a few generic vows, Elvis beamed. "Until today, you were two separate individuals. Now you will be one. By the power enthroned in me, by the state of Nevada, I now pronounce you husband and wife. You may kiss your bride."

Mia leaned in, expecting a chaste peck on the cheek, a pretend kiss for a pretend marriage. But there was nothing pretend about Nico's kiss. He wrapped his arms around her, sealed his mouth over hers and kissed her hard and deep. Mia melted against him as his tongue swept through her mouth, leaving no inch untouched. A claiming. In every sense of the word.

"Get a fucking room," Luca yelled.

Nico broke off the kiss with a scowl. "A little respect. You're talking to the new Mrs. Nico Toscani."

Mrs. Toscani? She hadn't agreed to change her name. Mia forced a smile. Her new life had just begun.

EIGHTEEN

"Go big or go home. That seems to be your motto." Mia walked around Nico's penthouse at the Casino Italia. He had brought her here after a few celebratory drinks, expecting they would be in bed together already. But she'd been wandering around for the last five minutes with no indication that she intended to sit down, much less get busy consummating the marriage with him.

He to admit, the penthouse was impressive. Soaring floor-to-ceiling windows gave him a 280-degree view of the city, while inside, thick Berber carpets and rich mahogany floors spread across three thousand square feet of space. He had already shown her the entertainment room, multiple seating areas, powder room, large master bedroom, dining room, and three massive bathrooms. Nico had given the designer a brief for understated elegance in neutral colors and let her run with it.

"I was kinda hoping to see your place," Mia said. "I don't know much about you. People usually know something about the man they marry before they tie the knot, other than that he's a mobster and runs a casino."

Nico shrugged off his leather jacket and hung it carefully in the closet. They had returned the rented wedding clothes on the way home, and he swore he'd never wear an ill-fitting tux again. "This is it." He'd never thought about his living environment before. It was a place to sleep and occasionally entertain.

"Seriously, you live in the hotel?"

"My office is downstairs. I'm available to handle any emergencies. It's efficient." He walked over to the polished granite wet bar in the corner and raised a quizzical eyebrow. She was unusually cagey, aloof, despite the vodka shots she drank with Jules before and after the ceremony. He understood her sense of disquiet, could almost hear the thoughts in her head because they were the same thoughts he was having.

What the hell had they done?

After this night, when they went public with their union, the fallout might be worse than either of them had anticipated. But no matter how bad it got, it couldn't be undone.

Yes, they had an attraction, an incredible chemistry that had sparked the night they first met. But for all that they had spent some time together, they were still strangers. Two people who had been walking different paths, now on the same road together. Nico had never expected to love his wife. Marriage was a contractual union, a business arrangement, a means of showing power and producing heirs. Love and intimacy were for mistresses. And yet, when he was with Mia, he imagined having both.

Mia shook her head. "I've had enough, thanks." She trailed her fingers over the wooden credenza. "Where is you in this suite? Magazines, pizza boxes, pictures, sports gear—the kind of stuff that tells a wife what kind of man she's just married, what he does on his time off, how he relaxes . . ."

"I'm here just to sleep," Nico said. "My days are taken up with work. There is no time for hobbies or relaxing."

"Liar," she teased, giving him a flash of the Mia he knew. "That motorcycle we rode on to get here is definitely for chilling out."

"Not when you're screaming at me to go faster. I didn't realize I had married a speed demon."

She grinned and Nico's tension eased the tiniest bit. Nothing in Nico's life had ever truly belonged to him. Even the casino had been built with Mafia money. But now Mia was his wife. His to have, his to hold, and his to protect. Although she insisted it was just a marriage of convenience, the words he spoke, the piece of paper he signed that evidenced their union, meant something to Nico—something he hadn't been prepared for when he agreed to the plan.

He watched her open doors and cabinets, peer behind curtains, and inspect the computer station and the electronics systems. She was stalling, trying to put some distance between them. So he gave her some space. He turned on one of the televisions, sat on the cold, beige leather couch, and stared at the football game on the screen as she walked around some more.

"What does this do?" She pushed a button and the window slid to the side, giving her access to a vast outdoor patio with a rooftop swimming pool, small garden, and hundreds of twinkling lights that Nico had never once walked through.

"Terrace." He came up behind her, looked out at the starry night.

"If I lived in this place, I would be out here every night," she said, stepping outside, her voice without the strain he'd heard since she said "I do." "It's so beautiful, peaceful."

"You do live here." He rested his hands on her shoulders. "This is your home now."

"I can't live in a hotel." She stiffened in his arms. "It's too . . . I mean . . . It's nice. Really nice. But it's kind of . . . bland. No character. And it's too clean and tidy. I'm not a tidy person. You saw my place. This isn't me."

"You can go to your place to visit whenever you wish. But you are my wife now, Mia. You live with me."

She shuddered and pulled away. "I forgot about that part for a minute there."

Nico felt a tightening in his gut and followed her back into the suite. He headed over to the bar, poured a shot of Johnnie Walker, and threw it back. Why the hell did he care whether she liked the place or not? It wasn't like they were going to spend a lot of time here. They were both busy people with businesses to run.

He joined Mia on the couch and looked out over the city spread out below them. His father thought of Vegas as a punishment, but Nico had always loved the city. It was all about glitz and glamour, hope and dreams, energy and opportunity, none of which were reflected in his presidential suite.

"If you were decorating, what would you do different?" Mia pulled a cushion on her lap and hugged it tight. "How would you make it yours?"

"Never thought about it."

"Oh."

He looked over, saw her face fall, realized his own walls had come up and she was trying to get them down. *Fuck*. He hadn't expected it to be as bad as this. It was like there was a bridge between them that they were both afraid to cross.

"Come here." He held out his hand, and she scooted sideways along the couch until she was only one cushion away. Nico leaned over, wrapped an arm around her shoulders, and pulled her close. Almost instantly, he felt something click, and she softened against him with a sigh.

"Try."

Nico twisted his lips, tried to remember a place he'd stayed or a picture he'd seen or something that had resonated with him when he was fitting out the hotel. "Il Tavolino."

She laughed, leaned against his shoulder. He felt an overwhelming need to carry her to the bedroom, strip off their clothes, and lie with her skin to skin, find the connection that had brought them together in the first place. But he knew better than to push. Sex was the white elephant in the room between them, the consummation of the marriage. If she needed to go slow, he would rein himself in. Control. He exercised it every minute of every day. It was just much harder with Mia, who made him want to let go and indulge the streak of wild that coursed through his veins.

"You want to live in a restaurant?"

"That restaurant. It's Old Vegas, Hollywood, and the golden days of the Mafia all wrapped up into one."

She rested her hand on his chest, right above his heart. "Let's say you have an Il Tavolino–style office where you can pretend you're an old-school gangsta. What about the rest of the home? What is modern Nico all about? Start with a color. How about black?" She sounded so hopeful he almost didn't want to answer.

"Deep purple." He waved his hand over the room. "Polished granite floors, dark walls, black furniture, purple furnishings, exposed pipes in the ceiling painted black, lots of small lights that would look like stars."

"Industrial," she said. "Modern."

"Fireplace." He started to get into it as a room took shape in his mind. "Thick purple rug in front of it."

"Romantic." She slid down until she lay with her head in his lap. Nico stroked her hair, contemplating the fictitious room of his dreams.

"Floor to ceiling windows everywhere and one wall taken up with a massive piece of art."

Mia looked up. "Street Art? Vintage? Pop Art? Fine Art?"

"Picasso. *Blue Nude*. Simple. Clean. But sensual."

She reached up, brushed her finger along his jaw. "Sad, but erotic. Primitive. He was one of the 'wild beasts,' Did you know that?"

"No." He caught her finger, brought it to his lips, smiling. "Are you saying I'm a wild beast?"

She laughed. "I think you have a wild side or we would have passed each other by. I'm the family black sheep, if you didn't notice. Even when I was a child, I didn't fit in. I was more interested in blocks and trains and math and computer games than clothes or makeup. I was a girl who was everything my father wanted in a son."

He pressed her palm against his cheek. "I was a boy who was everything my father wanted in a legitimate son. He didn't want any reminders of my mother after she died, so I learned how to hide that side of me."

"What was she like?"

"She was the love of his life." He leaned down and kissed Mia lightly on the lips. She tasted of vodka, naughty and sweet. "She didn't give a damn how a Mafia mistress was supposed to act. She drank whiskey instead of wine; she wore crazy, colorful clothes; she loved to gamble . . ." He felt uncharacteristically maudlin in his reminiscences, uncomfortably exposed, but if Mia needed this from him, he would not deny her.

"A hard liquor love like me. I think I would have liked her." Mia sat up, straddled his lap. Nico struggled against his instinct to shut down and take control. He didn't do vulnerable, and she was pushing him right to the edge.

"How did she die?"

"Drunk driver." He ran us off the road in the Valley of Fire. Our car went down a cliff. I survived without a scratch, but she didn't make it. He crashed on the next corner so he never paid for his crime."

"Oh God, Nico. How awful." She pressed a soft kiss to his neck and he stared out over the city, caught in a memory he had buried long ago. Hushed whispers. Angry voices. His nonna in a rage like he'd never seen before when his father brought Nico to live with her. Even as a child, he knew it would have been seen as a dishonor to his father's legitimate wife to have the evidence of his affair under her roof.

"You never had justice for your father, either," she said quietly.

"No." He realized then what had been bothering her all night, why she had been so wary around him. "You're worried about the vendetta."

"Are you going to kill my father?"

If she'd asked him that question before the ceremony, he would have answered yes. But he'd made a commitment in the chapel, an oath to join two families together and to protect this woman who had been joined to him forever. And even though it was before Elvis and not God, and in a tacky Vegas chapel instead of a church, it meant something to him. Something more than vengeance.

"I will withdraw the vendetta if he acknowledges me as head of the family and agrees to an alliance. Ending the feud will save many lives, and it will ensure you are safe."

"Oh." She let out a shuddering breath and wrapped her arms around him. "I know how hard that will be, and what it means to you. Thank you."

Nico held her soft body against him, looked around the stark, characterless room, seeing it through her eyes—the bland colors, neutral decor, soulless and detached from the light and life of the city below. She was right. It wasn't him, if he even knew who he was anymore. And clearly, it wasn't Mia either.

"Let's get out of here," he murmured against her hair. "It's our wedding night, and we're in Vegas. Let's make it something to remember."

He waited for her to remind him again that it wasn't forever. Instead she sat up and smiled. "Where?

"Take me somewhere you love to go."

A dive bar to end all dive bars, Red 27 was heaving when Mia walked in, dragging Nico behind her. If there was a heaven on earth, this was it. Goths with dreadhawks, Daken-fans with lazy hawks, and ravers with shark fins of all shapes and colors, were scattered through the dimly lit bar. Over on the small dance floor, a few punk fairies in frills and corsets strutted their stuff, and in the shadows near the restrooms, a tattered greaser wearing a suspiciously padded vest clocked Nico a wary look. Her favorite watering hole was a cornucopia of eccentric underworld delights with speakers blaring punk music loud enough to make ears bleed.

Mia leaned up to yell in Nico's ear. "Get ready for a sick night of punk, new wave, goth and rock heaven."

Nico took one look around and put a possessive arm around her shoulders. "This is where you like to go?"

"Love it," she yelled over the noise of the rowdy crowd. "It's raw, it's unadulterated, and it's sinful. It's the real Vegas that the tourists don't see, the polar opposite of glitz and glam." She pulled him over to the drinks menu scrawled in black marker on the torn paper wall.

"Punk rock and grime." Nico lifted a booted foot. Mia had insisted he wear his jeans, T-shirt and leather jacket with his kick-ass biker boots, but even dressed down he looked too tidy for Red 27 and she fought back an urge to reach up and mess his hair. "My feet are stuck to the floor and it looks like a tagger went crazy on the walls."

She laughed, not because of his words, but because he was clearly drinking it all in, from the psychedelic spray paint graffiti all over the walls, to the bras of all shapes and colors hanging from the pillars, and from the tacky mobiles on the ceilings, to the pennies pasted to the floor. The air was thick with smoke, the lighting barely enough to see, and with each breath, she drew in the scents of hops, dry ice, and the unmistakable peaty odor of pot.

"Let's go to the bar." She pulled him through the crowd, and past the worn, raised stage where a toothless long-haired banger was shredding his way through "Jesus of Suburbia." She skirted the pool table jammed into the far corner, and pulled up at the sticker-clad bar where the bartender, King, an aging hipster in a knit hat, his long beard dyed green, leaned over and gave her a kiss.

"Welcome back, my friend."

Wham. Nico had him by the throat and halfway over the bar before Mia had a chance to introduce him.

"Let him go." She tugged on Nico's wrist, dislodging his hand from King's throat.

"Sorry." She reached across the bar to straighten King's collar. "He doesn't get out much."

"Hey, no problem." King held up his hands, palms forward in the universal sign of surrender. "Just being friendly, man. We got a hands-off policy until five a.m. That's when the clubs shut down and the strippers come in looking for some fun."

"You." Mia turned and poked Nico in the chest. "Take it down about one thousand notches. I know these people, and they know me. Nothing's going to happen to me here."

Nico grunted but didn't look convinced. Mia ordered a couple of two-dollar drinks and found a small table near the back that wasn't covered in empties.

"Don't use the washroom unless you're desperate," Mia said, amused by how uptight her Mafia boss was in the pit of sin. Or maybe it was because he had left his bodyguards outside and he was alone for the first time in forever.

"I've got my piece." He patted his jacket, and Mia laughed. "Oh. It's a gun. I wondered what that was when you were pressed up against me at the bar. I thought you wanted me."

His eyes darkened and he reached over, dragged her chair toward him. "I wanted you back at the hotel. Now it's a fucking need."

Mia leaned over, kissed his neck. "Do you know what I need?"

He threaded his hand through her hair, pulled her closer. "What do you need, *bella*?"

"I need to dance." She pushed away and wound her way through the tables to the tiny dance floor in front of the stage. How the hell could she make this work if she wanted to jump him every time they were together? She didn't want to get emotionally involved in a fake marriage that tied her to the mob, especially when it was never meant to last. And yet, she was already emotionally involved. She could never have said 'I do' to a man she didn't trust, a man she liked and cared deeply about. There was so much more to Nico than the cold, ruthless mob boss he let the world see. He was passionate, protective, deeply committed to his family, and so damn sexy she couldn't keep her hands away.

Someone put the Clash on the jukebox and she danced

with two biker chicks as punk rock videos played on the projection screen behind the stage. She glanced over at the table, but Nico was already behind her.

"You trying to fucking kill me?" He wrapped one arm around her waist, and pulled her against him, as if they were alone and not in the middle of a dance floor in a grungy dive bar.

"I was trying to dance." Her nipples tightened as he ground his hips into her ass. "I see you want the X-rated version."

He kissed his way down her neck, and nipped the sensitive skin on her shoulder, sending a shiver down her spine. "I could fuck you right here and no one would bat an eye."

Mia turned to face him, wound her arms around his neck. "I knew you'd like it."

"I like watching you." He pulled her close and danced like his hips were unhinged, grinding against her until her clit throbbed and she was so wet for him, the thought of fucking him in the filthy bathroom held considerable appeal.

"Nico." She moaned softly, and he thrust his thick thigh between her legs, rocking her against the rough fabric of his jeans.

"Can you come like this?" His voice was a low, sensual rasp in her ear, his hands firm on her hips, his body hot and hard in her arms.

"I don't know, but I want to."

He twisted her hair in his hand, yanked her head back, and kissed her fiercely. "How bad is the restroom?"

"Bad."

She slid her hand down, smoothed it over his T-shirt, tracing over his rock hard pecs, the ripples of his abs. Nico's grip tightened and his voice dropped to a husky growl. "How much do you want me?"

"Worse." She rubbed the palm of her hand along his rock hard erection. People danced around them, laughed, and joked. Their R-rated behavior was nothing in a bar where she'd witnessed X-rated shenanigans.

"Come." He grabbed her hand, pulled her across the dance floor and through the maze of tables to the tiny, dark hall leading to the restrooms. He angled left and Mia pulled back.

"Women's."

He ducked his head in the men's washroom and chuckled. "Good call."

Moments later they were in the women's toilet, door closed, bare bulb flickering overhead. The walls were covered in spray-painted graffiti in a multitude of fluorescent colors, torn band posters, and stickers of all shapes and sizes. Two toilet stalls were set off in the corner, and a chipped enamel sink sat on a pedestal beneath a broken mirror.

Nico turned on the tap and grabbed a handful of paper towel from the dispenser.

"What are you doing?" Mia leaned against the door, frowning.

"Cleaning the sink?" He gave it an inexpert wipe, scrubbing along the edge.

"Why?"

He looked back over his shoulder. "So I can fuck you on it."

"I thought you knew. You didn't marry a princess." She came up behind him, slid her hand over his hip and tugged open his belt. "If you want to fuck me over a dirty sink, go for it."

She had barely finished her sentence before he ditched the paper towels, spun her around, and lifted her against him, bracing her against the door.

"Fuck the sink." With his free hand, he tugged open

his jeans and freed his cock from its restraint. Mia clung to his shoulders as he sheathed himself so she didn't land on her ass on the sticky floor.

"God." She rocked against him, desperate to feel him inside her. "I want you so bad, Nico. Hurry."

"You wanna fucking ride me, *bella,* you better be ready." He reached under her skirt and shoved her panties aside, slicking his thick finger along her folds.

"Jesus Christ. You're so wet for me. So hot." He thrust one finger inside her and she jerked back, slammed her head against the door.

"More."

He gave a strangled grunt, added a second finger, and curled them both to pulse against her sensitive inner walls. Mia fisted his hair, kissed him hard, furious, frantic, her heart pounding to the heavy bass of the music outside. She wanted this man like she'd never wanted anyone before, wanted to wrap herself around him, feel him deep inside her, take her pleasure from his hard, powerful body.

She felt the blunt head of his cock at her entrance, levered herself up on his shoulders to take him in. Desire became a raging inferno inside her. "Now, Nico."

"Ride me, *bella*. Ride hard."

She moaned as he entered her, swift and brutal, thrusting as deep as he could go. His face contorted in pleasure and he eased out and pushed inside again, sending sparks of pleasure dancing across her skin.

"You feel so good," she whispered. "Fuck me. Hard. Don't hold back with me. Give me everything you've got."

With one hand against the wall, and the other under her ass, he pounded into her, his powerful hips rocking back and forth. She lost herself in the delicious feel of him moving inside her, his firm strokes sending fire streaming through her blood.

Nico groaned, the sound wanton and erotic. She panted her breaths as he quickened his thrusts. Her muscles tightened, need spiraling out of control. Their lips met in a clashing, bruising, kiss, and as she neared her peak, he slid a hand between them and rubbed his slicked thumb over her clit.

"Oh God. Yes." She buried her face in his shoulder as she climaxed, an exquisite rush of pleasure that swept through her body, wiping everything away except the exquisite feel of his firm, thrusting cock, his heady, masculine scent, the rasp of his breaths, and the rock hard muscles that tensed when he came, pulsing and throbbing inside her.

He held her after the rush, possessing her with a gaze of intense pleasure and satisfaction as they panted their breaths, sweat soaked clothes clinging to their bodies.

"Not how I imagined a wedding night to be." He pressed a gentle kiss to her forehead.

"Me either."

"Fucking perfect."

Someone thudded on the door. "Hey! Get out of there. Some of us have to pee. Go fuck in the bar where everyone else does."

Nico gave her a quizzical look. "People fuck in the bar?"

"I've seen some X-rated scenes."

A slow, sly, sensual smile spread across his face. Pure mob boss. "You want to see another?"

NINETEEN

"You okay, Kat? You need anything?" Ben paused in the doorway to his living room. He'd brought Kat to his place after Nico's and Mia's wedding, and, after watching some television with her, he was ready for a cold shower and then bed.

Fucking hell. He hadn't been able to sleep since that encounter with Gabe and Mia, and he sure as hell wasn't going to be able to sleep with a beautiful woman in the next room. Although he was pretty sure he'd managed to talk his way out of Gabe's big reveal about his work as a cop, worry niggled at the back of his mind, and he had planned to meet Jack tonight to talk through his options. After a call with his lawyer, he realized his plan to wait out a custody hearing wasn't in the cards. He'd been thinking days, but his lawyer said it could take months

"Actually, I need help changing the dressing on my back if it won't squick you out." Kat looked up from the black leather couch and smiled.

Ben melted. God, she was beautiful. Tall and willowy, with long, chestnut hair, dark eyes, deep olive skin and a body to fucking die for. Die being the operative word.

Nico had instructed him to protect Kat until it was safe for her to go home, and he had a feeling taking advantage of Nico's innocent nineteen-year-old sister-in-law didn't count as keeping her safe.

"No problem. I did a first-aid course back in the day."

Kat pulled a first-aid kit from her overnight bag. "Back in the day? You aren't that old."

"Twenty-nine," he answered honestly.

"Not that old at all." She handed him the kit, and turned on the couch, lifting her filmy blouse. Ben tried not to look at the gentle curve of her hip, the smooth skin, the narrow dip of her waist. Instead, he focused his gaze on the large white bandage taped to her lower back.

Very carefully, Ben peeled it away.

"What the hell?" Her skin beneath the bandage was seared red in the shape of a letter C, the edges black and starting to scab.

"Sorry. I thought you knew. My dad ordered my brother to brand me. C for Cordano." Her voice tightened. "That was after he had Dante beat me with his belt. I'm popping the pain killers or I wouldn't even be able to sit down."

Bile rose in Ben's throat. What kind of family would do this to a beautiful young girl? "That's criminal assault," he blurted out without thinking.

She gave a resigned shrug. "I suppose if we lived in the normal world, it would be. But we don't. We live in a world where things like this happen, and no one can do anything about it."

Ben was tempted to assure her there were people who would do something about it, but who the fuck would that be? As with all the crime families, the Toscanis had cops on their payroll from Vegas all the way to LA—cops who would turn a blind eye to flagrant breaches of the law. It had been an eye-opening experience when Ben first worked his way into the mob, and it had taken him years to get a handle on his anger. Last year, he'd given Jack a list of all the dirty cops he knew. But big surprise, they were all still around.

"Well, nothing is gonna happen to you on my watch. I promise you that." He carefully examined the wound and replaced the bandage. "It isn't infected, and unless you want it to scar worse, it's best just to leave it alone."

"Thanks for looking at it." She dropped her blouse and turned to sit beside him on the couch. "Do you know what hurt worse?" She rested her hand on his thigh, rubbed her thumb back and forth over the rough denim. Desire shivered across Ben's skin, and he resisted the urge to knock her hand away. Maybe she was just needing some comfort. Lord knew, the poor girl needed it.

"What's that?"

"It was knowing that I'd spent my life in hiding for nothing. I was the perfect daughter. I did and said everything my father expected of a Mafia princess. But the other night, I realized it was a wasted effort. He hurt me to get to Mia, and it didn't matter that I had been everything he wanted me to be, because what he wanted me to be was nothing. I should have just been me. Like Mia." With her free hand, she undid the first two buttons on her blouse, and Ben's pulse kicked up a notch.

"Can't imagine a father doing what he did to you." He slid sideways across the couch, dislodging her hand, and reached for a pillow to put a barrier between them. She was so incredibly lovely, graceful, soft and gentle. Like an angel. And she'd been living in Hell.

"Well then I won't tell you about all the other things that went on in our house." She undid another button. "We are about as dysfunctional as a family can get. My father is a tyrant, a monster in every sense of the word, and so are the men who work with him."

Ben willed himself to look away from the exposed crescent of her perfect breast, the gentle slope, the lush swell of the forbidden fruit. He stared at the television, tried to focus on the screen and not the pulse of desire pounding through his veins.

"I'm not going to bite." Kat laughed lightly. "You can come closer."

"I'm good. Gonna take a shower and head off to bed." He fisted the pillow, breathed through his mouth so he wouldn't inhale the fresh, floral scent of her perfume. Something definitely wasn't right here. Did she think she owed him for looking after her? Or was she looking for some comfort?

She let her shirt slide down her arms to reveal a lacy, pink bra.

"Whoa." He held up his hands in a warding gesture. "I'll just go in the other room if you're wanting to change."

"I don't want to change." She tugged the pillow from his lap and clasped his hand. "I want to have some fun. With you. That's what I've been trying to tell you. What you see . . . this package . . . the girly clothes . . . it isn't me. It's what I did to survive. I want to find out who I really am with you."

Ben's stomach tightened and he gently released her hand. If he'd been another man in another place at another time he wouldn't have turned her down. But she was a vulnerable, young woman who had just been through a traumatic experience. It wasn't the right thing to do.

"Sweetheart. You're a beautiful girl, but I gave Nico my word I'd keep you safe, and that includes keeping you safe from me. He'd have my head if he knew I touched you."

She leaned across the couch; lay her head on his shoulder. "But he won't know. No one will know. I've never been with anyone. I was always too afraid after what happened to Mia's boyfriend, Danny. I'm free now. I want my first time to be with you."

Jesus Christ. His pulse thundered in his veins, and his erection pressed painfully against his jeans. He had never felt temptation like this before. And it wasn't because a beautiful half-naked virgin was begging him to be her first time; it was because he liked her. She was sweet and honest and genuine and kind. She was everything Ginger was not, everything he hoped little Daisy would grow up to be.

Daisy. His blood ran cold, putting out the fire that was raging in his veins.

"I can't, Kat. I want to. I won't lie to you about that. You're like a fantasy come to life. An angel. But you need to find yourself a nice, normal guy who cares about you and who's gonna look after you. And that's not me."

"Girls like me can't be with normal guys." She toyed with the button on his shirt. "I'm ruined, Ben. I've seen what the world is really like and it's not all sunny days and happy smiles; it's not all black and white. Good people do bad things and bad people do good things, and whether they are right or wrong depends on your point of view."

"You're wrong about that." He covered her hand with his, gently drew it away. "There's a line that you don't cross no matter what."

Kat laughed. "There is no line for us. It's just infinite shades of gray."

Ben pushed off the couch and grabbed his jacket. "Any man would want a beautiful, sweet girl like you. But what you're offering me is something you want to keep for a special guy—someone who wants to get to know you first, who'll treat you right, and appreciates all that you've got to give. You want to find someone who's gonna protect you above all things. Someone who loves you. I promise you, there are guys like that out there."

"Like Nico," she said.

"Yeah." Ben nodded, not unaware of the irony of holding a Mafia boss up to be the paragon of goodness. "Someone like him."

"Or someone like you." She pulled on her shirt, refastened the buttons.

"I'm not good, sweetheart." The thoughts he was thinking right now were definitely not the thoughts of a good man, nor were the thoughts he had every time he walked into Ginger's house and saw Gabe near his little girl.

She looked up and smiled. "Like I said. It depends on your point of view."

TWENTY

Nico woke to the smell of burned bacon and the worst hangover of his life. He scrubbed a hand over his face and sat up, last night as much of a haze as the smoke that filled the room.

He leaped up, stumbled over the clothes and computer equipment strewn across the floor. Where the fuck was he? He blinked, clearing his vision, took in the riot grrrl posters, on the walls, the sea of silver chains and bracelets on the chipped white dresser, the black lace-up boots sitting on a dismantled hard drive. Ah yes. He had spent the night at Mia's place.

Memories came back to him in a rush.

The wedding. The awkward hour at his hotel. The dive bar . . .

Fuck. The dive bar. He'd engaged in some X-rated activities he wasn't sure if he wanted to rehash right now, or he'd have a fire to put out of another sort.

The earsplitting shriek of a fire alarm filled the room and he waded through the debris to the open-plan living space of the tiny apartment. "Mia!"

"Sorry." She hurried toward him and pushed the

button on the alarm, plunging the room into silence. "I wanted to make breakfast for you before I leave for work, but as you can see, I'm not much of a cook."

Nico pushed open the window, drew in a breath of thick, smoggy air. Still, it was better than the smoke that charred his lungs.

"Uh . . ." Her voice thickened. "You might not want to do that?"

"Why?" He turned to face her, watched her blush.

"You're . . . um . . . naked. And my window is very visible from the street, and also to my elderly neighbors across the way. That's why I usually cover it." Her eyes widened and her blush deepened. "The window, I mean. I cover the window."

Nico became semi-erect under her scrutiny, aroused by her interest and the memory of what they'd done last night.

"You like what you see, *bella*?" He put his hands on his hips and gave her a full frontal view, proud that he was in no way lacking in size or girth.

She swallowed hard, and her voice thickened with desire. "I just . . . I've never seen you completely naked before. I didn't realize that dagger went all the way down. Last night, when we went to bed, it was . . . dark." She reached out and traced the dagger inked onto his stomach, following the lines down to his groin. He was ready for her before her fingers finished the journey, his cock rock hard, jutting against the soft cotton nightshirt she wore that barely skimmed the tops of her bare thighs. So cute. He liked the T-shirt paired with oversized socks. She looked soft, vulnerable, and very fuckable.

"Commitment to protect my family." He caught her hand, drew it to his cock. Mia smiled and wrapped her hand around his length.

"You feel very committed."

"And you look like you're wearing too many clothes." He reached for her shirt, tried to pull it over her head.

"No." She released him, and backed away. "I'm . . . How about I try breakfast again? Do you like cereal?"

Puzzled, Nico reached out and caught her wrist. "Why are you afraid to show me your body? There's very little I haven't seen already. There's nothing I don't like."

"Do you like burned bacon?"

He understood the question for what it was. Defensive. An attempt to hide. "I like finding out about you," he said softly. "I like knowing you can't cook, that your apartment looks like a bomb went off in it, and that you wear a Calamity Jane T-shirt to bed. I like listening to your music and fucking you in a filthy office and an even more disgusting dive bar. You've awakened the beast, *bella*. I won't be denied."

"Promise me you won't overreact." She nibbled on her bottom lip. "You do have a tendency to overreact in certain situations."

Overreact? He was always in control, prided himself on remaining calm in difficult circumstances. "What situations?"

"Kidnapping me. Beating up the Wolf in my office, fucking me in a restaurant just because I mentioned I was interested in what you were like in bed."

Nico gave an irritated huff. "You don't tell a man you want to get him into bed, and expect him to spend the rest of the evening thinking of anything else."

She glanced down at his cock, now fully erect. "I guess that means I'm in big trouble now."

"I want to see you. I want to see everything, your body, your ink, and your sweet curves. Show me who you are, or yes, there will be trouble." Part of him hoped she wouldn't undress so he could wrestle her into sweet submission, earn the reward of a body made for sin.

"Everything?"

"Now."

"Fine." Mia pulled off her shirt and toed off her socks. Nico drank her in, from her slightly tanned skin, to her beautiful breasts, the curves enhanced by the beautiful ink to the soft down of curls between her thighs. His gaze dropped to her long, lean legs and the flowers inked across her foot.

"Feet too?" He kneeled down to press a kiss to her instep. But what he saw made him recoil. "Dodgers fan?"

"Stay calm," she warned. "I saw the Giants' pennant in your office."

Nico lifted an eyebrow. "Of course the Giants. They lead 1210 wins to the Dodgers' 1184, eight World Series and twenty-three pennants versus the Dodgers' six and twenty-one. You're rooting for the wrong team."

"Am I?" She tried to pull away but he held her foot fast. "The Dodgers have won the National League West fourteen times compared to the Giants' eight."

"I'm taking you to a game," Nico said. "I'll convince you to cross over to the dark side. You'll find it's the more profitable side to be on."

She laughed, a soft throaty sound that made him feel warm all over.

"I already crossed over to the dark side when I got involved with you. And why do I think your interest in baseball isn't entirely because you have a love for sports?"

Unabashed he laughed. "I might know a bookmaker or two." He also knew some players, not just in baseball but in other sports as well. He had a couple of fixers on his crew who bribed young college basketball players to shave points by missing baskets to yield the greatest profit for their Toscani family fans.

"Such pretty feet totally ruined with Dodgers' ink," he teased. "We could have it removed."

"You touch that ink, and I'll remove something you are definitely going to miss."

Chuckling, Nico pressed a kiss to her instep. "I like these flowers."

"They match the ones on my boots."

He kissed his way up her leg, delighted when her breath hitched. "I wanted to fuck you in those boots from the moment I saw you in them."

"I thought you were afraid for your life since I was holding a gun to your chest." She dug her hand in his hair as he pushed her legs apart.

"My thoughts turned after you dropped the gun."

"When you thought I'd just murdered all those men?" Her teasing voice hitched when he pressed a kiss to her mound. "I didn't realize violence turned you on."

"I like it rough. Not violent."

"How rough?"

Nico looked up, his gaze assessing. "With you, last night was as far as I will go."

Mia had suffered a lot of abuse, but sex with Nico had been a revelation. The chase was exciting. Giving herself over to Nico, letting him take control, aroused her in a way she had never imagined before. She didn't feel less of a woman for giving in; she felt more simply because she knew that if she told him to stop, he would. She'd never felt that kind of trust with a man before. That kind of safe. Empowered.

But he hadn't given her everything. He hadn't let the beast free. His impressive self-control extended to the bedroom, too.

Her mouth watered at the thought of Nico, raw and

unrestrained. She tugged gently on his hair, urging him to stand. "So you would go farther? Rougher? If you didn't think I would break?"

"I wouldn't want to hurt you, *bella*. In any way."

"I'm hurting now." She took his hand, drew it down between her thighs so he could feel her wetness. Nico groaned and took over, as she knew he would, sliding a thick finger along her folds. His shaft was hard, jutting toward her from its nest of curls. With incredible force of will she pushed his hand away. "I guess I'd better get ready for work."

She turned, walked away, giving him a good Full Monty view. "You can see yourself out."

"Mia . . ." He gave a warning growl and her feet kicked into gear. Laughing she ran across the living space and headed for the bedroom.

He cursed in Italian as he stumbled over the books, computer gear, and clothes strewn across the floor. But he was fast, reaching the bedroom before she could slam the door closed. "You're going to be one sorry girl."

Mia's heart pounded, and she backed up to the bed. "How sorry?"

He lunged, reaching for her. Mia fell back on the bed, rolled out of his grasp. Their play was all the more exciting for the fact they were naked, nothing to stop him from claiming her if he could pin her to the bed. And wasn't that what she wanted? To fight and be subdued by a man strong enough to defeat her, gentle enough to cause her no pain?

"Christ, Mia. You don't want to play this game with me."

"Apparently I do or I wouldn't be wrestling with you naked on the bed." She pushed up only to have him body slam her back onto the mattress.

Mia twisted beneath him, scratched his back, pulled his hair, but her efforts just seemed to inflame him. Twice she wiggled from his grasp, but both times he caught her, pulled her back to the bed. She kicked out, rolling to the floor, and he cursed again. His muscles grew tauter, his jaw firmer, and his eyes blazed with sensual fire.

"Minx." He lifted her easily and dropped her on the bed. Sitting astride her hips, he grabbed her hands and pinned them over her head, forcing her to arch her back, offer her breasts for his licking pleasure. He took full advantage, drawing one nipple between his teeth, then the other, nipping just hard enough to make her moan.

"Condom. Drawer beside my bed."

Nico released her hands and reached for her bedside table. Taking advantage of his loss of balance. She twisted, jackknifed up, intending to roll off the bed again, but Nico was too fast. He grabbed her around the waist, and yanked her toward him, forcing her face down to the bed with a firm hand around her neck.

It was a primitive, primal position. Pinned on all fours, cheek to the bed, ass in the air, legs held apart by his thick thigh, forced into submission, she conceded defeat with a moan.

Nico gave a satisfied grunt. "You drive me out of my fucking mind. Nothing I like better than a bit of rough." Still holding her down, he reached for the nightstand, grabbed a condom, tore it open with his teeth, and sheathed himself.

"Was that rough?" she goaded him. "I thought we were playing nursery games."

"You don't know what you're asking of me." He grabbed her hands, bracketed her wrists, and pressed them against her lower back. "You already push me to the limit of my control."

"I want to push you further."

"And I want you to lift your ass, and show me your pussy."

She shifted to accommodate the new position and he thrust a thick finger inside her without warning.

"Oh God."

"I could fuck your sweet little cunt all day long and never get enough." With his free hand, he held her still as she bucked against him. "That's it. Fuck my fingers. Show me what you're going to do when I put my cock inside you."

He added a second finger, and then a third, stretching her, filling her, making her burn. He pumped his fingers swiftly, matching his rhythm to the frantic movement of her hips. She was climbing, climbing, desperate for the peak that still hovered out of reach.

And then he pulled away. She gasped at the fierce ache of unmet desire.

"I want to feel you come, *bella*. Open for me. Spread your legs and let me in." He pushed her legs apart with a rough shove of his thigh, and thrust his cock deep inside her, angling her hips so he could seat himself fully inside.

"You feel so good, Nico." She shuddered as her inner walls stretched to accommodate him, her body tight, muscles tense and desperate for release.

"And you have the softest, sweetest, wettest, most fuckable little cunt." He leaned over her, his hard body pressed against her back as he moved slowly inside her. He was everywhere. His lips on her skin, his body over her, dominating, protecting, his cock filling her so completely, they were one person, not two.

She spread her legs to take him deeper, pushed against the hand pinning her wrists to test her bonds. But he held her fast, held her safe, took the control she had given him and used it to drive her pleasure. "You're mine." He reached over her hip and pressed his thumb over her clit, circling and rubbing until she was frantic with need.

"Say it." He pressed his lips to her ear. "I want to hear you say it. Tell me you're mine. My wife."

Her orgasm hit her in a rush of white-hot heat, streaming through her veins to her fingers and toes, ripping a guttural scream from her throat. But she didn't say the words he wanted to hear. Yes, she was his wife, but she didn't belong to him, couldn't belong to him. Because all of this, everything they had in this moment, wouldn't last. For now they were together, hidden and safe in her apartment. When they walked out the door, they would be swallowed up by the bitter feud between their families.

A price would have to be paid. And it would tear them apart.

Nico's phone buzzed just as Mia stepped into the shower.

"It's Luca. I'm outside."

"Gimme a minute." Nico collected his clothing, strewn about the apartment, and quickly dressed. With all the high-tech surveillance equipment now available to law enforcement, his crew couldn't use their phones except for the most basic of calls. Everything else had to be dealt with in person.

He nodded to Mikey Muscles as he stepped outside into the crisp morning air. Luca waited across the street, leaning against his vehicle while two guards patrolled the block. Frankie had gone overboard with the security. He wasn't taking any chances.

"Let's take a walk."

"What's up?" Nico's eyes darted from side to side as they made their way down the street. When he returned to the apartment he would insist Mia pack up and move to his hotel. This area wasn't safe, and the farther they walked the more run-down and dangerous things became. He recognized the tags of two different street gangs on the crumbling brick walls, spotted a drug dealer he knew, and a couple of Albanians looking like they were about to cause a lot of trouble.

"I got a copy of the police report on the Wolf," Luca said. "His body was found in a vacant lot near the Spaghetti Bowl. He was wearing a Sicilian necktie. Was that us?"

"*Cristo.*" Now, fully awake, he gave Luca his full attention. *Cosa Nostra* only used that method of assassination—slitting the victim's throat and pulling his tongue through the hole—to send a message if they thought the victim was a rat.

"I left him half dead. Not fully dead. Although I didn't expect him to survive. Someone else must have found him." He stopped at the corner, allowing the guards behind them to catch up. He wasn't afraid of getting whacked. No one would dare. The guards were more for show and so Frankie could have a break from following him around.

"So what? You think he was a rat and the Cordanos used the opportunity to whack him and blame us? Their own *consigliere*?"

"It's what I would do." He didn't want to think about a day where Luca or Frankie or even Big Joe betrayed him. Mercy was for the weak, and he couldn't afford a repeat of the mercy he had shown Don Cordano the night of the massacre.

"So the fucking Cordanos owe us for finding their rat."

Nico chuckled. "I took their daughter. I'd say we're even."

"But you're just using her to get to Don Cordano." Luca followed Nico across the street. "Wasn't that the plan? I mean, the goal has always been to whack the bastard who killed your father and take your place as head of the family."

Nico gave a noncommittal answer, and they walked a few yards down the block. Last night, it had been easy to make the promise to Mia to spare her father. But now, in the light of day, with the expectations of his entire crew reflected in Luca's face, and yet more evidence of the brutality of Don Cordano, who was a threat to Mia as long as he drew a breath, Nico wondered if it was a promise he could truly keep.

"We'd better get moving on that plan," Luca persisted. "I got intel that Don Cordano is in New York right now. Three guesses why he's there, other than getting their blessing for a big fat Italian wedding that's going to be mysteriously missing a bride."

Nico didn't need three guesses. If Tony and Mia had married, Nico would have been considered a threat to the stability of the alliance. New York didn't like instability of any kind, and Don Cordano would have had no trouble getting their consent to whack him.

"We'll need to go public sooner rather than later." Nico had wanted to keep their union secret as long as possible, not just to give him time to break the news to the Scozzaris and smooth out the political situation, but because he wanted to keep Mia to himself, unburdened and untainted by the traditional expectations put on Mafia wives.

"Whaddya gonna do?" Luca snorted a laugh. "Take out an ad?"

"I'm going to do what everyone does after they elope." His stomach clenched. "We'll go meet the parents."

"And is that when you're gonna pop Don Cordano?"

Nico couldn't answer. He hadn't decided yet if he was going to whack the bastard or if he would shake his hand.

TWENTY-ONE

Mia's hand shook as she pushed open the front door to the family home.

"Don't talk," she said to Nico over her shoulder.

"Not unless I'm asked a question." He straightened his tie and smoothed his jacket before following her inside. Luca and Frankie joined them in the hallway along with the three armed Cordano guards who had followed them up the walk after patting them all down for weapons.

"Don't overreact. Dante's not the bad guy here. He might act a little officious because he's in charge while Papà is away, but he's nothing like my father."

Nico's jaw tightened, and she could see his pulse throb in his neck. "He beat and branded your sister, caused you to suffer, and didn't intervene when your father tried to force you to marry my cousin."

Mia turned to face him as one of the guards closed the door. "I know you can keep your cool under pressure. You saw my Dodgers tattoo, and I'm still alive."

Nico pressed his lips together. "If he touches you, or hurts you in any way, or if he says anything . . ."

She took a deep breath, and then another. "Maybe we

should have met with your family first. I have a feeling this isn't going to go very well."

"It's traditional to meet with the bride's family first," Nico pointed out.

"It's not traditional to elope." Mia sighed. "At least my father isn't here. He's not due back from New York until the end of the week."

"Mia, darling." Mia's mother walked toward them. She wore a cream sheath trimmed with gold, her hair perfectly coiffed, gold jewelry sparkling on her fingers. Impeccably dressed, as usual. "You didn't tell me you were coming to visit." She kissed Mia's cheeks. "Is Kat with you?" Her face fell when she saw Nico and his crew by the door. "You didn't tell me we were having company."

"This is Nico." She hesitated, unsure how her mother was going to take the news. "Nico Toscani."

When Mama didn't react, she continued to babble. "We're married. I married him. I have a ring." She held up her hand, but her mother still didn't move.

"Mama?"

"He'll kill you." Mama's face twisted in horror. "This time your father will kill you. How could you do this, Mia? It will be a matter of honor. You were promised to Tony Toscani."

Mia felt Nico's warm hand against her back, a small gesture of support that gave her strength. "He is a Toscani. He's Tony's cousin. Papà agreed to give the Toscanis a Cordano woman, and we've honored that agreement, but in a way I chose."

Mama's eyes went wide with shock and her face paled. "*Dio mio.* Tell me you're joking. Nico Toscani? And is he here to . . . ?" She backed away. "Your father isn't here."

"He's just here to meet you and Dante, Mama. He isn't going to kill anyone. He's very civilized."

Nico chuckled and leaned in to kiss Mama's cheeks. *"Piacere di conoscerla*—It's a pleasure to meet you."

"E Lei—And you," Mia's mother said stiffly, but there was no warmth in her voice.

"I called Dante's office and they said he was here. Is he in the study?" Mia had mixed feelings about introducing Nico to Dante, mostly guilt. Although Dante had done some terrible things, he was still her brother, and she had sworn to take his secret to the grave. But she felt sick hiding the truth from Nico. From what she had seen, Nico was a loyal, honorable man and breaking his trust was probably the one thing that he would never forgive.

Mia's mother's face smoothed to its usual implacable mask, and she transformed from horrified parent into the perfect hostess in a heartbeat. She clearly had more to say, but she was too polite to express her views in front of Nico.

"Yes, he is. Would your guests like to eat? I can make a little something."

Of course Nico and his men perked up at the offer of Italian home cooking, but Mia wanted to get in and out of the house as fast as possible. She'd never seen her mother react to a situation with anything less than perfect decorum, and it put her on edge.

"Not today. I just wanted to see Dante, and then we have to go." She took a step forward, and Mama grabbed her arm, drew her aside. "Is Kat safe? Where is she? I want to talk to her."

Disconcerted by her mother's harsh whisper and the firm grip on her arm, she pulled away. "She's fine. And safe. Much safer than here at home where she has no one to protect her."

Her mother glanced over at Nico and Luca, engaged in conversation, and lowered her voice. "There was nothing I could do."

"There was never anything you could do." Mia had never confronted her mother about her failure to protect her children from Papà's abuse before, and she was shocked at her own bitterness.

Mia's mother tugged her around the corner, and pain flickered across her face. "I felt every scream like a knife through my heart. I know you thought I wasn't there for you, that I was weak, and maybe that is part of the reason you are so committed to empowering women. But women can be strong in many different ways. Every obstacle doesn't need to be met head on. There were times I burnt a meal or broke a vase so he would turn his anger on me instead of you. I tried hard to keep him happy to keep you safe. Every minute of the day I spent trying to think of ways to keep you out of the house, to dissuade you from doing something I knew would anger him, to protect you the only way I could."

Shocked, Mia could only stare. "You could have taken us away. You could have stood up to him."

"If I'd taken you away he would have found us. You know that," Mama admonished. "And if I'd stood up to him, he would have killed me. After you all were born and I started to age, I was of no real use to him except to entertain his guests. I thought about it many times, but who would have protected you when I was gone? I stayed for you, to protect you, to help you find a way to be free."

Mia's heart sank to her stomach, and her words came out in a horrified whisper. "I didn't know."

"I didn't want you to know." Her mother twisted her bracelet around her wrist. "I'm not telling you to make you feel bad. I did what any mother would do. But never think a woman isn't strong because you can't see her fight. There is as much strength in enduring as there in engaging. There is strength in picking your battles and knowing when to walk away. There is strength in accepting your limitations and letting someone help you. A strong woman becomes strong because of the pain she has faced and won, because of the battles she has fought that no one sees, by falling down and getting back up again, by smiling in the morning like she wasn't crying last night. My biggest regret is that I didn't teach you that. You thought I had abandoned you when, in fact, I was behind you, supporting you, every step of the way."

"Mama . . ." Mia's voice cracked, broke, and she wrapped her mother in a hug.

"If this is real, then I'm happy because you'll be safe," Mama murmured in her ear. "But don't push him away. Some battles we can't fight alone." She kissed Mia on the cheek and pulled away. "I'll go make a little something for your guests. If we don't have a chance to talk before you leave, let Kat know I miss her."

"I will, Mama." Her anger subsided as quickly as it had flared, the empty space filling with admiration instead. "She misses you, too."

She joined Nico in the foyer and led him down the hall to her father's study with his men, and her father's guards taking up the rear.

"It's going pretty well," Nico whispered. "Maybe afterwards we can see your bedroom." He pinched her ass and Mia slapped his hand away while Luca and Frankie chuckled behind them.

"Behave. We still have to deal with Dante."

Nico's smile faded to be replaced a scowl. "He won't touch you. No one will touch you. No one will hurt you. You are my wife, and I will protect you with my last dying breath."

Mia laughed despite her anxiety. "You should be in the movies. Who talks like that? We've only been married for three days."

"I do."

She reached for his hand and gave it a squeeze. "I like it. Despite my commitment to empowering women, part of me still likes the whole alpha male gonna-protect-you thing. It makes me feel all warm and fuzzy inside. But save it for when you mean it."

"I mean it now, *bella*. Have no doubt you are safe with me."

Mia knocked before pushing open the door. Dante sat alone at her father's desk, a stack of files in front of him. Rev, stood nearby, his pumped, muscular body straining his blue silk shirt, short thick neck circled by a heavy gold chain. He gave her a lascivious look as she walked across the room, his leering gaze travelling down her body and back to her breasts. Nico growled softly behind her, and she cleared her throat in warning in case Nico pounced.

Dante looked up and his face twisted in a snarl as he registered the Toscani crew standing in front of him. "What's he doing here? What the fuck are the Toscanis doing in our house?"

Rev yanked Dante from his seat. "Behind me, Mr. Cordano. I'll rid this house of the Toscani scum."

"It's okay." Mia held up her hands. "We're not here to cause problems. We just came to let you know we're married."

"Married?" Shock, then horror crossed Dante's face and his voice rose to a shriek. "What the fuck do you mean? You were supposed to marry Tony Toscani. That was the agreement. Are you stupid? How did you marry the wrong man? Or is this just a sham marriage to get out of the agreement with Tony?"

Nico took a menacing step forward, and Mia put a warning hand on his arm.

"I married a man I chose. A man I care about. I've honored the family agreement as well, so come out from behind the desk and properly greet my husband." She felt curiously defensive about Nico and realized she had in-advertently revealed her true feelings about him when she had tried to justify their marriage to Dante. She cared about him. A lot. She just hoped Nico hadn't caught that little slip.

"What have you done?" Dante's eyes darted from side to side, as if he were looking to escape, and sweat beaded on his forehead.

Mia opened her mouth to assure him Nico meant no harm, but closed it when she realized what he was truly afraid of, a truth she had sworn to take to her grave.

"Dante. I haven't . . ."

"Rev." Dante's voice was panicked as he stepped away from the desk, shoving Rev in front of him. Rev yanked a gun from his holster, and within a heartbeat, Nico had shoved Mia behind his back.

"We didn't come here to fight." Nico's voice was calm and even. "We're unarmed. Your guards took our weap-ons before we came to the house."

"Papà will kill you both," Dante said from behind Rev's back. "You've made the biggest mistake of your life, Mia."

Mia cringed at his cowardice. If her mother had truly taken beatings to protect them all, then Dante had been hiding all his life. Even now he hid behind his bodyguard in front of an unarmed man. She didn't have to look at Nico and his men to see how little they respected Dante, because she had lost what little respect she had for him when he whipped Kat with his belt. He was spineless and weak, and if something happened to their father, the family wouldn't survive with Dante in charge.

"You won't even shake the hand of your brother-in-law?" Luca snorted in disgust. "You disrespect him. You disrespect your family. You disrespect the Toscani family. And you disrespect your sister."

Nico assessed Dante with a cool gaze. "This won't be forgotten."

Mia shot Nico an irritated glance. "You couldn't help yourself, could you?" She muttered under her breath. "You just had to threaten him."

Despite the tense and potentially volatile situation, Nico's lips quirked ever so slightly at the corners. "It's who I am." He threaded his fingers through hers. "We're done here."

"Wait." Dante came out from behind Rev's back. "It's not easy to put aside a vendetta that has lasted ten years, especially when it's directed at my father." He looked over at Mia. "This marriage is for real?"

"I have a marriage certificate." She pulled the official document from her purse and held it up for him to see. "And a ring. I've never lied to you, Dante, and you know I would never put you in danger."

Dante walked across the room to Nico and held out his hand. It wasn't the customary Italian form of congratulations or greeting, especially when welcoming someone to the family, but given the circumstances, she accepted that it was the best he could do.

Mia's chest tightened when Nico shook the hand of his father's killer. If there had been any way around this moment, she would have taken it. She felt sick inside about deceiving Nico who had come to her family home in good faith. But he had lived for his vendetta for ten long years. How could she take a risk? How could she gamble with her brother's life?

After the handshake, they made a quick exit. Mia apologized to her mother on the way out for not staying to eat, and promised to ask Kat to call.

"That went better than expected," Nico said after they were safely back in the vehicle.

"Are you kidding?" Mia stared at him aghast. "I thought it would be bad, but not that bad. I don't think he bought it."

Nico leaned down and whispered in her ear. "Then he missed the bit where you said you care for me."

Her cheeks flamed, and she glanced up at Luca and Frankie engaged in their own conversation in the front seat. Damn. He picked up on everything. "That was your takeaway from what could have been a fatal post-elopement meet and greet of the family?"

"That's all I remember. My girl cares for me." He puffed out his chest and gave her a smug, self-satisfied, oh-so-masculine smile.

She turned, rubbed her cheek along his jaw. "I guess she does."

"It's too bad she has to be punished tonight," he whispered as he inched her skirt up her thigh.

"What?" She slapped his hand down. "Why?"

"You tried to protect me. You risked your life. You need to learn never to do that again."

Mia huffed and tried to pull away. "Most men would say thank you."

"I'm not most men." He unclipped her seatbelt and tucked her into his side, her cheek against his chest.

"Apparently not."

"I'm your man. And it's my job to protect you. Not the other way around."

Mia looked up and laughed. "In that case, you'd better do up my seat belt if you want me alive for a repeat performance of 'Meet the Family' at your nonna's house tomorrow."

Nico sighed and clipped her seat belt. Mia leaned

against him, enjoying the quiet moment together as they sped through the city.

"*Bella*?"

"Yes?"

Nico pressed a soft kiss to her forehead. "Thank you."

Nico opened the car door for Mia and studied the vehicles on the street. He had requested a sit down with Tony at their grandmother's house because it was neutral ground. Not even Tony would disrespect Nonna Maria by drawing a weapon.

"Looks like we've got Tony, Charlie Nails, a couple of high-ranking capos and some bodyguards," Luca said. "Full house."

"You think Nonna Maria will feed us?" Frankie put out a hand holding them back as he checked the road.

Nico snorted a laugh. "She'll be in her element. A house full of hungry men? It's a nonna's dream come true."

"Well, at least there is one thing our families have in common." Mia stepped out onto the street and clasped his hand.

"She'll love you." Nico gave Mia an encouraging smile as they walked up the sidewalk. She had worn a simple black dress—no skulls or chains, tears, ribbons or lace—and black shoes with heels in a bid to appear respectable for the meeting with his family. He didn't mind the dress, although it wasn't her, but he planned to fuck her wearing just the heels when they got back to his hotel. There was just something about Mia in heels that got his blood pumping.

Not that he needed any help. They had spent last night recovering from the meeting with Dante by testing the strength of the various pieces of furniture in Nico's suite, including, just once, the bed. He had fucked her hard, loved her soft, and held her all night long wondering if it was possible to have it all—a woman he respected and admired, but wanted with an intensity that took his breath away—a Mafia wife and mistress all rolled into one.

"Uh no. I had two nonnas. I know what they're like. She'll probably ignore me because no woman is going to be good enough for her boy." Mia reached up and gave Nico's cheek a gentle nonna-style pinch.

Nico caught her hand and brought it to his lips. "Then she'll be wrong."

Nonna Maria came to the front door to greet them. She wore her usual red apron, her silver hair swept neatly back in a bun. Nico gave her the customary kisses, and introduced Mia.

"This is my new wife, Mia Cordano."

Nonna Maria looked Mia up and down, then turned her back and walked away.

"She's lovely," Mia whispered. "I feel welcome already."

Nico felt a surge of protective anger and put his arm around Mia's shoulders. Whether this marriage lasted one day or one year, Mia was his wife, and any disrespect of her was a disrespect of him, whether it came from the cousin he hated or the nonna he loved.

Conversation halted when Nico led Mia into the dining room where Tony and Charlie Nails sat with the four *capos* in the family. "*Permette che mi presenti mia moglie*—May I introduce my wife, Mia Cordano."

"Jesus Christ," Tony finally spluttered, after a moment of stunned silence. "When I first heard about this, I thought it was a fucking joke. You really have some balls."

"The size of my balls has never been in question."

Nico tossed a copy of the marriage certificate on the dining-room table.

"That piece of paper means nothing," Tony snapped without giving it a glance. "We had an agreement with the Cordanos. Would you dishonor our family by making us go back on our word?"

"The agreement was for a marriage between the Cordanos and Toscanis. That agreement has been fulfilled." He glanced over at Nonna Maria standing in the doorway to the kitchen. No words. No facial expression. No gestures. He hadn't expected support from the rest of the family, but his nonna was like a second mother to him, and he had hoped she would accept Mia as part of his life.

"Not in a way the New York bosses approve." Tony picked up his highball glass and drained the contents.

Nico's skin prickled in warning, and he motioned for Luca to stand closer to Mia. He had expected an outburst from Tony, expressions of surprise from his men, but the cold, calm that had settled in the room had him itching to draw his weapon.

"She's mine in every sense of the word." Crude, he knew, but it needed to be said, although he suspected no one would believe he'd consummated the marriage over a sink in the filthy restroom of a dive bar.

"Do you really intend to challenge me?" Tony stood so quickly his chair toppled over. "Are you going to drag this family into a civil war? Did you really think a bastard can become the *capofamiglia* and head this family when there is a Toscani of pure blood who has been groomed to lead? I've been the underboss for fuck sake. No one knows how this family works better than me."

Mia squeezed Nico's hand, but he wasn't leaving yet. Tony clearly had a card to play, and Nico wanted to see it. Tony was arrogant and impulsive, lacking the foresight, intelligence, and political awareness needed to be an effective leader. Nico would only have to push a few buttons to find out what was really going on.

"Better a bastard than a man who will destroy the family with his greed," Nico shot back. "I have nine crews working for me, each with ten soldiers and not one of them is involved in the drug trade, nor are their associates, because drugs are the fastest way to bring the family down." He was repeating what Tony already knew, but since both of them had declared as acting boss, the decision would come down to a vote by the five *capos* of the family, and he wanted them to know just how powerful he had become. In the event of a tie, Charlie Nails would have the deciding vote, and Nico knew which way the betraying bastard leaned.

"Drugs are where the money is at. This is the modern Mafia. We don't need to rely on protection rackets, loan sharking, petty deals, and real-estate scams." Tony smirked and looked to his men for support. "We don't need to build up legitimate business portfolios to support the family because the traditional ways aren't working anymore. I make more money in one week with my drug operation than you do in one month with all your rackets put together. And that's what this business is all about. Money. Making it. Keeping it. Spending it. And making fucking more."

He finished with a flourish, mocking a bow. Nico took note of which capos laughed, and which sat in stony silence, already planning how to direct his bid for leadership.

Luca shot Nico a quizzical glance, and Nico gave the slightest shake of his head. Tony had no idea how much money he really made. Nico had been careful to keep most of his high-performing rackets off the record, paying up only enough to Santo each week to keep him from becoming suspicious.

"And you know who agrees with me?" The consummate actor, Tony paused for effect. "Don Cordano. I had a meeting with him after he flew in from New York this morning. We agreed that there has been too much bloodshed, and the war between the Cordanos and the Toscanis must end. And the only way to do that is to honor the old agreements that were made before my father died. After your marriage is annulled, I will take your bride."

"You're crazy." Mia looked from Tony to Nico and back to Tony. "It can't be annulled without my consent and I won't give it."

"It can happen if one party agrees to the annulment, and I think Nico will." Tony gave them a sly smile, and Nico braced himself for the big reveal.

"After all," Tony continued. "Who wants to be married to a woman who would take you to the man who killed your father, a man you had been waiting ten years to destroy, the target of a vendetta that you were honor-bound to fulfill, and stand there and watch as you shook his hand?"

Dante.

Nico felt as if the floor had just dropped from under him. All these years, plotting and planning, frustrated because his requests to avenge his father were refused again and again, and he had been after the wrong man. No wonder the New York bosses had turned him down. They must have known.

Just as Mia knew.

One glance at her guilty expression was all the answer he needed, and her betrayal hurt more than the knowledge that vengeance had been close at hand.

"I don't think the New York bosses will refuse your request to whack your father's real killer," Tony said to Nico. "After all, he wasn't a made man when he shot your father in the back, and you have waited a very long time."

Nico forced back the emotion that welled in his chest, smoothed his face to an expressionless mask. He wouldn't give Tony the satisfaction of knowing how deep his blade had gone. He would show no weakness. No anger. No fear. Even though this charade with Mia was done, no one would see his pain. He would leave them with the impression he knew about Dante, and that nothing could tear Mia from his side. He would make them believe he had a master plan even though he had shattered inside.

"Come, *bella*. We are done here." For the very last time, Nico clasped the hand of the woman who had been his wife for a few, short, glorious days. The woman who had opened his heart.

The woman who had betrayed him.

TWENTY-TWO

"Where the fuck is he?" Nico thudded his fist on the hood of his SUV. He'd pulled out the larger vehicle to accommodate all the men and weapons he could carry after hearing that fucking Dante was the man he wanted. After signing the damn annulment papers ending his marriage to Mia, he had driven around the city with Frankie and Mikey Muscles looking for Dante. But so far they hadn't found their man.

His man. The end of his quest for vengeance. The fucking bastard who had shaken his hand.

Something niggled at the back of Nico's mind. How the fuck did Tony know he had shaken hands with Dante? It wasn't the traditional greeting a man would give to a new brother-in-law. Maybe Dante passed the details of the meeting to Don Cordano who passed them on to Tony. Maybe Tony had a spy in the Cordano house. Or maybe Mia's betrayal went even deeper than he had thought.

"What the fuck is taking Luca so long?" They had been waiting for ten minutes in the parking lot outside a bar Dante was rumored to frequent for its high-stakes back-room gambling, but so far Dante hadn't shown.

"There he is." Mikey Muscles pointed to Luca's black 300C.

Luca pulled up beside them, and Nico raged as soon as Luca opened the door.

"Christ. You drive like a nonna. Go with Mikey Muscles and see if he's in there." This was the sixth tip they'd had about Dante's favorite haunts, and so far, they'd struck out five times.

"On our way." Luca gave him a thumbs up before joining Mikey Muscles in a jog across the gravel.

Nico pulled out his phone and checked his messages while Frankie lit a cigarette. "Where is Big Joe? Why isn't he coming in? The whole fucking world is going to shit. The one person who is always on time, never misses a fucking call, is not there when I need him."

"He's guarding Kat," Frankie reminded him. "He can't be in two places at once."

"Tell him to take her home or to Mia's place or wherever she wants. We're done with the fucking Toscanis. And tell him to get his ass down to the clubhouse when he's finished. We'll meet him there."

He had no responsibility toward Kat any more. As soon as Mia signed her papers, the annulment would go through in one to three days, and he wouldn't have a sister-in-law in need of protecting. Nor would he have a wife.

Nico thudded his foot into a wooden fence bordering the parking lot. He hadn't spoken to Mia since leaving his nonna's house except to tell her he intended to get the marriage annulled before sending her home with Luca. He hadn't asked for an explanation, and she hadn't offered him one. It was clear why she'd kept quiet about Dante. She wanted to protect him from Nico's wrath. But she'd made the wrong fucking choice because Dante was a marked man from the moment he pulled the trigger. And now that Nico knew the truth, there was nowhere Dante could run, no where he could hide. Nico was going to hunt the bastard down and put a bullet through his brain.

Part of him knew he was out of control, but the only way to deal with this fucking mess was to unleash the beast or he'd goddamn implode. And the one person who could soothe his pain had betrayed him.

"Fuck." He kicked the fence again. "Dante can't just disappear off the face of the earth. What's the point in having hundreds of associates and soldiers when they can't find a single man?"

"I keep telling you, go for the bodyguard." Frankie puffed on his cigarette. "He's more visible, more recognizable. And he's not the kind of man who's going to hide. He'll lead you to Dante and then we can whack him. Rev is like a human shield. Dante will be vulnerable without him." He tested the wooden fence and pushed the board Nico had dislodged back in place, before blowing out a stream of smoke.

"We're not murderers, Frankie. There's only one man I want dead, and then I am going to try and end this fucking war. If we clip Rev, then they'll come after our guys, and we'll go after their guys. It won't stop until the streets run red with blood."

"With all due respect . . ."

Nico raised his hand. "I don't want to hear it. Everyone will be hitting the mattresses now. We need to focus our efforts on finding Dante before he disappears, if he hasn't already." He knew Frankie wanted him to lay low—hit the mattresses, too. But Nico didn't hide. He didn't run. And sure as hell didn't stop looking for the man who had taken his father's life.

"I'm trying to protect you," Frankie said. "Less chance of you getting clipped if the bodyguard is out of the way."

"I don't need protection," he snapped. "I need revenge. We're done with that topic."

"What about the topic of the girl you've been fucking brooding over all day. Why don't you just call her?" Frankie blew a smoke ring and watched it fade away.

"What the fuck?"

"Call your girl. Save a fence."

Nico punched the fence so hard, his hand went numb. "She's not my girl; she was my wife. Although it turns out I didn't know her at all."

"She was trying to save her shit-for-brains brother. Seems to me that's pretty consistent behavior for her." Frankie always seemed so calm, and yet when Nico looked in his eyes he saw nothing but darkness, anger, and rage.

"She betrayed me."

"And now you're going to kill her brother when only yesterday you were willing to put aside your quest for vengeance to have her." Frankie took another drag of his cigarette.

Irritated, his nerves frayed, Nico slapped the cigarette from Frankie's mouth. "I'm fucking sick of watching you try to kill yourself. My Uncle Ettore died of lung cancer. It is not a death I would wish on anyone and especially not you." He had lost everyone he cared about—his parents, Mia, friends, and family during the war—and the prospect of losing one of his two closest friends as well was unbearable.

"And I'm fucking sick of watching you lose yourself to the memory of a father who has been gone for ten years," Frankie shot back. "Yes, there is a matter of honor. But you have to live for something more than revenge, and Mia was that something. Now, you're going back instead of moving on. When does it end?"

"It will end with Dante dead, my father avenged and

the family honor restored." He clenched his fist and thudded his heart in a silent pledge.

"And you'll be alone with your vengeance, your honor, a war with both Tony and the Cordanos, and a stranger in your bed that you don't love."

Nico's heart thudded a protest beneath his hand. "Love isn't worth the pain. I should have heeded the lesson I learned long ago. Even you . . ." He gestured to the cigarette, directing his anger at the friend who never left his side. "Every day you make me watch you die."

Frankie dropped the cigarette and toed it with his boot. "You didn't seem to be in pain for the last coupla weeks."

"Forget about it." He waved Frankie off, even though he knew Frankie was right. He felt right with Mia. Happy. So fucking happy he had considered giving up the vendetta to be with her even though they'd known each other only a few weeks. *Stupido.* Dante's death might not bring his father back, but an eye for an eye had always been the traditional Mafia way. His father had been right. The old ways were best. Mia had spent her life fighting against tradition, and where had it led her? Back to the fucking beginning. Just like him.

"So what's on the menu today?" Jules handed Mia a cup of coffee and took a seat on the other side of Mia's desk. "Penetration test of a mob-run casino? Done that. Escape from a mob clubhouse? Done that. Getting hot and heavy with a mob boss? Triple check. Destruction of the office after the mob boss goes protective crazy? Check. Dressing up as a pretend mob wife? Done with miserable results. Escape from the mob? Vegas wedding? Something happens that you won't share with the best friend? Check, check, check, check. And now you're getting divorced.

It's been an exciting month. I can hardly wait to find out what's next."

"It's an annulment, not a divorce." Mia pushed the annulment form across the table. "If I contest it, then it can take four to six weeks. If I sign the paper, it is over in one to three days."

Jules stared at the annulment form and shook her head. "I don't get it. I thought you liked him. I thought he was the one."

"I never wanted to marry into the mob. It was just a way of protecting Kat and getting away from Tony." Mia shrugged. "It was a stupid plan."

"I've never known you to come up with a stupid plan." Jules took a pen from the holder on Mia's desk. "I also never saw you so happy as you were with him." She doodled a happy face on the form. "Oops. Look what I did. Now you can't get the marriage annulled. Silly me."

Mia groaned. "Jules . . . that's not going to change anything. I'll just print off another. I'm sure he's already filed his by now. He didn't say anything to me after we left his nonna's house except about getting the marriage annulled. He wouldn't even get in the car. He sent me home with Luca, and he and Frankie walked off down the street."

"What happened at his nonna's house?" Jules continued to doodle. "I'm pretty sure you didn't insult her cooking. I know there's a lot of mob stuff you don't want me to know, but it's not like I don't have a good understanding of what the underground world is like. I lived rough on the streets for six years. There's very little I didn't see. And if you're trying to protect me, don't. I can look after myself."

"I knew something." Mia swallowed past the lump in her throat. "I knew how his dad really died. I watched him shake hands with his father's killer, and I didn't say anything. Revenge is the one thing he's wanted for the last ten years, and I didn't tell him it was right in front of him."

Jules doodled another happy face and added a bow on top. "I'm sure you had a good reason."

"I did."

"Then give him some time to figure that out. Four to six weeks maybe." She drew a giant "L.O.V.E" on the paper, and then crushed it into a ball. "Don't sign this and make it easy."

"My father is going to make me marry Tony as soon as the annulment goes through." Mia sighed and rested her chin in her hands. "Why drag it out? I need to protect Kat, and I'm tired of all this. Tired of fighting an institution that I can't change. Tired of fighting the inevitable. Tired of watching people I care about get hurt. Women have no power in the Mafia. There's nothing we can do but accept it. "

"Bullshit." Jules threw the paper at Mia. "Stop the pity party. No one can force you into a marriage. You ran away with Kat before. Do it again."

"I'll put people at risk." Mia caught the paper and smoothed it out. "My father has only just realized that the best way to hurt me is through the people I care about. I can't protect everyone."

"You're right," Jules said. "But you don't need to keep protecting the people you've helped out along the way. At some point you have to let them go, and focus on taking care of yourself. I can look after myself. Your mom looks after herself. I'm sure your brother does, too. And your sister seemed pretty switched on when she climbed out her bedroom window so you guys could run away. She's not a little girl, Mia. I saw the same fire in her that I see in you. If you want to empower women, give us a push and let us fly, just like you do with the girls in your coding class. You give them the tools and leave them to find their way to hacker greatness."

"It's not the same."

"It is the same," Jules said. "If you want to be there to catch us when we fall, show us you've got someone to catch you, too. There's nothing wrong with needing a little help. I wouldn't be here working with you doing a job I love to do if I'd pushed you away. It doesn't make you less; it makes you more. It means you can see your limitations, and you'll do what has to be done to overcome them. You live in a crazy-ass world where the normal rules don't apply. It's a jungle, Mia, and you don't walk alone in the jungle with a stick when you need a lion by your side."

"He hates me, and I don't blame him." She tossed the paper in the waste bin.

"He's got a thorn in his paw," Jules said. "And he needs you to take it out."

TWENTY-THREE

"Hey, Big Joe!" Mikey Muscles waved from across the clubhouse. "You got a minute?"

Ben put down his pool cue and headed over to the door. He'd dropped Kat off at Mia's house last night after getting a text from Frankie. Although, Frankie told him Nico wasn't protecting her anymore, he'd exchanged phone numbers with her just in case. He couldn't just throw that sweet girl to the wolves, and he had a feeling Nico would agree when he calmed down. It was a bad situation for everyone. He could see both sides and he just wanted to keep his head down and ride out the next couple of weeks until he could find a way to get his little Daisy out of that house.

"Frankie's waiting outside." Mikey Muscles put his arm around Ben's shoulder in a gesture that would have been friendly but for Mike Muscles's firm grip and the way he steered Ben toward the door. "We're going for a ride."

This is it.

Ben tried not to tense up as they walked through the door. "Going for a ride" only ever meant one thing.

Someone was going to get whacked. And he had a very bad feeling it was going to be him.

"I just gotta go take a piss." He needed to send a message to Jack. A team was always on standby to tail Ben and pull him out in case of an emergency, and after his encounter with Gabe at the community center, he wasn't taking any chances.

"No time." Mikey Muscles gently pushed him forward to a beat-up vehicle parked on the street. One look and Ben knew it was stolen. And that meant whatever was going on needed to be covered up after the event.

"Sure thing." His heart pounded so loud, he could barely hear Frankie when he gestured to the front seat.

"You drive."

Fuck. Fuck. Fuck. Ben slipped into the front seat. He tried to swallow, but his mouth was dry. This was definitely it. Wiseguys were an alpha bunch. The only time they asked someone else to drive was when they were taking him to his own funeral. They were going to tell him to drive out to the sticks, park the car, and then Frankie was gonna pop him from behind.

If he was lucky.

If he wasn't, he'd be wearing the same kind of necktie they found on the Wolf.

"So, what's this all about?" He pulled the vehicle away from the curb, his mind spinning with options. He could crash the car and pray he got out alive. He could hope that Jack had someone watching the clubhouse, although his surveillance team had been cut back over the last year. He could speed the car or run a red light and maybe they'd get pulled over by the cops, but there was no guarantee that wouldn't invite them to just pull the trigger, or that the cop who pulled them over wouldn't be on Nico's payroll.

"Forget about it," Frankie said, settling in the back seat beside Mikey Muscles. "Just drive."

Ben's stomach knotted as Frankie directed him though the city and out to the east side. In a crazy way, he was almost relieved. He'd been waiting for this moment for the last ten years; always looking over his shoulder, always sleeping with a gun under his pillow, always knowing this day would come. If not for little Daisy, and his regret about betraying Nico, a man he liked and admired, he would almost have accepted his fate.

And Kat. Life was so fucking unfair. He'd finally met a girl who swept him off his feet, only to die the next day.

"Pull up here." Frankie directed him to a bar just off Charleston in the Naked City, one of the worst neighborhoods of Vegas, and the only place cabs or taxis would not go through after dark. It was a place where you could shoot a man in the street and no one would call the cops, because no one in the Naked City saw anything.

Ben parked the car in the gravel lot outside a stand-alone concrete building that had been spray painted black and tagged multiple times. Sweat beaded on his forehead. Could he ask them to do something for Daisy? Frankie was a cold, hard son-of-a-bitch, but Mikey Muscles was a good guy, with a couple of rescue dogs at home . . .

"Outside." Frankie waved his seven-inch Fixation Bowie knife in the direction of the door.

Jesus Christ. They weren't going to give him the mercy of a bullet to the head. It was going to be the fucking necktie like the Wolf. He wasn't afraid of the pain, but of Daisy one day reading the papers and knowing how her daddy died.

Forcing himself to be calm, he stepped out of the vehicle. He wouldn't run. He wouldn't beg. He had known the risks when he accepted the assignment. He would die with honor and pride, and the knowledge he was being punished for his betrayal.

"Here. Take these." Frankie offered him a pair of leather gloves.

Stunned, Ben just stared

"So you don't get prints on the gun."

Ben took the gloves and pulled them on, his mind spinning with possibilities. Was this a joke? A set up? Were they going to make him pull the trigger himself? Make it look like suicide?

Dare he hope?

Frankie handed him a 9mm Beretta. "Loaded. Serial number is gone. Can't be traced."

Ben's heart pounded, and he swallowed hard. "What's this all about?"

"Nico's opened his books. You got your contract," Frankie said. "You pull off this hit and you'll be allowed to go through the ceremony to become a made man."

God, no. He couldn't kill an innocent man. But if he refused to pull the trigger, Frankie would kill him. No questions asked.

"Who?"

Mikey Muscles patted him on the back. "Dante's bodyguard, Rev."

"The bartender is a friend of ours." Frankie sheathed his knife. "He says Rev is sitting at a table in the courtyard out back. We're gonna go in the front door, make our way through like nothing's going on. We get out back, you pop Rev, and we'll jump the fence."

"Are we whacking Rev to get to Dante? Is Dante inside?"

Frankie shook his head. "Rev's a threat to Nico. He's been asking around, trying to find places where Nico hangs out. He's gonna try and pop Nico before Nico pops Dante, and it's not gonna happen on my watch. He's also a drug trafficker who sold some bad shit to friends of mine and put them in an early grave. Bastard is a waste of space and the world will be a better place when he's gone."

Rev. Gabe. The man who'd got Ginger hooked on drugs so she couldn't be a mom to Daisy. The man who Ben was pretty damn sure had touched his little girl in a very bad way. And now Ben had a gun in his hand and it was going to be his life or the life of a piece of shit who deserved what was coming to him.

If he pulled the trigger, Daisy would be safe. He might be able to get Ginger clean. And there would be no threat to Nico. A criminal would have been brought to justice. But Ben would have crossed a line he thought he would never cross. He would become a made man.

"Nico wants this?" Although no stranger to violence, with a well-earned reputation for vicious and ruthless punishment of those who crossed him, Nico did not kill indiscriminately. Nor did he kill out of fear. Even if Rev was threat, this hit just wasn't Nico's style.

"Forget about it." Frankie brushed him off. "Nico's protection is the responsibility of this crew. You report to me and I'm telling you this isn't a fucking option. If you didn't want to be made, what the fuck have you been doing with the Toscanis for the last ten years, or with us for the last three?"

So Nico hadn't authorized the hit. Maybe that was his way out. Yes, he reported to Frankie because Frankie had recruited him, but he also worked with Nico directly. And if there was something he knew the boss wouldn't be happy about . . .

"You in, or are you dead?"

"Okay. Okay. Yeah, I'm in." He still had time to figure a way out—if he wanted a way out.

Mikey Muscles led them into the bar, a typical dingy

criminal hangout full of the worst elements of the Las Vegas underworld. The air was rank with the stench of hops, and unwashed bodies, and the screaming vocals of a death-metal song over the speakers drowned out all but the loudest of sounds. The bartender looked up from the worn, chipped bar, and nodded to the back.

"I see him," Mikey Muscles mumbled when they reached the back room. "He's at a table against the wall, facing the door. "He's gonna see us in 3 . . . 2 . . . 1." He stepped to the side and Ben lifted his gun.

Rev jumped up, his eyes darting from Ben to Frankie and Mikey Muscles, and back to Ben. He frowned, and then the bastard smiled. "So are you or are you not a cop?"

Ben thought about how proud he'd been to take his oath when he joined the police. How he was going to make the world a better place, just like his dad. He thought about walking the beat and seeing the same faces doing the same things day after day. He thought about the thrill of getting his undercover assignment, his enthusiasm for bringing Santo down, and his growing disillusionment when the department wouldn't act on the information he had given them.

He thought about ten years of anxiety-ridden days and sweat-soaked nights, and the day he'd joined Nico's crew and discovered a man who shared his moral compass, but who stood on the other side of the line. He thought about Ginger on the couch and Daisy in his arms, and he understood now what Kat had tried to say. After ten years in the mob, he couldn't see the lines.

He was walking in shades of gray.

TWENTY-FOUR

Thump. Thump. Thump. Mia knocked on the door of the Toscani clubhouse. She could see lights inside through the frosted-glass windows, hear the bass pounding through the walls, and see the shadows of mobsters enjoying their evening relaxation. They knew she was here. She knew they were there. But they weren't opening the damn door.

She contemplated trying to crawl in the bathroom window she'd escaped through four weeks ago, but she didn't want catching a mobster with his pants down, and getting in was going to be a hell of a lot harder than getting out.

"I don't think they want to see us," whispered Jules.

"They're just worried we're cops. Usually, the only women who would dare come to the clubhouse are hookers."

Jules gave her a wicked grin and yelled through the door. "Hey, in there. We're having a special tonight. Twenty for oral with a condom. Thirty without. One hundred for an hour and that's a deal because minimum at a brothel is one-fifty. And we call you Daddy for free."

"Oh. My. God. I can't believe you just did that." Mia

covered her mouth with her hand. "Prostitution is illegal in Nevada unless you're in a licensed brothel."

"Hacking into your husband's phone to find out his location is also illegal, but I didn't see you even batting an eye about doing that," Jules shot back. "How's that black hat feeling today?"

Mia dropped her hand. "It wasn't really a black hat hack. I was doing it for a good reason, so I'd say it's in the gray."

"It's illegal. Therefore, it's black. Your Mafioso husband has turned you to the dark side."

A deadbolt thudded and the heavy steel door opened a crack. "How much for an hour ungloved?"

Jules grabbed the door and pulled it open. "How about you go tell Nico you just asked his wife for an hour of ungloved sex?"

"Shit." A short dude wearing a wife beater vest and sporting a bad toupee stepped to the side, and Mia walked into the clubhouse with Jules at her heels. Almost instantly, all activity stopped, chatter died down, and the music faded away. Mafiosos of all shapes and sizes turned to look at them, and Mia shivered with the memory of the last time she was here.

"I'm looking for Nico."

Silence.

Jules nudged her in the back.

"I'm Mia."

"His wife," Jules added. "Mrs. Nico Toscani. And if you don't believe me, check out her ring."

Moments later Mia was surrounded by respectful well-wishers showering her with congratulations and kissing her cheeks. The man who had propositioned them at the door slithered away, and another mobster led them to the back of the clubhouse.

"That actually went better than I thought it would,"

Jules said. It was either get their respect and have them lead us to Nico, or death."

Nico was on the phone in a small office behind the pool table. Mia left Jules with Luca and Frankie, who were shooting a game, and sat in the seat across Nico's desk. He looked up, his face expressionless, as he listened to the person on the other end of the phone.

Mia mouthed a "hello," and Nico stood and walked to the other side of the room, his voice dropping to a hushed whisper. She caught the words hospital and surgery, but not much else.

He had taken off his jacket and tie and rolled up his shirtsleeves. Mia remembered how distracted she had been looking at his forearms when he helped her fix the car. She had never imagined that all her fantasies about him that day would come true. Or all her nightmares.

After he ended the call, he stayed at the far end of the room, staring out the window. For a man who was constantly in motion, his stillness alarmed her. She could see the stress etched in the lines on his face, the set of his jaw, and the lift of his shoulders. She could feel his pain. "Is everything all right?"

"It's business."

Her heart ached at his dismissive tone. She hoped she wouldn't add to his problems with what she had come here to do, although if she were honest with herself, it was just an excuse to see him.

"I came to return this." She pulled off the ring and placed it on his desk beside his silver pen as he turned to face her. "I don't feel right keeping it. And frankly, I'm relieved. It was so huge I felt like I was going to be jumped any minute by someone with a chain saw prepared to cut off my hand to get it."

She saw the faintest quiver of a smile, and then his face

went blank again. "It was temporary. Something I had lying around."

"Yeah, I have fifty-thousand-dollar engagement rings lying around my house, too, although I can't find them under the pizza boxes." Mia forced a laugh, although she could barely breathe for the tension in the room. Why the hell had she come? Jules had pumped her up with her rah rah speech, but now that she was sitting in front of the man who felt betrayed by her choices, she could see it was a huge mistake. She hadn't expected him to forgive her, and he clearly wasn't happy to have her here.

"I guess I'd better go. Jules is outside, probably causing trouble." She stood and walked to the door.

"If I'd had the chance, I would have picked something different for you," Nico said into the silence. "Platinum, not gold."

"Maybe some skulls on it?" she suggested, as a glimmer of hope flickered in her chest.

"Something unconventional. A bit of a steampunk design, with a black diamond in the center and pink ones on either side."

Emotion welled up in her throat. "Sounds very specific."

"It was."

"Well, now you can buy a dozen rings." She stared at the ring on the desk, already missing the connection it represented.

He crossed the floor to the desk, and picked up the pen. "I only need one."

"For your fiancée?" Embarrassed she put up her hand. "Don't answer that. It's not my business. I just came to return the ring and to tell you I'm sorry. I didn't get a chance to tell you before. But I am deeply sorry. It was an impossible choice. My brother isn't a good person.

He's weak and self-centered and cruel, and he did you a terrible, unspeakable, unforgiveable wrong that hurts my heart just thinking about it. But he is my brother, and although I think he should pay for what he did, I couldn't just offer him up to you on a silver platter. You said you were willing to put aside the vendetta against my father; I hoped you would extend that forgiveness to Dante. Death isn't the only way to get justice."

Nico flipped the pen around his thumb. "You didn't give me the choice."

"I know. And you deserved to have that choice. But I couldn't take the risk. I hope one day you can forgive me."

"You didn't trust me." He picked up the ring and put it in his pocket.

"I trusted you with me. I don't think you would ever hurt me. But no, I didn't trust you with Dante's life. Your reputation precedes you."

"So loyal." He stared at her intently as the pen twirled. "I wouldn't need an alliance if all my men were as loyal as you."

"They are." She gave him a quizzical look. "From what I've seen and heard, they admire and respect you, and they are proud to be part of your crew."

"Apparently not all of them." His corded throat tightened when he swallowed. "I have my own impossible choice to make."

Mia had never seen him so conflicted. She ached to hold him, but he'd taken the ring and made it clear that what they had was over. Giving him physical comfort wasn't the right thing to do. He wasn't hers any more. And she wasn't his. "I'm sorry, Nico."

"So the fuck am I."

She pulled a real estate brochure from her purse and dropped it on his desk, her far-reaching attempt to make good the damage she had done. "Here's something that might cheer you up. The Desert Dream is going up for sale."

When he didn't respond, she pushed it toward him. "It was one of the Rat Pack's favorite hotels and one of the last old Vegas-meets-Hollywood hotels left."

His jaw tightened. "I know what it is."

"It's going up for auction." She hesitated, waited for him to fill in the blanks, but he said nothing. Just stared at her as if she were trying to memorize everything about her, as she was trying to memorize him. After all, she didn't know if she would ever see him again.

"I know the realtor because his daughter is in my coding class," she continued. "It would be a shame if someone bought it and tore it down. It's Dante's favorite place to game. He's got a bit of a gambling problem. My father used to get so angry. Dante isn't very good with numbers and he would lose big. Really big. At one point he was so heavily indebted to one of Tony's bookies, my father had to whack the bookie to clear the debt before Tony found out. That's when he hired Rev. He said it was to guard Dante, but really, it was to keep him away from the tables. He was afraid Dante would ruin the family."

Silence.

Mia gritted her teeth. Either he wasn't understanding what she was trying to say, or he was still determined to put a bullet through Dante's heart. She didn't know what else she could do aside from spelling it out for him. Old Vegas hotel. Real estate deal. A casino. Dante's big weakness. A way to avenge his father without spilling blood. Justice. Everything he could want in one neat package. And Dante, although he didn't deserve it and would pay a heavy price, would be saved.

"I'd better go." She walked to the door and looked back over her shoulder. "It's a closed-bid auction. Apparently, the bids are submitted electronically and the computer spits out a winner."

There. She couldn't be clearer than that. He knew what she did for a living. She could hack the system and tell him the highest bid and he could bid higher. If he owned the casino he could let Dante run up his credit until the amount he owed was so high, Nico could take over his assets. He could ruin him financially. Maybe even the family, too. It wasn't black-hat hacking she was offering to do for him, just a shade of gray.

"Vito, get me a meeting with the realtor who's dealing with the sale of the Desert Dream Hotel." Nico stalked through his casino, barking orders at Vito over his shoulder.

"Yes, sir."

"Book it at Il Tavolino. Tell Lennie we'll be coming."

"Yes, sir."

"Louis reported a huge increase in the number of low-level drug dealers coming into the casino. Any idea what's attracting them? Or who?"

"No, sir, but I'll ask around." Vito pulled out a dove-gray handkerchief and mopped his brow. Nico had never seen Vito sweat. He'd never seen him ruffled or flustered in any way. He was always impeccably, albeit oddly, dressed in his silver-and gray suits, his hair perfectly coiffed, gray shoes polished to a shine. Maybe Nico was asking too much of him. Working him too hard. He had been an associate with Nico's crew for six years and a good casino manager, although Nico didn't think he had what it took to become a made man

"Are you sending any associates to deal with them?" Vito ran the handkerchief around the back of his neck.

Ah. That was it. Vito already had a heavy workload,

and policing the low-level dealers would stretch him too thin. Nico made a mental note to hire an assistant to give Vito a hand. "I'll send a few, but we need to find the source of the problem. And we need to find it before I buy the Desert Dream. I don't want any carry over."

Although Nico understood that Mia was willing to hack the realtor's database to find the highest offer, there was no way he was letting a woman get involved in family business. And especially not his woman. It was his job to protect her. He had ways of getting information that didn't involve his wife putting herself at risk or crossing a line she never wanted to cross. He hadn't decided if he would play Dante the way she suggested, but he certainly wasn't giving up the opportunity to purchase an iconic hotel.

"Where are Frankie and Luca?"

"Craps table, sir." Vito pointed out Frankie and Luca, who were at the center of a big crowd. No doubt Luca was on a roll again. He had a lucky streak when it came to dice. Nico just wished he would play that lucky streak somewhere else.

He groaned inwardly when he saw Luca's rack of chips. Every time he got lucky he threw his cash around like it was going out of style. One day he was going to attract the wrong kind of attention and he and Frankie wouldn't be there to save him.

After discussing more issues with Vito, he joined the crowd at the craps table. Frankie was playing it out on the pass-line bet, a safe strategy and one that had the best odds to win.

"What's happening with the capos?" he asked quietly.

Frankie stepped back, away from the crowd. "We've got five capos who are gonna vote between you and Tony on Sunday after church. You also get a vote, and Charlie Nails breaks a tie. We got four for you and one against if you can bring the Cordano alliance to the table."

A cheer rose up and the dealer pushed a stack of chips in Luca's direction.

"What if I don't bring the alliance?" Nico had been mulling over the alliance for the last few days. His personal issues aside, the Cordanos were not a good fit with the Toscanis, at least not the way Nico wanted to run things. They were heavily into the drug trade and he was determined not to go down that road. It was an easy temptation, his father had said, but easy money came with big risks.

Frankie lifted an eyebrow. "Without the alliance then you've got one vote for sure, maybe two on your side. The drug operation is a big earner and the kick-backs are gonna be hard for the capos to give up."

"If the vote doesn't go our way, I may have to break with the family," he said. "I'm not getting involved in the drug trade. There are too many players—triads, cartels, street gangs, Russians, Albanians—everyone wanting a piece of the pie. The feds will be all over us. And the risks of a long jail sentence will tear the family apart. You tell a guy he's got a choice of twenty years in lock-up or ratting out his crew, guess which road he's gonna take?"

He'd thought long and hard about his position after finding out the entire administration of the Las Vegas faction of the Cordano family had no honor. Nico had a solid crew. Loyal men—all but one. And a growing empire that now boasted fifty percent legitimate enterprise. Yes, he still thirsted for vengeance, but Mia had made him see how empty his life had become in the pursuit of that goal, and how tradition could be at once a comfort and burden. He could look ahead and not back, forge a new path. And if that meant breaking with the family to save them, then that's what he would do.

"Where you go, I go," Frankie said. "You need someone at your back even when you don't know you need
someone at your back."

They shared a glance, and Nico felt a tightening in his
chest. He still had to deal with Big Joe. And he couldn't
put it off much longer. Damn Frankie and his over-
protective nature.

Frankie had gone off the record and given Big Joe a
contract to whack Rev. It was meant to be a pre-emptive
strike to protect Nico. Frankie had heard rumblings in the
underground that Don Cordano had a contract out on
Nico, and Rev was his first choice for the job.

But Big Joe had fucked it up, freezing when he should
have pulled the trigger. Rev got away but not before calling Big Joe out as a cop. Big Joe had an easy explanation—
the cover he'd given his ex, now Rev's girlfriend, to get
her off his back—but the whole situation didn't sit right
with Nico. He needed to call Big Joe in to get to the bottom of it, but part of him didn't want to know if it was
true.

He liked Big Joe. Trusted him. Considered him a
friend. Before talking to him, he needed to have settled
in his mind what he would do if Big Joe was a cop. Don
Cordano clearly had no compunction ordering the traditional *Cosa Nostra* punishment for the Wolf, and over the
years, Nico had handed out his fair of Sicilian neckties.
But ten years of pursuing vengeance for his father had
almost cost Nico his soul. What would it cost him to have
to punish one of his closest friends, too?

After another ten painful minutes watching Luca rake
in more chips to the adulation of the drunken crowd, Nico
left the casino. He drove aimlessly up and down the
streets of Vegas, heading anywhere but the cold, austere
hotel penthouse he called home. When he finally wound
up outside Mia's apartment, he realized this was where

he'd been going all along. Despite everything that had happened, he needed her. Despite the pain he felt, he wanted her. She moved his soul and filled his heart and gave meaning to a life he had lost to revenge.

For ten years, Nico had buried his needs beneath layers of self-control. But Mia had stripped those layers one by one, laying him bare. Open. Vulnerable. Able to love.

He needed her support and her strength. Her caring and compassion. He needed the connection that calmed the beast, and made him feel whole. He needed to forgive and forget so he could see a clear path when it came time to face betrayal again.

He loved her. And he needed her to know.

Mia woke to a hand over her mouth. She drew in a deep breath to scream, and Nico murmured in her ear.

"Shh, *bella*. It's me."

Heart pounding, she clawed his hand away, trying to make out his face in the semi-darkness. With her mind still hazy from sleep, she had a split second of terror, wondering if he had come to punish her for betraying him. But when he stretched out on the bed, gently pulled her into his arms, she knew it wasn't pain he had come to give her.

"Kat is sleeping on the couch," she whispered. "The walls are so thin she'll be able to hear everything."

"*Ho bisogno di te*—I need you," he whispered.

He needed her. Nico Toscani—ruthless mobster, fearsome warrior, powerful capo—needed her. "I'm here for you, Mr. Mob Boss."

Mia rested her head on his chest, listened to the steady thump of his heart beneath the soft cotton of his T-shirt, breathed in the familiar scent of his cologne, and soaked up the warmth of the man who had been her husband for three short days.

He stroked his hand through her hair, down her back to the edge of her nightshirt, and then up again. Outside, she could hear the occasional rumble of a truck driving past, the bang of a car door, and the faint sound of music from one of the apartments downstairs.

Up and down. Up and down. Always to the edge of her nightshirt where it curled over her ass, pausing for a moment, and back again, as if he were trying to make a decision.

"The day my father died, we went to Prezzo for lunch," he said softly. "He ordered so much food, but he only ate the *pasta alla norma* and the *caponata*. He loved eggplant. I could never understand it. There is no vegetable I detest more. But we shared a sweet tooth and we finished a plate of cannoli between us."

Wary of interrupting, Mia relaxed against him, not wanting to push him further than he was ready to go.

"He showed me his pen and he told me the history of how it had passed down through our family from father to son when the son became a made man. He told me he knew one day the pen would come to me. He said it represented a commitment to honor tradition and to protect the family, and that a good leader, a good man, was one who could put his duty to his family above desire. There was nothing in life I wanted more than to please him. There was nobody I respected and admired more. But always in the back of my mind, I wondered if the price of holding that pen was too high, because after my mother died, he wasn't the same man."

Finally, his hand dipped lower, stroked the curve of her ass, and then up again. Her heart skipped a beat, anticipation or fear, she wasn't sure which.

"After he died, I thought of nothing but the weight of

his body in my arms, and the warmth of his blood as it ran over my hands. Revenge sustained me. It was the only reason I got up in the morning; it helped me make it through every day; it gave me something to live for. But I didn't realize it was all I lived for. Not until I met you."

Mia's breath hitched. She had never imagined a man like Nico could bare his very soul. Or that he would trust her with such a precious gift.

"*Sei tutto per me*—You are everything to me," he murmured, his Italian rolling over her in a soft caress. "I'm willing to put down that burden to be with you. I will find another way to restore the family honor." This time he tugged the nightshirt up, his hand smoothing over her skin, in and out of her curves, beneath the elastic of her panties.

Need heated her blood like a fever. She stretched and nuzzled his neck, tasting the salt on his skin, moaned softly in his ear.

"Shhh." He helped her slide the nightshirt over her head, and drew her down again until she lay on top of him. She shivered as her taut nipples brushed against his T-shirt, her hips pressed against the sharp edges of his belt, his hard length nestled firmly between her thighs.

She pushed herself up and stared at him, lost herself in the darkness of his eyes. Gently, she grazed his lower lip with the edge of her teeth. With a low groan, he brought his mouth up to hers, hard and hungry, his tongue thrusting inside.

He tasted strongly of the Johnnie Walker he loved to drink, sweet and spicy, dry and bitter, and she drew him in deeper, tangling her tongue with his, meeting each one of his strokes with her own. She'd missed him. Kissing him was like tasting him all over again.

He was bold, demanding, his fingers in her hair holding her in place, his tongue sweeping her mouth, claiming every inch with the ruthlessness of the mob boss he was.

Tremors of excitement rippled through her body. The silence of their encounter, secret, forbidden, stoked a fire inside her. She gave herself over to the sensation of his hot, wet mouth on hers, the rock and grind of his pelvis, the grip of his hand on the soft cheeks of her ass.

If he wanted to share his pain, she would welcome it. If he wanted to give her his body, she would open herself up and let him in.

With a low groan, he rolled until she lay on her back beneath him. Nico knelt between her parted legs, drank in her body like he was dying of thirst. His big hand cupped her wrists and pinned them to the bed above her head. She writhed in his grasp, fighting the pull of desire, his powerful grip. But he would not yield. He had bared himself to her, but he was still firmly in control.

With one leg between her thighs he leaned over and closed his mouth over her nipple, sucking with hard pulls of his mouth. She felt each exquisite tug low in her belly and arched her back, savoring the connection she felt when she was with him, that sense of rightness she'd experienced the first time they met.

He pressed her breasts together, licked one nipple and then the other, teasing them both until dampness trickled between her legs. Just when she thought she couldn't take anymore, he slid down, nibbling and kissing her stomach until she bucked her hips, trying to get him to the place she wanted to go.

With one hand still holding her wrists, Nico knelt between her legs and ran his thumb between the seam of her lips.

She licked his thumb, drew it into her mouth, sucked it deep to show him what she wanted to do, how she could take away his pain.

A low, husky growl rumbled through his chest. He stepped off the bed, and stripped off his clothes with quick efficiency. But when she sat up, moved to the edge of the bed, intending to make good the promise of her mouth, he pressed her back on the soft covers and positioned himself between her parted thighs.

Yield to me, his body silently demanded.

She yielded with a sigh, lay back, and opened herself to the most feared mobster in Vegas.

With gentle fingers he stroked along the sides of her labia, slicking her moisture up and around her clit. Her hips shifted restlessly on the bed, and she moaned, urging him toward her entrance. Nico settled between her thighs, his broad shoulders pushing her legs apart, his breath hot with promise. Mia threaded her fingers through his hair pushing him down with a silent plea.

He kissed her deeply, intimately, his tongue pushing inside her. She gasped and bucked against him, giving herself over to the pleasure of his sensual mouth. Lifting her hips, he took her to the brink as he licked and sucked, alternating deep thrusts of his tongue in her center, with butterfly touches over her clit. Her every muscle trembled with anticipation, her stomach tied in knots.

She felt his thick finger open her, sliding in slowly, torturing her with pleasure. Her legs shook uncontrollably and he added a second finger, drove into her hard and fast. Her ass pushed off the bed, and she strained toward him, hunger driving her out of control.

He pressed her back down, holding her in place. His fingers plunged in and out; his tongue rubbed hard and fast, sending her higher and higher, her arousal peaking just as he sucked her clit into his mouth.

She broke the silence with his name on her lips, undulating against him as pulse after pulse of pleasure sparked through her body, draining her of tension, stripping her of need, drugging her with passion.

He was up and on his knees before she had a chance to come down, reaching for a condom. Mia lay panting beneath him, drenched in sweat, her heart pounding beneath her ribs. She loved how he made her feel vulnerable and strong at the same time. Loved the silence of this encounter where he told her with his body what he couldn't say in words.

Sheathing himself quickly, he leaned over and took her mouth in a fierce kiss—tongues clashing, teething banging, hunger raging out of control—as he positioned himself on the bed. Lifting her legs easily to his shoulders, he thrust hard and fast into the wetness of her folds. Mia's pussy clenched at the intimate invasion, and a groan came from deep within her at the renewed rush of sensation as his thick cock pushed through her sensitive tissue.

With slow, measured strokes, Nico withdrew and thrust again, his muscles taut, chest slick with sweat, biceps straining as if he were struggling for control. Her head rolled from side to side, hips lifting, her body trembling as he gave her his power with the lightest of touch.

Wanton hunger burned through her, her lower body tight with need as her arousal shot higher and harder than before. Finally, he increased his speed, his balls slapping against her pussy with each hard thrust. Her legs quivered. Her body shuddered. She couldn't move and yet she felt empowered. Her mob boss had come to her. He needed her. And she wanted to give him the pleasure of her body, as she took her own pleasure from him.

With each merciless thrust, his powerful muscles bunched, his breathing labored, and yet his gaze never left hers.

Her climax came in an explosion of sensation, all the

more intense for the connection she felt as he watched her come apart around him.

"Mine." With a growling roar of pleasure, he hammered into her until he released, his cock throbbing inside her, pulsing as he came.

He collapsed on top of her, taking his weight on his arms as he feathered kisses along her jaw. She wrapped her arms around his body, desperate to keep the deep connection between them—the one she thought they had lost but now she hoped could be saved.

With one last soft kiss, he eased away to dispose of the condom. He returned to the bed moments later, pulling her against him to lie just as they had before.

"*Ti adoro,*" he murmured. "*Il mio cuore è solo tua*— My heart is yours."

"*Ti amo,* Nico." Mia drifted off to sleep soothed by the gentle rise and fall of his chest, the strength of his arms, the warmth of his body, and the soft murmur of his voice as he told her how he felt in the language of love.

When she woke the next morning, he was gone. Only the dent in the pillow beside her showed he'd been there at all. But his words stayed warm in her heart. She just wished it could be forever.

TWENTY-FIVE

Mia knocked on her father's office door. She hadn't been surprised to receive the summons after teaching her class at the community center. After all, she had brought her new husband home when her father wasn't around.

"I'll be right outside." Kat gave her a hug. She had returned home with Mia, worried about their mother being left alone. "If anything happens, I'll call Big Joe and he'll send Nico."

"Big Joe?" Mia gave her sister a puzzled glance.

Kat blushed. "He was so nice when I was at his place. It wasn't like being guarded. It was like finding a new friend. When I left, he gave me his number and he told me to call if I needed him."

"He has a little girl," Mia warned her. "And some messy ex drama going on. He's also a lot older than you. And in the mob. And there's also something else about him you should know."

"You're beginning to sound like Mama." Kat gave an exasperated sigh. "I'm nineteen, Mia. I understand the danger. But sometimes you can't help who you fall for, and when you do, the baggage doesn't matter."

"Come."

Mia swallowed hard at the sound of her father's voice. "Wish me luck."

"You don't need luck," Kat said. "You have strength. You have me. And now, you have Nico."

Heart pounding, Mia opened the door and walked into her father's office. This time there was no fire in the fireplace, although the curtains were still drawn. He had two guards with him she didn't recognize, and he was seated, as usual, behind his desk.

"I hear you married Nico Toscani." His dark eyes blazed as anger crept over his face.

"Yes."

"I'm not a fool, Mia. I know you did it to get out of the marriage to his cousin. You're a stupid girl if you thought you could defy me." He scrawled on a piece of paper in front of him, as if their conversation was nothing more than an idle chat.

"You're partly right." She straightened her shoulders. "At first, I did it so I didn't have to marry Tony, and to save Kat from any more of your abuse, but I cared for him when I married him, and now I love him. So if you think I'm going to agree to have the marriage annulled, think again. As with all *Cosa Nostra* marriages, it is forever."

"Forever only lasts until one of you is dead." He looked up and held her frozen with the cruel smile on his lips. "That gives you about one hour to enjoy your marital bliss."

Dread crept over her, leaving goose bumps in its wake. "What are you going to do?"

He gave her a haughty smirk. "The question is not what I am going to do, it's what have I done? I've sent someone to deal with the problem. I can't run a business when Dante is being chased around the city by that Toscani bastard who just can't give up the pathetic vendetta that he's clung to for ten fucking years." His calm facade slipped and he pounded his fist on the desk. "Nor will I tolerate being disrespected by my own daughter who is determined to dishonor the family."

"You put a contract on him?"

Her father laughed. "I didn't just put a contract on him; I baited him. I've turned his fucking quest for revenge against him. I've sent him around the city hunting down false leads on Dante, and tonight I'll put him out of his misery. He knows where Dante is, and he's on his way to whack him. Except Dante isn't the one who's going to be whacked. And just to be sure nothing goes wrong, I've enlisted some help. I'm not the only one who benefits if Nico Toscani is dead. The rest of his family wants rid of him, too."

She stared at him aghast. "You're working with Tony?"

"Soon to be my new son-in-law, and a man who shares my vision for how to make *Cosa Nostra* great again in Vegas."

Fury rose up in her chest like a fireball. "If you hurt him, I will destroy you. Everything you've built, everything you have, I'll take it away. I won't rest until you are nothing."

"Another vendetta." Her father raised an idle hand. "I am not afraid of you, Mia. You're a woman, and for some reason you've never been able to accept that. You are no threat to me. I am bigger than you, stronger than you, and more powerful than you can ever imagine. I've known you since the day you were born, and although you were desperate to prove yourself to me, your compassion was a fatal flaw. You would never be able to pull a trigger and take a man's life. And until you do, you will never be enough; you will never be worthy of my respect; you will never be as good as a son."

For some reason, his words didn't hurt her like they

usually did. Yes, she was a woman. And she had never realized just how strong a woman could be until she met Nico again. In the last few weeks, she had learned how to embrace what it meant to be a woman, and she had found a man who accepted her and loved her for who she was.

"I don't want your respect," she spat out. "And especially not if you measure a man's worth by his ability to take a life." Her hands balled into fists so tight her nails dug into her palms. "Character makes a man, not the circumstances of his birth or the power he holds or his ability to shoot a gun. It's about the choices you make and how you treat people around you; it's about the mercy you show when you've been wronged and the things you do when no one is around to see. You have no character. There is nothing about you I respect or admire. I don't care what you think of me anymore, because I think nothing of you."

She moved to leave, and one of the guards grabbed her arms. Before she could stop him, he snapped a pair of handcuffs around her wrists.

"What is this? What are you doing?" She tried to run but the guard grabbed her and forced her back down into the chair.

"You'll stay here until I get word that our little problem has been solved," her father said. Then you'll get ready for your wedding tomorrow. Tony and I didn't see any reason to waste time." He gestured to the guards. "Tie her to the chair. One of you comes with me. The other stays outside the door and guards her." He looked over at Mia and smiled. "I can honestly say nothing will please me more than giving you the fuck away at your wedding."

"We've got a location on Dante." Luca burst into Nico's casino office, uncharacteristically breathless, with Vito on his heels.

"I told everyone to stand down." Nico had stopped the hunt after spending the night with Mia, resolved to find a way to fulfill the family honor without spilling her brother's blood.

"We did. But Frankie got a tip and he called Vito to check it out. Dante's here. In the high stakes gaming room. Frankie's on his way."

Nico leaned back in his chair. Out of habit, he reached for his pen, but he had put it away last night as a statement to himself that he was letting his father go and moving on with a life that was more than a quest for revenge. "Is he fucking crazy? Why would he take such a risk when he knows there's a contract on him? I thought he'd hit the mattresses."

"He's got a gambling problem," Vito said, smoothing down his silvery suit jacket and crisp gray tie. "All the casino managers in the city know about him. There aren't many bookies who will deal with him because when he runs up the debts too high Don Cordano sends out one of his enforcers to clear them off, if you know what I mean."

"That's bad business."

Luca shrugged. "He's only got one son. What's he gonna do?"

Nico's father only had one son, and he'd expected him to fill his shoes by following the family traditions, as his father had followed before him. But now Nico had found the other half of his soul, the missing piece of his life. He was forging his own path—maybe even his own faction of the Toscani family—and he had resolved to find another way to make Dante pay for his crime.

Still, the man who had killed his father was sitting downstairs in his casino and it was too great a temptation to ignore.

"It's got to be a trap." Nico twisted his lips to the side. "Is he alone?"

"Yes, sir," Vito said. "I checked the security cameras after Frankie called. He came in alone and went straight to the high-stakes room where's he's been playing black-jack for the last hour. The other players at the table are regulars. I know them well."

"What about the facial-recognition database? Did it pick up any known Cordano associates?"

Vito shook his head. "No, sir. Nothing. We comped him the usual drinks, and he's almost made his way through a bottle of bourbon. He wasn't interested in food or the girls we sent over. Is it possible he doesn't know you own the casino?"

"Possible, but unlikely." Nico clicked to the live security feed on his computer and zoomed in on the high-stakes room. His eye-in-the-sky was so high-tech, he could watch the movements of the dealers' hands. The dealers were often the biggest cheaters in the casino, lured by the easy access to money and the distraction of the crowds.

He recognized Dante right away, studied his bloodshot eyes, the stubble on his chin. He looked like a man on self-destruct. If he really wanted to die, he had come to the right place.

Nico checked the weapon in his holster and pulled on his jacket. "Let's go."

"Maybe we should wait for Frankie." Luca checked his phone. "He texted to say he's on his way. Should be only twenty minutes."

"Dante might be gone in twenty minutes." Nico still hadn't decided what he was going to do when he met Dante face to face, this time knowing he had killed Nico's father. "Vito, call downstairs and make sure we have ex-tra security in the high-stakes room. Get them to clear everyone out except the players at Dante's table."

"Yes, sir. I'll go ahead and make sure everything is ready for you. Do you want the cameras off in that room?"

"Yes, turn them off. Louis is in charge of the control room tonight. Let him know what's going on."

"Very good, sir." Vito patted down his fluff of silver hair as he hurried from Nico's office.

"Luca, you've got my back." He stood, a brief image of Mia flickering through his mind. He still wanted her on this desk. Maybe when all this was done, he'd make every goddamned fantasy he'd had the first time she walked into his office come true.

"I always have your back." Luca followed him out of the office. "I might not be able to stop you from making stupid mistakes, but I can promise you won't face the consequences alone."

"That's fucking beautiful," Nico said dryly, looking over his shoulder.

Luca grinned. "Kinda like me."

TWENTY-SIX

"Jesus Christ, what a mess." Jack stepped to the side of the porch as the paramedics carried Ginger's body from the house. The forensics team had left a short while ago, and Ben had just been given clearance to go back inside.

Ben glanced over at the vehicle where Daisy was huddled in the backseat with her blanket. He'd made her promise to look at her storybook until he told her to lift her head. He didn't want her last memory of her mother to be of the ambulance attendants wheeling a body bag out on a stretcher.

"I'm sorry, Ben." Jack gave Ben an awkward pat on the back as they walked into the living room, where he'd found Ginger dead on the couch. Although they would have to wait for the autopsy results, the forensics team had been pretty certain she'd overdosed on the same tainted product that had recently flooded the streets.

"I feel bad that she's gone and Daisy's got no mom, but other than that she wasn't anything to me. And I'm fucking pissed at Rev for giving her that tainted shit." Ben shrugged Jack away. "Christ, Jack. If I'd put a bullet through him when I had the chance, this wouldn't have happened. I still think something was going on with him and Daisy. The bastard deserved to die."

"Don't say that." Jack stared out the window as the ambulance drove away. "You did the right thing. He wasn't a threat to you or anyone else at that moment. And, he probably didn't even know the drugs he'd bought Ginger were tainted. We've had a surge of calls about overdoses in the last few weeks from a lethal batch of drugs that came into the city—a toxic cocktail of fentanyl and other opiates. We had twenty-four overdoses in the first twenty-four hours, and the numbers are climbing."

"Nico still hasn't called me in." Ben stepped back into the doorway. "But when he does, it's gonna be the end of me." The call in was a formal order for a made man to report to his superiors, usually so he could be disciplined—in other words clipped. Ben wasn't made, but Frankie had used the terminology when he'd ordered him to stay in Vegas until Nico contacted him, so he figured the end result would be the same.

"The offer is still there to pull you out. You've got a little girl to think about and now she has no mom. I've talked to a judge and it's a simple formality now for you to have custody. She can go with you wherever you go."

Ben shook his head. "I'm not gonna be able to play happy families in suburbia when I'm constantly looking over my shoulder, sleeping with a fucking gun under my pillow, worrying about whether the guy across the street already washed his car yesterday, or whether that plumber's carrying a wrench or an assault rifle. You run from the Mafia and they assume you're guilty, so I know how that's gonna end. One day, a Chrysler 300C pulls up outside the door, two guys run in, pop pop, I'm dead, and Daisy's an orphan if they even let her live. What we talked about earlier is a better plan. Daisy stays with you and your wife, goes to the same school, sees the same friends, and

I take my chances with Nico. If it turns out bad, I've got an aunt in Florida who says she can take Daisy."

"How good are those odds if he finds out you've been undercover for ten years?" Jack turned back to Ben and folded his arms.

"He'll only care about the three years I was in his crew," Ben said, his watchful gaze on Daisy. "And I'm gonna let him know I didn't rat on him. He never got involved with drug trafficking, Jack. No prostitution. No human trafficking. No arms trading. He runs a clean casino. I'm not saying he hasn't crossed the line. I'm not saying he isn't a criminal—he's probably got one of the highest body counts in the city. And the things he's done to the people that crossed him—well, they scare the shit out of me. But he's fair, and there are lines he won't cross. He's not a fucking murderer like Tony, who kills just for the sake of killing. Nico's a bad guy who only whacks bad guys. He's no saint, but he's no sinner either."

"Are you trying to convince me or yourself?"

Good question. He had struggled for the last three years about the line between good and bad. How could he think of Nico as a good man when he made his living breaking the law? What was bad and what was good? Was a man who was honorable and respectable, who protected his family and stuck up for his friends, a bad man because he killed bad guys and ran protection rackets to keep the people in his territory safe? Ben didn't know anymore. All he knew was what felt right to him. Shooting Rev when he wasn't doing anything wrong didn't feel right. Just as leaving town without talking to Nico didn't feel right either.

"I dunno. That guy they found, the Wolf . . . the Cordanos gave him a traditional Sicilian necktie 'cause they found out he was a rat. Feds caught him smuggling cocaine and they offered him a deal—wear a wire or twenty years in jail. I'm not partial to neckties, but Nico . . . he kinda likes them, but only if someone's truly been a rat. And I didn't rat—at least not on his crew."

"I knew there was a reason you weren't filing the reports." Jack walked along the porch; dodging the broken tricycle Ben might never get a chance to fix. "So you're just going to hope he lets you off with a warning?"

"I'm gonna hope he lets me off with my hands and feet still attached. He caught this one dealer stealing from him, got a sledgehammer, and . . ." He trailed off, not wanting to give Jack any information that could be used to implicate Nico in a crime. "I know him like a brother," he continued. "He's changed over the last few weeks since he met Mia, chilled out a bit. I just pray some of that chilling rubs off on me."

He walked into Daisy's bedroom and packed her few clothes into a bag. On his way out, he grabbed one of her stuffed toys, a purple puppy with a large belly. It was surprisingly heavy and he put it back on the bed and lifted another, frowning at the weight. Curious, he lifted the toys one by one; noting they all had a similar weight. He pulled out his knife and sliced one open.

"Jack," he called out. "Get in here. I got something." He held up a brick of heroin as Jack walked in. "I think they're in all her toys. Might be the lethal batch that's just hit the streets. I'm gonna go find out if Daisy knew about it." He grabbed one of the toys and jogged out to the car where Daisy was still reading her book.

"Can I look up now, Daddy?"

"Yeah, sweetheart. I'm sorry I forgot about you there." He held up the toy. "Do you know anything about the packages inside these toys?"

Daisy's eyes went wide. "It's supposed to be a secret. Gabe said he would hurt me and Mommy if I told anyone. He used to come into my room at night and tell Mommy he was reading me a story, but he was really cutting up my toys and putting bricks in them. I couldn't play with them anymore, and he shouted really loud when I touched them. I felt lonely in my room when I couldn't touch my toys. I didn't have anything to cuddle at night, and I didn't want to be there alone."

Ben felt at once relieved that his worst nightmare hadn't come true, and angry that Gabe would use his daughter's toys—the toys he'd bought for her—as a place to stash his drugs. "Do you know what he did with them?"

Daisy nodded. "He gave them to his friend who came to visit all the time. They thought I wasn't listening, but I was because I liked to say good-bye to the toys Gabe's friend took away."

Ben felt the skin on the back of his neck prickle. "Did you ever see his friend? Do you remember what he looked like?"

"Yes. He was silver."

"Help!" Mia screamed as she rocked back and forth. The guard had tied her to the chair after handcuffing her, and she hadn't been able to work herself free. "Mama! Kat!" She had been shouting for at least twenty minutes, even though she knew the guard would never let them in.

She startled when the door opened, twisted her head to look back over her shoulder. God, if her father returned and told her Nico was dead, she would be tempted to prove to him on his own terms she was good enough after all.

"Kat!" Her face brightened when she saw her sister and her mother behind her. "Mama?"

"Mama made a little something for the guard and put a bottle of sleeping pills in it," Kat said, smiling. "We had to wait until they took effect before we could come in."

"Are you okay?" Mia's mother came around the chair and checked her for bruises.

"I'm good, Mama. I'm just so glad to see you. Nico's in danger. Papà's put a contract out on him, and they're planning to whack him tonight. I need my phone. It's in the bag on the floor."

"Kat, you get the phone. I'll find something to cut the ropes and open the handcuffs." Mama raced out of the room, and Kat pulled out the phone.

"Call Nico." Mia kicked her legs trying to loosen the ropes. "If you can't get him, try Vito. His is the only other number I have at the casino."

"No answer for Nico. I'll send a text." Kat quickly typed and then scrolled through Mia's phone and pressed Vito's number.

"Someone's answering." She held the phone up to Mia's ear, and she breathed out a sigh of relief when Vito said hello.

"I need to speak to Nico. It's urgent. I think someone is after him." Mia tried to keep her legs still as Kat pulled at the ropes around her ankles.

"Mr. Toscani is in a meeting in his office with Frankie and Luca," Vito assured her. "He gave strict instructions not to be disturbed. There are two guards outside his door and another two at the elevator." He chuckled. "I'm sure you, more than anyone, know how secure the casino is, especially after you sent us the final test report. We implemented all your suggestions immediately. I assure you, Mr. Toscani is perfectly safe, but I will make sure all the security guards know to watch for suspicious activity."

"Thanks, Vito."

"Pleasure, Ms. Mia."

Kat ended the call and cut through the ropes. "There you go."

Mia wiggled her feet to increase her circulation. "How long do we have before the guard wakes up?"

"Mama gave him a lot of pills so quite a while, but I don't think Papà was going out for long. He told Mama to keep the dinner warm."

"Help me up and turn on Papà's computer. I'll show him just how powerful a woman can be." She settled in her father's seat with her hands still cuffed behind her back, and stared at the screen. "He didn't log off. How convenient. That's one less password I have to hack."

"What are you going to do?" Kat asked

"Something I should have done a long time ago. Revenge and ruin all with the click of a button." She directed Kat to turn on the remote desktop connection and had her call Jules on her phone.

"I need some help cracking a couple of passwords and hacking into my dad's bank accounts. Are you up for a little black-hat fun? Just passwords. I don't want you to touch anything in the systems. I don't want you getting into trouble because of me."

Jules laughed. "I've been waiting for this moment since the day you caught me having a little black-hat fun at the public library. And I spent years getting into trouble. This is nothing compared to what I used to get up to." She tapped on her keyboard for a few minutes. "Okay I'm ready. Accept the connection, and we're off to the races."

"Jules is a password hacking pro," Mia explained to her sister. "She's written all sorts of code for uncovering hidden passwords. Plus, she's just really good at guessing."

"Hmmm." Jules mused over the phone. "What words would your daddy dearest use for his passwords? I don't think he's the exclamation mark dollar sign hashtag type. How about abusivebastard798? No. Fucktard332? No.

Ilovesicilianneckties4987? No. Where_are_my_cement_
shoes? No."

"Jules . . ."

"Shhh. I'm thinking. You do what you need to do.
Leave me to it for a few minutes. I watched *The Godfather* last night so I have lots of ideas."

Mia's mother ran in and held up the key. "I was looking for something to pick the lock when I realized your
father would have left the key with the guard. It took a
while to fish it out of his pocket." She knelt behind Mia's
chair and fiddled with the lock until the cuffs snapped
free.

"I'm worried about Nico." Mia rubbed her wrists.
"His casino manager said he's with his friends, but I still
want to go to the casino to check things out. Papà's not
working alone on this one. He's getting help from Nico's
cousin, and he seemed pretty confident about his plan."

"Don't go alone." Her mother put out a warning hand.
"Your father doesn't do things by half measures. If he
says he sent someone then he'll have sent someone who
is good at what he does."

"Who can I call?" She twisted her lips to the side,
considering. "I don't have phone numbers for anyone on
his crew."

"I have Big Joe's number." Kat held up her phone.
"Remember?"

Mia's tension eased the tiniest bit. "Perfect. Call him
and ask him to meet us there. Tell him Papà has put a
contract out on Nico for tonight."

Nico couldn't shake the feeling that something was off.
Everyone in the Vegas underworld knew he had put a
contract out on Dante. If Dante was so addicted to gam-

bling that he had to come out of hiding, there were dozens of casinos to choose from. His decision to come to the Casino Italia couldn't have been by chance.

"Hold up," he said to Luca when they passed the door leading to the staff locker rooms. "I'm gonna put on a vest." He insisted all his security guards wear Kevlar body armor after a rise in gun fights around the downtown casinos, mostly caused by disputes arising from the drug trade. "You should wear one, too."

"I'm good." Luca said. "Those things are so damn uncomfortable I can't move like I need to move."

Luca never wore a vest. He was still in self-destruct mode after his wife's death—too many women, too much booze, too much gambling. Although he had been younger when his father died, Nico remembered having similar feelings—taking on risky jobs for his father's capos because he didn't care if he lived or died. All he wanted was an end to the pain.

After Nico put on the vest beneath his shirt, they made their way down to the high-stakes room. Good as his word, Vito had cleared it out and the only people left were Dante, the dealer, and two casino regulars. Nico sat on the opposite end of the blackjack table from Dante and threw some money on the table. The dealer nodded and handed him a stack of chips.

"Gentleman, would you excuse us? Private game." Vito ushered the dealer and the two players out of the room, with murmured apologies. Although private gaming wasn't allowed in Vegas, Nico had outfitted the high-stakes table area with sliding doors and shuttered windows that could be closed to hide the room when the highest of the high rollers came to visit. Vito closed the doors and windows, and Luca clamped a hand on Nico's shoulder in warning.

"The guards are all outside. You want them in?"

Nico looked around the small room, his gaze resting on Dante. "I don't want anyone here but you, me and Vito."

"Jules, forget the passwords. I need you to login to our work system and hack into Nico's eye-in-the-sky at the casino." Mia ran through the house with her mother and Kat behind her, the phone to her ear. "I need to know where Nico is. I hacked his phone, so I know he's in the casino, but I can't pinpoint his location."

"I'm on it," Jules said. "This is all very exciting. I mean, the job is exciting but kidnappings, rescues, bad guys who aren't really bad, good guys who aren't really good, guns, embezzling money—"

"I'm not embezzling my father's money. I'm transferring it to a locked account for safekeeping. He won't be able to hide any money or liquidate his assets if everything goes south. I don't want his dirty money. If he gets arrested, I might hand it over to the police. Or maybe, I'll just give it to charity."

"You're a regular Robin Hood." Jules laughed. "I'd say that makes your black hat gray."

Mia gave her mother a hug, but when she turned to Kat, her sister was already pushing past her and out the door.

"I'm coming with you," Kat said. "You need someone on the phone, and I'm not sitting at home waiting for Papà to plan out my life like a good little Mafia princess. I'm not the girl you thought I was. Even if you say no, I'll jump in the car and follow you. This isn't something you can do alone."

Mia glanced at her mother for approval, and her

mother nodded. "Keep each other safe. I would come, too, but someone needs to be here when your father gets home."

"Mama . . ." Mia knew just what would happen when her father got home and found his guard drugged and Mia gone.

Mama smiled. "I think there's a little bit of the *pasta al forno* I gave to the guard. Your father will be hungry when he gets in, and he'll want to eat before he gets down to business." She reached out and gave Mia's hand a squeeze. "We are all strong in our different ways. Now, go save your man."

"I can only assume you came here looking for me." Nico had never seen a man who looked as utterly wrecked as Dante did now—tie askew, shirt untucked, hair mussed. So unlike the man who had shaken his hand at the Cordano family home.

"You were looking for me." Dante raised his weary, bloodshot eyes, his face pale and dull as though his life had been sucked away. "I thought I'd save you the trouble. Here I am."

So this was it. Face to face with his father's killer after ten long years. Security cameras turned off. No one to stop him. Two loyal men at his back. If he pulled out his gun and shot Dante now, his father would finally be avenged. It was all he had ever wanted, all he had dreamed about since the moment he held his father's lifeless body in his arms.

His hand hovered near his waist where his weapon was holstered. He'd made a promise to Mia. A promise to himself. If he pulled the trigger, he would be back where he started. There had to be another way.

"What are you doing here?" He lowered his hand, studied the man across the table. "A man who would shoot an unarmed man in the back, and then hide behind his father for ten years, isn't the kind of man with the courage to face his own death."

"Maybe you're wrong." Dante swirled the bourbon in his glass. "Maybe I'm done with the Mafia life and I wanted to do one courageous thing before I die."

"Circumstances can change," Nico said. "But not a man's character."

Dante gave a bitter laugh. "Once a coward. Always a coward. You're right about that. I was always too afraid to stand up to my father. I did whatever he told me to do even when inside I was screaming. Mia thinks my father tricked me into shooting your old man. But the reality is, I knew he wasn't armed. I just had no choice. Do you know what it does to a man when you go against your conscience? It eats at your soul until there's nothing left, until you become nothing more than the instrument for someone else's will."

"You're saying it wasn't your fault?" Nico snorted his derision. "That he made you do it? That's a coward's way out. We always have a choice. It's the choices we make in life that define us." His pushed himself off the stool. Dante was a pathetic, broken man. He didn't need Dante's death to fulfill him anymore. Mia had shown him a life beyond the emptiness of revenge.

"Or sometimes, it's the choices we make that kill us." Dante lifted his finger, looked over at Vito.

"No." Luca threw himself in front of Nico. A gunshot cracked the silence. Luca staggered forward. He grasped at the table and collapsed in Nico's arms, his shirt blooming red with blood.

Stunned, Nico looked up to see Vito with his gun pointed where Luca had been standing seconds ago.

Dante drew a weapon from beneath his jacket as Nico dropped to his knees with Luca in his arms.

"It's you or me. And I choose me."

Stay calm. Stay calm.

Mia ran through the casino with Kat, her phone plastered to her ear. "Where is he, Jules?"

"I'm looking. I'm looking. He's got one serious security system here. There are cameras everywhere. And so many people. How do you find just one person in all this?"

"The system is so sophisticated they can track individual people, but we don't have time to figure it out." She weaved in and out of the crowds, trying not to bump into anyone. "Try his office."

"Found it. There's no one there."

Mia's heart pounded, and she forced herself to slow down. Running wasn't going to get her anywhere if she didn't know where she was going.

"How about the back hallways, restrooms, or the alley outside? No one is going to whack him in the middle of a crowd."

"There are too many cameras showing too many things. You need a team of people to find him," Jules said.

A team. Led by an ass-pinching guard loyal to Nico.

"We're going to the control room. Keep looking." Mia waved for Kat to follow, and she headed for the control room. The last time she'd been there, she'd been trying to evade detection. Now, she didn't care if the whole damn world saw her.

"Louis." She banged on the steel security door. "It's Mia. Let me in."

The door opened, just a crack, and then wider. Louis stared at Mia and his eyes widened. "Jesus. The knife woman." He tried to push the door closed, but Mia stuck her foot in the crack and pushed her way through. "That's Mrs. Toscani to you. And I'm not here to cause trouble. I'm trying to find Nico. He's somewhere in the casino, and he's in trouble."

Louis glanced back at the sea of monitors behind him. "I can't let you in. This is a secure area."

"Are you kidding me? You let me in when I was dressed as a go-go dancer."

Louis's lips pressed together. "I paid a big price for that. I still got fucking bruises."

"Nico beat you?"

His face turned stony. "I don't talk business with the ladies."

Ah. That's right. She was a "lady." But not just any lady. She was a Mafia queen. "You go by the name Mikey Muscles, isn't that right?"

Louis gave her a wary look. "Yeah."

"Well, Mikey Muscles, your *capo's wife* is telling you to let her in. Do you really want him to find out you told me no? He might have beat you before, but that will be nothing compared to what he'll do to you when I tell him you refused to let me in. And when he's done with you, if there's anything left, it will be my turn. The knife I stabbed you with isn't my only weapon."

"Fuck." He opened the door. "Now it's like I got two fucking bosses."

"You're badass," Kat whispered as she reached for the door. "I want to be just like you."

"Leave it open," Louis directed. "I don't want anyone saying I was alone in a room with the boss's wife."

After wasting five minutes searching for Nico, Mia threw up her hands. "Where is he? What kind of system is this? I thought you could track a person from the minute they come into the casino."

"We can." Louis scratched his head. "But he's not here."

"He is here. I hacked his phone." Mia held up her phone with the little blue dot on the screen showing Nico somewhere in the building.

"What about these screens?" Kat pointed to six blank monitors. "What do those usually show?"

"High-stakes room. The casino manager, Vito, told me to turn them off on Mr. Toscani's orders."

Mia frowned. "Why?"

"I don't ask why," Louis said. "I just do."

"He must be in there. Turn them on."

Louis hesitated. "If Vito or Mr. Toscani find out . . ."

"Now."

He pushed a few buttons and Mia stared at the screens as they flickered on. A gasp from behind startled her. And then she heard a familiar chuckle. "I think you should listen to the nice security guard. You don't want to get him in trouble."

Mia spun around, and her heart dropped into her stomach. Rev had an arm around Kat's waist and a gun pressed to her temple.

"You." He lifted his chin toward Louis as he moved with Kat along the wall. "Close and lock the door. Then get down on the floor. Hands where I can see them."

Louis did as directed and dropped to his knees, hands in the air.

Kat opened her mouth as if to scream and Rev tightened his grip around her. "I know you're surprised to see me, kitty cat, but don't make a fuss. After all, we don't want to cause a commotion. People might get hurt."

TWENTY-SEVEN

Ben checked his text from Kat as he raced into the casino. She hadn't told him where in the casino they were headed, and given the sheer size of the place, it was going to be impossible to find her or Nico without some help.

He sent a quick text to Mikey Muscles and headed over to the control room. He would need back-up and Mikey could provide it. He could also help Ben find Nico before it was too late.

He couldn't believe he was doing this. If Nico had any reservations about who Ben was, he would have none after this evening was done. And yet Ben couldn't just sit around when he knew there was a chance to save him. Nico had given Ben the closest thing he'd had to a family. He'd given Ben his trust and his friendship. He's had Ben's back countless times, and he'd given Ben countless opportunities. In return, Ben had betrayed him. He figured he owed Nico at least this favor. And he was an officer of the law. He couldn't stand by when a crime was about to be committed.

He pulled up outside the door to the control room and peered through the window. Jesus Christ. There was fucking Gabe. And Mia, looking like she wanted to rip out his throat. And sweet, innocent Kat, with a goddamned gun to her head.

A surge of protective anger roared through his head. Gabe seemed to have no issue involving innocents in his crimes. Ben was momentarily overcome with regret for not pulling the trigger when he had the chance. But Gabe was now facing life in prison for the drug stash they'd found at Ginger's house. Justice would be served, and Ben's conscience would be clean.

Now, though, Kat was in danger. Not only that, Nico was somewhere in the casino with Vito, who he'd figured for Daisy's silver man—a Cordano and a traitor. He didn't know if Vito had the contract on Nico, but he was a threat, and Ben wasn't going to let Nico down.

He reached inside his jacket. *Christ.* If Gabe gave him even the hint of a reason, this time he wouldn't hesitate to shoot the bastard down.

"Police." He banged on the door. "Open up." He slammed Jack's badge against the window—he'd handed his in when he went undercover—and held his weapon ready. "I know it's you, Gabe. You're already facing time for the drugs. You want to add murder to your rap sheet? You'll never see the fucking sun again."

A few people looked down the hallway at him with mild interest, but for the most part people just passed by. Ben marveled at how they could be so blind to what was going on, but then, that was just a testament to the success of Nico's casino. He kept the customers so distracted with the music and the noise, the lights, the alcohol, and the games, they couldn't see a real show when it was staring them in the face.

He heard a deep voice, and then Mia pulled open the door, her face white, eyes wide in a silent plea. Gabe still had Kat at gunpoint. Louis was down on the floor.

Gabe's face rippled with amusement. "So, you are a cop."

"And you're a criminal. We found your heroin stash. You're facing a lot of time for drug offenses and maybe even Ginger's death, too, if she overdosed from the same shit you put in my daughter's toys. And if that stuff was tainted, there are twenty-four other deaths that might be added to your list of crimes."

Ben was prepared for anything, but not the shock or the pain that flickered across Gabe's face.

Gabe dropped his arm, releasing Kat. "Ginger's dead?"

Mia reached over and pulled Kat to her side. Taking advantage of Gabe's distraction, she slipped out the door, pulling Kat behind her.

"Yeah, she's dead." Ben's gaze flicked to Mikey Muscles who was slowly pushing himself to his feet. "Because of people like you who make it easy for addicts like her."

"I couldn't stop her." Gabe's shoulders slumped, defeated. "She started before she met me, and there was nothing I could do. I got into it because of her. So she wouldn't buy shit product from the streets."

"Give Mikey the gun." He needed to find Nico and make sure Kat and Mia were safe, but he couldn't leave until he made sure Gabe was no longer a threat.

Gabe drew in a ragged breath and handed Mikey the gun. Ben tossed Mikey the cuffs Jack had given him, along with the badge, after he'd received Kat's text and told Jack he needed to be a cop again for a few hours to save a friend. "Secure him and call 911. Where's Nico?"

Mikey snapped the cuffs around Gabe's wrists and looked up at the screens. "High-stakes room. And you'd better get there fast."

Heart pounding, Ben ran through the casino, hitting the sliding doors marking the entrance to the high-stakes area at a run.

He had only just stepped inside when he heard a scream.

Fuck. Was he too late?

TWENTY-EIGHT

"He's dead. Oh. My. God, Jules. He's dead."

Mia gasped for breath as she took in the scene in front of her. Nico on the floor with Luca on top of him. And blood. So much blood.

"I was too late. I want to die," she whispered into the phone, staring in disbelief at Dante with a gun in his hand and Vito standing only a short distance away.

"Don't go all Romeo and Juliet on me," Jules warned. Mia had called her after they left the control room to check that Nico was still in the building. The security monitors had shown bodies on the floor, but she couldn't make out faces. "Are you safe? If not get out of there."

Mia dropped the phone and took a step toward Nico, but Kat's firm hands pulled her back.

"Dante!" Kat turned on their brother, her face a mask of rage. "How could you do this?"

"The same way I did it to his father. The same way I hurt you." Dante's voice was thick with self-loathing. "My fate was sealed the first time I pulled the trigger. I wanted Papà to be proud of me, but I didn't realize the cost was going to be my soul. Once you cross that line, there's no going back. Once you make a wrong choice, you just keep sinking until you are in the pit of Hell."

Mia caught movement out of the corner of her eye. Nico's hand slid beneath his jacket. Relief flooded through her. She shoved Kat behind her and took a step back.

"Don't move." Dante lifted his gun and pointed at Mia. "Nico wasn't the only problem Papà asked us to take care of tonight."

"Us?"

"Vito, Rev, and me. He didn't trust me to handle it alone. He didn't trust me with anything. He said you would have made a better son." He spat on the floor, his nose wrinkled in disgust. "You were supposed to be waiting for me in his office, handcuffed to a chair so you couldn't get away. After you challenged him tonight, he decided Kat would be a better choice to marry Tony. She's does what she's told. She knows how to behave. You just cause too many problems. You never fucking listen. You never do what you're told. You would have been one hell of a hard wife to manage." He squeezed his eyes shut, his face contorted in agony. "*Addio, mia sorella.*"

"No." Nico rolled and fired his gun.

Kat screamed. Dante staggered back, his hand to his chest. Vito pulled the trigger, his bullet missing Nico by only an inch. Big Joe burst into the room and fired, dropping Vito to the floor with one clean shot to the head.

"Mia!" Jules shouted over the phone. "Mia!"

Mia dropped to her knees and picked up the phone. "I'm okay. Kat's okay, and Nico, too. But Dante . . . Oh God, Jules. Dante is dead."

"Park over there." Nico leaned over the seat and directed Big Joe down a dusty road on the Nevada border. "Turn off the lights."

Big Joe pulled the car to a stop. A full moon had risen behind them as they drove out of Vegas, casting a faint silvery glow through the ebony night. *Beautiful.* Nico made a mental note to come to the desert at night sometime when he wasn't planning to whack someone or dump a body.

Mikey Muscles turned on his powerful torch and placed it on the hood of the vehicle as Nico and Frankie exited the car. Frankie opened Big Joe's door and ushered him out with a wave of his gun.

"On your knees." Nico rounded the car and motioned Big Joe down. "Hands behind your head."

Big Joe dropped to his knees in front of Nico. He appeared neither afraid nor angry, but calm and resigned. Nico cursed the fates that had put this man he admired and respected on the wrong side of the law.

"Three years you were with me. Ten with my family." Nico gritted his teeth, his emotions still raw from finding out the truth. "I gave you my friendship. My trust. My respect. And you betrayed me. You would have known this day was coming."

"I did."

"You got anything to say?" He hoped Big Joe had something to say. Betraying *Cosa Nostra* was one of the most grievous of crimes, punishable by the harshest of punishments to deter anyone who thought of betraying the mob.

"Yeah." Big Joe swallowed hard. "It has been an honor. If there is another life after this one, I hope we meet again as friends."

"You're not gonna beg for mercy?" Frankie asked.

"No. I did you wrong," Big Joe said, directing his words to Nico. "I may not have given up any information about you or the closest members of your crew—and the bosses we were really after were killed by an unknown assailant at Vincenzo's—but there will still be a lot of people going to jail because of me."

"Including a few Cordanos." Mikey Muscles—now a Big Joe supporter after Big Joe saved his life in the control room—shot Nico a pleading look. "Don't forget that. The Cordanos are gonna be no more because of him."

Big Joe had been instrumental in the arrest of Don Cordano, and many of his capos and crew. Although the don was still nominal boss of the Cordano family, running his operations from his jail cell, his power was greatly diminished. Because of Mia's quick thinking, he had been unable to hide his money when he got wind of his impending arrest for his involvement with the drug trafficking operation he operated with the help of Rev and Vito. Nor was he able to make bail. Now, the remaining Cordano capos were fighting among themselves over who should take his place if he was slapped with a lifelong sentence, and the family was tearing itself apart.

"We know who killed my uncle and Don Falzone." Nico folded his arms. "Dante was responsible for the massacre at Vincenzo's. He had Rev—you knew him as Gabe—drive him back to the restaurant that night after they dropped off Mia and her father. From what Rev told Mikey Muscles before the cops came to take him away, it was a spur-of-the-moment thing. Dante told Rev he was just going to take out Don Toscani and Don Falzone so the Cordanos could take control of the city. But Rev knew him pretty well. Gambling was an escape for him because he felt trapped in the mob. He said Dante cared about Mia and couldn't stand the thought of her being married to Tony Crackers. He figured Dante thought that if he whacked everyone—his father, Tony, Don Toscani and all the witnesses—he could save Mia and be free. That's why Mia wasn't harmed and how the murder weapon wound up so far away. Rev said they wiped it down and tossed it from the car."

"It's a fucking hard life you chose to live," Big Joe said.

"It's a life I love." And it was a life that was going to see new challenges. After losing the capos' vote to Tony by a margin of three to two, Nico had broken with the family and declared himself boss of a new Toscani faction, starting a vicious civil war. But it was the only way to save the Las Vegas Toscanis from the same fate as had befallen every *Cosa Nostra* family who had become involved in the drug trade.

It was a war he believed he could win. At Mia's suggestion, Nico had contacted the Scozzaris with a proposal that would allow both families to save face, only to discover that Rosa's father had been dreading the day Nico called on him to honor the agreement. Rosa Scozzari was not, in fact, interested in coming over to America to marry him, and her father didn't want to lose her. Overjoyed by the termination of the agreement, the Scozzaris offered Nico their support in the form of soldiers and connections as he sought to establish his new faction in Las Vegas.

Big Joe gave a bitter laugh. "It's crazy, but I loved the life, too."

"Fuck." Frankie's head jerked around. "Someone's coming down the highway. Kill the light."

Mikey Muscles turned off the flashlight, and they watched a lone pair of headlights speed down the main road in the distance. But instead of continuing down the highway, the lights turned down the gravel road and headed toward them.

"*Cristo mio.* Someone knows we're here." Frankie

and Mikey Muscles crouched behind the open doors of the vehicle, weapons drawn. Nico directed Big Joe to put his hands behind his head and lie facedown in the sand while he waited with his weapon on the other side of the vehicle.

The car pulled to a stop on the road, and the driver stepped out, a slender shadow in the glare of the headlights.

"Stop. Stop. Don't do this." Waving her hands, Kat ran toward them, almost unrecognizable in tight jeans, black boots, and a leather jacket. "Please. Please." She stopped short when she saw Big Joe lying in the sand. "Oh. My. God. No. Nico. How could you?"

"I didn't," Nico said, bemused as he rounded the vehicle. "Not yet."

Kat crouched beside Big Joe as he pushed to kneeling in the sand. "Are you okay?"

"Kat, sweetheart." Big Joe stroked her cheek. "What are you doing here?"

"Saving you. Mia hacked Nico's phone so it wasn't hard to find him."

"Christ." Nico pulled out his phone and glared at it in disgust. "That's what I get for marrying a hacker."

"There is no saving me," Big Joe said.

"Don't do this." Kat stood in front of Big Joe, and for a moment Nico was back in Luigi's Restaurant ten years ago when another dark-haired girl begged for another man's life.

"Please. He's a good man, Nico. He has a daughter. He was just doing his job. Let him go."

Nico sighed. He had done this to himself. He had married into a family of strong women. The pain was just beginning.

"You don't need to beg for him." Nico motioned for

Big Joe to stand. "I'm giving him a pass. He saved my life and the life of one of my men. I owe him a debt." He turned to Big Joe. "Consider it paid."

Big Joe stood, his brow creased in a frown. "Then what's all this?"

"I couldn't let you just walk away without sweating a little." Nico grinned. "I have a reputation to protect. But I wasn't expecting you to be so stoic about it. We were hoping for a bit of a show. Maybe a few tears, begging, calling for your mama."

"Jesus Christ, you're a bastard." Big Joe leaned against the vehicle and took a deep breath. "I almost pissed myself."

"That would have been entertaining." Nico kicked at the sand beneath his feet. "I might embellish it a bit for Luca when he gets out of hospital. Especially since you're going to have to hitch a ride out of Nevada and it would make him laugh to think of you sitting in your piss in some trucker's cab." His voice dropped low with regret. He'd miss Big Joe. Couldn't imagine the crew without him. "You know you can't come back."

"He doesn't have to hitch a ride. He has me." Kat's hands found her hips and she glared at Nico. He couldn't believe how much she'd changed in such a short period of time. Gone was the soft, gentle kitten and in its place was a lioness just learning to use her claws. He hadn't told Mia about his plans for Big Joe, but now that Kat had got wind of them, he could just imagine her reaction.

And he could imagine just what he would do to calm his little tiger down.

"So this is good-bye." Big Joe shook Nico's hand. "I meant it when I said it was an honor."

Emotion welled up in Nico's chest. This was the part of the business he didn't enjoy. When the political became personal. When he lost a friend.

"If you ever stop being a cop, you know where to find me." Nico pulled open his door.

"If you ever stop being a wiseguy . . ." Big Joe shook his head. "Nah. It will never happen. You were born to be a wiseguy."

TWENTY-NINE

Act like a Mafia wife . . .
  . . . with a punk-rock attitude.

Mia swept past the security guards and into the high-stakes room at the Casino Italia, her high heels clicking firmly on the newly tiled floor. The police had come quickly after the 911 call, but not quickly enough. They had found only Vito's body, shot by an undercover officer in the line of duty, alongside an innocent guest, Luca, in the high-stakes room. Eyewitness, and consummate actress, Kat Cordano, explained she had been gaming alone with Luca when crazy Vito burst in and started shooting unprovoked after ordering the cameras turned off.

Dante's body was "found" in a burned-out car in the desert the next day, his death reported as fallout from the civil war between Mafia families. Although Mia couldn't forgive his crimes, she was glad that Dante had at least found peace, and she remembered him for the fun-loving brother he used to be.

She spotted Nico right away, sitting on the far side of a blackjack table. She studied him for a moment, intensely aware of the strength hidden behind that tailored suit, the power he now wielded as the boss of a new family faction, the fearlessness with which he had entered the war with Tony and his crew.

As if he knew she was watching, he looked up. His lazy gaze drifted over her body, taking in her vintage 1950's Paul Sachs black tuxedo lace cocktail dress, a little punk rock with a nod to Mafia-wife style. Since she couldn't wear her long socks with heels, she'd gone for stockings with a lacy garter belt that had tiny skulls stitched into the fabric, and chains instead of garters. She'd never worn lingerie for Nico before, but she suspected he'd appreciate her style.

Nico gestured for Mia to join him at the table. "You look very nice, *bella*."

"If you'd told me where we were going, I would have had a better idea how to dress." She checked out the cards in his hand and the bets that had been placed.

"You are perfect." He gestured to his stack of chips. "Bet."

Her lips quivered at the corners, and she pushed all his chips forward. "Go big or go home."

"I like a woman who's not afraid to take a risk."

She leaned over and pressed her lips to his ear. "I've taken much bigger risks than that."

Nico gave a soft growl of approval and put his arm around her waist, his thumb stroking in and out of her curves. Her hand tensed, ready in case he dived beneath her skirt and found the surprise waiting for him under the crinoline layer.

The dealer dealt him a seven. His up card was nine. Mia grimaced. Sixteen was too low to stand on but if he hit he'd probably bust. Nico's fingers skirted the edge of her dress and she gently slapped his hand away.

"This game is about emotional control," he said,

frowning at being denied the opportunity to feel her up in public. "Although around you, I find it a particular challenge." He tapped the table and got a five.

"Very nice, sir." The dealer counted out a huge stack of chips, and Nico waved for him to keep them.

The dealer smiled and retrieved the chips. "Much obliged, Mr. Toscani."

"You don't want all your money?" Mia looked back over her shoulder as Nico led her away from the table.

"I've got something worth much more." He guided her through the casino, pointing out the new improvements he was testing for his refurbishment of the Desert Dream Hotel. He opened the elevator with his key card, and moments later they were on the tenth floor.

"I thought we were going out." She looked around the newly decorated office, so different from the first time she was here. Dark wood, rich leather, and thick cream Berber carpet had replaced the cold, functional décor, and the walls were now a colorful mix of posters from old gangster movies and photographs from the days when the Mafia ruled the Strip.

"We're staying in." After closing the door, he settled in the leather chair behind his new reclaimed oak desk.

"Why did you ask me to dress up? I could have come straight from work. I had to leave Jules in charge so I could go home early and change."

A slow, sensual smile spread across his face. "I've been imagining this moment since the first time you walked into my office. The things I wanted to do to you that night, *bella* . . ." He licked his lips like a predator about to feast. "I want it all. Now."

"You want that night over again?"

"Yes, but this time you won't be walking out the door."

She shivered in delicious anticipation at the wicked

look in his eyes. Oh yeah. She was fully on board with his plan.

"Sit." He gestured to the chair in front of her, his tone laced with the same hint of command she'd heard that very first night.

Mia pressed her lips together, trying to remember how their first encounter had played out. "I prefer to stand."

Nico expressed his displeasure with a scowl. "Sit," he said curtly. "Or I'll make you sit."

"Are you trying to turn me on?"

He fought back a bark of amusement. "That's not what you said. I remember every word. You asked if I meant to break your nose, and I told you it was too lovely to break."

"Is that meant to be a compliment?" She arched an eyebrow and put one hand on her hip, tugging up her dress just enough to give him a hint of what was hidden below. Although she didn't let on, she remembered their conversation, too.

Nico's eyes widened and he sat forward in his chair. "Do you want compliments?"

"I want to give you this." She put her leg up on the chair nearest the door, and pulled back the dress to reveal her stocking, and the garter decorated with skulls and chains.

He drew in a ragged breath. "This is supposed to be my fantasy, *bella*. You're making it hard for me to stay in my chair."

"My apologies, Mr. Toscani." She slid her finger inside one of the garter straps, tugging on the little chain. "I didn't mean to make it . . . hard."

"Over here." He slapped his hand on the desk. "Now."

"Tsk. Tsk," she teased. "That's not how to play the game. I think you asked about my family next. And

Luigi's." She regretted the words as they dropped from her lips, worried she had ruined the game by bringing up such a painful memory.

Nico came around the desk and perched on the edge. "I made the mistake of thinking you weren't capable because you were a Cordano and a woman. I couldn't have been more wrong."

Mia walked toward him, working the heels and the dress until his mouth went slack. "Was that before or after I cupped my breasts and told you about stabbing your guard? Did you know I was incredibly turned on?" She paused for effect, loving the power she had right now. "Did you know I was wet? So wet. When I went home . . ." She trailed her fingers down her neck to the curve of her breast. "Well, I'm sure you can imagine."

His eyes blazed and he reached for her, only to swipe at the air when she stopped a few feet away. "I was so fucking hard I couldn't think. I told you a man couldn't be distracted, but you were the most distracting woman I'd ever met."

She stepped between his parted legs, the way she had done before. Electricity crackled between them, and she gave him a mischievous smile. "So you're saying . . ." She dropped her hand and cupped his erection, straining beneath the fabric of his fine wool pants. "When I dropped my hand that night, you wanted me to touch you like this?"

Nico growled, a low rumble that made her stomach tight with need. He curled his hand around her neck, and yanked her close, so close she could feel his breath on her cheek. Not wanting to give in so soon, she dragged her palm along his shaft, feeling it harden with each firm stroke.

"Yes, you did." She flicked her tongue along his earlobe and crooned. "You wanted me, Mr. Mob Boss. You wanted my hand stroking your cock. You wanted me on your desk, my dress hiked up, my panties gone, my pussy hot and wet—"

Before she even realized he had moved, Nico had her flat on her back on his desk, her skirt pushed up to bare her sexy skull garters.

"*Dio mio.*" He traced his finger along the edge of her garters, and then his hand tightened around her thigh like he was struggling to restrain himself. "You might just break me, yet."

"Then break." She pushed herself up on her elbows. "Here I am. Your fantasy come true."

He pounced, roughly pushing her panties aside. With a low growl of satisfaction, he slicked one finger through her labia, sending an exquisite shudder through her body. "Make no mistake. That part of my fantasy will come true tonight. I will have you on this desk in every possible way. But that comes after."

"After what?"

He pulled her up to sit, and she gave a disappointed moan.

"Shhh. You are entirely too sexy, too distracting. And tonight I have something I need to do." He settled her on the edge of his desk and smoothed down her dress. From his pocket, he pulled out a small black velvet box and then he went down on one knee.

Emotion welled up in Mia's chest. "You don't need to do this. We're already married. Elvis said so."

"You are worth so much more than a quickie elopement ceremony, *cara mia.*" He opened the box. "I want to do it again. Properly. When the words I say come from the heart.

Mia stared at the beautiful ring, platinum, with a black diamond in the center and two pink diamonds on the side, held in a punk-style setting. "If I had to design a ring, this would be it. This is me."

"I saw you the first time we met. And you saw me." He took the ring from the box. "*Ti adoro, Mia. Ti amo.* Make me the happiest man in the world by becoming my wife."

"Yes." She whispered the word without hesitation. If anyone had told her six weeks ago that she would wind up in a mobster's arms, tied to the life she'd fought so hard to escape, she wouldn't have believed them. But love made all the difference.

He slid the ring on her finger and stood, sweeping her into his arms for a smoldering kiss.

Mia melted against the heat and strength of his body. "I'd like three Elvises this time, two bottles of vodka, and a nice, long religious ceremony so I can watch you struggle with your self-control. And I would still like to consummate our marriage in the restroom at Red 27."

Nico chuckled. "Anything you want."

"Anything?" She looked up at him, at his tender expression, the softness in his eyes.

"Yes." He tightened his arms around her. "I will give you anything. My body. My heart. My soul. Everything I have, everything I am, is yours."

"I want forever," she whispered.

"*Cara mia.*" He brushed her lips with a gentle kiss. "You already have forever. I gave it to you the first time I held you in my arms."

Read on for an excerpt from the next book by

Sarah Castille

LUCA

Now available from St. Martin's Paperbacks

It started out like any other day in Vegas.

Luca rolled out of bed at noon, showered and shaved. There was nothing more important for a Mafia capo than *la bella figura*—looking good in the eyes of society. Once his knives were strapped to his body, he dressed in a new Italian wool suit, crisp white shirt, and red silk tie. He holstered two Glocks across his chest, an S&W500 and a Ruger GP100 around his waist, and a Walther P22 beside the knife on his ankle just above his Salvatore Ferragamo shoes. After meticulously checking his appearance, he walked back into the bedroom, ready to start his day.

That's when things started to go wrong.

First, the woman in his bed didn't want to leave. When charm and soft smiles failed to encourage her departure, he had to yank the covers off the bed and toss her money on the dresser, shattering the illusion that she was anything other the high-class escort she pretended not to be. Luca always tipped well so her feigned indignation lasted only as long as it took her to count the cash and wobble her way out of his penthouse suite.

After that, it had been one broken leg after another as he tried to call in a few business loans. The day had continued its downward slide when he had gone to collect protection money from a pawnshop on Las Vegas Boulevard only to discover that the Albanians had muscled in on his territory.

Whacking Albanians was never a good way to break

in a new suit, but the Toscani crime family didn't waste time when there were lessons to be learned.

Luca called up a couple of friends and they sent the Albanians back to their home country via the fiery pit of Hell.

With their arms missing.

And wearing cement shoes.

The last part wasn't his idea. But Frankie, the boss's right-hand man, was a mean SOB who had been in the concrete pouring business before he joined the Toscani crew. Frankie never gave up the opportunity to practice his trade, even if the nearest body of water was thirty miles away.

After he had changed his clothes, washed off the blood, and dropped off the suit at the dry cleaners, his day had gone from bad to worse.

He made a mistake.

Luca didn't make mistakes.

When Gina got pregnant after a one-night stand, he hadn't hesitated to do the right thing. After all, Gina ticked all the boxes for a desirable Mafia wife. She was a Mafia princess: pure Italian, well-versed in the culture, easy on the eye, and a good cook. Love wasn't part of the Mafia marriage equation so he felt no guilt about spending Friday nights engaged in the extra-curricular activities expected of a senior Mafia capo. A wife was a symbol of status. A mistress was a symbol of power. Gina understood how things worked and as long as the money rolled in, she had no complaints. Life was good.

And then she died.

Luca had been totally unprepared for the emotional trauma of Gina's death. Sure he cared for her, enjoyed spending some time with her, and they had an eighteen-month-old son, Matteo, together. But he hadn't loved her, and the guilt of failing to protect his new wife, and knowing she'd died without truly being loved, had destroyed him. He'd sent Matteo to live with his mother, and tried to lose himself in his work for the family, taking on the most dangerous of assignments, regardless of the risk.

Hence the mistake, which had led him to his current confinement.

Gritting his teeth, he shifted in the uncomfortable hospital bed, biting back a groan as pain sliced through his chest. When Dante Cordano fired the bullet meant for Nico's heart, Luca could have saved himself a whole a lot of pain if he'd worn a bulletproof vest. But sometimes, in the pit of despair, down was a hell of a lot more attractive than up.

A pale yellow glow flickered in the doorway, and his pulse kicked up a notch.

Nurse Rachel had visited him every night to give him pain relief of another kind. Even bruised and broken, his dignity ruffled by the continual poking and prodding of his person, he hadn't had to put much effort into convincing the young nursing assistant to get down on her knees and wrap her plump lips around the only part of his body that didn't ache.

When the door opened, he smoothed down his blue shirt and adjusted his belt. With a constant stream of visitors coming to his room, he had made it clear to the medical staff that he would not suffer the indignity of a hospital gown. Every morning, he washed, shaved and dressed with the assistance of his sister, Angela, and then he held court from his hospital bed. His mother set up some folding tables against the wall and brought food every day to feed his guests, and to ensure he didn't succumb to starvation. There was her food, or there was no food. That was her way.

"Rachel, sweetheart." His smile faded when an orderly

followed Rachel into the room pushing a hospital gurney in front of him. Luca's gaze narrowed on the sleeping woman in the bed. Her thick, blonde hair was strewn across the pillow, gleaming gold like the first autumn leaves. Her skin was pale in the harsh light, and her hospital gown gaped open at the collar, revealing a thin frame.

Rachel gave him an apologetic smile, and he watched as they settled the woman near the window—attaching wires to the monitors, adjusting the bed and checking her vital signs.

After the orderly left, Rachel leaned down and brushed a soft kiss over Luca's cheek. "I'm sorry, Mr. Rizzoli. I know you like your privacy, but there was a big shootout in the Naked City, and the ER is swamped. We don't have enough staff or rooms to accommodate everyone so the head nurse ordered us to double every one up. I suggested putting you two together because you've got the same type of injury."

Despite his irritation at losing his privacy, he graced her with a smile. He liked Rachel. She was a sweet girl, willing and compliant, and very skilled with her mouth. There was no point taking out his frustration on her. The Toscani crime family had friends everywhere. No doubt a couple of bills and a word in the right ear in the morning would restore the status quo with a minimum of fuss. In the meantime, he'd have company in the form of a beautiful woman who had, curiously, been shot in the chest.

After Rachel left, he canted his head and allowed his gaze to drift over his new companion. She had turned to face him in her sleep and the thin blanket dipped into her narrow waist and up over the curve of her hip. Her features were delicate, with high cheekbones and a slightly turned-up nose. She was the opposite of everything that attracted him to a woman: blonde instead of brunette, thin instead of curvy, frail instead of robust. Gina had been a big, loud, gregarious woman with an infectious laugh and a truckload of friends. She was the life of the party, talking non-stop even when the guests were gone.

"You're staring."

Her warm, rich voice slid through him like a smooth Canadian whiskey that finished the palate with a whisper of heat.

"I was just wondering, *bella*." He lifted his gaze to soft blue eyes framed in thick golden lashes. "Who would shoot an angel?"